LIAR'S MARKET

TAYLOR SMITH
LIAR'S MARKET

MIRA®

MIRA

ISBN 0-7783-2008-1

¥LIAR'S MARKET

Visit us at www.mirabooks.com

Printed in U.S.A.

First Printing: January 2004
10 9 8 7 6 5 4 3 2 1

Three may keep a secret—if two of them be dead.
—Benjamin Franklin

ACKNOWLEDGMENTS

My deep thanks for assistance and ongoing support to
Lieutenant Brian Bray and Officer Harry M. Saval (Washington, D.C.
Metropolitan Police), Nick Banks, Lee Roberts, D. P. Lyle, the Fictionaires,
Philip Spitzer and last but never least, Amy Moore-Benson. And as always,
Richard, Kate and Anna: I couldn't do it without you.

This book is dedicated to the memory of
Robert Kost
(1936–2003)
artist, musician and son of the prairie.

PROLOGUE

Hong Kong
August 27, 2001

Hong Kong radiated heat, sex and treachery in equal measures. Adding money and politics to that flammable mix guaranteed an explosion of murder.

From her twenty-eighth-floor penthouse terrace near the top of Victoria Park Alexandra Kim Lee gazed down on a city skyline that sparkled like diamonds strewn across a blueblack cape of velvet. Dazzling skyscrapers and light-strung yachts and fishing junks in the harbor made a festive display, specially contrived, it seemed, to mark her birthday. Her latest lover was expected any minute, and the plan was to celebrate at Fantin-Latour, Hong Kong's newest, most exclusive nightclub.

She'd been born in the harbor below exactly thirty-five years ago that night on board a junk that smelled of fish guts, rotting wood and wet rope. It had been the Year of the Dragon, the luckiest and most powerful of signs. And like the mighty dragon, which begins life in the narrow confines of the soupy egg, Alex had emerged from damp, humble beginnings to conquer her world.

Now, she had luxury homes in London, New York and Eleuthera, as well as this sprawling penthouse in the coveted residential sector high above Hong Kong. It wasn't so long ago that Chinese hadn't been permitted to live on the Peak, but the timing of Alex's life was as lucky as her sign. Schooling for young Chinese girls had become mandatory when she was a child, and she'd gone on to win scholarships at the London School of Economics. Afterward, she'd worked as an assistant to one of the leading British bankers in Hong Kong. When rule of the colony had reverted to China, she'd been in a prime position to strike out on her own, acting as go-between for western businesses looking for profit in the emerging modern China with its billion eager consumers.

Alex's ancestors had been fishermen and noodle makers, but she was on a first-name basis with British lords, American senators and international businessmen, with whom she was often photographed in the U.S. and European press. Her helpful introductions to leaders in the People's Republic led to lucrative commercial contracts for these influential Westerners. In return, she used her charm, as well as other incentives, to convince them to support trade accords and political treaties to Beijing's advantage. If those incentives sometimes included a financial donation or the passing of a secret gleaned in pillow talk with an influential friend…well, that was part of the business, too. In return for her efforts, Alexandra Kim Lee received the grateful largesse of Beijing and foreign businessmen alike—very grateful. Bank presidents from Zurich to the Cayman Islands were on her speed dial, and they took her calls personally.

Turning away from the railing and the stunning view of the city below, Alex reached up and lifted her silken black hair off pale, bare shoulders. The sun had set nearly an hour ago, but the air was still muggy and very warm. She lit a few sticks of fragrant sandalwood incense and set them in sand-filled brass dishes around the terrace to discourage those few hardy mosquitoes who might venture up to this altitude. Down in the harbor on a hot summer evening like this, fishermen would be shirtless, skin glistening with sweat as they prepared their nets for the night run. But up here among the Peak's green spaces, soft breezes carried delicate scents of jasmine, honeysuckle and orange blossom from well-tended terrace gardens.

The air stirred now, cooling Alex's body, naked under a lucky red silk Versace gown. The gossamer thin dress dipped low in front and back, held at her shoulders by the sheerest of filaments that looked as if they might give way at any second. Like Alex herself, their apparent fragility was deceptive.

If she looked closely enough in the mirror, she could see the beginnings of a few lines around her eyes and mouth, yet it was a common occurrence still to hear the squeal of rubber heels behind her as men stopped dead in their tracks to stare when she passed by. More important than beauty, though, she had brains, and what little was lost in looks was more than gained back in experience, connections and poise. She was probably at the peak of her operational effectiveness right now. She estimated that she had five, maybe eight good years left before the advantages afforded by her appearance began to dim. It was unfair that a woman's career should be shortened like that. Still, by the time her run was done, Alexandra calculated, she would have earned an extremely comfortable retirement.

Tonight, though, was an occasion to forget about business. Tonight belonged to her.

She peered once more over the filigreed-iron railing. City traffic sounded distant, muted in the steamy night air, but far below in the circular drive, a white limousine was gliding up to the building's front entrance. The blue-uniformed doorman rushed out to open the limo's back door, and as the passenger emerged, a hint of a smile touched the edges of Alex's crimson-painted lips.

When the door chime sounded a few minutes later, her maid emerged from the kitchen to answer it. Alex turned away from the city lights, leaning against the terrace's wrought-iron railing to face the richly furnished living room. The back of her silk dress draped to the cleft of her buttocks, and when the metal railing touched her bare skin, a shiver ran up her spine as if a shadow had passed over her grave. But then the maid opened the heavy, carved mahogany front door, and in spite of Alex's momentary chill of apprehension, a musical laugh escaped her lips. He was such a poseur, this one.

Dressed in an impeccable black tuxedo, he stood in the doorway, one elbow propped up against the doorframe, ankles crossed casually, doing his best Cary Grant, sophisticate-about-town imitation. In one arm, he clutched a sterling silver ice bucket with carved jade handles. Two champagne flutes dangled precariously, upside down, their flimsy stems threaded between the fingers of his other hand.

He glanced around in confusion for a second, seeking her out on the deep, tufted sofas and then over by the marble fireplace mantle. Every highly polished surface in the room held dense arrangements of birthday roses and lilies sent by less favored admirers, many of whose invitations she'd turned down in order to spend her special night with him.

When he finally caught sight of her out on the terrace, he grinned and strode across gleaming cherry wood floors. It was Dom Perignon in the silver bucket, she noted, tiny beads of condensation on the black bottle sparkling under the soft overhead lights. The exquisite flutes dangling between his fingers looked like Baccarat crystal.

Behind him, the maid remained at the entrance, staring, her mouth as open as the still yawning door. She was new, not yet accustomed to the kind of men Alexandra entertained. Still, you'd think the fool had never seen a man in a tuxedo before.

"Shut the door," Alex snapped in Cantonese. "Then go back to the kitchen."

"Oh, yes, madam! So sorry." The maid closed the door with a soft click of the latch, then shuffled away on slippered feet.

Alex turned her attention back where it belonged, on this silly, adorable, handsome man, as he leaned down to give her a kiss.

"Happy birthday, darling," he said.

He was almost a foot taller than she, and trimly built. Still, her small body and his large one fit together very nicely, she thought. He was quite a decent dancer, too. They would make a striking couple out on the floor at Fantin-Latour.

"You look good enough to eat," he added.

"Yes, please," she said demurely.

His grin widened. "Bad girl. Later. First, champagne, then dinner. After that, we'll see what else we can do for you."

He set the flutes on one of the low, glass patio tables. When he uncorked the bottle and poured the bubbles into the thin crystal, Alex pretended not to see the blue Tiffany box peeking out of his tuxedo jacket pocket. It didn't do to show too much excitement over such things or men might think you could be bought like some thoroughbred race horse—or worse, Kowloon whore. And Alexandra Kim Lee was certainly not that. She was a businesswoman, first, foremost and always.

He handed her one of the glasses, and the flutes chimed softly as the rims touched. "Many happy returns of the day, Alexandra."

"Thank you." She took a sip, savoring the perfect bubbles. Then she glanced over the rail once more. "Your car didn't wait?"

"I told the driver to park off to the side. Our reservation is for nine o'clock. I hope you don't mind not rushing right out."

She leaned back and studied him over the rim of her glass, smiling. "Not at all. The champagne is perfectly chilled, and I was just thinking what a lovely evening it was for enjoying the view."

"Gorgeous," he said, but he wasn't looking at the city or the harbor lights. "It's so quiet up here. And it's good to have you all to myself for a bit before we head back down into the heat and madness. It's an exciting city, Hong Kong, but it can be a little exhausting with all that frenetic bustle down there."

"Well, then, you should think of this as your refuge. Just you and me, all alone, floating on a cloud."

"And the maid."

She waved a delicate, dismissive hand, and her fine, woven gold bracelets sparkled.

He reached for the bottle and topped up their glasses. "Cheers, then. Here's to refuge in the clouds."

"Chin-chin," she said.

He moved beside her and they stood quietly, gazing down on the glistening city. A swath of swirling blue draped the star-dappled sky, a reflection of lights on the warm haze. Alex felt his hand come to rest briefly on her shoulder, then move slowly, sensuously down her back, raising a pleasant thrum on her skin.

"There's another reason I wanted a little time alone with you," he said quietly.

"Really?"

"Yes. I wanted to ask you something. Maybe now's as good a time as any."

"What did you want to ask me?"

"Well," he said, withdrawing his hand and looking down at his glass, suddenly boyish and coy. "I'll tell you in a minute. But before I do, I have a little surprise."

Aha, she thought, *the Tiffany box.* "Would it be a birthday surprise by any chance?"

"I think you could call it that." He took her glass from her hand and set both flutes aside on the low table. Then he lifted her fingers to his lips. "You're so very lovely, you know that?"

"Thank you. You're sweet."

He studied her face for a long moment and then, to her astonishment, he dropped to one knee. Alex's smile remained fixed, but inside, she felt a frisson of panic. The little blue Tiffany box in his pocket—it was probably the right size to hold a ring case.

Oh, please, don't tell me he's going to propose.

They hadn't even known each other all that long—not that longevity meant anything in cases like this. Last year, Hans

Dietermann, chairman of the board of München Deutsche Bank, had proposed to her during their first dinner together, only a few hours after they'd met. Then, as now, it was out of the question.

She touched his shoulders, a queen signaling her knight to rise. "Darling," she protested gently.

"Shhh, don't speak. Let me. What I wanted to say…"

She sighed and leaned back against the railing. What a way to ruin a perfectly good birthday.

His fingers slid lightly down the sides of her dress, as if he could find the words he needed written there in silk-stranded Braille. He leaned his head toward her knees, meekly, almost penitently, hands resting on her calves.

"What I wanted to say, my love, is this…"

He paused and exhaled heavily—working up his courage, she thought. Really, it was too tiresome. She wondered if it was too late to accept one of those other birthday dinner invitations. Finally, he found his voice again and looked up at her, a mischievous expression rising on his handsome face— handsome but not irresistible.

"You've been talking to people you shouldn't," he said, "telling tales out of school, bad girl. It's made your masters very angry."

This was not what she'd expected, but she had no more than a split second to even begin to comprehend his meaning before his grip tightened on her legs. He stood abruptly, and in one smooth movement, flipped her backward over the railing.

Shocked breathless, she made not a sound falling the two hundred and eighty-three feet to the pavement below.

He heard a faint thud as she landed, but didn't bother to look over the railing. What would be the point?

Instead, he dusted off the knees of his tuxedo pants, then picked up his champagne flute and downed the last dregs, slipping the drained glass into his jacket pocket next to the empty blue Tiffany box. He'd seen how her pupils had expanded when she'd spotted that stupid prop. He knew it would distract her.

Withdrawing a handkerchief, he wiped down the stem of her glass, the only part of it he'd touched, as well as the ice bucket and the bottle. Perhaps the initial thought would be that she'd been drinking alone, depressed on her birthday. The notion wouldn't stand up to five minutes of careful scrutiny, of course, but he didn't care. He'd be long gone, from the Peak, from Hong Kong, before the police ever got around to putting together a credible theory of what had happened here tonight—if they ever did.

Back inside, he crossed the living room quickly and silently. The place smelled like a bloody funeral parlor, he thought, with all those ostentatious floral arrangements. Appropriate, though, under the circumstances.

He withdrew a Sig-Sauer automatic from the holster at the small of his back, under his tuxedo jacket. The suppressor was in his other pocket, the one not holding the blue box. He screwed it onto the end of the barrel as he backed quietly along the wall, through the formal dining room and toward the kitchen.

He was at the swinging door when he heard the first faint yell of alarm rising from the front drive, twenty-eight floors below. A male voice. It wouldn't be the doorman, though. His driver would have long since taken him out, dumping the body in the trunk of the limo before leaving to dispose of it. It could be days before it floated to the surface of the harbor.

He gave the silencer one last, tightening twist. The motorcycle on which he himself would make his getaway had been pre-positioned near the servants' entrance at the back of the building. He calculated that he had as little as four minutes to get to it before the first police cars came up the Peak Road. In the meantime, the civilians on the scene would be pre-occupied with that silk-clad mess on the front drive.

Poor thing. She probably wasn't so gorgeous now.

When he burst through the kitchen door, the maid was sitting on a stool at the center island, a gossip magazine spread out in front of her, a bowl at her chin. Her chopsticks froze in mid-air and her mouth dropped open, grains of rice tumbling from her lips.

He put a single bullet in her forehead. The rice bowl sailed in one direction, the chopsticks in another, as the stool tipped backward. She slumped to the floor, her head wedged between the gleaming stainless steel stove and a maple cabinet.

Taking care to leave no prints, he left quietly through the rear kitchen door. The maid stared blindly after him, her black eyes milking over.

CHAPTER ONE

TOP SECRET
CODE WORD ACCESS ONLY
NOT FOR DISTRIBUTION

FEDERAL BUREAU OF INVESTIGATION
INTERVIEW TRANSCRIPTION

CASE NO. 1786521-02
CODE NAME: ACHILLES

DATE OF INTERVIEW: August 14, 2002
LEAD INTERROGATOR: FBI Special Agent
S. V. Andrews

(Special Agent Andrews) Okay, let's get started. Today is Wednesday, August 14, 2002, and this is interview number two with Mrs. Drummond MacNeil, also known as Carrie MacNeil.

I should note for the record that two witnesses are present: Mr. Frank Tucker, representing the office of the Director of Central Intelligence, and Mr. Mark Huxley, from

MI-6, the British foreign intelligence service. They're being allowed to observe this interview as part of their damage assessment on joint-intelligence operations resulting from the alleged activities of Mrs. MacNeil's husband. As of right now, Drummond MacNeil, CIA Deputy Director for Operations, is still at large, whereabouts unknown.

Okay, I think we're ready to begin now. So, for the record, please, state your full name and date of birth.

(Mrs. MacNeil) Didn't we establish that in the first interview?

We do it every time to keep the tapes properly identified for the transcribers.

Oh. That makes sense, I guess. So, once again then, it's Carrie Jane MacNeil. Originally Carolyn, but I've always been called Carrie. My maiden name was Morgan.

And your date of birth?

May 16, 1973.

So you're...um...twenty-nine years old, is that right?

Yes. I'll be thirty on my next birthday. The big three-oh. And don't I have a lot to be proud of approaching that landmark.

Such as?

I was being sarcastic, Agent Andrews. Obviously, my accomplishments are pretty limited. In fact, all things considered, I'd say I've made a real mess of things, wouldn't you?

In what way?

Take your pick. I've pretty much blown everything over the last decade—education, marriage, credibility. Abandoned my personal goals, so no career to speak of. And now, here I am, suspected of treason—and murder, too, if I understand correctly where you were heading when we talked yesterday. Good job, Carrie.

I told you yesterday, Mrs. MacNeil, the Bureau's official

position is that you're assisting our investigation into your husband's activities and subsequent disappearance. No one has said you're a suspect.

Not yet they haven't. You'll be sure to tell me when I am, though, won't you?

You'll be the first to know. But in the meantime, I want to confirm for the record that your participation in this debriefing is entirely voluntary. Is that right?

You mean, there's nothing I'd rather be doing?

No, I mean you're here of your own accord and we both understand that you're free of leave at any time.

Yes, fine, we both understand that. I can think of plenty of places I'd rather be, mind you. Having a root canal, for example.

No doubt. But getting back to the subject of your accomplishments, what about your son? You're proud of him, aren't you?

Oh, God, yes, I am. He's the best part of my life. All right, fair enough. I've messed up the rest of it, but I wouldn't have Jonah if it weren't for everything else. Let's just hope I haven't completely ruined his life, too.

That has to be a concern, for sure. But depending on the extent of your involvement in your husband's activities—

There was no involvement! I don't even know for sure that he was doing anything illegal. It's you people who keep insisting he sold state secrets and caused the deaths of I don't know how many people. Even if that's true, I had no idea anything was wrong until he vanished two days ago.

And you say he's gone into hiding, but what if you're wrong? What if he's been kidnapped? Isn't it possible he's innocent? That he's being held hostage—or worse—by terrorists? And you're just sitting here, wasting time, asking me questions I don't know the answers to?

We think it's highly unlikely he's been kidnapped, the evidence being what it is.

I'm still waiting to see all this supposed evidence.

All in good time. And if, in fact, it turns out you weren't involved, you'll be free to go home and raise your son and try to get past all this. But first, we have some information blanks to fill in and we think you can help.

So, let's just get back to the task at hand, shall we? State your address and place of employment once again for the record, if you don't mind.

What if I do?

Do what?

Mind.

Are you saying you won't cooperate with this investigation?

I'm just—never mind. It doesn't matter. My address—1221 Elcott Road, McLean, Virginia. At the moment, anyway.

You're planning to move?

I'm not sure. It's a little awkward there right now, and I've been offered the chance to house-sit for some family friends so... Well, I haven't decided yet what I'm going to do.

Do you own the house in McLean?

No. I think I mentioned yesterday that it belongs jointly to my husband and his mother. Actually, the house was left to Drum when his father died, but with the stipulation that my mother-in-law continue to live in it during her lifetime. Drum left her on the deed as co-owner because he was out of the country so much.

But this information you've already verified, I'm sure.

These are routine questions we have to ask. So, lastly, your employment.

None, at the moment. My son just turned six. With him so young and with us living abroad during my husband's last posting, I wasn't really able to work. I'm thinking about looking for something part-time in the fall, though, once Jonah's settled into first grade. Or, I was going to. But now that this has happened…

Sure. Things are up in the air, I can see that. Anyway, Mrs. MacNeil, I want to go back now to a subject we touched on yesterday before we had to wrap up—the murder of Alexandra Kim Lee in Hong Kong last summer.

I told you yesterday, I never met the woman.

But you know who she is.

Anyone who reads the papers or a newsmagazine would have heard of her. Her picture showed up there often enough, even before she died. I gather she was fairly well connected. Her murder was quite a little mystery back in the dog days of last summer. I seem to recall reading articles in *Time*—or *Newsweek*. Or both, I'm not sure. Weren't her maid and butler killed, too?

It wasn't a butler. It was the doorman of her building. Obviously, the killer wanted to eliminate witnesses.

Right. Anyway… I'm not sure why you keep asking me about her. It's not like I have anything original to offer.

You say most of what you know is from the papers. But not all, isn't that right? You have heard of Ms. Lee outside the media coverage of her murder, haven't you?

(unintelligible)

Pardon?

I said, yes, but it's still secondhand information. Until two days ago, when all hell broke loose, I only knew of her because of those newspaper stories. How would I have known her personally? She died in Hong Kong, right? At the time, we were living in London.

She had a home in London, too. Did you know that?

Not while we were there I didn't. I only just found that out.

At the same time you learned your husband knew her? (unintelligible)

What was that, Mrs. MacNeil? You'll have to speak up for the microphone.

I said, you really like to rub it in, don't you?

What do you mean?

The fact that Drum knew this woman—in the biblical sense, I suppose is what you're implying.

Is that true? Was he having an affair with her?

I have no idea. You're suggesting he was, apparently, but I have no proof of it.

Do you think it's possible?

Anything is possible. I would have had no way of knowing. You know what my husband's position was in London. He was CIA Chief of Station there. He had contact with all kinds of people, but I wasn't allowed to ask questions about any of it. That's how that game works, isn't it? Need to know—isn't that the operational term? Does your wife need to know about this conversation we're having right now, Agent Andrews? Are you going to go home tonight and talk it over with her? I'm guessing not. You guys and your precious little spy games and secrets. You just love them.

Mrs. MacNeil, if you and I were sleeping together, I guarantee you, my wife would know it in two minutes flat. She'd see the guilt in my face, for one thing, even before she found lipstick on my collar or whatever.

Ah, well, there's the problem—you just put your finger on it. You, Agent Andrews, would apparently feel guilty about sleeping with another woman and your wife would pick up on that. Bravo. She's a lucky woman. Nice to be married to a man you can count on.

Are you saying your husband was unreliable in a general sense? Or just that he didn't love you? Mrs. MacNeil? Carrie? Would you like some water?

No, I'm fine. I just—I thought—at the time... I knew there were other women. I did. Not because Drum showed any sign of guilt, mind you. Oh, there was a little pro forma remorse, maybe, on a couple of occasions when I tried to confront him about it, but I wouldn't call it guilt. He didn't even try all that hard to deny it. He said it was the nature of the job, that it didn't mean anything.

Not to him, maybe....

Look, you have to understand, Drum's twenty years older than me. His career and his habits were firmly established long before I came along. Not that I knew that when I married him, mind you. But from the time I found out what he really did for a living, I had to accept that he would be keeping odd hours and meeting people I'd know nothing about—his intelligence contacts, agents, sources—whatever you want to call them. Women in my position—it's mostly women, although these days, I suppose there are some husbands in the same boat, too—anyway, when you marry into this business, you soon learn not to ask questions.

And Alexandra Kim Lee?

Well, I guess it makes sense she was the kind of source Langley would want to cultivate. The papers said she was bribing western officials on behalf of Beijing.

So that's what you think your husband was doing? Cultivating a source? Or eliminating a threat?

I told you, I'm not even certain he knew her.

And if there were proof he did?

What kind of proof?

Copies of CIA contact reports on meetings he had with her. Surveillance photographs.

You have those? Do you have them here?

I can't show you the contact reports. Those are highly classified, obviously. But I do have these pictures I can show you—

Oh, God—then it's true.

This last one was taken three days before she was murdered.... Carrie? What is it?

The park they're in here? I recognize it. That statue of the soldier on the horse? Jonah, my son, used to call it the dancing horse statue. It's across the street from the American International School in London— Bloody hell! Drum took that woman to our son's school?

According to the surveillance report, they had been at her place in Mayfair that afternoon until your husband had to leave to pick up your son. The Brits had her apartment bugged. Apparently he told her you were at the British Museum—something about a seminar on African sculpture?

It was that day? I remember. I'd been updating the research on my master's thesis, trying to finish it. The British Museum was having a lecture series on African art that was right up my alley, so Drum agreed I should attend. Our housekeeper was off sick, so he said he'd take care of Jonah after kindergarten. Damn him! Then he goes and takes one of his bimbos to our son's school? What a bastard! Did he—

What? Introduce her to your son? No. Apparently she left when the school bell rang. Honestly, Carrie? I doubt this woman had much interest in playing stepmom to anyone.

Still—

Anyway, she flew back to Hong Kong the next day and two days after that, she was thrown off a twenty-eighth floor balcony.

And you think Drum had something to do with her murder?

What do you think?

I have no idea.

Do you remember where he was when it happened? Three days after you attended that lecture at the British Museum, it would have been.

Not the foggiest. I mean, I presume he would have been in his office at the embassy, but I can't be certain. Who can remember every little detail of a week that happened over a year ago?

Well, let me remind you then. His calendar for that week says he left London two days after this to attend a CIA regional meeting in Delhi.

Okay, I remember that, now that you mention it. He did go to India for a few days last summer. There you go, then. That's where he was.

Except he showed up late to the Delhi meeting. Arrived the day after Alexandra Kim Lee was murdered in Hong Kong. He said one of his connecting flights had been cancelled, but when we retrace his steps, there are thirty-eight hours unaccounted for. We have no idea where he was. He had no shortage of CIA aliases he could have been traveling under, but in checking flight manifests, we can't find any record of IDs sanctioned by the Agency. Thirty-eight hours, though, would have given him enough time to get from London to Hong Kong, murder Miss Lee, as well as the maid and doorman, then hightail it back to the Delhi meeting.

Sounds like a stretch to me. But even supposing you're right about all that, are you really surprised? She was bribing western officials, right? That's what the papers said, anyway. I know the CIA's not supposed to be assassinating people, but I gather there are exceptions to the rule. Langley could have ordered him to do it.

Oh, he was ordered to do it, all right, but not by the CIA. She was one of their own assets, you see—a double agent and a direct feed into the Chinese leadership. Whatever she did for Beijing was small potatoes compared to the influence she exerted on key Chinese officials and the gold mine of information she funneled back to Langley.

Now, we know from other sources that the Chinese found out she was playing both sides of the street, and so they ordered the hit on her. And how did they find out? Because your husband sold them the information.

You have proof of that?

Let's just say it looks like your husband has been selling out CIA assets for some time now—and some assets our British allies were sharing with us, too, which is why Mr. Huxley here from MI-6 is being allowed to observe these debriefings. And we're not just talking about Chinese operations, either.

It's so hard to believe. I mean, Drum's no angel, but I find it difficult to credit that he would commit treason, especially given his family's history of service to the country.

All I know for sure is that I had nothing to do with it. The only thing I've been doing for the past few years is trying to make a stable home for my son under circumstances that haven't always been ideal.

And yet, you do seem to be personally connected to a number of people who subsequently show up murdered.

What do you mean, a number of people? Who else? And while we're on the subject, let's not forget that my connection to Alexandra Kim Lee is secondhand, involuntary and after the fact. I don't know why anyone would think I had reason to want her dead.

She was sleeping with your husband and getting too close for comfort to your child.

Okay, that's it. I'm out of here.

You should sit down, Carrie.

No. This has gone far enough. I don't have to listen to this. I agreed to come in and tell you what I know about my husband's comings and goings. Now, I find myself being accused of God only knows what. You said I could leave anytime. Well, I want to leave now.

That's not a good idea. You leave now, it looks like you've got something to hide.

Like, I murdered this woman in Hong Kong? Are you out of your mind?

All right, all right. Let's forget about Alexandra Kim Lee for the moment.

Not until it's clear that I had nothing to do with her death— or anyone else's, for that matter.

Fine. If we leave her aside, will you sit back down?

No more stupid accusations?

Come on, Carrie, you know we have to ask you these questions if we're ever going to get to the bottom of what happened to your husband. Let's just do what we have to do so you can get back to your son, all right.

As long as it's understood…

Thank you. Now, if you'd take a look at another picture. What about this young woman? Do you recognize her?

Yes.

Where do you know her from?

I didn't say I knew her. I saw her—once, at the embassy in London. Just before it happened.

Before she was murdered, right? Her name was Karen Ann Hermann, by the way.

I know. I mean, I didn't know her name at the time—we barely spoke—but I learned it later. She was killed outside the embassy.

This past April 2, in fact. You were there when it happened. And then, right afterward, you skipped town— you and your husband both.

We didn't skip town! His posting in London was supposed to be up that summer, anyway. We left sooner than planned, that's all.

How convenient for you.

You're twisting this—

Let's just go over that day, Carrie—the day last spring when Karen Ann Hermann, a young American student who'd never hurt anyone in her life, was gunned down in cold blood outside the U.S. Embassy.

CHAPTER TWO

London, England
Tuesday, April 2, 2002

It wasn't meant to happen that way. No one so young or sweet or blameless should die like that, sprawled bleeding and terrified in a muddy puddle on a dark and rainy London street, far from home, surrounded by gaping strangers watching her life ebb away.

Karen Ann Hermann was only nineteen years old, a pretty young student from Maryland with a slim build, shy brown eyes, and a thick, nut brown braid that ran down her back nearly to her waist. She'd arrived in Britain only the day before, eagerly anticipating the sights—London Bridge, Buckingham Palace and all the other tourist draws ticked off in her dog-eared guidebook. An innocent abroad. She was only meant to spend ten days in England, and then go home to a long, happy, productive life.

Instead, only thirty-six hours after her plane landed at Heathrow, Karen Ann Hermann was cut down in a hail of bullets in rainy Grosvenor Square.

American Embassy, Grosvenor Square
4:15 p.m

A somber overcast sky shrouded the city. Cold dreary rain had been falling all afternoon. The roads and sidewalks were slick and treacherous. Stubby London cabs kept their headlamps lit in order to see and be seen through the dank, gray mist.

But ominous as the day was, city life trudged on and the streets were crowded with pedestrians. From the roof of the fortresslike American Embassy, surveillance cameras peered down on a steady stream of umbrellas that passed through Grosvenor Square like a river of bobbing wet multicolored mushrooms.

Gunnery Sergeant Brian Jenks of the United States Marine Corps stood watch just inside the embassy's main front doors, stationed in a booth fronted by an inch and a half of bulletproof glass. The receptionist at the window was locally engaged, the wife of one of the junior consular officers. At the moment, she was handing out temporary passport applications to a couple of American tourists who'd been scammed by a team of wallet-lifting pickpockets in the Earl's Court Underground station.

Sergeant Jenks, known to his men as "Gunny," was seated just behind and off to one side of her. It was his job to manage the security watch. A bank of closed-circuit monitors before him carried the feed from a dozen or so stationary and panoramic cameras located both inside and outside the chancery. The cameras were only a small component of the hardware mounted on the embassy, a spiny porcupine of a building bristling with antennae, sensors and filters attuned to the slightest noise, vibration, chemical or biological compound that might pose a threat to the building, its occupants, or the secrets it housed. Other equipment sent out a defensive array of silent, invisible beams to foil intrusions of the electronic, acoustic, microwave or infrared variety.

But none of this fancy equipment, the Gunny figured, was worth a damn without equal measures of human vigilance, precaution-taking, and plain old common sense. Overconfidence on technology opened the door to deadly intrusions of the low-tech variety, and when that happened, it was grunts like him and his men who paid the price with their lives. That's what had gone down in Beirut, Saudi, Nairobi and Dar es Salaam, and they were probably due for another nasty surprise any day now. If so, it wasn't going to happen on his watch.

The Gunny was five feet and seven inches of rock-solid muscle. As middle age loomed, it was getting harder to maintain the integrity of that bulldozer frame, but Jenks was proud of his powerful arms and rock-solid abs. "Small but mighty," he liked to think of himself, as he worked up a sweat every morning on the free weights and Universal set in the basement of Marine House, the nineteenth-century Victorian mansion where the embassy's twenty-eight-man Marine detachment bunked and where the Gunny and his family occupied a top-floor apartment.

The Gunny's head was shaved in classic Marine style, high and tight, with a circular patch of blond stubble on top waxed to ramrod attention. It made for a slightly pointed skull that seemed a little too small for his thick neck and broad shoulders, but in this, the Gunny was the perfect Jarhead, a well-

oiled machine of raw strength and pure military efficiency—
a role model for his men.

In the past, the Marine Guard had worn dress uniforms for
embassy duty, but with the heightened security climate now,
they manned their stations in battle dress, the better to intimi-
date. The Gunny's mottled cammies were starched to within
an inch of their lives and pressed into razor-sharp creases. His
webbed belt and holster cinched tight on his narrow waist, and
his pants were tucked into black combat boots that spit-polish
gleamed under the recessed overhead lights. His small forehead
was permanently pressed into a corrugated line of worry wrin-
kles as his sharp eyes scanned the bank of monitors before him.

In the marble-floored lobby on the other side of the bullet-
proof glass, hundreds of embassy visitors and staff passed
each day through security scanners operated by his men. At
the front gates, a guard hut stood inside a zigzagged row of
concrete barriers erected to thwart any determined terrorist
with an explosive-laden vehicle.

The Gunny's focus zeroed in now on the monitor display
of the guard hut out front, where two young Marines were
scrutinizing visitor IDs. A car bearing diplomatic plates had
just pulled past the concrete barricade and approached the
high, wrought-iron embassy gate.

Parking inside the embassy compound was at a premium.
Only the ambassador and selected senior diplomatic staff
were permitted to drive or be driven inside, along with a very
few high-level visitors, such as other ambassadors and rep-
resentatives from the Foreign Office. Agents from MI-5 and
MI-6, the British security and intelligence agencies, had also
been showing up ever more frequently in recent months to li-
aise with their American counterparts.

The Gunny could almost feel the cold drizzle running down

his shirt collar as one of his oilskin-jacketed boys bent low, rifles at the ready, to peer into the window of the chauffeur-driven Mercedes, whose tricolor flags fluttered wetly from staffs mounted on the front fenders. This would be the French ambassador, arriving for a private meeting with the visiting delegation of U.S. senators—late, of course, the Gunny thought, snorting lightly. A reception would follow the ambassadorial meeting, and it was scheduled to kick off shortly.

Trust the goddamn Frogs. If they couldn't even show up on time for a high level meeting, how the hell could you count on them to do their bit in the war on terrorism?

With his attention focused on the action at the front gate, the sergeant failed to hear the footsteps approaching from behind. "Hey there, Gunny. Who do we have here?"

The Marine, to his credit, didn't flinch.

When Drummond MacNeil peered over his shoulder at the screen, the Gunny noticed a flush rising on the receptionist's cheeks. Typical. Most of the women in the embassy seemed to hover near MacNeil at internal office get-togethers or follow him with their eyes whenever he passed in the hall. "Gorgeous," one girl had called him. Amazing how a mysterious job, six feet of lanky slouch, and a pair of blue eyes could turn some perfectly nice girls into total bimbos.

"Looks like the French ambassador, sir," the Gunny told him.

"Ah, oui, Monsieur Chevalier de la Haye." MacNeil's expression was arch, his accent fruity, but it sounded dead-on to the Gunny's untrained ear. "Fashionably late and ready to make a dramatic entrance, as always, I see."

"I guess."

They watched on the monitor as the young Marine at the gate waved the car through.

"Too bad he didn't just take a miss altogether," MacNeil

added. "I'm sure our visiting dignitaries could do without this guy and his constant whining."

"Don't care for our French allies, sir?"

"Avoid 'em as much as I can. My old man used to say, 'Count on the French to hide behind your back when the shooting starts and to stick a knife in it as soon as victory's declared.'"

The Gunny glanced up with interest. "Your father served over there during WWII?" MacNeil's much-decorated father, General Naughton MacNeil, had been a member of the Joint Chiefs of Staff during the early days of Vietnam, so it made sense that the old man would have seen service in the Big One.

MacNeil nodded. "He was with Patton's Eighth Army in North Africa, then arrived in Paris in time for the liberation. Not that the French ever thanked him for it. He said they drove him nuts when it came to working together in NATO."

MacNeil stepped back from the monitor and perched his long, lean frame on the corner of a desk near the door, his gaze shifting to the receptionist as she bent low to withdraw some paper from a bottom drawer of her desk, revealing a hint of cleavage and a lacy patch of pink bra. The girl seemed to feel his eyes on her, because she looked up and her face flushed even deeper. She turned back to the window as MacNeil gave the Gunny a sly wink. His suit jacket was unbuttoned, shoulders slouching as his hands slid into the pockets of soft gray pants that even the Gunny could tell were custom-made and must have cost a fortune.

"Your father was a great military leader, sir."

"Well, he died with his boots on, anyway. Dropped dead of a heart attack while reviewing the troops. All Army, all the way."

MacNeil didn't sound too broken up about it, the Gunny thought. Bad blood between them, maybe?

The younger MacNeil was about as different from the General as it was possible to be. Drummond MacNeil was in his late forties, with a thick head of hair that was considerably longer than the Gunny thought appropriate, even for a civilian. It took constant raking to keep the silvery mop from spilling into the man's perpetually amused eyes. MacNeil always looked like the whole world was walking around with "KICK ME" signs stuck to their backs while he was the only one in on the big yuck.

The Gunny focused on his monitors so MacNeil wouldn't see his frown of disapproval. The General, by contrast, had been a towering mountain of a man—not a Marine, of course, but pretty damn tough just the same. Once, on a visit to the Pentagon, Jenks had seen the old man's portrait hanging in a corridor. Built solid, buzz-cut and stern-looking, General MacNeil had radiated leadership. The Gunny would've followed that guy into any field of action he named, and so would just about every Marine he knew.

But the son was another kettle of fish. Had never even served in the military, which must have been a real disappointment to the old man. The Gunny had a son himself, and the kid's first words, swear to God, were *Semper Fi*. (Of course, Jenks had coached the baby for months, much to his wife's disgust, but still…) Now six, Connor practically slept in his miniature size cammies and could hardly wait to join the Corps.

MacNeil the younger hadn't gone the military route, though. Apparently he'd washed out of West Point and avoided the service altogether after that, trading instead on his rep as a Yale man. The Gunny had heard people in a position to know say Drummond MacNeil had done more partying than studying at the Ivy League school. Only the family's connections had swung his admission and protected a bare "C" average. After spending most of the seventies swanning around beaches, bars, and no-brainer jobs, MacNeil had apparently used those same connections to land himself a job at Langley.

Still, he must have done something right at the Agency, the

Gunny conceded, since he'd ended up with this plum London job and, by all reports, was on the fast track to the top. Go figure. Her Majesty's official diplomatic list identified MacNeil as a trade counselor, but a select few knew he was actually chief of the CIA's London station.

"Anyway, sir, did you need anything?" Jenks asked him.

"I just stepped out of the meeting to see this guy in," MacNeil said, nodding at the monitor as the French ambassador's car pulled up to the double front doors. "I was also hoping to spot my wife. Has she shown up yet, do you know?"

"I haven't seen her, sir."

Now, that's what wasn't fair, the Gunny thought. The guy was married to a great girl, his second wife, by all accounts. Carrie MacNeil was young, pretty, and nice as all get-out. The MacNeils' son, Jonah, was in Connor's kindergarten class at the American International School, and Carrie was one of the hardest working parent volunteers there. Their boys always ended up playing together at embassy family functions, like the Fourth of July picnic and the annual Christmas party, where by tradition the biggest Marine in the detachment dressed up as Santa and handed out presents to the diplobrats and assorted other embassy offspring. And when Carrie got herself done up to the nines for some fancy dress function, with her long, reddish hair and those shy, gray-green eyes— well, all the Gunny knew was that he'd had to warn several of his randier guys that wives of senior staff (especially the CIA head of station, for chrissakes) were strictly off-limits.

"She's supposed to be coming in for this reception and dinner of the ambassador's," MacNeil was saying. "Wives were originally invited to both, but then the ambassador's wife begged off dinner, so now the other wives are uninvited and it's turned into a working dinner. I tried calling Carrie to let her know, but there's no answer at the house and she doesn't seem to have her mobile turned on. What's the point of having a cell phone, I keep asking her, if you don't turn it on? That's why I got her the damn thing." MacNeil leaned closer to the monitors to scan the surrounding streets. "Jesus! Who can spot anybody under all these umbrellas. Anyway, Gunny," he added, straightening as the French ambassador swept into the lobby, "I've got to get back upstairs. Could you let her know when she comes in that dinner's off? As long as she's here, she might as well come up for the reception, though, meet a couple of senators."

"I'll pass the message on, sir."

But the Station Chief was already out the door, embracing the Parisian envoy like a long-lost brother and leading him back into the embassy's inner sanctum.

The Gunny sighed and turned again to his monitors, studying the feeds from the street outside, wondering which umbrella belonged to Carrie MacNeil, and how she'd feel about finding out she'd been uninvited to the ambassador's dinner after trekking out in this dismal weather.

Gunnery Sergeant Jenks wasn't the only one in Grosvenor Square on the lookout that afternoon.

Across from the embassy, a hard-eyed man was parked in a squat London cab with its service lights switched to the "Off Duty" position. The cab was parked out of sight next to a London branch of the Canton-Shanghai Bank. A knit black watch cap was pulled low over his forehead, completely obscuring his hairline, but the thick black stubble on his chin and his heavy moustache suggested a heritage rooted anywhere around the Mediterranean or beyond—which could mean Spain, Italy, Greece, India, or any one of half a dozen

Middle Eastern countries. There were so many immigrants in London nowadays that the man's swarthy appearance was completely unremarkable.

In fact, this man's ancestors hailed from the Caucuses, but he himself had been born and bred in an east-end London suburb only four miles from where he now sat waiting for his target to appear out of the mist.

National Gallery, Trafalgar Square
4:28 p.m.

The clerk at the youth hostel near St. Paul's Cathedral had told Karen Ann Hermann and her two girlfriends that morning that heavy rain was predicted to begin in the afternoon and continue for the next couple of days, so the girls had decided to see the changing of the guard at Buckingham Palace first thing, while the weather was still on their side. From there, they'd wandered up to Trafalgar Square to feed the pigeons, then ducked into the National Gallery across the road as the rain moved in.

It was late afternoon when Karen, sitting on a padded bench near the gallery's Leonardo etchings, consulted her much-thumbed guide book, her finger tracing a map of central London.

"The American Embassy's just a few blocks from here," she told her friends. "I think I could run over there and be back in an hour or so."

Kristina Finch looked doubtful. "Maybe we should go with you." The girls had been roommates at the University of Maryland.

"Seems like a waste of time for you guys if you're going to bother registering," said Karen.

Caitlin Bercha, the third in the group, had lived across the hall from the other two. "You don't really have to, you know. That's just something you do in places where there might be a revolution or something. Not much chance of that here."

"Yeah, plus we're only going to be here for ten days," Kristina added.

Karen hesitated, then exhaled wearily, the much-put-upon sigh of youth everywhere. "I know, but I promised my parents."

"But it's pouring out there. You'll get soaked walking all that way."

"Why don't you just *tell* them you registered?" Kristina suggested brightly.

"Yeah! How are they ever going to know?" Caitlin asked. "Then we can see if we can get some stand-by tickets for the theater tonight. The guy at the youth hostel said they disappear fast, so we should get to the box office early."

Karen looked from one eager face to the other, sorely tempted. But then her conscience kicked in. She was an only child and her parents worried more than most. She couldn't lie to them.

"I can't. I promised. Look, I'll tell you what. How about if you guys go over and see about the tickets, and I'll do this embassy thing, and then we'll meet up at, umm…" Her forefinger slid across her guidebook map. "Leicester Square. That's in the theater district."

The two other girls exchanged glances. "I don't know," Caitlin said. "Maybe we'd better stick together."

"No, really, guys, this is a good idea. You go for the tickets and I'll do this. No point in all of us wasting what little time we have."

"Are you sure you'll be all right?"

Karen waved away their worries and gathered up her things. "I'll be fine." She shrugged into her long tan raincoat, leaving her braid inside and flipping up the collar. From her pocket she withdrew a black knit tam which she pulled onto her head. "Watch for me at Leicester Square—say around six-thirty, just to be on the safe side. I don't want to leave you guys hanging around in the rain."

So, the plans were made.

Karen left her friends with a smile on her face, secretly glad for a little quiet time as she stepped out onto the wide, white front steps of the National Gallery and popped open her black travel umbrella. Not that the streets around Trafalgar Square were all that quiet, what with the swish of tires on wet pavement and the roar and honking of rush hour traffic. But the average teenage girl abhors a conversational vacuum, so Karen had been inundated with high-pitched chatter almost non-stop since she and her two friends had met up at Dulles Airport three days earlier to catch their flight for London. At this point, her craving for quiet was almost physical.

Life had given Karen Ann Hermann an unusual appreciation for silence. The only child of parents who were both profoundly deaf, her early childhood had been spent in a world as still and serene as it was warm and loving. Karen had no hearing deficit of her own, but long before a preschool tutor had been brought in to help bring her speech up to par, she'd been signing fluently, and she still moved easily between the hearing and non-hearing worlds. Every summer since the age of thirteen, she'd worked at a camp for hearing-impaired youngsters, first as a volunteer, then as a paid counselor.

Karen's parents had never been encouraged to cultivate a sense of adventure themselves, but a couple of those kids their daughter worked with, they'd been astonished to discover, had traveled around the world. They skied and scuba dived and parasailed, and got downright snippy if you suggested there was anything surprising in that. Times had definitely changed. The Hermanns had never even been on bicycles for fear they might be struck by an unheard car coming up on them from behind. And though they now ran a small but moderately successful home-based Web site management business, neither had ever traveled beyond a sixty-or-so-mile radius of Washington, D.C.

Karen was already determined to help give the next generation of hearing-impaired kids more opportunities than her parents had had. She was even considering pursuing a doctorate and then teaching at Gallaudet University, the only one in the country dedicated to the needs of deaf students. Now *there,* the Hermanns thought, was a hot-bed of militancy. Both were Gallaudet graduated, but would a hearing-enabled professor, even one as sign-fluent and accomplished as Karen, be welcomed there these days, when so many students insisted that hearing people couldn't relate to the issues they faced? They didn't want their precious daughter targeted by reverse discrimination.

It was a source of constant worry, but they comforted themselves with the realization that Karen's final career decisions were some way off.

In the meantime, she'd gotten it into her head to do some traveling. Having passed her freshman year at the University of Maryland with flying colors and the start of her summer job still a month off, she'd been eager to join two girlfriends on a spring vacation in England. She was a good kid, an honor roll student who'd never given them a moment of worry. What's more, she was an adult now, for all intents and purposes, and she'd saved the money for the trip herself from the part-time tutoring she'd done all year. How could her nervous parents forbid her from going, much as they wanted to?

Before they would agree, though, they'd gone onto the Internet to do their homework. The State Department Web site posted travel warnings to Americans traveling abroad, but Britain, they were relieved to see, fell into a low-risk category. Fair enough. The IRA seemed to prefer negotiation to bombs these days, and London was as security-conscious as Washington where other hot-button populations were concerned. If their daughter must go abroad, England was probably as safe a bet as anywhere.

Still, the State Department Web site did advise U.S. travelers to register with the embassy on arrival in a foreign country so that they could be notified in case of emergency. If the advice was rarely heeded in the more popular tourist destinations, the Hermanns didn't know that.

Afterward, they would bitterly regret extracting the promise that took Karen to the embassy that day. Had they been a little more worldly, they might not have, but Mr. and Mrs. Hermann had never been out of the country themselves.

Thus it was that Karen Ann Hermann came to be outside the American Embassy that dark and rainy London afternoon when all hell broke loose.

CHAPTER THREE

FEDERAL BUREAU OF INVESTIGATION
INTERVIEW TRANSCRIPTION

(continued...)

So when you arrived for the reception that afternoon, Carrie, you didn't know you wouldn't be attending the ambassador's dinner?

No. Apparently Drum had left messages for me on my mobile and at home, but for some reason, I hadn't gotten either of them. I gather he'd also asked the Gunny to watch out for me—that's the Gunnery Sergeant, head of the Marine Guard detachment.

Sergeant Jenks, yes. He's been interviewed on several occasions. We've got his full testimony covering that day.

Right. Well then, you know he was on duty in the lobby. He was tied up when I came in, so it was Drum's secretary who took me upstairs to the reception. She was also the one who told me I wasn't needed at the dinner.

Would it surprise you to learn there's no record your husband ever called your cell phone that day?

He said he did. I thought the voice-mail system must have been down.

It was working just fine, according to company records. And although the phone at your apartment did receive one call at about...let's see...12:27 p.m. GMT—

That's when he called to tell me I was invited to the reception and dinner.

Right. According to your home-phone records, that was the only incoming call that day.

So, what are you saying?

I'm saying he lied. Your husband's real purpose was to lure you out that afternoon.

Lure me out?

Yes. That's why he didn't bother calling back when the dinner requirement disappeared. He made a special point of going down to the lobby and telling Sergeant Jenks he'd called you to try to cancel, but we think he was just covering his tracks.

You make it sound like he was laying a trap for me. What are you—

Let's just carry on with that day, Carrie. Did you see anything out of the ordinary when you arrived? Anyone who seemed to be watching you as you went in?

No. Not that I would have noticed, probably. It was a horrible day, pouring rain. I was hunched down under an umbrella and so was everyone else in the street.

Did you take a taxi?

No, it was just a few blocks. I probably should have, but I didn't realize how hard it was raining. I walked over.

So you weren't approached by a taxi or anyone else in the street? Didn't notice that you were being followed?

Not that I recall. I talked briefly to the Marines at the front gate when I got to the embassy. I knew them, of course. And then, the receptionist at the front desk, who called up to say I'd arrived. That's when Drum's secretary came down to take me up and told me about the cancellation.

And how did your husband seem when you saw him?

I don't know. Fine. Normal, I guess.

He didn't seem surprised that you'd actually made it over? You didn't notice anything unusual about his reaction?

Not really...unless... I don't know...

So there was something?

I'm not sure. It was a busy day for him. High profile, you know, with the senators in town and him responsible for their program while they were in London. And it was a tense time for everyone, of course with the heightened security climate since September 11.

But there was something else. What was it?

I'm not sure. It's hard to put my finger on it.

Try. Tell me about that afternoon, Carrie. What happened when you attended the reception for those visiting politicians?

CHAPTER FOUR

American Embassy, Grosvenor Square, London
5:41 p.m.

Carrie's facial muscles were beginning to ache from the effort of so much forced smiling. Her feet, perched on impractical three-inch heels, were wet and cold, and as she shifted her weight on the thick pile carpet, she felt water squishing in the toes of her strappy black Manolos. She'd probably ruined her most expensive shoes, wearing them out on such a rainy afternoon, but Drum had told her to "spiff it up" when he'd called unexpectedly and pressed her to put in an appearance at this late afternoon reception and the dinner to follow.

Now, it turned out she wasn't needed at dinner.

The expendable chair-filler, that's me, she thought, dodging the frond of one of the tall, potted palms that dotted the perimeter of the long room. She kept finding herself backed into the thing, wedged into a corner by two of the reception's more garrulous guests, and it felt as if a persistent spider were landing on her bare neck every few minutes. It was beginning to get really irritating.

She took a dangerous sip from her wineglass—dangerous because she was starving and now there wasn't even the prospect of a good meal to fill her empty stomach. Not that the wine did anything to improve her mood, which was becoming grumpier by the minute, knowing she'd trudged out in the pouring rain for nothing more than a tepid glass of mediocre California Chardonnay and yet another chance to observe the diplomatic version of that ancient male ritual, the pissing contest.

In this environment, it meant feigning to possess more insider access than the other guy—with "feign" being the operative word here, Carrie decided, watching her two companions over the rim of her wineglass. One was an ambitious young Bostonian, who had to be fresh out of college, with that thick, shining mop of Ivy League hair and those darting, nervous eyes that belied a self-promoting line of patter. Carrie had already forgotten his name. *David? Douglas... something?* He was a junior aide to one of the visiting senators. She was guessing it was his first official trip abroad.

The other was Nigel St. John (pronounced "Sin-jin," she had to keep reminding herself, like that actor who always insisted that "Ralph" was really "Rafe"—God, but some Brits could be pretentious...). St. John was a minor British Foreign Office functionary who always seemed to latch on to her whenever she was dragooned into attending one of these official cocktails.

Carrie would have been happy to leave the two of them to their own devices, now that she'd done her duty and made introductions and a little small talk, except that Nigel kept clutching her arm and drawing her back into the circle of their conversation every time her gaze drifted over his shoulder in search of some avenue of escape.

The embassy's top-floor reception area was a large, open room painted a pale antique yellow, with cherry wainscoting and crown moldings imported from the Carolinas and deep blue broadloom woven in the carpet mills of Georgia. Occasional chairs, chests and tables scattered around the room were eighteenth- and nineteenth-century Philadelphia Hepplewhite and Chippendale pieces. An ever-changing array of canvases by contemporary American artists lined the gallery-like walls.

This was where America put its best foot forward in the British capital. Guests were expected to do no less.

The scent of hot seafood canapés and expensive colognes drifted over the assembled crowd of sixty or so guests invited to meet the visiting senators this afternoon. Tinkling glasses provided a high counterpoint to the deep drone of mostly male voice holding forth from every part of the room, punctuated by the occasional eruption of mock-hearty laughter.

As she looked over the room, seeking out her husband, Carrie recognized a number of faces belonging to the usual crowd of Brits and officials from other friendly embassies who regularly showed up at these functions and hosted their own in return. One or two returned Carrie's glance with acknowledging nods that ranged from merely polite to downright lascivious—the latter from a randy Australian charge who smirked as he checked her out from head to toe and back up again, with pointed pauses at breast level. Carrie was tempted to offer a stiff-fingered salute in return, but that would have been considered poor protocol and, in any case, took more nerve than she possessed.

Instead, she turned away from him, and as she did, she spotted Drum over by the tall, arched windows with Senator Watkins, head of the Senate's select intelligence committee.

Her husband's raised eyebrows when Carrie had first walked in the room, followed by a quick smile and nod, told her she'd probably passed muster—maybe even exceeded his expectations. Well, fine. With the exception of an ambassador's spouse, whose role as chatelaine made her something of a social force to be reckoned with, nobody on the diplomatic circuit paid much attention to a mere "wife of." After seven years of marriage, the last three spent here in the British capital, she'd long since resigned herself to the fact that her primary job at these affairs was to serve as ornamentation.

She'd worn a green silk wrap dress that Drum said turned her gray-green eyes catlike. Her long, coppery hair was clipped up in a loose twist impaled by a jeweled stick. There hadn't been time to do much else with it, given the last-minute nature of this command performance. In any case, it had seemed the safest bet to survive the sleety rainstorm she'd had to brave to get over here from their Kensington town house. A few soft tendrils had shaken loose in the bluster.

"Don't you agree, Carrie?" St. John asked out of the blue.

Carrie shifted her focus back and offered what she hoped was a convincing nod. She'd dropped the thread of the conversation, which seemed at the moment to consist of the usual complaints about the fickle French. Her two companions were so busy upping the ante of their mutual indignation that she knew they sought her input only as a matter of courtesy.

"No doubt," she said. She had no idea what she'd agreed with, but it didn't matter. They required only an appreciative audience.

Her gaze shifted back to her husband. She could have tried begging off this reception when he'd called at the last minute like that. She had work of her own to finish, pulling together the bibliography on her master's thesis, which was almost ready to be shipped back to her advisor at Georgetown, if only she could quit her nervous tinkering. If he thought it was ready to defend, she'd finally complete the program she'd abandoned six years earlier when her son was born. And then…well, first finish the thesis, she told herself. One step at a time.

The lowering clouds outside had added another disincentive to coming out this afternoon, plus the fact that she liked to be home when the embassy van brought Jonah home from kindergarten. In the end, though, she'd done what Drum asked, as she always did. After all, this was an important occasion for him and it wouldn't kill her to be amiable.

Like all intelligence officials abroad, he operated under cover in a milieu where "Spot the Spook" was the favorite game of bored diplomats. Officials in the know sometimes referred to Drum archly as the post's "resident intellectual," but his cover story said he was a commercial counselor. As his wife, Carrie was required to maintain that charade, while at the same time taking special precautions not to compromise his position or station operations. Most of the carefully selected guests to this particular reception, of course, knew what his real function was, but she'd long since learned that the safest path in all situations was to neither confirm nor deny anything.

The delegation of American politicians had arrived in London that morning, their first stop on a whirlwind fact-finding tour in the latest round of the war on terrorism. Drum would be leading them through their briefings with his intelligence contacts in MI-5 and MI-6, as well as the Foreign and Prime Minister's offices and the Ministry of Defense.

His present companion across the room was the head of the delegation. An overweight, blustering powerhouse from Arizona, Senator Watkins was obviously in lecture mode at the moment, but Carrie knew there was no need to worry about Drum. He'd lived his entire life among powerful movers and shakers. Not only had his father been a five-star general and member of the Joint Chiefs of Staff, but the MacNeil family had been wealthy and influential Virginia landowners, businessmen and community leaders for generations. Drum could hold his own with anyone.

His body language now, as he leaned a shoulder against a leaded glass window frame, told Carrie he was just waiting for the senator to run out of breath. His bespoke Savile Row suit, a soft, dove gray pinstripe, draped his tall, lean body beautifully. His shirt and silk tie were likewise understated but elegant. His silver hair was slightly tousled, as befits a busy man, but it gleamed in the glow of the dropped crystal chandeliers that lit the high-ceilinged reception room.

Carrie knew from old photographs that Drum's hair had once been nearly blue-black, but he was twenty years her senior and it had already been more salt than pepper when they'd met. They'd married after a whirlwind courtship in East Africa, where she'd been working with the Peace Corps and he'd ostensibly been an embassy aid official. It was only after they were married that he'd confessed his real profession.

Would it have made a difference if she'd known before? Carrie often wondered. Hard to say. She'd been a different person then, and Drum had seemed to exude a self-confident, protective strength sorely needed in that difficult period of her life. She wasn't that frightened young girl anymore, however.

Still, there was no question that he was still, at forty-nine, a very attractive man, with a high forehead, even features, and intense, cobalt-blue eyes that seemed to mesmerize men and women alike. Watching the hint of a smile playing at the corner of Drum's lips, Carrie knew that Senator Watkins was about to feel the full force of that determined Southern charm. She almost pitied the man. Before the evening was over, the senator would be spouting the MacNeil view of the world as if it were gospel, and he wouldn't even know he'd been co-opted.

Through the tall windows behind Drum and the senator, the lights of London were already beginning to twinkle, daylight driven out early by the dark, heavy-laden clouds that had loomed over the city all week. Taking care not to spill her wine, Carrie took a discreet peek at the thin platinum watch on her left wrist. Five-forty-five. Surely this would be winding up soon. The congressmen would want to go back to their hotels and freshen up before the cars came to take them to the residence for the ambassador's working dinner.

It was hours since she'd grabbed a quick apple in lieu of lunch. She was tempted to lunge when a tray of hors d'oeuvres passed her way, but there was a special corollary to Murphy's Law that went into effect whenever she found herself at one of these embassy receptions—if she grabbed one of the tempting canapés, it was a sure bet that someone would choose that exact moment to stick out a hand to introduce themselves. And then, there was always the risk of ending up wearing the thing when this dull, alcoholic Brit beside her decided to move in and try to get a little cozier, as he inevitably would if she didn't escape his clutches soon.

There wasn't much to eat back at their flat, though. Grocery shopping had been on her list of things to do later that afternoon, before Drum had called and changed her plans. She'd left soup and peanut butter sandwiches for the housekeeper to give Jonah when the van brought him back from his kindergarten class at the American International School, but if Carrie wanted dinner, she was going to have to pick it up on the way home.

She was just debating how soon she could make her escape when she felt an arm slip around her shoulders and turned to find an old friend at her side.

"Tom!" she cried, genuinely delighted. "I didn't know you were coming!'

She and Tom Bent exchanged kisses on either cheek. "Came to herd the senators," he said, "though to be honest, it's a bit like herding cats." He leaned in closer and whispered in her ear, "I spotted you as soon as I walked in. You look beautiful, Carrie. You also look like you need rescuing, poor thing."

"Oh, God, yes," she whispered back, glancing at her two companions, who had abandoned their pontificating long enough to show an interest in the new arrival.

The Bostonian obviously knew him. "Tom! I wondered where you'd disappeared to after the ambassadors' meeting." He turned to the Brit beside him. "Nigel, this is Tom Bent, the CIA's Director of Congressional Liaison. He's the man who decides which secrets those nasty spooks will share with their political masters. Tom, Nigel St. John from the British Foreign Office."

"Sin-jin," the Brit corrected as he held out his hand. "How do you do?"

"I do wetly, thank you," Bent said, shaking.

"Excuse me?"

"I snuck out for a quick run over to Harrod's."

He retrieved his hand and smoothed down his poker straight hair—unnecessarily, since it was perfectly gelled in place, as always. Despite the fact that Tom was Drum's age, his hair was still nut brown, only his temples running a little to gray, lending just a hint of mature gravitas. Carrie suspected the color was maintained by an artful stylist, since Tom was very careful about his appearance—and, she suspected, a little vain about his thick head of hair.

It didn't detract in the least from her affection for the man. Unlike most of her husband's old crowd, Tom had welcomed her warmly right from the start after she and Drum had come home from Africa, and he'd always gone out of his way to be kind. Maybe it was because he, too, had come from humbler roots and "married up," as Drum's mother like to say. Whatever the reason, Tom was always a ray of sunshine for Carrie, and never more so than on this gloomy day.

"My wife made me promise to bring her back some Oxford marmalade," Tom was saying, "orange, extra chunky. Swears only Harrod's has the real McCoy, so off I went. The senators have such a tight schedule, I didn't think I'd have another chance if I didn't do it this afternoon. But Lord, it's not a fit day for ducks out there!'

He had a pleasant, always-smiling face, with warm, coffee-colored eyes and an air of scrubbed earnestness, his cheeks flushed and glowing. Carrie knew it was mild rosacea and not the weather that put those blooms there. Regardless of the season, Tom always looked like he'd just come back from taking a brisk autumn constitutional in his impeccable Brooks Brothers finery.

Tom and Drum had been friends since their days at Yale, although Carrie had the impression that this hard-working West Virginian, a coal-miner's son on a full scholarship, had never been the hell-raiser her husband was reputed to have been back then.

"You should have called me," Carrie said. "I would have picked up whatever you needed."

"Well, I would have, darlin', but to be honest, I needed to get away from all this hot air, even if just for an hour."

"Are you traveling with the delegation?" St. John asked.

"For my sins, alas, I am. Somebody needs to keep an eye on 'em, you see, make sure they don't alienate our friends and give comfort to our enemies—and don't you repeat that to your boss, young Daniel," he added, shaking a finger at the aid to the senator from Massachusetts.

Daniel! Daniel Boone? No...Brown, that's it, Carrie suddenly remembered.

As she glanced over toward the windows once more, she caught Drum watching them soberly. She gave him the smile he expected, and he cocked an eyebrow. She looped her hand through Tom's arm.

"Would you excuse us?" she asked the other two.

"You're abandoning us?" St. John asked plaintively.

"Sorry, Nigel. Duty calls. I think my husband would like to talk to his old friend, Tom, here."

"Good to meet you, Nigel," Tom added. "Dan, catch you later."

"I wish I'd known you were coming," Carrie said as they detached from the others and drifted across the floor.

"It was a last-minute decision. Things are incredibly hectic back in Washington, what with all the new anti-terrorism legislation on the table and the military situation dicey as it is right now. But the Oval Office wanted somebody along to keep an eye on these cowboys. I got drafted."

"How's Lorraine?"

Tom had been married for twenty-five years to the daughter of the Right Reverend Arthur Merriam, Episcopal Bishop of Washington, based at the Cathedral of Saint Peter and Saint Paul, also known as the National Cathedral.

"She's just fine," Tom said. "Helping her mother most of the time, running one committee or another."

"Her mother must be getting on."

"She'll be seventy-six in August, but don't let her hear you suggest she's elderly. The women in Lorraine's family live to a ripe old age. Her grandmother lasted to ninety-one and was still playing bridge three times a week. Liked her gin and tonics right up to the end, too."

"Ah, well, that's the secret ingredient, I guess."

Tom rolled his eyes. "Must be. God knows, Lorraine and her mother swear by them." He stopped and turned to Carrie. "How about you and Drum, darlin'? How are things?"

"All right. We're going home this summer, you know."

"Yes, I heard. Drum's being promoted. That's great."

"I guess," Carrie said.

"You're not pleased about it?"

"I'm happy for him. It's what he wants. It's a little tough for Jonah, though. Drum's hardly around now, and I can only imagine he'll be even busier once he takes on the Deputy Director's job. Like you said, these are crazy times. Plus, poor Jonah has to give up the friends he's made here."

"And how is my godson? I mustn't forget, by the way, Lorraine sent along some little goodies for him. I've got them in my suitcase back at the hotel."

Carrie smiled. "I hope you get a chance to come over and

see him while you're here, Tom. He's a great little guy. He's just bloomed in kindergarten this year. Absolutely loves school. Our flat is covered with his paintings and drawings."

"An artist, like his mom. But kindergarten? Already? Seems to me he was just taking his first steps."

"I know. I can hardly believe it myself. Come September, my baby's going to be in first grade."

"Big changes. And what about you, Carrie? Are you okay? It's not easy, I know, being a diplomatic dependant in a strange city."

"It's a great city, though. Impossible to be bored. Mind you, I'm a little tied down by Jonah's half-day schedule. He's at school from one to four each afternoon, and I try to help out there whenever they need an extra pair of hands, so it doesn't leave a lot of time for gallivanting. Still," she added brightly, "I have been busy this past winter. I re-registered at Georgetown for a remote study program, and I've gone back to the thesis I abandoned after Drum and I got married."

"No kidding. That's great. How's it going?"

"Pretty well, I think. I hope. It's kind of hard to tell. Can't see the forest for the trees and all that. But I'd already done a good chunk of the first draft, and I had a lot of original research from when I was with the Peace Corps. My advisor seemed to think I'd be able to pull it together."

"You were running some kind of a gallery out there in Africa, weren't you?"

She nodded. "We helped local artists set up a cooperative to market their sculptures and paintings to tourists. My thesis dealt with marketing art from the Third World, so I had really good primary source material. It needed to be updated, of course. New trends emerge in seven years. But Oxfam here in London has been promoting developing country art and handicrafts for some time now, and they've been really helpful."

"So you've been able to finish?"

"Well, you know what they say, a thesis is never really finished, only abandoned. But I'm working up the courage to send it to my advisor. If he thinks it's ready for prime time, I should be able to defend it when we get back to D.C."

"Carrie, that's great. Drum must be so proud of you."

"Oh, I guess so…" She glanced over to the window where Drum stood watching them expectantly. "I think we're being beckoned."

Drum reached out to her as they approached. Senator Watkins, spotting the movement, broke off in mid-sentence, his face opening up into the guileless smile seen in countless election year posters. Drum drew Carrie close into the circle of his free arm. He was just over six feet tall, so that she tucked neatly into his side, as a good accessory should.

"Sweetheart, I'd like to introduce Senator Paul Watkins. Senator, this is my wife, Carrie. And of course, you know Tom Bent. Tom, we were just about to send out a search party."

"Well, it's a wild, wet day out there, but I can safely report that Harrod's managed to relieve me of a sizeable chunk of change and my marital shopping obligations have been successfully discharged."

Watkins's huge, fleshy hand swallowed Carrie's. "I'm so pleased to meet you, Mrs. MacNeil." His face was flushed, his bald head perspiring. He nodded at Tom, then turned back to give her a long, appraising once-over before shooting a mischievous wink at Drum. "Aren't *you* the lucky man, Mr. MacNeil?"

Tom gave Carrie's arm a gentle squeeze, and when Carrie risked a glance at him, she saw his eyes roll subtly. She felt better, knowing she had at least one ally here. Tom knew what some people said about her improbable marriage to Drummond MacNeil and he was sympathetic.

And maybe the senator didn't mean to imply anything, anyway. Maybe she was just overly sensitive—although, in point of fact, she'd actually heard the words "trophy wife" whispered behind her back on more than one occasion. It was one of the hazards of marrying a much older man. Everyone presumed you were the bimbo he'd dumped his long-suffering first wife for. And Drum had, in fact, been married before, but he'd been widowed two years when Carrie had met him in Africa. It didn't matter. To anyone who didn't know her, she was just the young airhead who decorated his arm and who'd given him the heir his first wife hadn't.

Nor did it help now that Drum suddenly took it into his head to kiss her far more warmly than their surroundings warranted, letting his gaze linger on her in the kind of long, wistful glance she'd rarely seen since they'd left Africa—and virtually never in the last couple of years. What was that all about?

Drum turned back to the senator with a sigh and an uncharacteristically silly smile on his face. "You're right, Senator. I'm the luckiest man in the world."

Carrie didn't dare risk glancing over at Tom Bent to see what he made of that.

It was approaching six when the senators finally began to gather up their coats to return to their hotel and freshen up before the ambassador's dinner. After Tom Bent had herded them all out to their waiting cars, Drum accompanied Carrie down the elevator to the embassy's main floor and out through the solid steel door that divided the secure area from the public lobby.

As he held up her buff-colored Burberry raincoat for her

to slip her arms into, the smoked glass lobby windows rattled under an ominous peal of deep, rolling thunder.

"Are those the shoes you came in?" Drum asked.

Carrie gave her Manolos a rueful glance. "Yes. I'm an idiot. I've been sloshing around for the past two hours."

"Well, make sure you grab a cab. Don't try to walk in this weather."

She nodded, tucking her hair inside a dark chocolate-colored beret and slipping her hands into soft brown kidskin gloves. "Do you know what time you'll be home?"

"Pretty late, I imagine. Don't wait up for me."

"The story of my life," Carrie said, with no real trace of bitterness.

She was long past questioning his late nights, and complaining was a waste of time. Drum said it was a hazard of his profession. Generally speaking, that was probably true. Generally, but not always. At this point, Carrie had given up trying to reconcile his work with the lingering scents that sometimes accompanied him when he slipped into bed late at night—scents of passion Carrie hadn't shared and perfume she didn't own, scents a shower couldn't quite mask. Lately, he'd been gone more and more, caught up in crisis after crisis as terrorist threats continued to mount. He could make Carrie feel positively un-American for questioning anything he did. She no longer bothered.

She reached up to offer the kind of perfunctory peck on the cheek that was habitual by now, but he held her close, once again giving her a more lingering kiss than a public venue and seven years of marriage normally inspired. His arms stayed around her as he studied her.

"What?" she asked, resisting the urge to squirm out of his grasp.

"Nothing. I just wanted to look at you. You're really something, you know that?"

She frowned. "Drum, are you all right?"

He smiled and kissed her once more, lightly, then released her. "I'm fine. I'd better get back upstairs and get a little work done before I have to go baby-sit those visiting clowns. I'll see you at home."

"Right. See you later."

Carrie watched him walk back to the heavy steel door, where he slipped his hand under the keypad cover and entered the four-digit security combination. The lock clicked and he wrenched the handle open, pausing briefly to give her a last look and a wave before disappearing back into the secure womb of the building.

Exhaling wearily, she slipped her handbag over her arm and headed for the front doors, but before she'd gone a few steps on the marble tile, a muffled voice called her name. Carrie looked around for the source of the hail and saw a familiar figure waving her over to the reception window.

At this hour, with the embassy closed for the day, the civilian receptionist had left and the Gunny was alone on duty behind the bullet-proof glass. A Marine corporal stood by the front doors, opening them and then re-locking them behind staff leaving the building.

The last public straggler was still at the window with the Gunny. A young woman, she was hunched over at the counter, madly writing on a white file card. Her wet umbrella was propped against the wall, while her coat dripped water on the gold-streaked marble tiles.

"Hey, Gunny," Carrie said, smiling as she walked gingerly over to the booth, taking care to avoid the death-trap puddles on the slippery floor. "What's up?"

His voice crackled back at her through the speaker set into the glass. "I heard you were going to be in the building, but I was on the phone when you came in. I been working on the team rosters for the kids' softball league. Is Jonah gonna go out for Pee Wees?" The Gunny's son Connor was Jonah's best buddy and the two boys often slept over at each other's flats.

"He wants to," Carrie said, "but you know we're going home this summer?"

"Yeah. Connor's really bummed about that."

She sighed. "That's the worst thing about this life, isn't it? The poor kids have to keep making new friends."

People who married into the business knew what they were getting into, Carrie thought—theoretically, at least. But the kids had no choice in the matter. Drum had been an Army brat himself, but he was philosophical about it. The tough ones survived it just fine, he always said, and the weaklings were going to stumble whether or not they stayed in one place all their lives. Carrie wasn't sure about that, but she had noticed that relationships in Drum's life all seemed vaguely disposable. Was it the impermanence of his childhood friendships that made him always seem to be holding something back even now?

The Gunny held up a finger for her to wait while he dealt with the girl at the window. She'd straightened and seemed to have finished what she was writing. Carrie peeked over her shoulder. It looked like a consular registration form.

"All done?" the Gunny asked.

"I think so," the girl said, sliding the white card into the metal drawer under the triple-paned window that separated her from the Marine.

The Gunny pulled a lever and the drawer slid back to his side of the glass. "Looks good," he said, picking out the form.

"I'll leave it for the consular section to file tomorrow. They're all gone for the day now."

"Thanks a lot for letting me in." The girl slipped her pen back into the bag slung over her shoulder. "It took me longer to get over here than I thought it would, but I promised my parents I'd do this."

"No problem. We wouldn't want you to have to tramp back over here again tomorrow."

"Is it supposed to rain again?" she asked, buttoning up her tan raincoat.

"That's what I hear. Welcome to jolly old England."

"Rats. I guess we'll have to do some museums."

The Gunny's buzzed head gave a nod. "You don't wanna lose that umbrella. You'll be needing it."

Watching the girl tuck a few loose hairs into her knit tam, Carrie felt a sudden plunge in the pit of her stomach. They were about the same height, and although their coloring up close was different, dressed in rain gear as they were, they would be almost indistinguishable from a distance.

It gave Carrie the sort of brief shock she got every time her own reflection surprised her in passing a mirror or window. She'd had an identical twin sister once. When they were small, they were always dressed in matching frilly outfits, to be cooed at and admired in their tandem stroller.

"It made me so proud," her mother used to say with a sigh. "My two little Strawberry Shortcakes—identical and perfect."

As if anything less than a matched pair fell somehow short of the mark, Carrie had felt ever since.

Isabel, her twin, had died when they were eighteen—about this girl's age, by the look of her. But even now, more than a decade later, the pain of losing her other half could still overwhelm her unexpectedly, like the phantom ache of a severed limb.

The girl in the lobby smiled shyly at the Gunny and Carrie in turn. "Well, thanks again. Bye."

Carrie returned her smile and the Gunny gave a brief salute. As the young corporal at the front door unlocked it to let the girl out, Carrie turned back to the window.

"Anyway, Gunny, on the softball thing, I guess it depends how long the commitment is. We'll be here till the end of the school year, for sure. I will, anyway. Drum says he may have to head back to Washington earlier. But if it means Jonah can be on a team with Connor, I'd try to hang in as long as possible and let him do that."

"That should work out okay. We're going to set up the schedule so the games are all done by the end of June. A lot of people are in the same boat, what with transfers and summer vacations. It makes for a pretty short season, but at least the kids get to play."

"That would be great." It was one last thing she could do to help Jonah through the transition they were about to make, Carrie thought—one that might turn out to be even more disruptive than a move from London back to Washington, if she followed through on her growing resolve to make some real changes in her life. "Put Jonah down then. He'll be so happy when I tell him."

The Gunny grinned and started to reply, but just then, a sharp bang shattered the hollow stillness of the empty lobby. Three or four more ear-splitting cracks followed in rapid succession. To Carrie's ears, it sounded like firecrackers exploding outside, but to the two Marines in the lobby, it obviously meant something else altogether.

"Weapons fire!" The Gunny's sidearm was already out of

its holster. "What's going on out there?" he hollered to the corporal at the door.

The young Marine had his nose to the glass, but he ducked back and pasted himself against the interior marble wall, his eyes huge. "We got a shooter, Gunny! It looks like at least one civilian's down."

"Oh, shit!" The Gunny grabbed the phone beside him and started yelling for backup.

Karen Ann Hermann had just left the embassy grounds, rounding the concrete barriers at the perimeter. She was running very late, but at the zebra crossing, she hesitated, confused by the glare of lights on the wet pavement and by the honking cars whizzing by on the rain-slickened road, all of them coming from the wrong direction.

She was getting her bearings, trying to remember the layout of the map in her guidebook in order to plan her route to Leicester Square, when she heard someone call her name. She glanced around. A black London cab slowed as it approached her from the left, its passenger side window down.

How could a cab driver know her name? She must have misheard. Unless maybe he had Kristina and Caitlin with him? Had they decided to come and get her? She ducked low to peek into the back seat of the cab. It looked empty, but the driver was staring at her expectantly.

Had she imagined it, hearing her name called? She must have. There was no way the other girls would have splurged on a taxi, and neither would Karen, rain or no rain. A luxury like that wasn't in any of their budgets. Theater tickets and souvenirs for her parents were the only big-ticket items she'd bargained on, but a taxi would set her back a bundle.

Head shaking, she waved the driver on, but instead of

pulling back out into the line of traffic, the squat little car pulled up closer until it stood directly in front of her.

She shook her head again. "No, thanks anyway! I don't need—"

Before she could finish the sentence, the inside of the cab exploded in a flash of light. Karen felt a stinging slap to her throat and her head kicked back. A split second later, before she even had time to reach a hand up to feel what had stung her neck, a double smack to the chest sent her flying back as if she'd been kicked by a horse.

It was only as she hit the pavement that her ears finally registered the loud retorts. Her head bounced on the cobblestones, and then she lay on her back, the wind knocked out of her, heavy rain soaking her face and smearing the lights in her eyes. She felt an icy splash on her legs as the taxi sped away.

It was cold on the ground. Her sprawled arms and legs were wet and chilled, but across her chest, she felt a spreading pool of warmth. When she was finally able to catch her breath a little, it came in ragged gasps.

Faces appeared above her, a man and a couple of women, then two soldiers. No, not soldiers. Marines. She'd spoken to the cute one when she'd arrived. He'd been manning the sentry box at the front gate. At first, he'd said she'd have to come back the next day, but when she told him she just wanted to fill out a consular registration form, he'd called and gotten permission for her to go in. On her way out, when she'd stopped to thank him, he'd told her about a club near Piccadilly that he and the other Marines liked to go to. Maybe they could meet up there later?

Karen had promised to ask her friends. Then, she'd headed for the zebra crossing. That was when the cab had pulled up and the driver had called her name.

The Marines were standing over her now, guns drawn, looking nervously from the street and down to her, then back to the street again. She saw their mouths move, but her ears were still ringing from the crack of the thunder that had exploded in her face and she couldn't hear what they were saying. One of the women was crying.

"I'm okay," Karen told her. Or tried to, except no sound came out.

She rolled onto her side, her hand reaching for her throat. Her neck felt mushy and wet, like soggy oatmeal, and she was feeling so dizzy she thought she might fall off the earth. But she had to get moving. She was going to be so late. She was supposed to be...somewhere.

Where was she supposed to be?

Tears sprang to her eyes as she tried to remember, cold rain mixing with the warmth running down her cheeks and with that other warmth that covered her front now. Bright lights swam around her. She wasn't sure where she was anymore. All she really knew was that she wanted to go home. She was tired...so tired.

She curled herself up into a ball, nestling into the cobblestones, her lower arm tucking into her side. Her hand curled up beside her face, the movement instinctive. She had no awareness of her thumb settling instinctively on her chin, nor of her fingers waving laxly.

Feet shuffled around her, and worried faces swam in and out of her line of sight, lips moving soundlessly. She strained to make out their fading features, but none of these was the face she wanted to see. Her thumb was still on her chin, her four fingers waggling limply as she called out in her primal language. To the confused faces, it was probably just random fluttering, but for Karen, it was her first word, rising out of the deepest recesses of her fear and sadness and intense lone-liness—*Mommy*.

She signed it over and over, a silent cry from long ago, a small child calling mutely in the only language her mother could recognize. But this time, there were no comforting arms to take the little girl up and hold her close to let her know she was safe.

Then, Karen Ann Hermann's eyes closed for the last time, and her fluttering hand fell still on the wet, hard cobblestones, silenced for all time.

The sky wept.

CHAPTER FIVE

London Embassy Shooting
Was cabbie Al Qaeda assassin, lone wolf or second victim?

BY J. P. TOWLE
Special to the Washington Post

LONDON—Nearly four months after the shooting outside the U.S. Embassy in London that took the life of a young American tourist, questions remained as to the motive of the Pakistan-born taxi driver blamed in the attack.

U.S. and British intelligence officials say there is little doubt Ibn Mussa Ibrahim attacked to protest American foreign policy.

But if so, skeptics ask, why shoot an unarmed civilian? And why was Ibrahim himself later found shot to death and stuffed in the boot of his taxi?

Security cameras outside the embassy captured the attack on video. The tapes show a shadowy, bearded figure behind the wheel of the black London taxi. The cab pulled up at the embassy's outer gates just before the driver let loose with a spray of automatic gunfire.

The embassy had already closed for the day when 19-year-old Karen Ann Hermann of Oakview, MD, who had just left the building, was caught in the hail of bullets fired from the cab. She died at the scene.

But friends of the 26-year-old cabbie insist he had no interest in politics. Ibrahim immigrated to the U.K. in 1996.

"All he wanted was to earn enough money to bring his fiancée from Peshawar," said Ibrahim's roommate, Farid Zacharias. "Al Qaeda? No way. He loved American movies and Burger King."

An alternate theory is that Ibrahim's taxi was hijacked before the embassy attack.

"You can't tell me that's him in those videos," Zacharias argued. "It was dark and raining. How can they be sure?"

But security spokesmen say Ibrahim's were the only fingerprints found in the cab and on the murder weapon, later recovered in London's High Park.

"We think he was a sleeper, like the Sept. 11 hijackers," a senior intelligence source said. "Several have been inserted into Western Europe and the U.S. to await assassination orders."

As to why the cabbie was subsequently killed, it may be because he missed embassy personnel in the April attack.

"Murdering one young tourist probably didn't pack the political punch his Al Qaeda masters were looking for," the same high-level source said.

FEDERAL BUREAU OF INVESTIGATION
INTERVIEW TRANSCRIPTION

(continued...)

So, Carrie, we were talking about the murder of Karen Ann Hermann.

Right. As I said, I didn't learn her name until later, but she was there in the lobby when I came out of the reception for the visiting senators. She left the building ahead of me. If I hadn't gotten held up talking to the Gunny at the front desk, I probably would have been outside, too, when it happened.

You might have even been shot. Has that ever occurred to you?

Of course it has. It's amazing more people weren't hurt in that attack. It was really bad luck that she happened to be there the moment that terrorist drove up.

And so Karen Hermann died in your place.

I—what? In my place? Wait a minute, what are you saying? Are you suggesting he had a specific target? And I was it?

What do you think?

That's not what the papers have been saying, and my husband never mentioned there was any suspicion it could have been something like that. Why would a terrorist target me specifically?

You said yourself you were struck by the similarity in your appearances that evening—yours and Karen Hermann's.

Strictly superficial similarities.

You said you were taken aback by how much you looked alike.

It was a rainy day. Raincoats and umbrellas tend to be pretty generic. Plus, we both had our hair tucked up under berets, so, yes, we looked a little alike.

Enough that you were struck by it. You said it spooked you for a second.

Yes, but that's because I'm a twin.

You have a twin? An identical twin?

Yes—or rather, I did have. Isabel died when we were eighteen, along with our parents. When you grow up with an identical twin, though, you never quite lose that sense that there's supposed to be a mirror image of you out there somewhere. Even now, I get a shock when I accidentally see myself reflected in a store window or something, thinking it's Izzie. Except, of course, it can't be. She's been gone over ten years. Still, I never seem to stop looking for her.

Was it a car accident she and your parents died in?

You must have this somewhere in those thick files of yours.

If so, I haven't seen it. I mean, we try to be thorough, but unless it's directly relevant to this investigation, the Bureau hasn't got resources to waste on trivial details.

It isn't trivial to me.

No, I'm sure. Sorry. That's not what I meant. How did they die?

A fire. Our house burned down just after New Year's in 1993. I was back at school by then. It was during my freshman year at Georgetown.

Your sister didn't go?

No. She was still living at home with our parents back in San

Diego. She didn't go to college because she—well, she just didn't go, that's all. Anyway, the fire broke out in the middle of the night. No one survived.

I'm sorry.

Yes, well, anyway—as I said, after spending the first eighteen years of your life as half of a twosome, something always seems incomplete when you're alone. That's why I was momentarily struck by the similarity in Karen's and my appearance that day at the embassy.

And it never occurred to you that someone else might have been confused by it, as well. The shooter in the cab, for example? And shot the wrong person?

But that would mean—wait a minute, are you serious? Is there any proof at all that man was lying in wait for me?

I'm asking if it might have occurred to you.

Well, the answer is, no, it didn't. What possible evidence could you have that he was?

Security cameras at the embassy recorded the attack. We've analyzed those tapes six ways to Sunday. There's no audio, but when the cab pulls up in front of Karen, she ducks down and looks inside, like the driver hailed her. And the Marines at the front gate said they heard the driver call out to her just before he opened fire.

He called her by name?

He called out a name. It might have been Karen, the Marines thought. Then again, it could just as easily have been Carrie.

You're serious, aren't you?

Dead serious. We even called in a lip-reader to look at the tapes. She confirms the Marines' story, although she couldn't be sure, either, exactly what name he called.

My God. You mean...? That poor girl.

Yeah, that poor girl. And her poor family back home. Did you know Karen Hermann's parents are both deaf?

I think I read that, yes.

Here's something you probably didn't read. Her father? He had a stroke three days after her funeral. He's back home now, but paralyzed, they say. He can't sign anymore, so even though his wife can still talk to him, he can't answer. Can you imagine the mom? She lost her only child, and now, on top of the grief of that, she hasn't even got her husband's support.

That's awful. I'm so sorry.

You're sorry. Yeah, well—anyway—let's put Karen Hermann back in the file for the moment and move on, shall we? You were saying that you and your family were supposed to stay on in London until the summer. But then, right after this shooting, you left early and came back to D.C.

That's right. Drum had already been notified that he was being promoted to Operations Deputy at Langley. We'd been delaying our departure so our son could finish out the school year. But after the attack at the embassy, the official threat level was notched up and dependents and non-essential personnel were being shipped out. Drum decided there was no point in sticking around any longer, so we left a couple of weeks later.

And then?

Then, nothing. He started his new job at CIA headquarters. I was tied up with getting us settled after the move.

You went to live with your husband's mother?

Yes. The MacNeils have a big old family home over in Virginia, right on the Potomac—but you know already that, don't you? Anyway, it's just a few miles from Langley, so it was convenient for Drum. His mother has been rattling around in it by herself ever since his father died. She has a daughter, as well—Drum's sister, Eleanor—but she lives in New York and hardly ever returns to D.C. Anyway, I think I said that Drum inherited the house when his father died. When he was posted back to Langley, neither he nor his mother would hear of us living anywhere else.

How did you feel about that?

It wasn't the first time. We'd lived there before the posting to London, too—after Africa, when Jonah, our son, was a baby.

I know, but I asked how you felt about it. Not many young wives would want to live with their mothers-in-law.

Well, no, neither did I particularly, to be honest. But we left London so suddenly, I didn't have time to convince Drum we should be looking for our own place.

So you just went along with what he wanted?

To begin with, yes. You have to understand, I had a lot on my plate. There's a ton of personal admin that has to be taken care when these transfers come through. With Drum as busy as he was at work, that all fell on me—the shipment of our personal effects, getting what we'd left behind out of storage. Drum's Jag was in storage, but I had to find a car for myself. I also had Jonah to get settled. Had to try to find a summer day camp that was still accepting registration. There was no way a six-year-old could be expected to hang around the house all summer. He would have been bored silly, and Althea—that's Drum's mother—she wasn't used to having noisy children underfoot, either.

Anyway, bottom line—living there wasn't ideal, as far as I was concerned, but with our rushed departure from London, it's what I was handed. I tried to make the best of it.

And your husband? How did he seem when you got back to D.C.?

He was even busier than he'd been in London, just as I suspected he'd be—which was another reason he had no interest in house hunting.

How did he settle in?

It's been tough for him, the past two or three months.

How so?

Well, being back at headquarters is not like being out in the field. You're a lot more independent out there. Back here—well, you must know this yourself. The FBI can't be that different from the rest of the government. There's a lot of bureaucracy to deal with. Political gamesmanship, that sort of thing. Drum hates all that.

So he wasn't happy?

He was showing signs of stress, I'd say. It wasn't that he couldn't handle the deputy's job, mind you. He was really pleased to have been promoted. It was more like, he was champing at the bit to get to it. He wanted to put his mark on things, he said. Travel out to the posts, get to know all the station chiefs.

And what was stopping him?

As I say, bureaucracy. It seems there was some big organizational review underway—still the fallout from September 11, I gather. You know—trying to decide what the Agency did wrong, coming up with recommendations on what they might do differently in future. When Drum got back from London, the Director asked him to take on the running of that task force for a few weeks. Said it needed a little fire put under it. Drum felt he couldn't say no, especially when the Director stressed how high profile it was, and how important to the Agency's future. But Drum was more and more frustrated with every passing week. Said he was spending his days pushing paper around, chairing endless meetings—except not the ones he wanted to be in on.

And which were those?

The ones dealing with day-to-day operations, I suppose.

And so?

So, nothing. What could he do? He had to get the damn job finished, he said. That's what he was trying to do. All I know is, we hardly ever saw him. Most days, he left home before Jonah was up and came back long after he was in bed. After I'd gone to bed, too, for the most part.

He left at what time in the morning, generally?

About seven. He liked to beat the traffic and be at his desk before seven-thirty.

Always?

Whenever he was in town, yes. As I say, he was almost always gone by the time Jonah came downstairs for breakfast.

So, he had a routine that never varied.

Not really.

And then two days ago, something changed. Right, Carrie?

You know it did. That was the day everything changed.

CHAPTER SIX

Washington, D.C.
August 12, 2002

The buzzing of the cicadas was relentless, maddening, like an electric drill to the brain. Sweltering air hung thick and hazy, even at this early hour, a reminder that the nation's capital was a southern city, albeit one overlaid with a more northern ethic of naked ambition. Summer heat and the drone of the insects in the treetops only amplified the sense of urgency that coursed through Washington like a permanent adrenaline feed.

Every cop on the beat knew that in D.C.'s rougher eastern neighborhoods, there would be blood on the pavement before the day was out. It was the same every summer. People couldn't live day after day, week after week in such close quarters and suffocating humidity without snapping.

But it wasn't just a problem of the concrete inner city. Even in green, leafy suburbs of neighboring Virginia, tension was rising.

McLean, Virginia
7:32 a.m.

Knowing Drum's impatience with anything or anyone in his way in the morning, Carrie had gotten in the habit of either waiting to get up until after he'd left for work, or showering and dressing in the front guest room so he could have the master bedroom and bath to himself. On that morning in particular, she was anxious to avoid him. She'd been awake since a little after five and had slipped out of bed as soon as she'd felt him stirring for fear her brittle nerves would betray her.

The previous night, as happened more often than not, she'd been in bed when he got in. But going to bed wasn't the same as going to sleep, not with her body thrumming in anticipation of what the dawn would bring. Her head, too, had spun with doubts, wondering whether she was doing the right thing. And even if she was, she wondered if she shouldn't just screw up her courage and tell him about her appointment the next morning—assuming he didn't already know.

Despite the fact that he was so rarely around, Drum had an unnerving ability to pick up information by osmosis—or maybe it was his mother who served as his inside source here on the home front. Althea's formidable determination to stay on top of everything that went on under her roof was only one of the drawbacks of living in that house, as far as Carrie was concerned. As far as Drum was concerned, though, the notion of a place of their own had been a non-starter.

"I haven't got time to look for a house we don't need, Car-

rie. MacNeils have been living on Elcott Road for generations, and the house really belongs to me now, anyway. My
God, do you have any idea what it's worth these days? Over
an acre of land in an area of million-dollar-plus homes? Surrounded by parkland, and fronting on the Potomac, no less?"

"But I always feel like we're crowding your mother."

"That's ridiculous. The place is way too big for her alone.
Anyway, she'd be the first to insist it's where Jonah belongs.
Not to mention how close it is to Langley. Christ! Haven't I
got enough on my plate without adding a long commute every
day?"

End of discussion. But if Carrie had been wavering for
months about whether or not to take back her life, this one-
sided debate had pretty much tipped the scales. When the dust
had settled on the move and Jonah was safely enrolled in summer camp, she'd quietly made—then canceled—several appointments with the partner of her former college roommate,
who now had a legal practice in Alexandria specializing in
family law.

After the third time Carrie had chickened out, Tracy Overturf had met her for lunch, where, to her own horror, Carrie
had broken down in tears over her Cobb salad.

"Oh, God, Carrie, this can't go on," Tracy said. "Look how
unhappy he's made you."

"I can't just blame it on Drum. I let myself go down this
road."

"You met him at a vulnerable time. You'd lost your whole
family. If ever someone was looking for a port in a storm, that
was you back then. And no wonder."

"Still, I didn't have to abdicate my life. Look at you. You've
had a solid relationship with Alan for years, but that didn't
keep you from starting your own legal practice."

"I wouldn't read too much into that. The only reason Heather and I formed Childers and Overturf after we passed the bar is because there were no jobs to be had. And you haven't seen our offices yet—bankruptcy auction furnishings in three small rooms in a renovated cotton mill. It's not fancy. I'm warning you. Look, Carrie, I care about you too much to keep it on a professional level where Drum's concerned, but Heather doesn't know you like I do, and she's really good— a pit bull in divorce cases. If you decide you need her, she'll do a great job for you and make sure you get a fair deal."

"I don't need that much. I'm not even sure divorce is the right answer. If it were just me, but there's Jonah to think about. This could really mess up his life."

"What about your life? How happily can he grow up with a mother who's so frustrated? Look, just talk to Heather, all right? Explore your options. Then, whatever you decide to do, at least you'll be making an informed decision."

So Carrie had thought about it for a few days, then called and rebooked with Tracy's partner—just to explore her options, she told herself. Now, she worried Drum would get wind of her plans before she had a chance to figure out what she wanted to do.

She and Jonah had been out at the Pentagon City Mall the previous afternoon, buying new running shoes to replace yet anther pair he'd outgrown before he could even wear down the treads. When they got home, Carrie had seen the message light flashing on the answering machine next to the telephone in the kitchen. Her heart had begun to pound when she'd played it back and realized it was Heather Childers's secretary calling to confirm her appointment for the next morning.

Althea said nothing about having heard the message, but to Carrie's worried mind, she seemed cool that evening. Her

mother-in-law had exchanged only the most cursory of greet-
ings, then taken her dinner up in her room, pleading fatigue.
But much later, a light had been burning under her door well
past her usual nine-thirty bedtime.

Carrie knew she should wait up and talk to Drum herself,
heading her mother-in-law off at the pass. But ever since their
return from London, days could pass without their paths
crossing between 7:00 a.m. and midnight or without exchanging more than a few words face-to-face.

In the end, Drum had returned home in the wee hours of
the morning, long after everyone was asleep. Not even the
dreaded Althea had that kind of staying power.

The MacNeil home was a century-old Georgian residence
built on a choice promontory overlooking the Potomac River.
The family was old Virginia stock, descended from a Scots
ancestor who had purchased a large tract of land in the late
1700s from the original Lord Fairfax, for whom the county
was named.

An even larger house had once stood on the site, the cor-
nerstone of a sprawling tobacco and lumber plantation. The
first time Drum had brought Carrie home, his mother had
pulled out an album of old sepiatone photographs to impress
his new bride with the history of the clan into which she'd
somehow finagled herself. One showed an earlier generation
of MacNeils standing before a grandiose Greek Revival mansion, complete with Ionic columns, a full-width front porch,
and weeping magnolias lining both sides of a long and stately
gravel drive—sort of a Virginia version of Tara.

But after the insult of the Civil War, the plantation had
never really recovered its former glory. When the big house
had burned down during the economic depression of the

1890s, Drum's great-grandfather had rebuilt a smaller place on the same site, looking across the river to Maryland and, downstream, to the heights of Georgetown.

At the time of the fire, there'd been whispers that old Elcott MacNeil had torched the place for the insurance money. It was certainly coincidental that a number of irreplaceable items, including those rare old photographs, the family bible, and a few of the better pieces of furniture just happened to be out on loan or away for refurbishing when the fire broke out. Virginia gentlemen, however, do not publicly accuse one another of arson, especially when the gentleman under suspicion is an ardent supporter of the incumbent political party. And old Elcott MacNeil, solvent once more, was certainly in a position to be generous—all the more so when the federal government showed a sudden interest in buying up his tired plantation acreage for parkland and home sites for senior Union officers.

Elcott MacNeil was also one of the chief advocates for the construction of the Great Falls and Old Dominion Railroad. Built at the turn of the last century, the railroad had drawn vacationers from the miasma of Washington summers, as well as year-round residents from among those government officials in the upper levels of a burgeoning federal bureaucracy who preferred to live outside the capital. Of course, railroad access to northern Virginia had only increased the value of the MacNeil acreage, which had been mostly sold off, forming the basis of the family's wealth ever since.

Over the years, the replacement house had been expanded in architecturally tasteful bits and pieces, becoming the new seat of the dynasty. If the old plantation with its rolling drive was gone, the house and its prime location still marked the MacNeil family as Fairfax County gentry.

* * *

Carrie tiptoed past her mother-in-law's closed door on her way to the guest bathroom. Althea had moved out of the master bedroom when Drum had announced their return from London. Carrie would have been happier if she would have stayed put, but Althea had insisted on moving into her daughter's old room down the hall. By the time the family arrived back in town, the switch was a *fait accompli*.

"This house is really Drum's now, anyway," she told Carrie as she showed off new burgundy and pink floral bed linens, drapes and matching lampshades she'd bought for the heavy, carved walnut bedroom suite that was now to be theirs.

The walls had been newly painted in a matching shade of dark burgundy that to Carrie's eye resembled dried blood. With its dark Victorian furnishings and heavy floral draperies, the room, despite its size, felt claustrophobic and funereal. But now that it had been redecorated especially for their arrival, Carrie knew there was no question of touching a thing in it without causing grievous offense to her mother-in-law.

"But there's no reason for you to give up your bedroom, Althea," she protested. "Drum and I were fine in the room we had before."

"Oh, no. He works so hard. He needs his rest, and the master bedroom is so much quieter than the ones at the front of the house. You don't hear the street noises back there at all."

The house sat on an acre of land on a riverfront cul-de-sac which had only five homes on it, all with equally large lots. The small, exclusive neighborhood had been carved out of a parklike wedge of land at the end of Chain Bridge Road, but the way Althea spoke of street noises, Carrie thought, a person might think the house was smack in the middle of Piccadilly Circus.

"We've never been bothered by noise," she told her mother-in-law. "And you always say what a light sleeper you are. Wouldn't you be better off staying put?"

Althea would not be moved. "No, this is yours now. I'll be fine in Ellie's old room. I'm sure I'll get used to the noise in time."

And she did seem to be coping admirably, Carrie thought. Despite the racket made by those few well-tuned luxury cars that constituted morning rush hour in this quiet neighborhood, her mother-in-law's room seemed dark and silent when Carrie passed her door, as it was most mornings at this hour. Althea almost never rose before ten. Carrie was anxious that this day not prove the exception to the rule.

From the guest room window, she peered out over the street, trying to judge what the weather would bring that day. No surprises there. Thick haze filtering the early morning light told her it would be another hot and sticky one.

A semicircular driveway covered in crushed white rock led from the house's porticoed front door to the edge of Elcott Road. At the curb, bluebottle flies were flitting lazily around the lids of the fifty-gallon trash bins Carrie had wheeled out the night before—a gray one for regular garbage, green for garden waste, and a blue bin for recyclables. Up and down the street, identical tri-colored trios of bins dotted the ends of other well-manicured drives, the only sign that the pristine neighborhood housed real people with normal requirements for food, drink and bathroom products.

Across the road, a green van sat in the driveway of Bernice and Morrie Klein's house. The old couple had lived opposite the MacNeils for thirty years now, but they were getting on. Carrie had seen them only once or twice since she and Drum and Jonah had returned from London—and not at all in the last few weeks, she suddenly realized. Maybe she should run over and check on them? If their cleaning service was there, though, they must be all right.

For all intents and purpose, the rest of the street seemed deserted.

Carrie turned from the window and headed into the bathroom for her shower. Afterward, wrapped in a fluffy white towel, she did her makeup and hair carefully. Then, calculating that Drum must have left by now, she debated slipping back into the master bedroom to choose something appropriate for her appointment with the lawyer.

But a glance at the clock on one of the side tables told her it was getting late. There was no telling when Jonah would decide it was a morning to dawdle, so instead, she pulled on the tank top and track shorts she'd left hooked on the back of the bathroom door after her run the previous morning. Best to get him moving first. Then, she could slip back upstairs and change while he was eating his breakfast.

The large attic had long ago been converted into nursery space for successive generations of MacNeil children. Drum and his younger sister had occupied the two big rooms up here from the time they were born until they'd left home for college. Jonah's bedroom and playroom were long, high-ceilinged spaces with steeply pitched rooflines. A small bathroom between the two rooms had been set into a dormer that looked down over the front of the house.

When Drum and Carrie had moved into the house after Tanzania, Carrie had redone the rooms in a bright circus motif for their own baby boy. On Jonah's bedroom walls, she'd painted striped tents, elephants, lion-tamers, clowns and balloon-carrying children, all cavorting on a soft yellow background. The ceiling was pale blue with fluffy white clouds.

Over his yellow circus-truck bed, she'd hung a red-and-white-striped canopy. The playroom was done up to look like the inside of one of those circus tents, with feather-harnessed horses, dancing bears, chimps on bicycles, more brilliantly costumed clowns, and a strawberry-headed ringmaster whose black top hat had "JONAH" written in gold leaf across the peak.

As a toddler and preschooler, Jonah had loved his bedroom and playroom, but when they'd been posted back from London that summer, the first thing he'd asked was whether they could redecorate his "baby rooms." He thought a combined Spider-Man–Incredible Hulk theme would be just the ticket, but Carrie had been stalling. If she went forward with these on-again, off-again intentions of hers, he might soon have another room in a different house and it would be important to make that new place as special as possible.

She found him curled at the foot of his bed, his favorite Spider-Man action figure tucked in the crook of his arm. His sandy red hair was tousled on the rumpled blue sheets, and he looked more angelic than fifty-seven pounds of pure energy normally allowed.

She gave him a kiss and a tickle. "Hey there, Jonah-man. Are you and Spidey going to get up today, old sleepyheads?"

He grunted and rolled over, his SpongeBob pajama bottoms twisting around his chubby legs.

"Come on, little guy. It's a great day out there. Today you make volcanoes at camp."

She moved to his bureau, humming *Good Day, Sunshine* to coax him out of rumpled sleep as she laid out his clothes on a chair—a blue-and-green-striped tank top and tan cotton duck shorts. She hesitated over the sock drawer.

"Do you want to wear your new sneakers today or sandals?"

"Sneakers," he mumbled.

She laid some blue tube socks on the pile of clothes and a pair of his miniature-size blue jockey shorts, and parked the running shoes next to the chair. "Okeydoke, buddy. All your clothes are here. If I leave them and go down to get your breakfast ready, can I count on you to get yourself dressed?"

"Uh-huh."

"You sure?" she said, leaning over him with a smile and another tickle. "You're really, truly, for sure awake? Or do I need to dress my superhero this morning?"

He giggled and rolled over on his stomach once more. "Mom! Really, truly, for sure. I can do it myself."

"You'll wash your face? And brush your hair? Cause I've gotta tell you, bud, you are not a pretty sight at the moment. You don't want to be giving Miss Mindy a fright attack."

"Mo-om!"

"Okay, okay. I'm going down to make your breakfast. But you've got ten minutes, all right? Up and at 'em, Adam ant."

She left him rolling off the bed with a grunt as she headed downstairs, fully expecting to have the kitchen to herself.

In his time, it seemed, General MacNeil had lectured his own son on the importance of being known as a man who didn't waste valuable time. There'd been a period in Drum's wild youth, Carrie knew, when he'd had no interest in the old man's advice, but then he'd been recruited by the CIA and his outlook had apparently undergone a transformation.

By the time Carrie had met him, he was already rising through the Agency's ranks. In the seven years they'd been married, he'd rarely taken breakfast at home, preferring to have his "girl" bring something to his desk while he read the daily intelligence brief and the overnight cables.

So that morning, she was taken aback when she came downstairs to find Drum sitting at the table in the breakfast nook, reading the *Washington Post* and looking as unhurried as she'd ever seen him.

The breakfast room in which he sat was a glassed-in solarium set off to one side of the big, wood-paneled kitchen. The house had been refurbished several times since its original construction in order to keep up with modern amenities. The solarium had been added in 1968, the year General MacNeil had been named to the Joint Chiefs of Staff.

Carrie could see Drum's blue shirt reflected in the wide bay of lead-lined windows behind the round oak table, but other than that and his long, sprawling legs crossed one over the other, he was completely hidden from view. Sun shone through the glass panes behind him, casting a patchwork rainbow across the kitchen's terrazzo tile floor.

"You're still here," she said.

"Mmm…" he murmured from behind his paper. "You have a real knack for pointing out the obvious, sweetie."

"I thought you'd be long gone. Is Margaret on vacation?"

These days, Drum's "girl" was a forty-eight-year-old executive assistant with steel wool for hair and, according to him, a swaying, pickup-size rear end that made him wince every time she left his office. Neither tact nor political correctness had ever been his strong suits.

"No. I'm sure she's busy grumbling as we speak about the coffee I'm not there to drink."

Apparently Margaret had bristled his first day back at headquarters, when Drum had interrupted her admin spiel and sent her out to the directors' mess to fetch coffee and a bagel while he made some calls. He had no use, he said, for her "feminazi attitude." His secretary in London had fetched his meals during the four years he'd been there; and so had his previous girl at Langley when he'd been head of the counterintelligence unit, as well as the one before that, who'd taken care of him in Dar es Salaam, Tanzania.

"Now I get an EA with delusions of grandeur and a chip on her shoulder," he'd complained that first week back. "Is that what comes with a promotion these days? A seventh floor office with a view to kingdom come and clerical staff with attitude? EA, my ass. Whatever happened to secretaries?"

He'd left no room for doubt that if Margaret wanted to continue as assistant to the Operations Deputy, she'd carry out her duties in the way he expected. At the same time, he told Carrie, he'd put in a personnel order for someone less prickly to occupy his outer office. Easier on the eyes, too, while they were at it.

His newspaper rustled now as Drum set it down on his lap, closed his eyes and massaged his temples.

"Another headache?" Carrie asked.

He nodded.

"Can I get you some Tylenol?"

He exhaled heavily. "Already took three."

"Do you think you should see a doctor about these headaches, Drum? You've been getting them ever since—"

He picked up his paper, shook it out, and went back behind it. "It's just a headache."

Carrie took a cup from a hook under the wooden shelf that ran the length of the kitchen's brick-lined inner wall. The display rack held part of the collection of brightly colored handthrown pottery that Drum's mother had amassed in the course of the General's military postings around the world.

"So you didn't call in sick or anything?" she asked, pouring out her coffee.

"I'm not sick. I'm going in."

"You don't need to let Margaret know?"

"I'm not there to answer to my staff. Pays to keep them off balance. Anyway, if she checks my calendar, she'll know I've got a meeting across the river this morning."

"Oh." Carrie moved to the walk-in pantry and withdrew a box of Cheerios. Could she possibly have worse luck?

On the other hand, she thought, studying the deep vertical tension lines atop the bridge of his nose, Drum was not exactly a happy camper these days, either. After the tragic end to his posting in London with the murder of the young student from Maryland, he'd landed back home in the middle of another political firestorm. Everyone was looking for a scapegoat for the security lapses that had brought the nation's morale so low. Congress and the press were calling for heads to roll. For the past eleven months, Washington seemed to have been seized by endless rounds of self-examination, mutual recrimination and accountability reviews as every department, agency, official and politician tried to avoid being stuck with the hot potato of blame. And rather than take up the operations position he'd been angling to obtain for so long, Drum found himself saddled with make-work projects that seemed designed to do little more than provide the illusion of CIA industriousness and hold the Agency's critics at bay.

"Is it another one of those committee meetings of yours?" Carrie asked.

"Something like that," Drum said wearily.

Before she could probe further, Jonah burst into the kitchen with an ear-piercing cry. "Nyaow!" His arms propellered two toy star fighters, one gripped in each small hand. The two craft wheeled and dipped, exchanging imaginary phaser fire. "Chinnng! Chinnng!"

He bounded across the terrazzo tiles, ready to take his usual leap onto one of the bar stools lined up along the long baker's table that served as the kitchen's center island, but at the last moment, he caught sight of his father. The rubber soles of his new blue Nikes squealed to a halt, the lights in the heels flashing wildly.

"Daddy?"

Drum turned another page, glancing up. "Hey, sport."

"How come you're home?"

"Obviously, because I haven't left yet."

Jonah climbed up onto one of the tall bar stools and sat quietly, his star cruisers in silent running mode now as he waited for his breakfast.

Carrie took a blue bowl from one of the glass-fronted cupboards, and set it on the island in front of Jonah, studying him and his father surreptitiously as she poured out his Cheerios. Her son was strawberry-haired, gap-toothed, freckled. His coloring had come from her end of the genetic pool, as had his mischievous green eyes. He was wearing the blue-and-green-striped tank top and tan shorts she'd put out for him, and his stocky little body fairly purred, now that he'd thrown off sleep.

Drum, by contrast, was forced to sit sideways at the breakfast table in order to cross his long legs, the polished toe of his soft, black Italian brogues tapping a chronically impatient beat in the air. Would Jonah eventually stretch out like that? Carrie wondered, trying to imagine what it would be like to have a son who towered over her the way his father did.

"Can I get you some breakfast, Drum?" she asked.

Mistake. When he finally looked directly at her, his deep blue eyes narrowed and the paper fell into his lap. "You look very nice this morning."

"Oh…thanks." Despite the old shorts and tank top, wasn't it obvious she was too carefully groomed for someone planning nothing more than to drive their son over to his summer day camp a few blocks away?

"How about some toast or a bagel?" she asked, anxious to deflect attention. "Or cereal? I could do up some eggs."

"No," Drum said, his appraising gaze never wavering. "I will take some more coffee, though."

"In the travel cup?" Every evening, she set up the coffeemaker to brew by 6:00 a.m. and left a clean, lidded travel mug on the counter next to it in case Drum wanted coffee for his ten-minute ride over to Langley.

But he picked up a ceramic mug sitting on the table beside him and held it out. "No, just refill this, would you?"

Carrie collected the coffeepot and carried it over.

The tall windows behind him overlooked a long lawn dotted with weeping willows whose branches swept the lush grass, kept green by an automatic underground sprinkler system that even now was chuck-chucking rainbow sprays into the early morning air. But the windows in the house were all shut up tight against the heat and humidity that never seemed to dissipate in the long Washington summer. Nights here were too warm and the pollen too thick for Jonah, who suffered from mild asthma, to sleep comfortably without air-conditioning.

The lawn ran down to the banks of the Potomac. A couple of sculling teams were out on the water, oars moving in smooth unison as the shells passed the MacNeils' boat slip. The dock was repaired and re-varnished every year, although in the time Carrie had been married to Drum, they'd never had a boat. When they'd come back from London, she'd asked him about getting a kayak or sailboat she and Jonah could paddle around in that summer, but Drum had said something about currents in the river and the matter had been dropped.

Carrie set his refilled cup in front of him, cursing the tremble in her hand that made it clatter, trying to read his body language and gauge his mood. "So, you have a meeting downtown?"

"Mmm..."

"Where?"

"The Bureau."

"What time?"

He'd gone back to reading his paper, but he set it down again, frowning. "Why do you ask?"

She turned away. "No reason. It's just unusual to have you here in the morning, that's all."

"Well, the meeting's at nine." He dropped behind his news-paper screen once more.

On the way to the fridge, Carrie glanced at the antique rail-way clock on the wall. It was now seven-fifty-five. The FBI was...where? Pennsylvania Avenue, wasn't it? It would take him at least forty-five minutes in rush hour to get across the river and down the Mall and park the car. Surely he'd have to head out shortly.

If he left in the next few minutes, there'd still be time for her to run up and change into something more appropriate— a skirt and blouse, at the very least. No lawyer, friend of a friend or not, was going to take a woman in shorts and a tank top seriously. Could she change later? Her appointment wasn't until ten-fifteen, and even though it was over in Alexandria, there was probably time to come back after she'd dropped off Jonah. But if she did that, she ran the risk of run-ning into Althea and her inevitable barrage of questions and small complaints. How would she explain to her mother-in-law why she was getting so dressed up this morning?

Why was nothing ever simple?

Propping the fridge door open with a hip, Carrie reached for the milk with one hand and the carton of orange juice with the other, trying to estimate how long it would take her to negotiate the traffic she herself would face. She kept one nervous eye on Drum as she poured juice into a glass.

"I want some banana on my cereal," Jonah said.

She added milk to his bowl and replaced the cap on the jug. "Please may I have...?"

Jonah rolled his enormous gray-green eyes. "Please may I have some banana on my cereal?" He'd lost one of his top front teeth the previous week and the resulting gap had given him a lisp and a lop-sided cant to his sweet mouth.

Carrie smiled and pushed back his sandy hair, leaning over to kiss him on the forehead. "Yes, you may, you handsome devil, you."

He started to smile before he remembered to grimace and wipe his forehead with the back of one hand. Then he turned his attention back to his star cruisers, dive-bombing them over the bobbing oat circles in his cereal bowl.

Across the way in the solarium, Drum lowered his newspaper once more. "Jonah, what's the rule about toys at the table?"

Two chubby hands whipped into his small lap, then reappeared a moment later without the spaceships. "Sorry. I thought that was at dinnertime."

"You think good manners only get brought out once a day? Your mother lets you get away with that?"

"No, sir."

Carrie was already at the refrigerator, putting away the milk and juice, and her back was to the table, but she winced as she lifted a banana from the hanging wire fruit basket and a paring knife out of a rack over the counter. Avoiding the critical gaze that now encompassed her as well as her son, she returned to the center island. Silence hung heavy in the room while she peeled back the skin and sliced the fruit with quick strokes, the sun glinting off the steel blade as each creamy piece tumbled into the bowl.

"Eat up now, sweetie," she murmured. "It's almost time to go."

"Carrie?"

She'd moved back to the sink and was slicing the peel into small pieces, letting them fall into the plastic bin where she saved vegetable scraps, egg shells and coffee grounds for the garden compost pile. She paused. Would she even be here come fall to turn the last ripe batch of compost into the flower beds?

"Carrie, would you have the courtesy to face me when I'm addressing you, please?" Drum's voice was dangerously polite.

She straightened and turned. *Don't provoke him. Not today.*

He'd folded the paper and set it aside, focused solely on her now. Hard to believe she'd once felt protected and safe inside the tight cocoon of that icy gaze. Out of the corner of her eye, she noted Jonah sitting very straight on his stool, towhead down, concentrating intently on the spoon moving rhythmically up and down between the blue bowl and his mouth.

"I was going to make Jonah's lunch and tidy up," she said evenly. "Rose will be in at nine and your mother likes to leave a neat kitchen for her."

Althea's housekeeper had been with the family for over thirty years. For the first twenty of those, she'd lived in the small servants' quarters out behind the kitchen, but now, she just worked weekdays from nine to two, doing cleaning, laundry and light cooking, and she lived with her daughter in Arlington. At one time, Carrie had thought the unoccupied maid's room at the back of the house would make an ideal studio for her own use, but that plan, like so much else in her marriage, had died of neglect.

"I've never understood why my mother feels it necessary to clean the place for the maid," Drum said.

"Pride, I guess. She doesn't like Rose to think we live like animals."

"Like I care what a servant thinks."

"Well, your mother does, and since I may not be back from driving Jonah before Rose gets here, I'd better do it now."

"Why wouldn't you be back? It takes five minutes to get over to the rec center."

Carrie was gathering up ingredients for Jonah's lunch. *Keep it simple.* "I have some errands to run after I drop him off."

"Such as…?"

"Well, I need to pick up your suit at the dry cleaners and return some books to the library. And I need to drop by the pharmacy and the grocery store. The refill on your mother's blood pressure medication should be ready, and I wanted to get some chicken breasts for dinner. Are you going to be home, do you think? I was thinking of doing them on the grill."

"Doubtful. How long are you planning to be gallivanting around this morning?"

"Not long. Maybe an hour or so. Could you let me have some money?" she added. He'd never believe her otherwise. He wouldn't expect her to have enough cash on hand to buy groceries and pay for the prescription and he didn't like her to have a debit or credit card. She could write checks on her household account, but carrying plastic was just an invitation to strangers to steal your personal information, he said. She didn't dare point out the Amex and Visa cards in *his* wallet. That was never the same thing. She just prayed he wouldn't tell her to wake Althea for the prescription money. That carried its own set of hazards.

"Can I be excused?" Jonah asked meekly.

His bowl was scraped clean, though it was hard to say whether that was indicative of a sudden growth spurt or a desire to escape the tension in the room.

"Did you have enough to eat?" Carrie asked him. "How about some toast or a bagel?"

"No, thank you, ma'am," he said, glancing at Drum. "I should go and brush my teeth now."

When Carrie smiled and nodded at him, he scrambled off the stool. He was already halfway to the door when Drum's voice called, "Jonah?"

The red lights embedded in the heels of his sneakers flashed as he squealed to a stop and turned to face his father once more. "Yes, sir?"

"How about a hug for your old man?"

Jonah hesitated, then hurried over, heel lights flashing with every step.

His father set the paper aside and hoisted him onto his lap. "How's that summer camp going?"

"It's good. I can dive head first off the diving board."

"You can? Head first?"

"Uh-huh. The low one, anyway. And I jumped off the high board yesterday, too. Three times. I didn't go head first, though. But I did off the low board, lots of times. I can show you if you want. You can come and watch when we have our swimming lesson."

"I don't know about that, pardner."

Jonah's face fell and he nodded. "Yeah, I guess not."

Drum studied him for a moment. "You know what I've been thinking, though?"

"What?"

"I've been thinking it's about time we had a boat. Got a dock, we should have something to tie up to it, shouldn't we?"

"Wow! Yeah! You mean it? Can we get a motorboat, with a steering wheel and everything?"

"Why not? With a steering wheel and everything. Maybe we'll get a chance to go out on the weekend and take a look. Would you like that?"

"Yeah, Dad! That would be cool."

"Okay. You better get a move on now, but we'll talk about it later, okay?"

"Okay!"

"Big hug?"

Jonah threw his arms around his father's neck and Drum held him close. When Jonah scrambled off his lap again, Drum's silver head gave a curt nod in the direction of the center island and its abandoned dishes. "Something you forgot over there, pardner?"

"Sorry," Jonah said, returning to stack them.

"It's all right, sweetie. I'll do that this morning," Carrie told him. "It's getting late and you need to gather up those newspapers Miss Mindy asked you to bring in. They're making papier-mâché volcanoes at camp today," she explained to Drum. Then, to her son, "Go on up and brush your teeth, but don't make a racket, please. Let Nana sleep."

As Jonah headed out the door, Carrie turned back to the counter and started packing his sandwich, applesauce, juice and cookies into his red-and-blue Spider-Man lunch box. Behind her, she heard the legs of Drum's chair scrape on the terrazzo floor.

"You're spoiling him, you know."

"I just—"

"I'm trying to encourage him to take on some responsibility. I don't appreciate it when you undermine me like that."

She turned. "Drum, he's barely six years old, and he's a really good little guy. All his teachers say how much they enjoy having him in class."

Once more, Carrie felt herself pinned by the ice-blue stare. "Don't do that again, Carrie. Don't try to turn me into the heavy while you play the good cop. Just because you get to be with him all day while I work my butt off to put food in your mouths, doesn't mean I don't know my own son or what's best for him. I have no intention of being an irrelevancy in his life, you know."

"I didn't mean—"

"Just don't do it again. I don't appreciate it." He picked up his suit coat from the back of his chair and turned to go. As an afterthought he stopped and reached into his pocket, withdrawing a wad of bills from which he peeled off a few twenties and laid them on the table.

Carrie knew she should just leave well enough alone, but if good sense were part of her nature, she wouldn't be in the pickle she was now. "Drum?"

"What?"

"A boat? Didn't I suggest getting a boat?"

"Did you?"

"Yes, I did, when we were coming back from London. I wanted something to make up to Jonah for leaving early and him missing out on being on the softball team with Connor Jenks. But you said the currents were too dangerous."

"Oh, I don't think I said that, Carrie. You must have misunderstood. I always ran boats off that dock when I was a kid. There's no problem in good weather."

Like hell she'd misunderstood. "So now you think Jonah should have a boat?"

"Maybe. Under close supervision, of course. We'll see."

Carrie sighed, shook her head and started gathering up the dirty dishes and loading them in the dishwasher. Fine. If he wanted to be the hero now, let him. It might make what she had to do easier. Or harder, she thought suddenly. If she left, surely Drum wouldn't fight her for custody, would he? On what grounds?

"Make sure you take your cell phone with you when you go out," Drum said. "And Carrie?"

"What?"

"It doesn't do any good if it's not turned on. I need to be able to reach you in case of an emergency. Do you understand?"

"It'll be on."

"Good." He came up behind her, one arm slipping around her waist as he pulled her toward him. She tensed, waiting for the routine kiss she thought was coming.

Instead, he hissed softly in her ear, "Don't think I don't know what you're up to."

Her head snapped up, her heart hammering in her chest. "What are you talking about?"

Instead of answering, he stepped away from her and flipped his suit jacket over his shoulder, his smile fixed, enigmatic and irritating. "I have to go now," he said. "I'll call you later."

He never did.

CHAPTER SEVEN

TOP SECRET
CODE WORD ACCESS ONLY
NOT FOR DISTRIBUTION

FEDERAL BUREAU OF INVESTIGATION
INTERVIEW TRANSCRIPTION

(continued...)

What was that business about getting a boat, Carrie?

Oh, just an idea I'd had. I knew that the dock behind the house had been used in the past. There's plenty of pictures of Drum and his sister when they were growing up, sculling and boating with friends on that section of the Potomac. I could understand Drum being nervous about a boat when Jonah was very small, but now that he's bigger, I thought it would be a nice thing for us to do together as a family. But up to then, Drum had always turned the idea down flat. That's why I was so taken aback when he suggested the other morning that he and Jonah might go out and look at boats.

Did you know that your husband's first wife had drowned in a boating accident?

Yes, I did. That's why I never pushed the subject. I thought it must be painful for him.

It says here in the files that she died in November of 1993. The death was officially ruled accidental, but the circumstances look to have been a little murky. Seems there was a fairly lengthy investigation.

I suppose so.

You suppose so?

Well, yes. I wasn't around at the time, you know. I didn't even meet Drum until two years later, and in Africa, besides. His wife's death was still a pretty raw subject for him, so he didn't really talk about it. What little I know comes from comments my mother-in-law or family friends have dropped in passing.

To the effect that...?

To the effect that Theresa might have been depressed before she died. You have to admit, it's a little strange, taking a boat out in the middle of the night in November. Not exactly prime boating season.

So, they think she killed herself?

I don't know. Maybe. The boat was found hung up on the shoreline several miles downstream, but the body wasn't found until a month or two later, apparently, so it was difficult to say whether her drowning was accidental or intentional.

Why was she depressed?

I don't really know. As I say, I'm not even sure she was, or whether it was just something people decided later to try to explain what happened to her. I gather she couldn't have children, but I'm not sure if that was the source of the problem. My mother-in-law has suggested she was unstable, but you have to take that with a grain of salt, so who knows?

You think she made that up?

Let's just say my mother-in-law's approval is an elusive commodity. I'm not sure she approved of Theresa any more than she does of me. I doubt anyone would really be good enough for her son—but then, that's a mother for you. I do know that when it comes time for my own son to be bringing home a bride, I'm going to try to remember what I've learned from my own experience and handle things a little differently.

So, getting back to the other morning, your husband left for this supposed meeting at the Bureau and said he'd call you later, right?

Right.

And that was the last time you saw him? You haven't heard from him since?

You know I haven't. I left shortly after he did to take my son to day camp and run errands. By the time I got back home, police cars were blocking the driveway and the house was crawling with FBI agents and CIA Security. They've been flitting around me like flies ever since, so if he had been in touch, you guys would be the first to know.

And you're saying you had no idea what he was really up to that morning?

Not a clue. When I first saw the police cars at the house, I thought there'd been a break-in. Then I panicked, thinking my son had been in some sort of accident.

It never occurred to you that something might have happened to your husband?

Not until I got inside and the people there showed me their IDs. When I realized some of them were CIA, I knew it must be about Drum, and I guessed it had to be serious. I thought maybe another terrorist attack. After everything we've been through in the past few years, it wouldn't have surprised me.

In fact, it would have solved a lot of problems, wouldn't it?

What are you talking about?

If your husband were killed in something like a terrorist attack—it would be very convenient.

That's a terrible thing to say! I didn't want anything bad to happen to him.

Come on, Carrie. You weren't just running errands that morning. You went to see a divorce lawyer. Divorce is messy. How much easier if he suffered a fatal mishap, instead.

That's truly perverse, you know that?

Trust me, it happens more often than you might think.

Yeah, well, not with me, it doesn't. In the first place, if I were organized enough to plan something like that—not to mention connected enough—don't you think I would have done it before I had to write a two thousand dollar retainer check to that lawyer?

Maybe you're just dumb like a fox.

All I wanted was some space to figure out what to do with the rest of my life. I wasn't even sure I wanted a divorce when I walked into the lawyer's office that morning. I didn't particularly relish the thought of raising my son in a single-parent household—although for all intents and purposes, that's what I was doing, anyway. I certainly never wanted him to grow up without a father, though.

Go ahead and talk to the lawyer if you don't believe me. Heather Childers is her name. I give up my lawyer-client privilege. I've got nothing to hide.

I can think of one person who might beg to differ.

Who's that?

Your mother-in-law.

Oh, Lord... Althea...

CHAPTER EIGHT

McLean, Virginia
August 12, 2002—8:09 a.m.

A tomblike gloom hung over Althea MacNeil's bedroom. The draperies were navy blue and lined with blackout fabric, so that only a bleak hint of the sunny day managed to peek around the dark edges of the heavy silk.

She lay on her narrow bed in the dim light, studying the silver-framed photograph on her bedside table. The portrait of her late husband in full dress uniform had been taken the day he'd been named to the Joint Chiefs of Staff. It had been his proudest moment. Hers, as well.

The whole family had attended the Oval Office ceremony. President Nixon had shaken hands with her and the children in turn, solemnly asking Drummond, who was sixteen at the time, whether he planned to follow his father into a military career. Obviously, the President hadn't been briefed about their son's recent run-in with the Fairfax County Police, who'd found a plastic bag of marijuana in his car when they'd pulled him over for speeding. Naughton had managed to get the incident hushed up, but even so, Drummond's flowing, shoulder-length hair should have been a tip-off to the President that this apple had rolled some distance from the paternal tree. Althea cringed in mortification even now at the memory of her son's scruffy appearance that day.

Eleanor, by contrast, had stood ramrod straight in her professional-looking brown tweed suit, hair pulled back into a tight bun that made her seem older than her nineteen years. She really should have been a boy, Althea thought. She was Naughton's true heir. She'd always been a little daunting, just like her father, both of them knowing exactly what they wanted and where they were going. Vice president of a New York brokerage firm, Eleanor lived in a penthouse overlooking Central Park. A couple of years ago, when *Businessweek* had put her on their cover after she engineered some corporate merger or another, they'd called her "Ironside's Daughter."

Althea had no idea how she'd managed to raise such an unladylike girl—so excruciatingly blunt. In fact, Ellie, she was sorry to say, had turned into the kind of woman men called a "ball-buster." Althea had tried to tell her many times that there are other ways for a woman to get what she wants, but her daughter, she knew, found her utterly vapid. Ellie rarely came home anymore, now that Naughton was gone.

She'd never married, although there had been a couple of long-term relationships—not to mention numerous casual affairs, Althea suspected. She really didn't care to know the details. But at fifty-two, the ship of motherhood had sailed without Ellie aboard, so it looked as if Jonah was the only grandchild Althea would ever have. Thank goodness Drummond had produced a boy to carry on the family name.

There'd been a time when both Althea and her husband had despaired that Drummond would ever make anything of himself. In his own way, though, their son had followed his father, after all, becoming a sort of warrior and a leader of men. Of course, Naughton had never really approved of the CIA. They all seemed a little shifty over there, he used to say. But surely he'd have been pleased to see how far Drummond's career had advanced.

From the kitchen downstairs came the addictive scent of fresh coffee brewing and the faint clatter of dishes and cutlery. She'd lived mostly on her own since Naughton had passed away twelve years earlier, but old habits die hard. Morning activity in the house could still cause long-dormant instincts to kick in. It was maternal guilt, she supposed, whispering that she should be down there making someone's breakfast, ironing a last-minute shirt or packing lunches. But they didn't need her anymore. She'd just be in the way if she went down now.

In any case, she was loathe to move and didn't really feel like facing anyone. Let them head off for their respective days. Then, she'd get up, make herself a cup of tea, and enjoy the quiet until they all burst back in on her again. Quiet was a rare enough treat.

Rolling onto her back with a sibilant grunt, Althea nestled deeper into the pillows, inventorying her aches and twinges. Her hips, neck and back felt as if she'd slept wrong. When was it that there started being a wrong way to sleep? Children never did. They slept like logs and woke full of that pent-up energy that blew them out of bed and carried them through their frenetic days. Not her, though. Relentless arthritis was advancing on every joint in her body like some unstoppable army of dry rot.

Bette Davis was right—old age is not for sissies.

Althea hadn't had an uninterrupted night's sleep in years. Each evening, she fell into bed by nine-thirty or ten to watch the news on the television. These days, the set was perched on the cherry highboy opposite her bed, too close for comfort in this smaller room she'd had to squeeze into after giving up the master bedroom. But she never managed to stay awake long, anyway, and the television would shut itself off after the weather report that she always seemed to miss. Then, some time around midnight, her bladder would wake her, and after that, those insomniac twin devils, regret and worry, would take over, taunting her for hours.

The devilish glow of her bedside radio clock had read nearly 5:00 a.m. the last time she'd looked at it early this morning. She'd finally dropped off again, only to be woken by the clump of her grandson's feet careening past her door and down the stairs to the kitchen. Really. Did no one teach children to *walk* indoors anymore?

She was especially achy and stiff, she realized, more tired than when she'd lain down the night before. It must be the air-conditioning. When it was just her in the house, she never kept it on all night. She'd been raised in the South, and on muggy summer nights, you opened all the windows wide to catch whatever fresh breeze you could. If there was none, you slept out on the porch, but you never shut yourself up inside.

Of course, she wasn't on her own now. Drum was back with his family and their needs had to be considered. Carrie said the air-conditioning was better for Jonah's asthma. As far as

Althea was concerned, all this talk about asthma nowadays was just so much hooey—another scheme by drug companies to peddle medicine. Another excuse for inexperienced young mothers to pamper their little darlings. Children should breathe natural air. That was how Althea had raised her own children and they'd obviously turned out fine.

But the young girls these days had different ways of doing things and thought they knew better. Carrie certainly never seemed willing to take advice. Just nodded thoughtfully when Althea gave her the benefit of her experience, then went ahead and did what she'd planned to do all along. Well fine. Althea was not one of those interfering mothers-in-law, no matter how many blunders the girl made.

The furnace fan was already humming, pushing air-conditioned chill through the house's massive system of ductwork. Not a good sign. Obviously it was going to be another scorcher.

There'd been a time in Althea's life when it couldn't be too warm. She could stay out on the deck in the summer sun from morning till night, her skin turning as brown as an old nut, hair bleaching out to a soft, golden straw color, and never mind the heat or the intense humidity. But those days were long gone. For many years, now, she'd found the too-long summers oppressive and stifling. It was her heart, she supposed, and those extra pounds she'd gained during the change and never managed to shed. At seventy-three, her body no longer managed heat very well, and she found herself puffing and feeling faint after even the shortest excursions outside.

She'd had to give up gardening completely, except in the early spring when it was still cool enough in the morning to putter around a little, tugging up a weed here and there and potting a few marigolds for the back patio. This year, even that had been more than she could handle. When the children had arrived back home, the patio pots had held nothing but dried-out weeds.

Althea had planned to have the fellow who took care of the lawns replant the pots, but then Carrie had volunteered to do them herself. Her intentions had been good, Althea supposed, but really, the colors she chose to put together! It wasn't the way Althea would have done it—all those pink asters and blue salvia mixed together like that, the effect so gaudy and un-structured. Althea's idea of gardening was neat, straight rows of red begonias and that silver-gray dusty miller in front of the clipped boxwood hedges lining the drive. That was the way she'd always done it, and it had looked very orderly.

But Carrie—well, this wasn't the first time Althea had had to suffer through the girl's gardening efforts. Drummond had first brought her home from his posting in Africa the summer Althea had had her gall bladder removed. While she was laid up, Carrie had started redoing the flower beds with all sorts of new varieties of daylilies and climbing roses and impatiens and heaven only knew what else—a riot of colors.

"A get-well surprise," she'd called it, obviously delighted with the effect.

It certainly was. It had taken Althea three bottles of Roundup, secretly applied, before the blessed things had all finally died off. She'd thought she had her new daughter-in-law convinced her choices weren't suitable here, however they might have fared back in California where she'd been raised. But then the next thing she knew, Carrie was back and those gaudy pots had started sprouting all over the patio again.

Was there any of that plant-killing spray left in the garden shed? Althea wondered.

She heard voices murmuring down in the kitchen and suddenly realized one of them was Drummond's. She glanced at the clock, frowning. This was awfully late for him to be at home.

Something was going on. She couldn't quite put her finger on it, but both her son and his young wife had been acting strangely of late. Nothing overt, mind you. No loud arguments or angry whispering behind closed doors. Just a dangerous politeness that to Althea's ears didn't ring true.

Of course, she'd thought from the start that the marriage was a poor idea—not that Drummond or his sister had ever been interested in any advice their mother had to offer. Althea had long since learned to keep her opinions to herself. But when she'd first received the news of Drummond's second marriage, along with that photograph of him and the girl in the Serengeti—her in a gauzy top and African print skirt, that wild red hair tumbling everywhere, and Drum with his arm around her, grinning like an old fool—all she could think was that his father would have been appalled.

What had he been thinking, a forty-two-year old man taking up with a girl barely out of her teens? Well, there was the obvious explanation, of course—men did go for a pretty face and a firm, young body—but just because he wanted to have his fun didn't mean the fool should marry her.

Was it grief that had driven him into her clutches? His first wife, Theresa, had died two years earlier, and Althea suspected that Drum felt guilty about not having been home the night she'd taken it into her head to go out on the river by herself, but the girl had always been a little clueless, and if it hadn't been that night she did some damn foolish thing, it would have been another.

But why rush into another marriage? Althea had done the

math. Carrie hadn't gotten pregnant until a couple of months later, so it wasn't as if Drum had *had* to get himself tied down to someone so unsuitable. Really, she had no idea what he'd been thinking. Still, she'd set her own feelings aside and tried to be as welcoming as she could when they came home.

But then yesterday, there'd been that odd telephone message left on the machine. Althea had gone to the phone book to look up the name of the office calling to confirm an appointment Carrie had apparently made for this morning. Childers and Overturf was a legal firm, according to the listing. A small ad in the Yellow Pages said the practice, based in Alexandria, specialized in family law—wills and estates, adoptions, divorce and child custody cases.

So which of these services was her daughter-in-law after? Althea wondered. Adoption? She had it easy with only one child to care for and Jonah off at camp or sports or some other activity more often than not. It was a mystery to Althea how the girl planned to fill her day once Jonah started school, especially with Rose handling the household chores. It was often when their children entered first grade, though, that young mothers started to think about a second baby.

Neither Carrie nor Drummond had ever mentioned giving Jonah a little brother or sister before now. Althea had begun to suspect there was some physical problem. Carrie had delivered Jonah in a hospital in Nairobi, despite Althea's warning to Drum about getting her back to the States well before her due date. Were there complications at the birth they hadn't chosen to tell her about? Well, Althea wouldn't be surprised. Who knew how a woman's inside might get butchered in a godforsaken backwater like that?

But at the thought of an adoption, Althea felt a dread chill. *Oh, please, let them not bring a strange child into the house.*

A real grandchild was one thing. Jonah could be rambunctious, of course, but when it was your own flesh and blood, you made allowances. But a stranger's child? A drug addict's, perhaps, or some trailer trash floozy's? Really, it wasn't to be borne.

Then, she had another indignant thought. Childers and Overturf also handled divorce. Surely Carrie wasn't thinking about that? On what grounds? Because Drummond worked long hours and wasn't there to entertain her? Althea had no sympathy for that kind of nonsense—not when she herself had been married for thirty-six years to a soldier who was often gone for months at a time. Of course, Carrie was young, and young girls these days didn't seem equipped to handle the kind of sacrifices generations before them had. Still, there was no excuse for irresponsibility. What could she be thinking, when there was a child to consider? When it came to the needs of children…

The toilet flushed in the upstairs bathroom. Althea hadn't heard her grandson go back up. He must have been told to tiptoe, unlike his noisy descent earlier.

She sighed. His mother would be driving him to camp shortly. They would go out and the house would be hers again for a little while—at least for as long as it took Carrie to attend to that appointment. But an appointment to do what? That was the question.

Well, if the marriage was falling apart, Althea couldn't say she was surprised. It was what she'd secretly predicted all along. That seemed to be the way things went these days, wasn't it? She was only surprised it had lasted as long as it had.

Still, there was the child. If it came to divorce, Drum would get custody, of course. It only made sense that his son would grow up in the house that had sent so many generations of MacNeils out into the world. Which meant, Althea thought wearily, that she would be called upon to assist in caring for the boy.

Well, it couldn't be helped. She would have to put her own interests and needs aside, just as she'd always done. That was the kind of person she was.

CHAPTER NINE

FEDERAL BUREAU OF INVESTIGATION
INTERVIEW TRANSCRIPTION

(continued...)

Why not a marriage counselor instead of a divorce lawyer, Carrie?

I tried to suggest counseling to Drum. Several times, in fact.

And?

He didn't see that we had a problem.

But it sounds like you were fighting most of the time. How could he not see a problem?

I never said we were fighting. That wouldn't be true. We never fought.

Never? Come on, Carrie, all married people fight sometimes.

Not us. Not really. I wish we had.

Why is that?

Because it might have shown there was some emotion other

than indifference at work there. Oh, we had arguments, of course, but when we did, it was Drum who usually made the deciding call.

You just went along with whatever he said?

Pretty much, especially in the beginning. After that, I guess it became our default mode—my fault as much as his.

Look, I married a man twenty years older than me who was smart, sophisticated and articulate. And me, I had zero self-confidence. Most of the time, especially in the early years, I just assumed he knew better. Even on those occasions where I had doubts, I couldn't out-argue him, so I didn't often try.

But you'd attended Georgetown University, Carrie. You'd gone on to graduate school. You were working again on your master's thesis. You also had enough guts to see a lawyer to safeguard your rights in case you and he split. That doesn't sound like someone with zero self-confidence.

Maybe I finally grew up. God knows, it took me long enough to do it. But even so, it wouldn't be accurate to say he and I fought. Maybe I couldn't be bothered. I was on my own so much that for the most part, I just waited until he was gone, then went ahead and did what I wanted to do, anyway.

So, when did you decide that wasn't enough?

It was something I'd been thinking about for a while—even before we went to London, in fact. Things hadn't been going well for a long time. We were happy in Dar es Salaam, I think, when we first met and got married. I got pregnant pretty quickly. We were both thrilled about it—Drum, too. But then, everything started to change.

Change how?

I guess we started to grow apart after Jonah was born. He was colicky for the first six or seven months, so I had to be up with him most nights. Even when he slept, I was exhausted so I didn't really have any time or energy left over for Drum.

Jonah eventually outgrew the colic and things started to settle down, right about the time we were scheduled to leave Dar. But then the embassy was bombed and after that, the situation at home took another nosedive.

We wanted to talk about that. We've noted that you were there the day the embassies in Nairobi and Dar es Salaam were bombed.

What a horrible day that was. We were... Wait a minute... what? What's that expression supposed to mean?

What expression?

The smug, "gee, why am I not surprised?" expression on your face. So now what? You think Drum had something to do with the bombing of the embassies in Africa?

We don't know when his extracurricular business dealings began. It could go back that far.

Get real. Eleven people died in the Tanzania embassy bombing that morning. Several dozen in Nairobi, if I recall correctly. Drum and I were both in the building when the truck bomb drove into the yard and detonated. You think he would have set himself up to be killed?

Call it unintended consequences. You play with fire, there's always a chance you get burned.

That's crazy. If he was supplying information to—who? I still haven't figured out who exactly he's supposed to have been dealing with in these supposed treasonous activities of his. You said he blew that Chinese double agent. I gather we know that it was Middle Eastern terrorists who bombed the embassies in Africa. And the shooting in London—well, I'm still not sure who that was. If you guys have figured that one out, I never heard about it.

That investigation is still ongoing.

So what's the link between all these far-flung fiascoes you're trying to dump at Drum's door? Who exactly is he supposed to have been dealing with? The Chinese? Al Qaeda? Al Capone? Good Lord, why not pin the Kennedy assassination on him, too, as long as you're blaming him for everything else? This makes no sense to me at all.

Well, let me put it this way, Carrie. You know that countries spy on other countries, collecting intelligence for their own military and other purposes. But these days, obviously, there are a lot of non-state actors out there, too. Terrorist groups, anti-government rebels of one sort and another, that sort of thing. That being the case, there's an active market for certain kinds of inside information. And whenever you get a market for anything developing, you're going to have not only sellers and buyers, but eventually you're going to see middlemen popping up, people who deal in the bulk acquisition of a product—in this case political and military intelligence—that they then re-package and re-sell to interested buyers. These middlemen have operations that function sort of like an espionage vacuum cleaner. They suck up every bit of secret information they can get hold of, shake it all out on the floor, figure out which bit of information is worth how much to who, then turn those bits around and re-sell them, piecemeal, to interested parties.

Terrorist middlemen?

Let's call them information brokers. They maintain the connections with interested buyers, so they set the market in terms of demand. And recently, we got wind of one broker who was rumored to have had a high-level source inside the American intelligence community.

And you're thinking that source was my husband? Tell me, Agent Andrews, did this brilliant theory occur to you guys before or after this past Monday, when Drum went missing?

You asked who we thought he was dealing with, Carrie. Without getting into specifics, I'm just trying to put this all in context for you. Let's just get back to what we were talking about.

You were asking some very personal questions about the state of my marriage, for reasons I've yet to fathom, unless you're planning a mid-career switch to marriage counseling, Agent Andrews.

I'm interested in any changes you noted in your husband's behavior, Carrie, because the timing could provide a clue as to when he started dealing with this broker I mentioned. So, let's go back to the morning the embassies were bombed. Where were you and he when the bomb went off in Dar es Salaam, for example?

I told you, in the embassy. Drum was in a meeting on the third floor. I was on the main floor with the admin officer, handing in our shipping inventory. As I said, we were getting ready to leave the country. Fortunately, I'd left the baby at home with the ayah.

That's when the bomb went off. It was horrible. Eleven people died, and dozens of others were injured by flying glass and falling walls and furniture—myself included. I've still got scars here, on my arms and neck, from windows shattering in the office I was in.

And what about your husband?

He wasn't really hurt. Not physically, anyway. It was after that, though, that he started having headaches.

You mentioned his headaches. He had one on Monday,

just before he disappeared, you said. So, were they migraines?

No, tension headaches, I think. He seemed to get them whenever he was stressed. I kept trying to get him to see a doctor about them.

So he must have been stressed on Monday morning—which would suggest he had something more on his agenda than a routine meeting of bureaucrats.

Not necessarily. I told you, he hated all that committee work he'd been saddled with.

Right. And they started after the embassy was bombed? How did he react that day?

How do you think? It shook him up. Badly.

Because he felt responsible?

My God, you really are accusing him of being somehow involved in that. I can't believe it.

Not necessarily. But the bomber breached the security perimeter. That was a failure of the post's physical security precautions, for sure, but it was also a major intelligence failure, wasn't it? Nobody saw it coming, after all, and your husband was in charge of intelligence operations there.

Well, maybe that had something to do with it. He seemed—it was as if—oh, I'm not sure. It was a horrible day all around. And now, after everything else that's happened—September 11 and attack on the USS *Kohl* and all—it seems pretty clear that it was the beginning of a trend that nobody really saw coming. But maybe Drum did feel partly responsible. Whatever the case, it does seem to be when the headaches started.

What happened right after the bombing? What exactly did he do that morning? How did he respond in the first few minutes?

How do you think? It was terrifying. The whole building shook, and not just once. It went on and on—wave after wave of noise and pressure. Glass and debris flying everywhere. People screaming. Smoke. Lights gone. Even after the main blast finally stopped reverberating, there were still smaller explosions outside—tires and gas tanks blowing on the cars in the parking lot. Everyone was traumatized. Who wouldn't be?

And Drum? Was he traumatized, too? Carrie? What?

I told you, we were in different parts of the embassy when it happened.

But you do know something, Carrie. What? What did he do?

(unintelligible)

Come on, Carrie—speak up, dammit! What did Drum do after the truck bomb went off?

Oh, God...he panicked. There. Are you happy? When the admin officer and I finally made our way to the emergency exit, I stumbled away from the smoke, and that was when I spotted him. Near the edge of the parking lot. He must have been one of the first people out of the building. I don't think anyone else noticed him.

What was he doing?

He was in his car.

In his car? Doing what? Carrie? Louder, please.

I only realized it when I got up close to the car. He was freaking out. Desperate to get away. It didn't mean anything, though. He was disoriented. He didn't even seem to realize that the tires on the car had blown out. He was screaming that he couldn't find his keys, although frankly, I doubt the car would have started, anyway, and even if it turned over, it wasn't going anywhere on four blown tires. I couldn't convince him, though. It was all I could do to keep him from taking off on foot.

Are you saying he was hysterical?

He was scared...terrified. But so what? We all were.

I see. So what you're saying is that Drummond MacNeil— son of Naughton MacNeil, a five-star general, one of the great American military men of the twentieth century— Drummond MacNeil panicked under fire.

That's such a crock. He's been getting that his whole life, you know, that "son of the great general" bull. He could never just be himself. He always had to live up to what his father had done. It's not fair.

Yeah, well, who said life was fair? It had to have been humiliating, though. He was the CIA Station Chief, after all. A guy in that position has a rep of his own to maintain.

It didn't mean anything! He was in shock. We all were. For God's sake, there were body parts everywhere. We had to step over severed arms and legs and heads just to get down the stairwell. Anyone would have panicked. That's what I told him.

What you told him when? When he was trying to run away? Or later, when he realized he'd lost it?

Nobody saw. He pulled himself together and we went back to help the others. Nobody else saw what happened.

But somebody did see, Carrie. You did. His pretty young wife, who looked up to him and who he was so proud of. You saw him fall apart, shaking and cringing and trying to run away like a coward. He must have been crushed.

So is that why the marriage went sour? Because he hated the reflected image of himself he saw every time he looked at you, knowing how he'd behaved that day?

I never, ever made anything of it or held it against him.

It wouldn't matter. He knew he'd lost face. That would be enough.

I don't know. Maybe. Maybe that's why he stayed out so much. Why—

Pardon...? Carrie, once again, I have to ask you to speak up.

All that time.

All what time?

Damn. You know, I always thought it was my fault he worked such long hours—and that he looked for company elsewhere. With other women. My fault, because I was preoccupied with the baby. I thought it would get better once Jonah got a little older, but when we came back to D.C. after Africa, Drum just dumped me in that house with his mother and a toddler and he disappeared, for all intents and purposes. After a while, I guess I became resentful and less inclined to pay attention to him even when he was there, so he stayed away even more.

So maybe it was a combination of the baby and the bomb?

I guess so, a little of both. All I know is that I was wondering why I was bothering trying to be a wife when he seemed to have so little interest in us as a family. When he was posted to London, though, I saw it as a chance for a new beginning. After all, we'd been happy on our last posting—most of it, anyway. It didn't turn out that way, though. It was just more of the same.

And so you came home and made the appointment with the lawyer.

Yes.

It didn't occur to you that there might be a better way to solve the problem.

What do you mean?

Widowhood would be more lucrative than trying to

*wrestle alimony and child support out of a controlling guy
like that, don't you think?*

Oh, so now I had something to do with his disappearance
the other morning?

*I'm just wondering. The MacNeils are a pretty well-to-
do family. You stood to inherit nicely if anything
happened to your husband. More than you'd get in child
support or alimony.*

You're way off base. In the first place, assuming we did go
ahead and split up, it would be for a judge to set and enforce
child support. That's what I believed and it's what the lawyer I
met with that morning confirmed. As for alimony, I'll tell you the
same thing I told Heather Childers, the lawyer: I didn't want it.

You weren't going to ask for alimony?

Nope. Didn't want it, don't need it. And if I didn't need his
alimony, I sure don't need his estate, either.

*What did you think you were going to live on? You said
yourself, you've got no career to speak of.*

That's true, but I do have assets, money that belongs to me
alone. My father was a pharmacist in San Diego and he owned
a drugstore and a few properties there. Most of my parents'
estate and life insurance proceeds are still banked and
invested. I lived on them for a while when I was a student, but
my expenses weren't much. After Drum and I were married,
he never wanted me to touch them. Male pride, you know. He
needed to be the family breadwinner. Anyway, it's not a
fortune, especially since the stock market went south, but it's
enough to keep me going for a few years while I raise my son
and try to get myself started on a career.

*I see. As long as you didn't blow the entire wad on a
long, drawn-out custody battle, right?*

Oh, God—what a nightmare that would be. Okay, fair enough. But you know what? Call me naive, but it never occurred to me that custody would be an issue. How could it be, when I obviously had the stronger claim? Even the lawyer said it looked like Drum wouldn't have a leg to stand on.

So what did you think that morning, Carrie, when Drum said he knew what you were up to? Did you think he'd found out about the lawyer?

Maybe. He could have. There'd been a phone message that I was afraid his mother might have heard. It would have been just like her to tell him about it.

Did you really imagine he'd let you just walk away with your son?

I don't know. At that point, I got scared, I admit it. I should have realized when I saw him with Jonah that morning, trying to connect, obviously resenting me for having more time to spend with him. But I swear, it really was the first time it occurred to me that I might have to fight to keep my son. So that being the case, the idea that I could have had anything to do with plotting his disappearance is just loony tunes.

So, where is he now, Carrie?

I keep telling you, I have no idea. He said, "I'll call you later," he left, and that was it.

He said he was going to a meeting at FBI headquarters that morning?

That's what he said, yes.

But there was no such meeting. He started out in that general direction, but before he even got to the bridges, he doubled back and ended up at Tyson's Corner. Why do you suppose he did that?

I have no—wait a minute, how is it you know what route he

took? You couldn't possibly, unless... Oh, my God. Was he being watched? How long?

How long what?

How long has he been under surveillance? Since we arrived back in the States? Or longer? Since the girl—Karen Hermann—was killed in front of the embassy? Or since that woman in Hong Kong was thrown off her balcony? Oh, God—tell me it's not since the embassy bombings in Africa. I can't believe it. And to think I used to tease Drum about being paranoid.

Paranoid about what?

Everything.

That's an occupational hazard for CIA types, isn't it? Comes from overestimating their own importance in the grand scheme of things.

So, you had him under surveillance that morning, but you lost him. That wasn't too bright now, was it?

No, I agree it wasn't. It wasn't the FBI who was watching him, though. Until the incident at Tyson's Corner, we knew nothing about the allegations surrounding your husband. If we had, you can be sure things wouldn't have gotten so out of hand.

Aha, I see. Is that a little interagency rivalry I'm hearing there, Agent Andrews? Everybody knows the FBI doesn't have much use for the CIA—and vice versa. So that's it, is it? Langley began to suspect Drum was up to no good. It must have been the Brits who accused him, right? That's why Mr. Huxley here is being allowed in on this. But the CIA being the CIA, they didn't want you guys sticking your noses in their business. They decided to keep it in-house, watch him themselves until they could figure out what, if anything, he was up to. Only they blew it and he got away on them. Good job, guys.

But it figures, you know? Drum kept saying he was going to end up the scapegoat.

For what?

Everything that went wrong, starting with the embassy bombing in Dar es Salaam. It got worse after September 11, but maybe that wasn't so paranoid. Everybody really was looking for a scapegoat after that disaster. London was a major listening post, so Drum was one of those called back to testify about why the intelligence community missed the warning signs. In the end, he was cleared of any blame, but it certainly didn't help his paranoia to be put on the hot seat like that.

I kept telling him he wouldn't have been tapped for the operations job at headquarters if there'd been any concern about his loyalty. What did I know? Who'd have guessed they were watching his every move?

So please, Agent Andrews, you tell me what's happened to my husband? And how the hell, if he was already under investigation, did these brilliant watchers manage to lose him that morning?

CHAPTER TEN

McLean, Virginia
August 12, 2002—8:12 a.m.

The forest-green Town & Country van parked across the road from the MacNeil residence was something a suburban soccer mom might drive, the kind of minivan that hauled kids, snacks and juice coolers to neighborhood playing fields all over America every weekend. The magnetic signs mounted on the sliding doors suggested an especially enterprising soccer mom, one who cleaned houses on the side to earn a few extra bucks for the kids' college or orthodontist funds. Cheerful red-and-yellow script on the placards proclaimed the services of *MIGHTY MAID—MIGHTY GOOD!* A cartoon drawing of a stout woman in a black-and-white uniform grinned at passersby as she wielded a feather duster in one muscular arm and a broom in the other.

But although this van did serve multiple purposes, they weren't the obvious ones.

It was parked in the driveway of a sprawling, periwinkle blue Cape Cod style home owned by Bernice and Morrie Klein. The elderly couple had lived across Elcott Road from the MacNeils since the two Klein daughters, now grown and married, had been toddlers. The towering blue spruces, hickory trees and willows dotting the rolling green lawn had been saplings when the Kleins moved in, and extensive flower beds on the half-acre lot had been Bernice Klein's pride and joy. But she and Morrie could no longer keep up with the weeding, feeding and dead-heading, and the mow-and-blow gardeners who took care of yards in that neighborhood couldn't be trusted to do it properly, either, so the colorful beds had been replanted with low-maintenance shrubs.

The Kleins' tan Cadillac Seville was parked next to the Mighty Maid van. The nine-year-old sedan carried handicapped plates front and rear, but these days, it rarely left the black-topped driveway. Bernice had a heart condition and crippling arthritis. Morrie had emphysema. Most of the time, it was either too hot and muggy or too cold and damp for either of them to be comfortable out of doors. Morrie thought they should keep the car in the garage, but Bernice had the idea that a vehicle in the driveway added a measure of security, lending the impression someone might be coming or going at any moment. Given her bum ticker, Morrie didn't like to argue, even though it meant the Caddy's paint job suffered from too much exposure to the elements. Who knew how much longer they'd even be able to manage the car? he thought. Let it stay outside already, if that made Bernice happy.

Morrie had been vice president of a major auditing firm back in the days when that meant something, integrity-wise, but he'd retired from the business nearly twenty years earlier. Then, up until 1990, when the General had passed away, he and Naughton MacNeil from across the road had played golf twice a week at the Army-Navy Club.

Bernice and the General's wife had also been friendly at one time, exchanging recipes and plant cuttings, and taking occasional shopping excursions together when the boys were out golfing. But then, there'd been a falling out over some imagined slight Bernice couldn't even remember anymore—hadn't been aware of at the time, either, for that matter. Althea MacNeil always had been quick to sense insult where none was intended, and the time finally came when poor Bernice simply ran out of energy to deal with her prickly moods. As a result, the Kleins had more or less lost touch with the family across the road—although if they happened to be outside when the son's pretty second wife passed by, she always gave them a friendly wave.

On the whole, the neighborhood wasn't as chummy as it used to be. Bernice and Morrie had once had a wide circle of interesting friends, but in recent years, company had slowed to a trickle as health problems and the Grim Reaper took their toll on everyone of their generation. With their two daughters living out of state and busy with their own families, the old couple didn't get many visits.

The cleaning van showed up three days a week. In between, an oxygen delivery company and the St. John Home Nursing Association came by. In recent weeks, a panel truck belonging to a fix-it service called Handy Andy had also been on site.

So although the Kleins appeared to be virtual shut-ins, any busy neighbor who took the time to notice would have been reassured that their needs were being attended to. Not that the

residents of the manicured homes on Elcott Road felt obliged
to take much notice. It was one of the pluses of living in an
upscale area—you didn't have to be your brother's keeper.
That's what people had checkbooks for.

East Hampton, New York
8:12 a.m.

In point of fact, however, the Kleins had long since decamped.

Not long after Memorial Day, Bernice and Morrie had been
spirited away in the middle of the night and flown up to the
Hamptons, where they'd been settled for the duration into a
luxury waterfront seniors' apartment complex. Daily maid
service was provided, and gourmet meals were served in the
palm court dining room. A shuttle bus took residents to and
from local shopping areas, movie houses and community theater. The on-site activities club included a book group for Bernice and regular poker games for Morrie.

That particular morning, the Kleins, early risers, were out
on the double swing on their front balcony, enjoying their first
and only coffee of the day. The cool, salty air smelled tangy
as breakers crashed on the rocky Atlantic shoreline. At each
corner of the porch, hanging pots of trailing red geraniums
and sweetly scented alyssum swung gently in the mild on-
shore breeze. Through the screened balcony door, Frank Sina-
tra serenaded them from the stereo. Bernice warbled along to
As Time Goes By, images of a smoky Casablanca cabaret
floating through her thoughts.

Morrie held up his coffee cup and did his best stiff-lipped
Bogey impression. "Here's lookin' at you, kid."

Bernice smiled. "Isn't this the life?"

"You can say that again."

"I forgot to tell you, I talked to Susan yesterday." The younger of their two daughters lived in Boston.

"How's she doing?" Morrie asked.

"Good. The kids are in summer camp and Eric's off on a business trip somewhere…San Francisco? Seattle? I forget. He's back in a couple of days. She says they might drive out to see us next weekend."

"That would be nice. We could squeeze them in here, I guess?"

"Oh, sure. Susan and Eric in the spare room, the kids on the blow-up mattress in the sitting-room. Or vice versa…I don't know. Whatever they want. The kids will love the water."

"So, does she think the old folks have gone ga-ga?" Morrie asked.

"Not Susan, no. You know her. She was the one who always told us we should get out of D.C. for the summer. It's Valerie who thinks one or both of us must have had a stroke, the way we decided on the spur of the moment like that to come up here. She keeps asking me, are we all right? I told her, 'Honey, your father and I are having more fun and feeling younger than we have since the Truman administration.'"

"She believe you?"

Bernice's blue eyes twinkled. "Well, I might have mentioned the tango lesson."

"Oh, sweetie, you shouldn't have. Now she'll really think the blood's not washing over the old brains."

"I said we only went out on the floor the one time—though I did let it slip that this Saturday was bossa nova night."

Morrie grinned. "You're a very naughty girl, you know that?"

"Don't be surprised if people in white coats show up. I think she thinks we're a danger to ourselves."

"She's going to have us declared mentally incompetent."

Bernice gave a dismissive wave. "Hmph! No one's more competent than you, honey."

He took her hand and kissed the inside of her wrist. She snuggled into his side, resting her snow white head on his shoulder as they rocked contentedly, humming along with Frank while seagulls wheeled and swooped over the waves.

It was a real tonic, this surprise vacation. They'd been cautioned not to reveal the real reason for it, nor did either of them feel it prudent or necessary to mention to anyone, including their daughters, that the whole shebang was thoughtfully being provided free of charge. That was their own business.

Besides, Morrie thought, *stroking his wife's soft, warm fingers, getting it for free is just the icing on the cake.*

McLean, Virginia
8:17 a.m.

Back in Bernice and Morrie's living room on Elcott Road, a stabbing pain woke Mark Huxley. He shifted position, but the cramp in his back was relentless. One bloodshot eye forced itself open and focused blearily on the dial of the heavy chronometer strapped to his wrist. A little over two hours gone.

His arm dropped across his eyes. "Bloody hell."

He'd fallen asleep draped awkwardly on the chintz-covered sofa. It wasn't that he was overly tall, just five-ten, but clearly even that was too long, and he was too solidly built for the overstuffed couch to do double duty as a cot. His head had gotten wedged into the corner of one arm, while his legs hung awkwardly off the end, boots planted on the thick Chinese carpet. Now he had a crick in his neck and a spasm in his lower back.

He shifted position, trying to find a reasonably comfortable angle, loathe to wake up any more than he already had. He'd done twenty-three straight hours of surveillance, and at this point, he could happily sleep the next twenty.

Getting too old to be pulling all-nighters, mate.

It had been after 5:00 a.m. when they'd finally finished up out in the van. The others had only come on shift at three, so they'd offered to hold the fort while Huxley slipped into the house to grab forty winks. He'd opted to crash in the living room rather than crawl under the covers in one of the upstairs bedrooms, since their target would be on the move again in a couple of hours. In any case, even though they'd been camped out there for several weeks now, Huxley had yet to find a mattress in the place that felt right. His bones had spent too much time on rough terrain, he supposed, to appreciate the comforts of the Klein's lovely home.

Another angry spasm forced him to shift again. His legs ached after hanging off the edge of the couch for the past couple of hours. But, although he might be just a carpenter's son from Yorkshire, with rough hands and simple habits, his schoolteacher mum had raised him to observe the niceties of civil decorum, so he wasn't a complete barbarian, now was he? He knew enough not to put his combat boots up on the flowered upholstery. While Mrs. Klein might appreciate the courtesy, however, his spine clearly didn't.

Huxley reached out and pushed away the dark mahogany coffee table set in front of the couch, then slid down with a grunt onto the sculpted pink oriental rug beneath it. He took a few deep breaths, wincing as his muscles unkinked and his body finally began to relax, settling into the dense wool pile laid over a polished hardwood floor. A contented smile tugged at the corners of his mouth as the pain dissipated. *All right, then. This is more like it.* From here on in, this was going to be his personal kip spot.

He was just beginning to drift off again when the radio on his belt crackled. *"Leapfrog, this is Auntie. Come in, over."*

When he didn't answer right away, the voice came back, more insistent this time. *"Sun's well over the yardarm back in Old Blighty, fella. Get it in gear. Over."*

Huxley sighed and unclipped the radio. "Leapfrog here," he grunted, "and the point is, I'm not on bloody Greenwich time, am I? What's going on?"

They'd chosen their radio code names early on, when the CIA Director had agreed to a limited surveillance operation on Drummond MacNeil. Huxley was "Leapfrog" because it rhymed with "Bulldog," as in the old English bulldog, which he'd modified with a little Cockney rhyming slang. He'd given the partner-slash-baby-sitter the Agency had assigned him the name "Auntie," a twist on "Uncle" as in "Uncle Sam." It wasn't brilliant, but brilliance wasn't required, so long as the operation accomplished its objective—bringing down a traitor.

The American-accented voice on the other end of the radio frequency resonated with a deep bass that was as far from anyone's auntie's as it could possibly be. *"Looks like we're getting ready to rock and roll out here."*

Huxley yawned. "Roger. On my way. Over and out."

He stared at the inside of his gritty eyelids for a moment, then exhaled heavily and pulled himself to a sitting position. His broad, flat hands rubbed the sleep from his eyes. Pale stubble bristled on his cheeks and chin. He could use a shower, too, but it would have to wait. With one hand on the table and one on the couch, he hoisted himself to standing.

His shoulders were broad, his torso densely packed, like a boxer's. He took a moment to tuck his black T-shirt back into the webbed military belt that held up his khaki trousers, then patted down his close-cropped hair. It was fair and wooly-thick, showing no sign, he was pleased to note, of imitating his old da's thin, receded mop. But then, male pattern baldness came through the maternal line, didn't it? Must've been sheep on his mum's side of the family tree.

Although so far he'd dodged hair loss and graying, the lines in his face betrayed his thirty-seven years and then some. Like his dense body, the face, too, had a bit of the boxer about it. Maybe it was the old scar across his left eyebrow, a souvenir of a knife attack in a back alley in Khartoum, or the slightly off-center cant of his nose, whose bridge took a small zigzag detour on its path southward.

Over the years, Huxley had offered various explanations for how the nose had been battered. The more pints of Guinness he put away, the more creative the stories got, and anyone with an inkling of his murky background seemed prepared to buy whatever nonsense he chose to make up. The truth was pretty banal, however—a long-ago girlfriend had elbowed him accidentally as they wrestled out of their clothes in the back seat of her father's little red Morris Minor. They'd had a devil of a time explaining the bloodstains on the upholstery to the old man.

Heading out through Mrs. Klein's cheery yellow kitchen on his way to the side door, Huxley braked suddenly and detoured when his abused nose picked up the aroma of fresh-brewed coffee. Someone, bless their merciful heart, had slipped in and put a pot on the machine. But he frowned as he grabbed a rinsed mug from the drain board and lifted the pot off the burner. Someone had come into the house to make this and he hadn't heard a thing. So how good was his game, really? Not for the first time, he wondered if he was losing his touch.

He poured himself a cup of the strong black brew, then stepped outside, blowing over the top to cool it down. The AC was on in the house, but even at this early hour, muggy heat already had the street wrapped in a warm, wet shroud. The air was thick and green-smelling like new mown grass. The high-pitched whine of a thousand cicadas countered the low, barely audible hum of the morning commute on the George Washington Parkway, a mile or so away.

Taking care to keep himself hidden from the street, Huxley made his way over to the green van parked just a few feet from the door. A side panel carrying one of the gaudy, magnetic Mighty Maid signs slid open at his approach.

Inside, not a mop or bucket was to be found. The windows, tinted an opaque and reflective shade of black, concealed the fact that all the seats except the driver's had been removed from the vehicle and that the rear cargo area held a couple of tons of high-tech surveillance gear. One side wall of the stripped-down interior had been rigged out with long counters and an instrument bank of computers, monitors and video and audio recording devices. Custom-fitted storage lockers below and on the opposite wall held back-up generators, spare tapes and film, and a veritable arsenal of rifles, shotguns, pistols, ammo, flares and flash-bangs.

The van was parked nose-in so that the rear window enjoyed a clear line of sight to the house across the road. A thirty-five-millimeter camera with telephoto lens sat atop a tripod aimed out the back gate window. Next to it, a video camera was fastened to a second tripod. A young woman in blue jeans and a black tank top was fiddling with the video camera's telephoto lens.

As Huxley climbed up into the tight space and pulled the sliding door shut behind him, she glanced back at him and gave him a self-conscious smile. Her fizzled blond hair was pulled up in a tight ponytail bound with a rubber band. Her face and shoulders were covered with so many freckles that Huxley was always tempted to ask if she'd been caught behind a screen door when a paint sprayer blew up.

He nodded at her and at the bald man sitting at the console. Then he got a whiff of the place and his nose wrinkled. "Phew! A little ripe in here, isn't it?"

"You saying we need a shower?" Frank Tucker asked.

"It's nowt personal," Huxley told him.

Tucker opened his mouth to reply, then paused, raising a beetle black eyebrow that told Huxley his Yorkshire brogue must be coming through strong. Well, fair enough. He was functioning on only a couple hours of sleep. The accent would flatten out once the caffeine kicked in, in deference to his partners' thick Yankee ears.

Tucker was "Auntie" who'd radioed over a few minutes earlier. Even hunched as he was on a rolling stool, his legs doubled up and barely able to squeeze under the countertop running the length of the van, it was obvious the man was huge. Under his shining bald dome and thick black eyebrows were the most ferocious coal dark eyes Huxley had ever seen.

In one of the quiet moments since the two of them were first thrown together four months earlier, the older man had told him he'd once been a Navy diver. Huxley guessed that experience had to be thirty years in the past of a career that seemed to be well beyond its glory days. He looked to be in his early fifties, and while Huxley hadn't probed, a few casual comments Tucker had dropped led him to believe the fellow wasn't exactly one of the CIA's big movers and shakers these days. As for the ponytailed blonde at the back, Brianne Tengwall could have stepped out of one of those old American *Gidget* movies Huxley had watched as a teenager, she was that young and green. Fresh off the Farm, was his guess—the CIA's training compound for new recruits at Camp Meade, Maryland.

And that was the full extent of the assistance Huxley had been extended over here—one burn-out case, one rookie, and a little technical support.

Fair enough, he thought. It was more than he might have expected. Even at that, Sir Roger Cambridge, also known as "C," the head of MI-6, had pulled in some very big favors to get them to go this far. He'd warned Huxley from the start that it was a very dicey time for the CIA, and the last thing the Director had wanted to hear from the cousins were accusations that one of their top officers was a sell-out.

Huxley also knew that this surveillance was on very shaky ground, politically and legally. In the first place, it was a basic tenet of the relationship between these longtime allies that they didn't spy on each other. The agreement was sometimes honored in the breach when a security risk was suspected, but one didn't want to cry wolf unless one was pretty damn certain of one's facts. That took quiet legwork carried out with the utmost discretion, because to get caught spying on the cousins guaranteed a firestorm on both sides of the Atlantic—one that could prove disastrous to mutually beneficial intelligence pooling arrangements that had been in place since the early days of WWII and had lasted throughout the long, tense period of the Cold War.

Equally serious—perhaps more serious, from an American point of view—was that fact that when MI-6 surveillance had followed Drummond MacNeil back onto American soil, it was the CIA that had elected to provide backup support. Under U.S. law, CIA operations on domestic soil were strictly forbidden. From the moment Drummond MacNeil had arrived back on home turf, the FBI should have been notified of the suspicions surrounding him and taken over the case.

But there was a long history of bad blood between the Agency and the Bureau. A skeptical CIA Director had flatly refused to notify the FBI and weaken his hand in the great bureaucratic poker game they played here in Washington until there was firm proof his newly appointed Operations Deputy was betraying state secrets to enemy agents. The last thing the CIA needed at this critical juncture was a treason scandal, with the Agency already pedaling as fast as it could to stay ahead of accusations it had dropped the ball on threat prediction and management. Revealing a mole in the ranks, especially one as high up the ladder as Drummond MacNeil, could sound the death knell for the Agency as it presently existed. Far too many people had vested interests in the current arrangement to see that happen.

Huxley suspected this was why the Director had assigned a past-his-prime operative and a rank rookie to back up his surveillance on MacNeil. If the under-staffed team failed to come up with sufficient evidence to warrant kicking the investigation up to the next level, the Agency's reputation would be protected. Just to be on the safe side, MacNeil has already been quietly sidelined with some sort of make-work project. Regardless of the outcome of the surveillance, he would gradually be shuffled even further out of commission. No CIA Director was going to tolerate a deputy with even the faintest whiff of scandal about him. So one way or another, even if he didn't know it yet, MacNeil's career was over.

And if they did get irrefutable goods on him, enough to satisfy the Director? Huxley had a feeling CIA Security would move in fast, neutralize the bastard—a convenient heart attack maybe—tell the FBI nothing, and blandly assure MI-6 and anyone else who cared to ask that there were no traitors in its ranks because the CIA knew how to police itself, end of story.

It was all politics, Huxley knew. He didn't care. He'd take what he could get. He just wanted MacNeil and any possible co-conspirators he might have put out of commission.

Pulling out another rolling stool, Huxley settled next to Frank Tucker at the monitors. As for this fellow, burn-out case or not, few people would want to run into the ex-frogman in a dark alley, he was that daunting. Not the kind of man at whom you wanted to lob casual insults about personal hygiene, regardless of how funky the place smelled.

"It's not you," Huxley assured him. "It's this vehicle that could stand a good fumigating." He lifted his mug and inhaled the scent of coffee, trying to clear his nostrils of the ripe fug lingering in the air.

The unmistakable odors of spoiled food and wet paper were a pungent reminder of their night's work. Tucker and Tengwall had brought the van up the street a little before 3:00 a.m., slowing just long enough at the MacNeils' driveway for Huxley, who'd slipped over from his surveillance post across the road, to slide open the side door and help them grab up the big plastic trash bins MacNeil's wife had left out at the curb the night before. In their place, the team had left identical bins filled with paper-stuffed white plastic kitchen bags.

Tucker had won the coin toss, staying back at the Kleins' to keep an eye on the MacNeil residence while Huxley and Tengwall took the garbage-filled van to a vacant garage behind a safe house the CIA owned a couple of miles from Elcott Road. There, they'd dumped a week's worth of smelly waste onto plastic sheets spread over the floor, sifting for evidence of MacNeil's movements and contacts, removing every receipt, note and bill they found. Just before dawn, they'd refilled the trash bins once more, then driven back to Elcott Road and swapped them back to await pick up by the municipal garbage service. After that, Tucker had come back outside while Huxley went in the house to grab a couple of hours sleep. The only reminder of their earlier efforts now was the swamp gas stench that seemed to permeate every nook and cranny.

"We don't even notice it, do we, Tengwall?" Tucker asked the young woman at the rear window.

Like the two men, she had military experience, but her Air Force stint was much more recent. She couldn't be much older than twenty-three or -four, Huxley estimated, and at barely five feet tall, she looked even younger—all of seventeen or eighteen, maybe, with that perky blond ponytail, the spray of freckles, and the tank top and jeans she'd shown up in last night.

"Your mistake was going out and breathing fresh air," she told Huxley as she fidgeted with the focus ring on the camera aimed out the back window.

"Yeah, well, a person does need a little shut-eye once in a while."

"Slacker." She sniffed her fingers and wrinkled her nose. "But thanks, anyway, for the reminder of what a disgusting job that was. I may never get the smell of sour milk out of my hands. It went right through the latex gloves. Next time, you get to do the kitchen bags."

"Let's hope there won't be a next time," Huxley said, peering at the bank of monitors.

The screens displayed a shifting selection of perspectives

on the house across the road, inside and out. Several weeks earlier, while the entire MacNeil family was attending Sunday services at the National Cathedral over in Washington, Huxley and Tucker had carried out a black bag job on the house across the way, salting the interior with tiny, voice-activated microphones, pinhole cameras, and solar-powered, fingernail-size transmitters, the equipment concealed in wood moldings, wall switches and light fixtures. While Drummond MacNeil seemed to possess the normal quotient of paranoia for someone in his business, there was no indication so far that he'd picked up on the fact he was being watched.

Huxley only hoped they would get a break soon. He'd been on the case nearly a year now, his punishment for an operation gone horribly wrong. At least, it felt like punishment. And so it should. People who'd trusted him had ended up dead, all because of that bastard across the road.

Mark Huxley hadn't even heard about the murder of Alexandra Kim Lee, the female double agent in Hong Kong, when he first began to suspect there was a deadly leak in the intelligence flow between London and Washington.

At the time, he'd been the newly appointed head of Middle East operations at MI-6 Headquarters overlooking the Thames River in London. Prior to taking up that job, he'd spent nearly a decade out in the field, running joes from Khartoum to Tehran to Cairo.

Of all the assets Huxley had ever recruited, Amina Habib was one of the most useful. He'd met the young Palestinian woman when she was a business major at the University of Cairo. Bright and hardworking, Amina had pragmatic views on Middle East politics, unlike many of her compatriots. Israel was a fact of life, she said. Her people could either figure out a way to coexist with the Jewish state or continue to sacrifice one generation after another in a war of attrition that couldn't be won.

After her graduation, Huxley had lined her up with a very useful friend of his who ran a discreet and fairly specialized travel agency in Beirut, Lebanon. When Danny Mahmoud, owner of the agency, died of cancer a few years later, Huxley arranged MI-6 financing to allow Amina to buy the travel agency from Danny's widow. Thereafter, Amina became a gold mine of information on the movements of the Palestinian and other Arab politicos whose names crossed her desk.

Eighteen months earlier, when she'd alerted Huxley to an unusually high number of older "students" suddenly booking flights to select cities on the American eastern seaboard, her worth as an asset had suddenly soared. Sir Roger Cambridge himself had briefed Drummond MacNeil, the CIA Station Chief in London, on the information they were receiving from their impeccable Beirut source.

Three weeks after that CIA briefing, Amina Habib's body washed up on a beach under the Corniche, the popular promenade along Beirut's Mediterranean coast. She was reported to have drowned accidentally during a weekend yachting excursion—except Huxley knew Amina was terrified of water. As a child, she'd been aboard an overloaded refugee boat that had capsized, claiming the life of her mother and two brothers. Amina herself had been saved by an uncle, but ever since, she'd always refused to set foot on a beach or boat. Huxley knew she would never willingly have gone onto anyone's yacht.

Nor were antemortem injuries she suffered ever adequately explained by the Lebanese authorities, who could only suggest she must have hit her head on some rocks while she was in the water. Another of Huxley's operatives had stolen a copy of the Lebanese autopsy report. Huxley had taken it to MI-6's own medical examiner, who'd scoffed at the official verdict on the cause of death.

"Weren't any rocks that gave her that bump on the noggin," the ME said, peering at the X rays attached to the autopsy report. "Given the amount of bleeding and brain swelling, I'd say these head injuries happened six or eight hours before she actually drowned. Probably would have killed her eventually if the water hadn't gotten her first."

"Maybe she hit her head and fell overboard?" Huxley suggested.

"Well, if so, then it's a miracle," the examiner said wryly.

"How do you mean?"

"She had a fractured skull—and not just from one knock on the head, either. Several there were. She'd have been out cold, no doubt about it. But the cause of death was drowning. Plenty of salt water in the lungs, it says here. But you tell me: if she hit her head on entering the water, how did she manage to avoid drowning for the six or eight hours it took to produce this much intercranial bleeding? She was unconscious but still treading water? Oh, yeah...right. Like I said, a bleedin' miracle."

The only credible conclusion was that Amina Habib had been attacked and beaten unconscious, then taken out to sea and dumped overboard. And the most logical motive for her murder, Huxley had to conclude, was that her jumpy customers had uncovered her connection to western intelligence.

A couple of months after her unlikely accident, Huxley was contacted by another of his joes, an Iranian diplomat posted in Paris, who sent word that a broker in Zurich was offering timely information on allied anti-terrorist efforts, information that had been obtained from a pristine source high in the western intelligence net. Offering to sell this information to the highest bidder, of course. But when Huxley flew over to Paris to debrief the Iranian and try to winkle out who the western intelligence source might be, he found the man dead of an apparent suicide by hanging. The staging was just about perfect. The only question was why the knife with which he'd apparently cut the rope, the chair kicked out from under his feet, and the steel light fixture holding the rope and body had all been wiped meticulously clean of fingerprints.

After the fact, Huxley discovered that the Iranian had sent an identical warning to a contact at the American Embassy in London.

There'd been other losses, as well, including Alexandra Kim Lee in Hong Kong, and the talkative, helpful son of a mobbed-up Russian arms dealer, a young man who was very fond of the London night scene until the evening he was discovered drowned, his head in a loo at the Club Taj Mahal on Carnaby Street.

Slowly, as MI-6 began to connect the dots, it became clear that, despite differences in regional focus and the mode of assassination, the common denominator to all these far-flung cases was the broker in Zurich and a history of contact, direct or indirect, with the CIA Station Chief in London, Drummond MacNeil.

Huxley eyed the silver Jaguar XKE parked in the drive across Elcott Road. The car's license plates said DRUMR.

"He's still home? Awfully late this morning, isn't he?"

Tengwall nodded. "He's been taking his time, reading the paper, hanging with wifey and the kid."

"A change in routine. Something's getting ready to go down. I can feel it in my aching bones."

"You've been saying that for weeks," Tucker pointed out.

"I know, but I've been watching this bloke for months now. He's ready to make a move, I'm certain of it."

The surveillance had started back while MacNeil was still CIA Station Chief in London. His every movement had been tracked, his phones tapped. It had gotten trickier when he suddenly returned to Washington. After a hasty series of calls between the heads of MI-6 and the CIA, Huxley had been given permission to come over and continue his watch with limited Agency support. But outside of the three watchers in the van, apparently only a small handful of officials in the CIA knew what they were up to.

Tucker had told Huxley that it was the Director himself, a family friend of the Kleins, who'd personally prevailed upon the couple to make their home available for a sensitive operation of national importance. The Director had authorized a secret Agency slush fund, impervious to Congressional oversight, to cover the costs of the Kleins' stay in the Hamptons. He'd also handpicked Tucker to ensure that their guest from MI-6 had what he needed. Rather than rescind MacNeil's appointment and arouse his suspicion, however, the Director had decided to keep MacNeil on a very short leash until the allegations were resolved one way or the other.

"He told his wife he had a meeting over at FBI headquarters this morning," Tucker said.

Huxley frowned. "We didn't know anything about that, did we?"

Tucker and Tengwall both shook their heads.

"So maybe that's bogus. How did he sound?"

"Totally relaxed," Tucker said. "We'll see soon enough what he's up to this morning, but our boy is smooth."

"Wifey's not so relaxed, though," Tengwall noted.

"Well, we know she's off to see a divorce lawyer this morning," Huxley said. "Did she tell him?"

"Not that we heard. She seems to be walking on eggshells, though."

Huxley sipped his coffee as he peered at the monitor showing a wide-angle view of the kitchen across the road. He and Tucker had placed the camera over the range hood in the course of that Sunday morning black bag job. MacNeil's wife could be seen on the screen, picking up dishes and wiping down countertops. She was lithe and supple in shorts and a sleeveless top. The black-and-white monitor didn't do justice to that long, coppery hair, Huxley thought. There was no question this was a very attractive woman. When he'd first started surveillance on her husband and began to watch her, as well, Huxley had put her down as the typical vacuous gold digger that older men with egos like MacNeil's generally hooked up with. But as time went on, he'd had to concede that Carrie MacNeil seemed brighter than most trophy wives. She was also a genuinely loving mother to her little boy, who was better behaved than most diplobrats Huxley had run across in his day.

Had he encountered Carrie MacNeil under other circumstances, Huxley thought, he might even have found her appealing. But like attracts like. If this woman had hooked up with an operator like MacNeil, what did that make her? A woman willing to turn a blind eye to some pretty grievous character traits just so she could live an easy life in comfortable digs? Well, a bad call that turned out to be. She didn't look so comfortable now.

"I think we established back in London that the MacNeil marriage is not the model it seems to be," he told Tucker and Tengwall. "We've never actually seen them scrap, but there's not much evidence of warmth there."

As they watched the screen, Drummond MacNeil, who'd risen from the table on the far side of the room, approached his wife from behind and planted his hand on her shoulder.

She seemed to freeze as he leaned down and whispered into her ear.

"Turn up the volume," Huxley said, gesturing rapidly.

Tengwall dived for the volume control on the console, but it was too late. MacNeil was already stepping away. His wife turned and stared at him, a look of shock on her face as he made his way out the door of the kitchen, heading for the front hall.

Tengwall frowned at the image on the screen. "Now what was that all about? You ask me, these people are just weird."

"Weird and up to no good," Huxley said.

The camera in the entry hall chandelier provided a bird's eye perspective on MacNeil picking up his briefcase.

Huxley placed his coffee cup on the console and bent low to withdraw a motorcycle helmet parked underneath it. "All right then, boys and girls. It's show time."

"Why don't I tail him this morning?" Tucker said. "You've been up all night. You can hang back and review the tapes of his conversation in the kitchen with his wife. There's not a lot there, so it won't take long, but you might want to take a look, see if anything strikes you. Tengwall can tail the wife when she leaves. Once she gets back, you can go inside and catch a few more hours shut-eye."

Huxley shook his head. "Thanks, mate, but I'm fine. I'll take him this morning. Once I'm awake, I won't sleep again and I could use the fresh air."

Just then, MacNeil emerged from the front door across the road. Tengwall had her thumb on the camera's shutter cable. It clicked and the film advance whirred as their target pulled the door shut behind him, squinted up into the sky, then pulled a pair of opaque black designer sunglasses from the breast pocket of his suit. He put them on, raked back his hair, then took the red brick steps two at a time down to the silver-gray

Jag on the gravel drive. The headlights flashed twice as he aimed a key fob at the car. MacNeil opened the driver's side door and tossed his briefcase across to the passenger's seat, then dropped into his own side. A muffled thwump sounded across the road as he climbed in and pulled the door closed behind him.

"God, he's a real smoothie, ain't he?" Tengwall said to no one in particular.

Huxley pulled on the helmet and headed out the door of the van. "Later then, mates."

A modified police edition Harley-Davidson was parked off to one side of the Kleins' garage, hidden behind a high, fragrant juniper bush. Straddling the motorcycle, Huxley stuck the key in the ignition, then finished buckling the helmet, waiting to hit the start switch until the radio message from Tucker told him the target was on the move.

Tapping the side of the helmet, he adjusted the microphone set into the mouthpiece. "Leapfrog here, Auntie. You reading? Over."

"Loud and clear. Hang tight for a second. There's a garbage truck coming up the street."

Huxley heard it before he saw it, the strain of the big engines and the grating, mechanical whine of its bin lifters as it paused at the end of the next drive down from the Mac-Neils'. Huxley peered through the juniper bush at the target. Between the motorcycle helmet, the radio static and the roar of the garbage truck, he hadn't heard the Jag's ignition come to life, but it had already rolled to the bottom of the drive when the garbage truck pulled forward and blocked it from view.

Huxley lifted the kickstand on the bike and waited, but the truck seemed to be taking an inordinately long time to pick up the MacNeils' bin. Maybe it was just fatigue making his nerve ends bristle like this. "Auntie, what's going on over there? Can you see the target? Over."

"Negative. The truck's in the way."

"What's taking so long?"

"Don't know. It's just sitting there. I can see the Jag's tires behind it, but that's about it."

"I don't like this."

"Hang on, something's happening...okay, looks like trouble with the lift arm, that's all. It's picking up the trash can now."

A loud, grating whir sounded as the blue bin rose high in the air and was tipped over the open back of the garbage truck, releasing a torrent of the cartons, plastic junk and loose paper that Huxley and Tengwall had sifted through just a couple of hours earlier. The mechanical arms ground again and the bin reversed direction, landing back on the drive with a thud.

Then, nothing. Instead of moving on to the next drive, the truck just sat there.

Huxley didn't like it. He knocked the kickstand back to the ground and leaned the bike over to rest on it. He was just about to climb off and sprint out to the road to see what the hell MacNeil was up to when Tucker called a warning in his ear.

"Hold tight, Leapfrog. The truck's moving now. It's okay. The target's in sight."

Huxley saw MacNeil now, too, at the edge of the roadway, ready to pull out. He ducked back out of sight just as the Jag peeled away from the drive and headed up the street. Huxley raised the bike's kickstand once more and switched the key to the "on" position. Between the roar of the Jaguar and the racket of the next garbage pick-up, he felt confident no one would notice the deep-throated hum of the bike purring to life when he pressed the electronic ignition button.

"Okay, you're clear to go, Leapfrog."

"Right-o. I'm off then," Huxley said.

"Roger. Keep me posted. Oh! By the way…"

"What?"

"We drive on the right side of the road here. You'll keep that in mind, won't you?"

"Bugger off," Huxley replied, grinning as he rolled the Harley down Bernice and Morrie Klein's driveway. "Over and out."

CHAPTER ELEVEN

McLean, Virginia
8:29 a.m.

After Drum left, Carrie flew through the kitchen, wiping down surface, putting dishes in the machine, tidying for the housekeeper. As she took one last glance around to see that everything was shipshape, she tried to quell the butterflies in her stomach—and, just maybe, muster up some nostalgia for the place. But it didn't feel like home and probably never would.

Except for the third floor nursery she'd done over for Jonah, every single room in this house had been fitted out by others who came before her. Most of the current decor had been chosen by Althea. The apple-green-and-white-checked wallpaper above the oak wainscoting, the eclectic international pottery collection on the display shelves, the Depression glass dishes in the glass-fronted cabinets—they all reflected someone else's tastes and experiences. There was nothing of Carrie here, and if she were to move out tomorrow, there would be no hint she'd ever passed this way. Even the flower beds beyond the solarium windows had rejected her efforts to put down a few fragile roots of her own.

What had she done wrong?

Althea had also come into this veritable institution of a family as a callow young bride, but frankly, Carrie thought, her mother-in-law had done a better job of finding a way to fit in. Althea was strong-willed and opinionated, but she made her wants known and didn't allow people to take advantage of her.

Maybe she'd been luckier, too. She and Drum's father had spent the first half of their marriage living in a succession of base houses as the Army moved him around the country and around the world. By the time he was posted back to the Pentagon and they moved into the house on Elcott Road, the General's mother was already deceased and his father was in a rest home suffering from galloping dementia. There'd been nothing to stop Althea from making this place over in her own image.

Carrie had brought little into her marriage by way of experience or material goods—certainly no furniture or old photos or other family items, all of which had been destroyed in the fire that had claimed her parents and twin sister. Nor had she felt comfortable making changes to a household that had obviously been running smoothly for years. Fixing up the dusty, long unused space on the third floor was as much as she'd dared attempt. That, and her laughable attempts at gardening.

"I don't know what your problem is," Drum had said when

she'd suggested they get a place of their own after returning home from London. "Anyone would thing you were being forced to live in a grass hut."

I wouldn't mind, Carrie thought. *At least, it would be* my *grass hut.* As far as she was concerned, she might as well be living in a hotel.

It sounded ridiculous, she knew, the notion that she should be disgruntled because she couldn't mark her territory like some restless cat. In any case, it was only symbolic of what was really wrong in the marriage. Drum didn't notice the faded drapes in the dining room or the sagging sofa springs in the gloomy living room, much less the sense of defeat that gripped Carrie's heart and mind whenever she looked into the future.

She'd once had ambition and plans. She'd double-majored in business and art history at Georgetown University, planning to get into curatorial work, maybe open up a gallery of her own one day. But three years after losing her family, still trying to come to terms with the grief and anger she'd been swallowing since it happened, going forward because there was no way to go back, she'd finally given up on grad school and joined the Peace Corps.

But even if she'd run away from her problems, she'd still done a creditable job of managing the artists' cooperative in Tanzania, she reminded herself. For a while, she'd even dreamed about introducing Americans to the work of some of the more talented sculptors and painters she'd met over there. Except that the longer she was away, the more terrified she became at the notion of stepping alone off a plane back in the States. She had no home anymore, and no idea what she was if not a daughter and a sister and a twin.

The guilt was almost unbearable, being the only one to have

escaped the fate that had destroyed the other members of her family—a blaze that should never have happened. And wouldn't have, Carrie knew, if only she'd been there.

She should have seen it coming when she'd gone home for Christmas that December. It was her freshman year at George-town University. Isabel had seemed fine at first, thrilled to have her back, but it didn't take long before Carrie realized that her twin sister was depressed—clinically depressed, her father confided in a quiet moment alone with her.

What she didn't guess at first was how much of Izzie's de-pression was her doing—how much her sister resented the fact that Carrie had run off and abandoned her. And why shouldn't Isabel be resentful? After all, Carrie was the lucky twin. The twin who got to go away. Who got it *all,* even in their mother's womb, where the doctors said Isabel had been crowded and blood-starved, as sometimes happens in twin pregnancies, so that one fetus is deprived while the other one thrives.

In this case, oxygen deprivation had damaged the motor centers of Isabel's brain while Carrie claimed the lion's share of the placental blood supply. The damage wasn't obvious at birth, except for a ten ounce weight difference between the babies. Isabel's weight soon caught up and as infants, the twins seemed virtually interchangeable. Within a few months, though, it became apparent that Isabel wasn't meeting the physical development mileposts expected of healthy babies. At eighteen months of age, cerebral palsy had been diag-nosed. With each year that passed, she fell further and further behind, while Carrie—the healthy twin, the greedy twin—crawled and chattered and walked and ran on schedule and with an ease her sister would never possess, her own body stiff and uncooperative. At ten, Isabel began suffering seizures that stole many of the limited physical abilities left to her. By fourteen, she was confined almost full-time to a wheelchair and near-total dependence on others.

Still, the sisters were as close as twins generally are, with a secret language of their own and a contentment with each other's company that, in their earliest years, tended to exclude outsiders. Their parents, especially their father, anxious that both girls realize their full potential, encouraged them to pursue independent interests and friendships. And as time went on, ability levels alone meant the twins would lead very different lives.

Carrie was allowed—encouraged—to attend sleepovers at other children's houses, but never Isabel because their mother worried about medication and possible falls and the potential embarrassment of incontinence. Instead, she would take Isabel out to a movie or stay up late playing *Sorry!* with her. When the twins were in Girl Scouts, Carrie went to all the rallies and campouts, while Isabel stayed behind with their mother, who helped her complete all the merit badges that didn't require running or jumping or climbing.

Once, in junior high, Carrie had talked Isabel into attending a dance with her and her friends—but only once. Carrie had always tried to match her pace to Isabel's, and she only chose friends who were relaxed about including her sister. But that night, after hearing sniggers from the sidelines over her jerky attempts to move with the music, Isabel had withdrawn to the far end of the bleachers, rejecting Carrie's efforts to coax her back or cheer her up, spending what remained of a miserable evening watching couples avert their eyes as they slow-danced past her. She never attended another school event again.

From then on, whenever friends came to pick up Carrie, Isabel's mouth smiled, but her gray-green eyes smoldered. Carrie, the spoiled twin, got dates, prom corsages, and kisses under the front porch light, while Isabel, the wounded doppelganger, stayed behind and fumed.

Their father worked ridiculously long hours, six or seven days a week, building his business, but their mother tried hard to make it up to Isabel, almost pushing Carrie out the door, as if her mere presence were a painful reminder to mother and sister alike of what Isabel might have been, if only she hadn't been robbed of her blood supply.

"You two go on now," their mother might say to Carrie and a date. "Isabel and I have a lot to do, don't we? We thought we'd head over to the mall and check out that sale at Macy's. Maybe get our makeup done, hmm? And have dinner out, since your father's working late again. What do you think, Izzie? Italian, maybe? Then…well, better take a house key, Carrie, just in case we're not here when you get back."

She meant well, Carrie knew, focusing all her love and attention on Isabel like that, but maybe their mother's desperate attempts to compensate only served to remind Isabel that she was different and somehow pitiable.

When it came time to apply for college, their father encouraged Carrie to apply to Georgetown, his alma mater. Isabel, whose medical absences had left her still several credits shy of her high school diploma, pretended to be fine with it when Carrie was accepted. Secretly, though, she must have been seething.

Sometime around 3:00 a.m. on January 7, 1992, fifteen hours after Carrie's plane left to take her back to her second semester at Georgetown, her twin sister managed to splash a trail of lamp oil along the entire length of the carpeted hallway leading to the bedrooms of their San Diego bungalow, as well as all over herself. Then, the fire marshal concluded, Isabel dropped the empty lamp oil can, propped herself against their sleeping parents' door and struck a wooden fireplace match against the frame. The matchstick, which welded itself to the skin of Isabel's melted fingers, came from a full box later found burned but intact in the pocket of what remained of her cotton flannel nightgown.

When the D.C. Police showed up at Carrie's dorm the next day to relay the terrible news from the San Diego Police Department, they said her twin had suffered fatal third-degree burns to eighty percent of her body. Her parents had died in their sleep of smoke inhalation.

Carrie had been living in a fog of guilt ever since.

Giving the kitchen counter one last swipe, she glanced up at the old railway clock on the wall. Eight-thirty. Time to get going. Jonah's day camp started at nine, but they'd promised his counselor to arrive a few minutes early that morning to deliver the newspaper for the volcano project.

The front hall smelled of lemon oil, roses, and the slight mustiness of air endlessly recirculated through the central AC unit. The place needed to have all the windows thrown wide for a while, Carrie thought. Maybe she could do it before Jonah got home from camp. He'd have the pool and the center's air-conditioned indoor facilities to keep him cooled down during the day. Even so, Carrie reminded herself to double-check the asthma inhaler in his red nylon backpack and make sure it was fully charged.

Going up the stairs, she tried, as always, to ignore the reflection as she passed the antique gilt-edged mirror hanging over the first landing. Isabel might have been around to lend moral support with this Drum dilemma if Carrie hadn't ruined her life. Izzie had always been a good observer of human nature, with a clearer take on the personal problems her sister used to bring her to help puzzle out. Carrie could have used her advice now.

Althea's door was still closed when Carrie passed the second-floor landing, and although the room had an eastern exposure that got bright morning sun, the heavy lined curtains were obviously still drawn because no light escaped from the crack under the door. Nor could Carrie hear the classical music station Althea often had her radio tuned to when she was awake.

Instinctively, her heels lifted and she went the rest of the way up on tiptoe. Best to let sleeping mothers-in-law lie.

Automatically picking up Jonah's dropped sock, toys and discarded drawings as she mounted the stairs to the third floor, Carrie heard him humming tunelessly in the bathroom. She felt a familiar ache in the middle of her chest even as she smiled at the sound—the smile for Jonah, the ache for Isabel, who would have loved her little nephew. Even after all this time, Carrie thought about Izzie and her parents every day. But that morning, as it had so many times before, the question crossed her mind—if they hadn't died, would she even be here? Maybe not.

When she'd met Drum in Africa—handsome, self-confident, and seemingly so attentive and protective—she'd been bruised and grief-stricken still, only too ready to hide out in his shadow and let her own shaky ambitions slip away. She had no one but herself to blame for having drifted into this sleepwalking state, Carrie thought. No one but herself to pull her out of it, either. If she didn't make her move now, she sensed she might disappear completely.

The third-floor bathroom was set into a dormer that looked down over the front of the house. The mirror over the white pedestal sink was capped with a striped awning. The towels and bathmats were in bold red and white, the walls a sky-blue. All around the room, she'd hand-painted a parade of circus clowns and animals.

Jonah stood at the sink on a red plastic step stool, watching himself in the mirror as his brush moved dutifully up and down his small white teeth—taking extra care, possibly because he'd spotted his mother's reflection in the mirror. She smiled at him. He'd recently discovered the wonders of hair gel, and his strawberry curls lay slicked down and shining against his scalp at the moment.

Carrie felt a wave of emotion course through her like a warm tide. Whatever else she regretted in her life, she didn't regret this little boy. If losing her family, not to mention her independence, had been the price of gaining her son, then who was to say that fate didn't give back as much as it took away?

"Hey, bud," she asked, pushing her voice past the lump in her throat, "are you almost ready to go?"

He nodded.

"Did you get the newspapers for your volcanoes that I left out last night?"

"Dere inna front hall," he mumbled through toothpaste foam, spraying white flecks everywhere.

"Yikes," Carrie said, grabbing a facecloth to wipe them off the mirror. "Sorry, I didn't mean to interrupt you. Finish up here and I'll meet you downstairs. And don't forget your bathing suit and towel. They're on top of the dryer."

"'kay."

Carrie wiped that last spray off the mirror, then hung the cloth over the shower door. "I'm just going to finish getting myself ready. I'll meet you downstairs in a few minutes. Don't start any new games, please. Just put your lunch and your swimming stuff in your backpack. I want to check your inhaler before we go, too. And Jonah? Quietly, please. Don't wake Nana."

His head bobbed up and down.

"That's my boy," she said, planting a kiss on her fingertips and transferring to his slicked-down curls.

She ducked into his bedroom to give it a lick and promise, pulling the blue-striped duvet up over his bed, lobbing his discarded SpongeBob pajamas into the white wicker laundry hamper. There were space cruisers, trucks, paper and markers strewn across his desk and window seat, but they would have to wait for later.

Back downstairs in the master bedroom, she tore off her shorts and tank top and stood in her underwear, rummaging through her closet. Rapidly, she chose and rejected a haltered sundress—too ditsy—and a tailored linen pant suit—too severe, too hot-looking when she was already in a sweat—settling finally on a hip-belted, sleeveless white silk shell over a calf-length green-and-white batik print skirt, and espadrilles for her bare, tanned feet. Cool, modest, functional.

She'd canceled three appointments with Tracy Overturf's partner in the past two weeks, her nerve failing at the last moment. But Tracy, who was the closest thing to a sister she'd had since Isabel's death, would know if she chickened out again. This time, there was no going back.

In the Mighty Maid van across the road, the two remaining watchers had binoculars trained on the garage door when it began to rise. The rear gate of the blue Passat station wagon was up, and MacNeil's wife and the little boy were loading a large stack of newspapers inside. After they were done, she opened the back seat passenger door and her son scrambled in. She tossed a backpack across the seat from him and lobbed a straw purse into the front seat, then leaned into the car to buckle the little boy's seat belt. Tucker and Tengwall could see his tousled hair peeking over the back headrest, which told them the kid had to be sitting on a booster seat. This was a safety-conscious mom.

Tengwall got to her feet, ducking under the van's low ceiling, and gathered up her own backpack and a set of keys from the console.

"Are you sure you don't want me to do the tail on her this morning?" Tucker asked.

"No, I'm good. I'll take the Kleins' Caddy?"

Tucker nodded. "I gassed it up yesterday. It hasn't been out of the drive for a few days, and we did promise to give it a run now and then. Got your radio?"

"Oops, almost forgot." Tengwall snagged a transmitter/receiver from one of the recharging units under the console. After checking the frequency, she snapped it onto the belt of her jeans and headed for the van's sliding side door.

Tucker held up a hand. "Hold on. Wait'll she pulls out."

The garage door was dropping and the Passat was rolling down the crushed stone drive. It paused at the end, and they saw the woman craning her neck to examine the trash bins at the curb.

Tucker's black eyes flashed. "Shit. Did we put the cans back in the right order?"

Tengwall crab-walked back to her station at the back window and rummaged around until she found a stack of Polaroids on the fold-down workbench. She rifled through them, then withdrew one she'd shot the night before showing the woman, wearing shorts, a tank top and clogs, her wavy red hair spilling up and over the clip at the back of her head, wheeling a blue recycling bin into place next to a green waste container and a gray trash can. Taken at dusk, the shot was dim and a little blurry due to the low shutter speed, but using a flash would have drawn too much attention.

"Looks right," she said, her gaze moving back and forth between the Polaroid and scene across the road, where the Passat's engine was idling. "I don't think it's the bins that are the problem. She looks like she's waiting for someone."

They heard what it was before they saw it come around the curve in the road—grinding gears, the squeal of metal sliding, then the bang of heavy-gauge plastic hitting the road. A powerful engine revved as the Waste Management Industries truck pulled up, brakes shrieking at the MacNeils' drive. Tucker and Tengwall watched as the mechanical arms on the side of the garbage truck reached for the green garden waste container.

"Ah, that's it," Tucker said, finally exhaling. "The kid wants to watch."

"What is it about little boys and trucks?"

"Don't know, but it seems like they've all got that fascination with the big machinery."

The six-year-old across the way had obviously unbuckled his seat belt because he was hanging over the front seat now, grinning broadly as the big truck's mechanical arms screeched and lifted the bin, tipping it upside down and dumping grass clippings, leaves and pruned branches into the back. Seeing that he had an audience, the driver gave the bin a few wild up-and-down shakes before finally lowering it back to the curb. The little boy's face lit up with delight.

Tengwall returned the Polaroids to their place and gathered

up the car keys once more as the garbage truck pulled ahead to the next drive. She and Tucker watched the boy's mother turn in her seat, presumably supervising as he buckled himself back in. Then, after glancing both ways, she pulled the station wagon out into the street and headed up the road.

"Lift-off. I'll be in touch," Tengwall said, flying out the door of the Mighty Maid van.

Tucker watched her climb into the Caddy, and heard it roar to life. He frowned as the big tan sedan peeled down the driveway on a squeal of rubber. He clamped the transmit button on his radio.

"Hey, Tinkerbell, surveillance is supposed to be subtle," he said. "Not to mention the fact that car belongs to a taxpayer. Take it easy, will you?"

"Yessir, boss. Slowin' up here," Tengwall's voice came back as she turned sedately out into the road and headed off after the station wagon.

CHAPTER TWELVE

McLean, Virginia
August 12, 2002—8:31 a.m.

Huxley, meanwhile, still had MacNeil's silver-gray Jaguar in sight. For a while, everything went along just fine, but when it began to go bad, it went bad with a speed that was mind-boggling, as these things are wont to do.

Huxley kept the bike a respectable distance back as they drove toward the George Washington Parkway. Like any good military-trained operative, he had a map of the terrain firmly embedded in his memory, and between that mental image and more than three months of tailing MacNeil on his home turf, he knew the most logical route to FBI headquarters was to take the GW south to one of the bridges leading across the Potomac to the D.C. side. The George Mason Bridge near the

Pentagon would be Huxley's choice, since it was the most direct route with the least amount of downtown traffic to negotiate.

On the other hand, direct wasn't necessarily the name of the game here. The target's habits, like Huxley's own, showed the effects of years of personal security briefings. MacNeil varied his route frequently, often taking circuitous paths to arrive at his destination. And then, of course, there were times when his destination turned out to be one the watchers hadn't expected—not so surprising, given what they knew about MacNeil's extracurricular activities and his penchant for unexplained intrigues, including a taste for women to whom he was unencumbered by the bonds of matrimony.

Today would turn out to be one of those days where the unexpected should have been expected.

The Harley was gunning around a curve along the George Washington Parkway, a couple of car lengths behind the Jag, heading south, as predicted, toward the D.C.-bound bridges. Suddenly, a merging Ryder moving van switched lanes and cut Huxley off, apparently deciding that size trumped right of way. Huxley slammed on the brakes just in time to avoid running the bike up the truck's rear bumper like some ambitious Chihuahua mounting a St. Bernard.

He was tempted to blast his horn in protest, but the first rule of surveillance was not to draw attention. Besides which, there was always a chance that the move had been deliberate, and that this was a confederate of MacNeil's, here to nail potential threats. But when Huxley pulled out and caught the driver's reflection in the rental truck's side mirror, the guy's panicked eyes and nervous lip-chewing suggested he was inexperienced at handling a big vehicle in heavy traffic. Not malicious, just stupid.

Huxley fell back and watched for an opportunity to get away from the fool. A break in the lane to the right came about twenty seconds later and he took it, shooting around the big Ryder van and darting ahead, eyes peering through his black tinted helmet visor to locate the silver-gray Jaguar once more. When he spotted it, Huxley was surprised to see MacNeil talking on his cell phone.

He frowned. The call had been initiated in the thirty seconds or so Huxley had been stuck behind the Ryder truck, but he had no idea whether it was inbound or outbound. MacNeil's home and office telephones were being tapped, all calls recorded, but ironically, when he was on his cell phone out in the open, generally the most insecure of environments, he was relatively safe from prying ears.

Ridiculous, Huxley thought, not for the first time. Even the tabloids back home had resources to eavesdrop on mobile conversations between gossip targets like Prince Charles and Camilla. But the Director had ruled that ongoing mobile electronic surveillance required more people in the loop than he was prepared to tolerate at this point, given the sensitivity of the investigation. So unless MacNeil was talking to someone at his house—which seemed unlikely, since he'd left his wife a few minutes earlier and she herself should be on the road by now—there was no way of knowing what this present conversation was about. Huxley made a mental note to have Tucker pull the cell-phone records as soon as possible to try to determine who was on the other end of what appeared to be an intense conversation, if MacNeil's agitated gesticulating was any indication.

When the call ended and MacNeil set the mobile aside, it soon became clear that his plans had changed. The Jag was in the center lane of traffic, but it veered without warning over to the right and then, a few moments later, peeled down an off-ramp marked for the Potomac Overlook Regional Park. It was all Huxley could do to make the same switch in time to catch the off-ramp. Behind him, brakes squealed and a horn blared angrily as he cut the bike over and careened off the roadway.

Coming down the ramp, he spotted the Jag with its DRUMR plate a few hundred yards ahead, brake lights flashing as it approached a red traffic light at a T-intersection. MacNeil slowed briefly as a couple of cars passed through the green light at right angles to him at the top of the T. Then, the Jag's engines roared and its tires kicked up gravel as it crossed the center lane and shot around the two cars ahead of him, careening through the intersection against the light, turning left and disappearing into the underpass beneath the Parkway.

So there was one possibility eliminated, Huxley thought, calculating rapidly. This wasn't a dead drop in the park or a contact meeting. It looked like MacNeil was simply making a U-turn.

Huxley reached the line of cars at the bottom of the ramp just as the light changed to green. Taking the shoulder, he gunned the Harley past the vehicles ahead. The bike skidded on loose gravel, narrowly missing the bumper of a Miata convertible as he took the left turn that dipped beneath the Parkway. The blonde at the wheel of the convertible smacked the horn and the little car bleated in impotent fury. The Harley's big engine roared back defiance as the bike charged through the echoing underpass.

The Jag was up ahead, already merging back onto the GW Parkway, northbound now. Huxley was far enough behind that he didn't think MacNeil had necessarily noticed the motorcycle maneuvering abruptly in the background, but now that he was safely contained on the Parkway once again, Huxley slowed the pace and proceeded a little more sedately up the ramp. At the same time, he activated the microphone in his helmet.

"Auntie, this is Leapfrog. Come in, over."

After a few seconds of static, Tucker came back. *"Auntie here. What's up?"*

"Looks like we've got a change in plans. We were en route when our boy suddenly had a phone conversation. Soon as he hung up, he turned himself around. Don't know if it was his idea or somebody else's, though."

"Where are you now?"

"Northbound on the GW. Could be going back home, but my guess is he's inbound to Agency."

"Nothing going on here. Wife and kid left a few minutes ago. Let me check in with the office see if anyone there called him in. You carry on and I'll get back to you as soon as I know anything. You're okay otherwise? Do you want additional support?"

"No, it's under control."

"Okay, let me know if anything changes. Meantime, I'll check the cell-phone logs, too, see what I can find out about that call."

"Roger that, Auntie. Over and out."

It was a missed opportunity, Huxley later realized. Had he taken Tucker up on the offer of additional backup, they might yet have prevented what followed. But he didn't, and so, the die was cast.

CHAPTER THIRTEEN

Asbury Park Recreation Center, McLean, Virginia
8:48 a.m.

Carrie had helped Jonah carry a week's worth of old *Washington Post* newspapers into the craft room at the rec center. There they found Miss Mindy, counselor for the six-year-olds who had named themselves The Sharks, getting materials together for their arts and crafts project for that day.

"Knock, knock," Carrie said, her hands too full of newsprint to rap on the door. "Paper delivery!"

Mindy was pretty and dark-haired, about seventeen, Carrie guessed, because she'd mentioned at their first meeting that she'd be a senior in high school that fall. The girl's big brown eyes lit up when she spotted them at the door.

"Hi, there!" she said brightly. "Oh, Jonah, yay! You remembered the newspapers. I'm so glad. I was worried we wouldn't have enough for everybody. This is such a cool project, and it would be really neat if everyone gets to make their own volcano so you guys can take 'em home to show your moms and dads when they're done. Here, let me help you with that."

She rushed over and relieved Jonah's failing arms of its load, setting it aside on a table.

"I've got this," Carrie said, adding her own pile to the stack with a grunt of relief. "Jonah's really been looking forward to this, haven't you, sweetie?" She turned to her son, only to find him tongue-tied and blushing as he gazed up, open-mouthed, at his counselor.

Mindy gave him a hug, then helped him off with his backpack. "They're going to be great, aren't they, buddy? Today we'll mix the papier-mâché and put them together. After they dry, tomorrow or Wednesday, we'll paint them. Then, on Friday, when they're really, really dry, we mix up our special, top secret chemicals. And then, when we put them in the volcanoes, what happens?"

"Ka-boom!" Jonah cried happily, flinging his arms into the air.

Carrie feigned shock. "Chemicals? Ka-boom? You're going to blow the place up?"

Mindy laughed and she leaned forward, hand cupping her mouth conspiratorially. "Vinegar, baking soda and red food coloring. Bubbles over, sort of looks like lava." Then she straightened and smiled down at Jonah once more. "But it's going to be really cool, right, bud?"

"Yeah, really cool," Jonah sighed, his eyes still locked on this object of obvious adoration.

Well, Carrie thought, this explained why he was so cooperative about getting out of bed in the morning—and why he seemed to spend so much time in front of the mirror lately, brushing teeth and fussing with hair gel. Buckling him into his booster seat this morning, she'd also caught a distinct whiff of his father's expensive aftershave.

"I can hardly wait to see," she told them. "I leave you to it then. Honey, maybe you should go out in the playground with Zack and your other buddies until Miss Mindy's ready for you guys?"

"Or you could help me get supplies out," Mindy suggested. "It's up to you. If you'd rather go with the guys…"

Jonah waved his hand for his mom to bend down, and when she did, he stood on his tiptoes and whispered in her ear, *"I wanna help."*

"No problem," Carrie told him, "if Miss Mindy's sure that's okay?"

"Oh, yeah, for sure. Jonah rocks."

His beaming face was a wonder to behold. Carrie tried not to grin, and only wished she had a camera. "Well, all right, then. Me, I'm off. You guys have a great day."

Jonah waved distractedly at her as Mindy reached out a hand. "Come on, Jonah. I'll show you where the water cups are. Think you could fill them at the sink for me, one for each kid?"

"Yeah," he whispered, slipping his hand into the teenager's as she led him over to one of the craft cupboards.

"Anyway…bye, then," Carrie called after them, already forgotten. Lost him to another woman already.

"Thanks a bunch again for bringing in the papers," Mindy said over her shoulder.

"No problem."

Back in the parking lot, Carrie fumbled in her skirt pocket

for the car keys she'd slipped in there after locking the Passat and grabbing up her load of paper. One of the keys had tangled itself in a loose thread inside the pocket, so it took a moment to get it free. As she worked it loose, she watched several parents dropping kids off for day camp. One of the other mothers Carrie recognized. She had a daughter who was also a Shark—Zoë was her name. But although Carrie had seen Zoë's mom here every day since camp had started, she'd never managed to get more than a couple of words out of the extremely shy woman. She lifted a hand now to wave, but Zoë's mom climbed into her minivan without ever looking up.

Carrie glanced at her watch. Eight-fifty-five. She'd be on the GW Parkway by nine—then, maybe thirty minutes to get to Tracy and her partner's law offices in Old Town Alexandria? Less if the traffic was moving. Summertime, a lot of bureaucrats were on vacation. She and Tracy might even have a few minutes to grab a quick coffee before her appointment with Heather.

Carrie fished her cell phone out of her straw bag and pulled up her friend's office number from the contact list and hit the phone's "send" button. When the receptionist answered at the other end, she said Tracy was in.

"Hey, girlfriend!" Tracy's cheerful voice said a few moments later. "Don't you dare say you're calling to cancel yet another appointment."

"No, I think I'm finally ready to take the bull by the horns. I just dropped Jonah off at his day camp and I'm on my way now. I may even be early."

"Attagirl! Progress. That's what we like to see."

"Any chance you're free for coffee if I do get there early?"

"You betcha. I've got a light day today. No court appearances. There's a Starbucks right downstairs in the building, so just give me a shout when you're parking and I'll meet you there. You remember where we are? Across from the Torpedo Factory?"

It was a renovated nineteenth century armaments manu-facturer, a sprawling two-hundred-year-old brick building on the Old Town riverfront. In the 1980s, the building had been converted to artists' lofts and galleries, and if ever Carrie had a dream to open a gallery of her own, the Torpedo Factory was probably near the top of her list of desirable locations.

"It's a plan," she told Tracy. "I'll call you when I get there."

"You doing okay this morning?"

"You know, not bad, as a matter of fact. Just watched my son gushing over his camp counselor, who he's obviously got a huge crush on. Who knew?"

Tracy laughed. "It starts already. I can't say I'm surprised, mind you. That one's going to be a heartbreaker. You're going to have to beat off the babes in a few years."

"Oh, please, no. Don't tell me that."

"Whoops. Nope, cancel that, maybe not," Tracy agreed.

"God forbid he should take after his father," Carrie said grimly.

"Not gonna happen, kiddo. You're raising a fine young man."

"That's the aim, anyway. Okay, Trace. I'm on my way. See you shortly."

Carrie was almost to the GW Parkway when, braking for a red light, she heard something roll on the floor under her seat. Fishing around with her hand as she sat at the light, her fingers closed on a small metal canister. Retrieving it, she opened her hand to find Jonah's asthma inhaler, fallen from his backpack.

"Damn!"

The light changed, but instead of heading toward the Parkway on-ramp, Carrie maneuvered the Passat into position for a U-turn and headed back to the rec center.

Pulling into the parking lot a few minutes later, she saw that the drop-off rush was over. Zoë's mom was still there, though, sitting in her van in the shade of a leafy oak, seat angled back, apparently dozing. Come to think of it, Carrie thought, that was exactly where she found the woman's van parked every day when she returned to pick up Jonah. Did Zoë's mother have no other life?

Carrie parked the Passat and grabbed the inhaler from the cup holder, then climbed out, locked the car, and started across the parking lot at a sprint. It was only then that she noticed the silver-gray Jaguar parked across the lot—a Jag with Virginia vanity plates that read DRUMR. She hesitated on the roadway, staring in stunned silence at her husband's empty car. What was he doing here?

The Sharks were in the craft room inside the building. Carrie peered through the thick glass window in the door at a dozen or so six-year-olds decked out in oversize men's shirts with rolled up sleeves whose tails hung nearly to their ankles. Their hands were already gluey with the flour and water paste they were mixing, obviously loving the stuff. One kid had a tell-tale streak of white around his lips that suggested he'd given the stuff a taste test. Mindy was distributing newsprint to each table and showing the kids how to tear it into long strips.

But as Carrie's eyes roved up and down the rows of tables, she couldn't see Jonah anywhere. Heart pounding, she opened the door and stepped into the room. And then she spotted them, Drum and Jonah, off in one corner, Jonah with his head down, looking at his shoes, Drum bending low and whispering to him.

"Mrs. MacNeil, hi, again," Mindy called, looking both surprised and a little nonplussed as she glanced back at Jonah and his father in the corner.

"Hi," Carrie said distractedly. "Sorry to interrupt, but I found Jonah's asthma inhaler after I left. It must have fallen out of his bag. I…I'll just go and put it back in there…in case he needs it. I mean, probably he won't…but on the other hand, don't you just know that the day he hasn't got it will turn out to be the day he has an attack?" She was crossing the room even as she spoke.

Drum had looked up as soon as Mindy had called out her name. As she approached, Carrie saw his expression shift from surprise to annoyance to bland neutrality in the blink of an eye.

"What are you doing here?" she whispered to him.

"My meeting downtown was canceled," he said. Then he looked down at their son. "It's okay, Jonah, you go work on your project with the other kids."

"Yeah?" Jonah said, his glum expression brightening.

"Yeah, for sure. We'll do it another time."

"Okay!" Jonah said eagerly. "Hi, Mom. Watcha doin' back here?"

"Your inhaler," she said, holding it up. "It was rolling around on the floor of the car. I'll put it away in the pocket of your backpack, but make sure you keep it zipped in there so it doesn't fall out again, okay?"

"Okay. Can I go make my volcano now?"

"Sure thing. I'll see you this afternoon."

"Bye, Mom. Bye, Dad," he added as an afterthought, glancing at his father before making his escape.

Drum was already on his feet and making moves to leave. Carrie waved a second goodbye to Mindy, then paused by Jonah's hook on her own way out the door to slip the inhaler securely inside the backpack and zip the pocket. She followed Drum out the door and they paused on the other side for a moment, watching through the small window as Jonah pulled one of his father's discarded pinstripe dress shirts out of his cubby and shrugged into it.

"You'll do what another time?" Carrie asked quietly.

Drum had been watching the children, but he turned to her now, his expression puzzled. "What's that?"

"You told Jonah 'we'll do it another time.' Do what?"

He turned and started walking toward the exit. Carrie hurried after him.

"Oh, that. Nothing," he said blandly. "My meeting at the Bureau was canceled, as I said, so I thought as long as I was out on the road, anyway, I'd drop by here on my way back to the office and watch Jonah jump off the diving board. You remember, he was telling me all about it this morning at breakfast."

"But they don't have swimming until the afternoon."

"No, so I discovered. I guess I'll have to do it another time."

"And that's what you came here for?"

"Isn't that what I just said? Anyway, I'd better be off. What about you? You're looking very dressed up."

"A skirt's cooler on a day like this."

"You're going shopping?"

"Just to pick up a couple of things." Carrie hesitated then added, "And Tracy called. We're going for coffee."

Drum scowled. "Oh, joy. The legal beagle."

"She's my best friend, Drum, and I don't get to see her very often. She's working by the Torpedo Factory over in Alexandria now. I haven't been in those galleries in a while. I'm curious to see what's new there." Not a single lie in the bunch, Carrie thought—well, except for the little one about Tracy calling her, rather than the other way around.

"Fine. You have fun. Just don't forget to pick up my dry cleaning, will you?"

"I won't."

She left him at his car and crossed over to her own blue Passat, frowning as the silver Jag peeled out of the rec center parking lot.

Across the way, Carrie noticed, Zoë's mother was still dozing in her minivan, a brown stuffed bear clutched in her arms, waiting for the children to be dismissed so her life could start up again.

CHAPTER FOURTEEN

Asbury Park Recreation Center, McLean, Virginia
9:08 a.m.

Huxley and Tengwall had met up across the parking lot from the rec center, the Harley and the Caddy nestled deep in the shadows of a dense clump of willows near the roller hockey rink. Huxley had pulled out his portable radio and they were in touch with Tucker back at the house as they tried to puzzle out the significance of MacNeil and his wife rendezvousing unexpectedly like this.

"Escape plan?" Tengwall wondered. "MacNeil discovered the bugs at the house, so they decided to meet up and make a run for it?"

"MacNeil didn't have luggage when he left," Huxley pointed out.

"He could have put it in the trunk of the Passat when it was in the garage."

"I don't think so."

"Me, neither," Tucker agreed. *"My gut tells me that if—when—he runs, he's not taking her with him."*

"Agreed," Huxley said. "And I saw her when she pulled in and spotted his car. She was stunned to see it there. No way she was expecting him. But, on the other hand—"

"The kid," Tucker said.

"—the kid!" Huxley echoed.

"Better get in there."

"Right-o," Huxley said. "I'll go in and Bree will...no, hang on, here they come now. It's MacNeil and the wife, but *sans* the kid."

The MacNeils emerged from the building, deep in sober conversation. A few moments later, they parted, heading to their respective cars.

"Okay, I'm off," Huxley told Tengwall.

The radio crackled again. *"Maybe I should call in more support?"*

"I don't know," Huxley said. "We may be back on track here. I'd hate to cry wolf prematurely."

"Fair enough, but let me know if anything else gets hinky out there. Like it or not, I think the boss is going to have to consider kicking this up another notch."

"I'll be in touch," Huxley agreed. He loped back over to the Harley and rolled it quietly behind the rink fence before kicking it to life and tailing MacNeil out of the rec center lot, leaving Tengwall to continue her surveillance on the wife.

When the Jaguar turned onto Dolley Madison Boulevard a few minutes later, it looked as if MacNeil was returning to Langley, after all, where he could be safely contained and observed. Whatever else had been going on, Huxley decided, it seemed MacNeil was in for another routine day at the CIA salt mine, after all.

He couldn't have been more wrong.

Seen from above, the CIA site is shaped like a clenched fist. By accident or design, the fist seems to rise out of Dolley Madison Boulevard in angry defiance of all the Agency's enemies, internal and external.

From the ground, however, the Agency is shrouded in dense landscaping, its own and the thick woods of Langley Fork Park, which hide the top-secret facility from prying eyes. To pass through the well-guarded gates and pierce that woody veil is to discover a complex of fortified buildings bristling with antennae. Every second of every day, those sprawling arrays of roof-mounted steel hum with the inbound and outbound encrypted signals that form the Agency's pulsing lifeblood.

Drummond MacNeil had spent most of his adult life riding the ebb and flow of those secret signals that thrummed the air, setting Langley's supersensitive electronic ears atingle. From out in the field, operatives with their ears close to the ground reported back every whisper of political intrigue, every hint of shifting power bases, every rumor of military thinking that might give the U.S. a tactical edge, whether in a fight or in sensitive international negotiations. Inside Agency walls, thousands of analysts weighed and sifted communiqués from around the world, massaging discreet bits of information plucked from the vibrating airwaves into coherent strategies designed to safeguard America's position as the only superpower worthy of the name.

As MacNeil's car approached the main CIA entrance on

Dolley Madison, Huxley wondered if the man had any inkling of what he had, in fact, already lost. As Operations Deputy, those antennae would have hummed with a tune MacNeil himself conducted, sending instructions to operatives, overt and covert, in every major city and political hot spot on the globe. Did the man guess yet that the baton had already been snatched from his grasp, and that he would never get to conduct that secret symphony?

There was no way to be sure. But in the end, it was the electronic buzz from those bristling antennae that was probably the undoing of Huxley's year-long surveillance, allowing the once-and-never Operations Deputy just enough leeway to finally give him the slip.

Huxley knew something was amiss the moment MacNeil sailed past the CIA turnoff without ever giving it a sideways glance. Gut sinking, he switched on the radio to call Tucker for the backup that he now realized he should have asked for back when MacNeil pulled that sudden U-turn on the George Washington Parkway.

No, even before that, Huxley decided. It should have been in place that morning from the moment they'd realized that MacNeil's routine was undergoing a sudden and unexpected shift. Always be suspicious of any change in the status quo, however minor or innocuous it may seem. Wasn't that one of the prime directives of surveillance?

So Huxley put in the call for backup—or tried to. But as anyone knows who's ever tried to have a cell or radio conversation near CIA headquarters, the area is an electronic Bermuda Triangle because of the intense interference generated by its vast communications array.

Huxley tried over and over again to raise Tucker, but there was nothing but static on his headset. For four and a half agonizing minutes as he chased the silver-gray Jag south and west through dense traffic, Huxley experienced the sickening premonition that all the watchers' work and effort—not to mention a year of his own life—was about to crumble to dust in front of his eyes.

He was halfway to the expressway leading to Dulles Airport, weaving in and out of traffic to keep the Jag in sight, when the static finally lifted and he was able to raise Tucker and let him know what was happening.

"I'm on it," Tucker said. *"Keep on him, but at a safe distance. Don't get yourself killed. The GPS tracker on his car is functioning just fine. I'll order up a copter and we'll cover all the airport access points. He'll never make it onto a plane."*

There was a mile to go until they reached the junction for the Hirst Brault Expressway, which would take MacNeil directly to Dulles International Airport. Huxley's mind was racing, keeping an eye on the Jaguar in the center lane up ahead, at the same time glancing overhead for the surveillance helicopter that Tucker had called in. Would the chopper come from Dulles? Highly unlikely. From the Agency itself? There was a landing pad there, he knew. Or would it be based all the way over at Bolling Air Force Base in D.C.? Or, farther away, at Andrews AFB?

One way or another, MacNeil would be nearly to Dulles by the time it arrived, Huxley calculated. All the more reason not to lose the guy now.

He started making contingency plans for when and how he would stop MacNeil if he made a run for it inside the airport. How fast could Tucker get his people into position? Would he have all the exits and entrances covered?

A sign for the airport expressway flashed by. Half a mile. The traffic was dense with commercial vehicles but moving steadily. Fighting his instinct to look for the exit on the left, where it would be back home, Huxley moved the bike over into the right lane, not giving any of the twelve-wheelers around him the chance to box him out of his escape route.

Dulles Airport—Next Exit 1/4 Mile

Huxley frowned. Up ahead, the silver-gray Jag still hadn't moved out of the center lane. Was MacNeil planning another last second charge to confound any tail following him? If so, then he clearly wasn't aware of the motorcycle that had been on him since he left home.

The exit was in sight now, but the Jaguar never budged from its center lane position. So if it wasn't the airport expressway, then what...? Huxley consulted his mental map of the surrounding area.

The Beltway, he decided. The junction for the ring road that looped around the capital was about a mile beyond the exit for Dulles, if he wasn't mistaken. And if MacNeil was taking the Beltway, who knew what his ultimate destination might be. He could be going anywhere.

He couldn't just vanish, though. Tucker had attached a Global Positioning System tracking device to the Jag's undercarriage weeks ago, and the GPS had been pinging out MacNeil's location ever since. Even if he were to decide to drive all the way to Mexico, they'd pinpoint his position within a radius of ten feet. So let him take the Beltway, Huxley thought. The Harley had a full tank of gas and he could drive for as long as that smug bastard could, with or without backup.

But it wasn't the Beltway, either. Huxley was just getting ready to alert Tucker when the Jaguar sailed right past that exit, as well. A few seconds later, however, it veered over to the right at last and took the next exit leading to Tyson's Corner. Huxley followed several car lengths behind as MacNeil turned left next to a big red Circuit City store, then wheeled along the outer roadway of the Tyson's Corner Center shopping mall as if trying to decide where to park.

Huxley glanced at his watch. Not yet 10:00 a.m. The stores wouldn't be open yet, but employees were streaming in. And even at opening time, he estimated, the mall would be busy enough, with kids still on summer holiday and harried moms checking out back-to-school sales. If MacNeil forced their hand here, it was not the ideal location to have to round up a suspect who could be armed and dangerous.

Huxley clicked on his radio transmitter. "Leapfrog here, come in."

"Auntie here. Where are you?"

"Tyson's Corner Center. Looks like our boy's planning a spot of shopping. Or a meet. Over."

"Can you stay on him? We had additional support heading for Dulles, but I'll divert them and have them to you there ASAP."

"Shouldn't be a problem. I haven't seen any obvious sign he's spotted me, and as far as we're aware, he doesn't know me from Adam."

It was the one advantage he'd had throughout the surveillance, Huxley thought. They'd had to presume that MacNeil knew Tucker by sight, since the big fellow had been with the Agency forever, it seemed, and the two had actually met once or twice. But Huxley's and MacNeil's paths had never crossed in London, except at the discreet distances Huxley himself had choreographed, once MI-6 had put the American under surveillance in the wake of one too many sacrificed assets.

"Looks like he's pulling in to a parking structure," Huxley told Tucker now. "Terrace C, it is."

"Stay on him. You've got a handheld unit with you, right? Don't bother with the cell phone. They're useless in there."

"Got it."

"Okay, go. I'll be in touch as soon as the backup's in position."

"Roger. Over and out."

Inside the parking structure, Huxley drove the Harley behind a pillar half a level down from where MacNeil had parked the Jag, still in his line of sight. He watched the lights on the Jag blink as MacNeil locked it. He was empty-handed, and if he was glancing around the lot behind those dark glasses he had on, looking for a tail, he was being subtle about it. A light but steady stream of cars was flowing into the lot, and while MacNeil held back to let a couple of them pass by him, he showed no sign of having spotted Huxley.

Watching MacNeil out of the corner of his eye as he headed for the mall entrance, Huxley removed his helmet and busied himself with clamping it to the bike's backrest. He took his time dusting himself off, then slipped a portable radio unit out of the bike's saddlebag and onto his webbed khaki belt, checking first to make sure the unit was turned on and the battery charged. By the time he reached the exit, MacNeil was at the pedestrian bridge leading over to the mall.

They were at the second level, but on the other side of the bridge, MacNeil ducked down a staircase and entered on the lower level. Huxley followed, blending into the background behind a couple of young mothers pushing toddlers in strollers and three black-clad teenage boys in hip-hanging baggy pants who loped along, punching each other in the shoulder with every couple of steps.

The mall's bottom level housed a food court, illuminated by bright sunlight from the arched glass roofline two stories overhead. Take-out places around a spacious black-and-white-tiled seating area were serving their first customers of the day. Huxley's stomach rumbled at the smell of bacon and cinnamon rolls. He'd had nothing that morning but that cup of coffee from the Kleins' kitchen—but then, neither had MacNeil eaten breakfast at home, come to think of it.

Good. If he settled in for breakfast, it would give Tucker's backup time to get over here and make up for the time Huxley had lost when he was out of radio contact around CIA headquarters.

But MacNeil wasn't stopping. Slipping his sunglasses off and into the breast pocket of his suit jacket, he bypassed the fast food places in the atrium and headed deeper into the mall. Huge potted palm trees in buff-colored marble planters stretched over the second level, fronds dangling greenly, oddly thriving in the mall's cool, recycled air. Steel security grills were still rolled down on most of the stores, although one or two were lifted halfway, allowing employees to duck under and enter the premises.

MacNeil approached a gourmet coffee shop whose grill was already up. A young girl was working alone inside at the steaming, spitting machines behind the counter. Huxley hung back next to a jeweler's across the way and around the corner while MacNeil spoke to the flustered-looking teenager. She nodded and reached for a foam cup. As he waited for her to make up his order, MacNeil proceeded to flirt with and tease the girl. Even from his distant vantage point, Huxley could see that she was giggling and blushing to beat the band.

He pretended to examine the diamond rings in the jewelry store window. From all appearances, he might have been some anxious suitor eager to pop the question just as soon as he found the right ring for his girl. Through the glass corner window, he kept one eye on MacNeil as he peered at the solitaires and gem-studded bands in gold and platinum scattered across a rippling bed of royal blue satin, sparkling and gleaming under display spotlights.

There'd been no diamond rings for Phyllis, Huxley recalled. His late wife had been a no-nonsense Dublin nurse who worked for Doctors Without Borders in a refugee camp in Lebanon. Phyllis had made it very clear that she hated diamonds and everything associated with them.

"All that De Beers marketing hype for a colorless rock that's common as dirt and plain as water," she said one night, head shaking as they watched the sunset off the Corniche. "And yet, all those poor souls are dyin' for 'em over in Africa. Don't you even think about buyin' me a diamond ring, Mark Huxley, when you ask me to marry you."

Huxley had been taken aback as much by her ability to read him as by her cheek. "You're pretty sure of yourself," he'd answered, grinning. "Who says I'm going to ask, then?"

"Oh, you'll get around to it," she said, her warm brown eyes crinkling with laughter, "soon as you work up a little nerve."

"Is that so? And what'll you say when I do?"

"I'll say yes, of course, you daft fool. What else would I say?"

And that was it. He hadn't even had to go down on one knee. She hadn't wanted a diamond, but he'd tried to make her happy in other ways. He thought he had, too—although if he'd known how little time they would have together, he thought, he would have done so much more.

The black-and-white floor tiles and marble planters echoed with the clang of steel as grills rose on stores opening for business up and down the mall. The crowd was still light, but when MaNeil emerged from the coffee shop, blowing across the top of his uncapped foam cup, there were enough shoppers about that Huxley was able to blend into the surroundings as he followed the other man's stroll down the mall.

MacNeil walked slowly, tentatively sipping his coffee that seemed to be lawsuit hot. Now and then, his silver head tuned to follow the gait of a pretty girl passing, but he seemed otherwise to be a man with nowhere special to go and no particular time to be there.

The radio on Huxley's belt suddenly crackled and his nerve endings thudded. He dropped back a few more paces and lowered the volume, ducking behind the sound blind of a splashing fountain to try to mask the noise as he unclipped it and held it to his mouth. "Leapfrog here."

"You're backup's arriving as we speak and monitoring on this channel," Tucker said. *"Where are you?"*

"Lower lever, beyond the food court. There's an atrium near Lord & Taylor. The target's just passing through, heading east."

"Watchers one and two here," an unfamiliar voice said. *"On the lower level, approaching subject's location now."*

Huxley saw them before they saw him, two bland suits in Ray-Bans who might have been inconspicuous had it not been for the coiled wires rising out of their collars, connected to plastic ear pieces. That, plus the fact that one of them was muttering into his shirt cuff like some mad accountant who'd tallied one too many spreadsheets. None of the shoppers seemed to take any notice of them, though, so maybe you had to be in the business.

When Huxley lifted a hand, the non-mutterer spotted him, elbowing his partner, who dropped his cuff back to his side.

Huxley pointed at MacNeil up ahead, brought his two index fingers together, then separated them and circled each hand around in opposing directions, signaling them to spread out but keep the target in sight. The two suits nodded and their paths instantly diverged.

MacNeil wandered on, apparently oblivious, sipping his coffee. Huxley had a moment of unease when he stopped at the window of a pen store, apparently studying the Cross sets in the window, but if he was checking the reflection in the glass for watchers, he showed no sign that he'd spotted Huxley or the suits on opposite sides of the corridor, who'd both chosen that moment to become engrossed in a little window-shopping of their own.

MacNeil moved on, rounding a corner at a Hecht's anchor store, then heading down a southbound corridor, followed at a distance by the others. Huxley hurried over to an information kiosk.

"Can I help you, sir?" a young clerk behind the desk asked.

"Can I see a layout of the mall?"

"Certainly, sir. There's a directory right here," the clerk said, lifting a folded brochure from a rack. "Were you looking for something in particular?"

"Just getting the lay of the land, thanks," Huxley said, taking the brochure and unfolding it as he followed the others around the corner.

The mall was huge, he realized. The corridor MacNeil was following looked to be a few hundred yards long, passing through another atrium area and then continuing on until it terminated at a large Bloomingdale's department store.

What the hell was the man up to? If it was a meet he had planned, he must be early, because he appeared to be in no hurry whatsoever.

MacNeil paused outside a store featuring science and educational toys and sipped his coffee as he watched a young salesman spin a large, Mylar disc that resembled a flying saucer designed, it seemed, for no other purpose than to catch the attention of children and other gullible passersby, drawing them into the store. The salesman apparently tried out his line of patter on MacNeil, but without success, because MacNeil shook his head and walked on.

You can't con a con man, Huxley thought.

Tucker's Ray-Ban watchers maintained a discreet distance and Huxley stayed even farther back behind them. As the corridor widened around another babbling fountain at the next atrium, MacNeil paused again, this time to watch a young boy held firmly in hand by his father toddle around the lip of the pool, giggling with delight as the spray stopped and started.

MacNeil's expression was unreadable from this distance. Was he thinking of his own boy as he watched the father and son? Did it occur to the man, Huxley wondered, that his son would have to bear the stigma of his father's treachery for the rest of his days? Did a man like that care?

No way of knowing, but at that moment, MacNeil seemed to come to a decision. With a speed that was startling, he turned and headed down an eastbound spur off the atrium that led, according the Huxley's directory, to a Nordstrom's, another anchor store whose outside exits, he realized with a start, led directly back to the Terrace C structure where Huxley had parked the Jag.

The man was no fool and he wasn't wandering aimlessly. He'd taken nearly a full circle back to his point of origin. This was the problem of tailing a subject on his own turf, Huxley thought, mentally kicking himself for letting down his guard. He yanked his radio off his belt. "He's heading back to his car!"

The two suits picked up the pace, and then the radio crackled to the sound of yet another unfamiliar voice. *"Watcher three, here. I'm in the parking lot and I've located the subject's vehicle. I'm on it."*

"Bloody good thing," Huxley muttered back. "Okay, let's not lose him now."

MacNeil was at the Nordstrom entrance now, but he paused there, glancing back. Huxley managed to duck into a Washington Redskins merchandise store. He watched through the store window as one of the suits, caught out in the center of the corridor, practically screeched to a halt in front of a cellphone sales kiosk in his effort to avoid being noticed. The other one, Huxley noted, was across the way, ogling pastries in a high-end deli.

When his gaze shifted back to MacNeil, Huxley saw him withdraw something that looked like a sugar packet from his suit coat pocket. Ripping it open with his teeth, MacNeil dumped the contents into his coffee cup and stirred it around with his finger. Then, a wry smile on his lips, MacNeil swung his arm wide, spreading the cup's content across the bottleneck of the store entrance. Two teenage girls were leaving just at that moment, and they squealed.

"Sorry, ladies," MacNeil told them. "How clumsy of me."

One of the girls went down at once. The other tried to tiptoe around the spill, but a split second later, her feet flew out from under her and she landed with a painful sounding thud on the hard marble.

MacNeil turned and ran into the store.

The two suits dropped all pretense of disinterest now. "Go, go, go!" the suit at the deli hollered.

"No, wait!" Huxley called after them.

Too late. Tall, strapping fellows that they were, they

reached the store entrance in a couple of strides—and the next instant, they were sprawled on the floor, arms and legs akimbo. One of them went down so hard on his face that Huxley heard his jawbone crack on the marble from twenty paces back.

It was all the evidence Huxley needed to know what they were dealing with. The compound MacNeil had spilled on the floor had been developed by MI-6's own labs. MacNeil must have been given a sample during one of his liaison visits in London. Clear and granular, the stuff looked like silica gel in its dry form, and it even tasted a little sweet, which was why the boys and girls in Tactical liked to disguise it by putting it in the sort of sugar packet ordinarily found in restaurants. But when mixed with a hot liquid, such as coffee, tea, or even reasonably warm tap water, the polymer compound dissolved instantly and became a super-slippery lubricant with a multitude of purpose—not least of which was the property observed here, of spreading out rapidly to form a wickedly slick sheen over any contained surface, rendering that surface nearly impassable with the use of a mountain climber's crampons. The boys in the lab called the stuff LBB—liquid ball bearings.

By the time Huxley reached the store entrance, half a dozen people had already gone down in the clear slime. He paused for a second to calculate the width of the LBB slick, then backtracked to get a running start. Hurdles had always been his event so he sailed over, but even so, the heel of one boot caught the very edge of the slick and he had a heart-stopping second before finally regaining his balance.

He searched in vain for MacNeil, then finally spotted his gray pant cuffs and black Italian shoes just before they disappeared at the top of the escalator straight ahead. Taking care to stay on his toes so as not to skid on any remaining polymer compound that had adhered to his boots, Huxley sprinted to the escalator, pushing shoppers aside as he took the rolling steps two at a time.

"Do you *mind*?" one matron asked frostily.

"Pardon me, mum. Pardon…pardon… Oy! Out of the blood way!" Huxley bellowed, chivalry failing at last.

Bounding off the top of the escalator, he went straight forward, knowing MacNeil had to be heading for the exit. Dodging a couple of slow-moving strollers and a display of cut glass ornaments, Huxley flew through the aisles. Sure enough, he saw the silver head pass through one of the heavy glass doorways.

Still running, Huxley ripped the radio off his belt and slammed the talk button. "Watcher three! He's heading your way. Do not let him get in that Jag! Repeat, do not let him get away. Do you copy? Over."

Silence. Huxley flew out the door then stood, breathing hard as he looked left and right. "Watcher three!" he snapped at the radio. "Have you got him?"

"Negative. He didn't come this way."

Huxley started running toward the parking structure. "What do you mean, he didn't come that way? I thought you were with his car."

"Uh, roger that. It's right here in front of me. A silver Jag, Virginia license plate DRUMR. But the subject didn't come this way."

"Bloody hell," Huxley muttered, just as a squeal of tires sounded off in the distance. He turned and ran over to the ramp leading away from the parking structure, but all he saw was a steady parade of nondescript foreign and domestic sedans and SUVs on the ring road circling the mall, either arriving for a day of that great American pastime, shopping, or heading off toward the anonymity of the surrounding highways.

MacNeil was gone.

CHAPTER FIFTEEN

McLean, Virginia
August 12, 2002—1:15 p.m.

Two black-and-white Fairfax County police cruisers stood nose to tail across the entrance to the MacNeils' white rock driveway, blocking access. Carrie spotted them the moment she turned up Elcott Road and her anxiety level rocketed.

It didn't help that her nerves were already thrumming after Drum's surprise appearance at Jonah's day camp and then her subsequent meeting with the divorce lawyer. How had it come to this? Was she going to have to fight to keep her son?

Heather Childers had advised her to note down every example she could remember of Drum's absences and her own presence as the stabilizing force in Jonah's young life. "From what you tell me, Carrie, I can't imagine the courts won't grant you custody. Mothers still have distinct advantage in these cases, especially where one partner has a career that's as time-consuming as your husband's seems to be. In circumstances like that, in fact, the working partner often concedes that the child is better off with the other parent. One way or another, there's not much question that Jonah is better off living with you. Your husband is bound to realize that."

"You don't know Drum. In the first place, he genuinely loves his son. He really does, I know that. For all I know, Jonah may be the only reason he hasn't left me long before now." Carrie shook her head. "I don't know what Drum expected out of a wife. Whatever it was, I haven't met the specs. Aside from having me show up dressed to the nines on those rare occasions when circumstances demanded a spouse on his arm, he hasn't needed me in a very long time."

Yet, there had been a time when he couldn't get enough of her, Carrie thought. When he'd wanted her body, and even included her in his other, secret life. Back in Tanzania, before Jonah was born, Drum had often taken her along on his upcountry intelligence gathering trips. It had started on their honeymoon. Even that trip, she now suspected, remembering "chance" meetings with some well-connected local figures, had been partly about his business.

It was during their honeymoon, on safari in the Serengeti, that he'd told her what he really did for a living. "But you can be part of it, Carrie," he added.

It was early morning, just after sunrise. They were in an embassy Land Rover, standing up in the back through the open roof, photographing a pride of lions dozing less than ten feet from the vehicle's nubby tires. The lions—one male, three females and a couple of cubs—lay bloated and panting in the shade of a baobab tree, waiting out the heat of the day, unconcerned about the prying lenses of human interlopers who they knew by now posed neither challenge nor threat. The ravaged carcass of an antelope brought down during the night lay a short distance away, hyenas and vultures picking at the scattered bones. Every once in a while, the male lion raised his matted mane and sent a desultory growl in the direction of the scavengers, who scattered briefly, waiting to see if he was serious about protecting the kill. When it became clear that all the lions were too satiated to move, the sly, ugly birds and grinning hyenas moved back in to squabble amongst themselves over the remains.

"Here we are," Drum had said, wrapping himself around her back, "cruising around, seeing the sights. Maybe seeking out new artists for your gallery? What could be better?"

Carrie adjusted the long telephoto lens of his Nikon, focusing on a herd of zebras grazing warily at a cautious distance from the lions. "So, I'm…what?" she asked, smiling as he nuzzled her neck. "Your cover? You married me to provide an alibi for nosing around places you're not supposed to go?"

He pinned her tightly in his arms, pressing her against the edge of the open roof, kissing her ear even as the metal rim dug painfully into her ribs—threat and caress intermingled even then, Carrie realized now. "You make a great Mata Hari," he murmured. "And the debriefings are so much fun."

It had been exciting, Carrie recalled, disgusted now to think how titillating she'd found the notion of being married to a spy—the intrigue, the undertones of danger. But in her clearer moments, it had all seemed so benign, just a game, really. After all, America wasn't on a war footing. At that point, even the Cold War was ancient history—no more using hapless Third World countries to fight proxy wars. And if she'd married a spy—well, he was out there in the field to gather intelligence, wasn't he? And intelligence was just another word for information. Washington didn't need pawns, anymore. Now, maybe, there was a chance to do some good, unselfish work in the world, setting policies based on the real needs of real people instead of on strategic games and stupid stereotypes. There wasn't a whole lot wrong with that, was there?

My God, girl, but you were naive, Carrie thought. *Twenty-two years old and dumb as dirt.*

"Anyway," she added to Heather Childers, "Drum's extremely touchy about any suggestion he's not the perfect *paterfamilias*. I walk away, and his ego gets a big-time bruising. And when Drum's backed into a corner, his instinct is to come out fighting. Believe me, he doesn't like to lose."

"You think he'd seek custody just to spite you?"

"Maybe," Carrie said, recalling Drum's behavior that morning. Why was he suddenly so prickly and competitive on the subject of Jonah?

"All the more reason to have our ducks in a row," Heather said. "So you go home and do that homework. Tell me, how would you feel about shared custody?"

"I'm not sure. How would that work?"

"However we set it up. Some kids spend three days a week with dad, four with mom, then vice versa the following week."

"That sounds pretty disruptive. Kids need stability."

Heather shrugged. "Sometimes a non-custodial parent gets the child on alternate weekends and certain specified holidays. And once in a while, we run into cases where a parent gives up parental rights and custody entirely—gives them up willingly or has them taken away."

"Drum will never give up access to his son. And to be honest, I wouldn't want him cut out of Jonah's life, anyway. A little boy needs a father." Carrie groaned. "God, this is horrible no matter how you slice it, isn't it? What am I doing to my poor baby?"

"In my experience, Carrie, these things go as well or as badly as the parents decide. Contrary to popular opinion, many kids adjust reasonably well to their parents splitting up. There's always an initial shakedown period, of course, while everyone gets used to the new arrangements, but eventually it settles into a routine. If the parents handle it well and don't use the children to emotionally blackmail one another, then they adjust. The important thing is for Jonah to understand that it's not his fault and that his parents still love him unconditionally. And when the situation at home has been really tense, having two homes actually seems to beat the alternative."

"But that's the thing. I don't think our home life has been horrible. It's just...I don't know...bleak, somehow. Probably more from my perspective than Jonah's, in fact. I'm not even sure how aware he is of the tension between his dad and me."

"I'm sure you've made every effort to protect him."

"I really have. And Drum hasn't been terrible, either. He may not be around all that much, and he's a fairly stern father because that was the example he grew up with, but he loves Jonah, there's no question of that."

"Well, it's up to you to decide what you think is best, Carrie. Just keep in mind that sacrificing your life isn't necessarily going to make Jonah a happier human being. You also have to consider what kind of example you're setting as far as self-respect is concerned, given what you tell me about your husband's track record for extramarital affairs."

Carrie sighed. "There is that. I don't want Jonah to grow up thinking it's all right to behave the way his father does. Or, for that matter, that women are supposed to be his personal playthings and doormats."

"Your future daughter-in-law and granddaughters wouldn't thank you for it," Heather agreed. "Anyway, what you need to do now, Carrie, is try to come to a decision on how you'd like to see this unfold. And one other thing…"

"What's that?"

"Does Drum know you're considering leaving?"

"I don't think so. At least, I didn't, before now. There's a chance he might have gotten wind of it, though. I should have given you my cell-phone number instead of the one at the house, where anyone can hear messages. Your secretary left a message for me yesterday and I think my mother-in-law may have picked it up."

"Oops. Sorry about that. Let me get your cell number and I'll make sure no one here calls the house again. But the reason I asked if Drum knows you're looking to walk away…well…I hesitate to raise it. I don't want to scare you. But we should at least consider the possibility."

"Of what?"

"That he might try to take Jonah away."

"But you said the courts—"

"I don't mean through a legal custody decision. As far as those proceedings are concerned, we always have to presume that the other parent will resist any attempt to strip him of custodial rights. That's why we have to have our arguments and evidence well prepared in advance. But your circumstances are a little more complicated. In this particular case, it's action outside the legal venue I'm concerned about."

Carrie sat back, uncomprehending for a moment. And then, as it dawned on her what Heather was suggesting, she was horrified. "You think Drum might try to kidnap Jonah?"

"You said he doesn't like to lose. From what Tracy has told me about him, I've got a pretty good idea of his line of work.

If anyone has the skill set to pull off something like that, it would be someone with that kind of background."

Carrie felt an icy chill run through her veins. "Oh, my God. After I dropped off Jonah at day camp this morning…"

"What? What happened?"

"I realized he'd left his asthma inhaler in the car. When I went back to the rec center to give it to him, I found Drum there."

"Trying to take Jonah out?"

"No, I don't think so. At least, he said he just came to see Jonah swim. But his timing was off. The kids were getting ready to do an arts and crafts project. I found Drum and Jonah sitting off to one side of the classroom when I got there. I got the impression Jonah wasn't too happy about whatever they were talking about."

"Has Drum ever done that before—shown up at your son's school in the middle of the day?"

"Not that I can remember, but I suppose there's a first time for everything."

"A little suspicious, though."

"If I were really paranoid, I'd say it was. He'd been on his way to a meeting downtown when he got word it was canceled, apparently. The rec center's more or less on the way back to the office, so it's not unthinkable he would have taken advantage of some unexpected free time to drop in. He had no way of knowing the kids didn't have their swim session until the afternoon."

"Still, Carrie," Heather said, "you might want to think about telling the camp administrators not to let Jonah leave with anyone but you."

"You really think Drum might try to kidnap Jonah?"

"It's been known to happen."

Carrie sat quietly for a moment, thinking, then shook her head. "No, I can't see it happening. It would be out of character."

"Why is that? You said he wouldn't want to lose a custody battle. He'd have to realize he was playing with a weak hand."

"That's true. But I can't see Drum pulling a vanishing act, walking away from everything he knows," Carrie said. "He likes his position in life too much—being a Virginia MacNeil. Living in the big house on the Potomac. Getting a CIA deputy's job after years of working his way up the organization. You have to understand, this is a man who's spent his whole life trying to prove—mostly to himself—that he was as good a man as his father and worthy of the MacNeil name. He may fight me over custody, but he's not going to give up everything he's worked for. Not now, when he's finally getting the recognition he feels he deserves." She shook her head firmly. "No, I don't think so. It couldn't happen."

Even as the words left her mouth, Carrie had the sinking realization that it sounded like famous last words.

It was well after noon when she finally got home. As she came up Elcott Road and turned in at the driveway, a uniformed police officer climbed out of one of the cruisers and walked toward her car, one hand raised, the other hovering over the gun holstered at his hip. Carrie rolled down her window and was blasted by a hot wave of thick, muggy summer air, hardly relieved by the cooling effects of the Potomac just a few dozen yards away.

"Can I help you?" the cop asked.

"I live here," Carrie told him. "What's going on?" Her first thought was Jonah. After the conversation in Heather Childer's office, it had been all she could do to resist the temptation to join Zoë's mother in her daylong parking lot vigil. Instead, she'd skipped her planned tour of the Torpedo Factory art galleries but had forced herself to carry on with her other errands, including the visit to the dry cleaner's and the grocery store. Now, she had ice cream and other frozen food in the back of the station wagon that needed to be unloaded.

"Your name?" the policeman asked.

"Carrie MacNeil."

"Can I see your driver's license, please?"

"Yes, sure. But what's going on here?"

The lawyer had set off her nerves with horror stories about custody battles and kidnapping, but even without those dire warnings, Carrie's mind was quite capable of creating nightmare scenarios all by itself after surviving a bombing in Africa and the shooting at the London Embassy. A sociopath could have attacked the rec center—Zoë's mother, perhaps, stewing out there in the parking lot until her brain finally cooked and she snapped. Or maybe Althea had foiled a daytime robbery, or had suffered a heart attack or stroke. Or maybe someone had attacked the house, knowing it was the home of a senior CIA official. Far-fetched as all of these possibilities sounded, they were no more unlikely than some of the events Carrie had already lived through in the last few years.

She withdrew her wallet and then her driver's license, and handed it over with a trembling hand, waiting impatiently while the cop scrutinized and compared the photo and her face. At the top of the drive, she noticed a couple of unfamiliar cars parked near the front entrance of the house.

The cop handed back the license. "Okay, Mrs. MacNeil, you can go on in."

"But what—"

"There are people up there waiting to talk to you."

He backed away from her car, waving at the cop behind the wheel of the second cruiser, who started it up, put it in reverse and edged away, clearing a path for Carrie to get by with the Passat.

She parked beside the garage, grabbing what she could of the frozen foods in the back before hurrying toward the front steps. As she crossed the drive, she noticed a white Mercedes parked in the shade under the trees. It had D.C. plates and, unlike the other vehicles in the drive, it looked familiar. The other two cars parked alongside it were black Ford Tauruses with radio antennae, and even if she hadn't spotted their government plates, there was no mistaking the air of officialdom that clung to them.

So it had to be something to do with Drum, she decided. Was he hurt? She felt guilty suddenly, unable to dodge the notion that her meeting with the lawyer had somehow brought a plague down on him.

Tucked off to the far side of the garage, invisible before now, she spotted one other vehicle, but although this one wasn't entirely unfamiliar, it was out of place. It was a green minivan with a removable magnetic sign on the sliding side door that read, *MIGHTY MAID—MIGHTY GOOD!* Where had she seen it before? She racked her brain to remember, and then it came to her. Across the road, at the Kleins'. So, maybe the problem was there, she told herself hopefully, feeling sheepish for wishing ill fortune on the nice old couple.

But as she made her way up the circular, red brick steps to the wide front porch, the door opened, and when Carrie saw who it was, she knew why the Mercedes had seemed familiar. She'd seen Tom Bent and his wife Lorraine a couple of times since returning from London, mostly while attending Sunday services with Althea at the National Cathedral where Lorraine's father, Bishop Merriam, had presided. The last time Carrie and Tom had really talked was at the embassy reception in London for the visiting senators—the night that young student from Maryland had been gunned down outside in the rain.

"Tom," Carrie said, "thank God, a friendly face—although you're the last person I expected to see this morning. What's going on here?"

"Hi, darlin'," he said. "Let me help you with those groceries. Is this it, or are there more?"

"There's a couple more bags in the back of the car," Carrie replied, her stomach knotting at Tom's sober tone. "But—"

"Let me just run and grab them," he said. "I'll be right back."

Carrie waited, holding the heavy front door open with her hip while he ran out and gathered up the white Safeway bags she'd left in the station wagon. He was jacketless, the sleeves of his blue pinstripe cotton shirt rolled up to his elbows, red tie loosened at the collar. A lock of his brown hair flopped over his forehead. For tidy Tom Bent, the look was shockingly disheveled.

"Tom, what—"

He remounted the steps and held the door to let her enter first. "Come inside. We'll talk there."

Turning to enter, she spotted someone else from the corner of her eye, walking up the drive. The freckled blonde looked barely out of her teens, dressed in blue jeans and a black tank top, her hair pulled back in a ponytail. She was watching Carrie and Tom with a frank look that straddled curiosity and suspicion. She seemed so young that the first thought that crossed Carrie's mind was that she must be selling high school raffle tickets. But if so, how had she managed to talk her way past those burly, unsmiling cops at the bottom of the drive?

"Can I help you?" Carrie asked.

"No, I'm fine, Mrs. MacNeil. I was told to report over here, that's all. You two go ahead on in. I'm right behind you."

Carrie frowned and was about to argue the point—except what, exactly, was the point? Whatever was going on, clearly she was not in charge here. And how did this girl know her name?

The house was a center hall plan, with a spacious entry and a black-and-white checkerboard of marble tile covering the vestibule floor. A round mahogany table at its center held an arrangement of the fresh flowers that Althea had delivered every week from a local florist. A large, formal living room stood off to one side of the entry hall, overlooking the front of the house, but its carved sliding panel doors were pulled shut at the moment. The dining room and a wood-lined study were on the other side of the hall, while the winding oak staircase rose up from across the vestibule. The kitchen with its solarium addition was straight ahead, at the end of a short hall.

It was from that direction that Rose, the housekeeper, emerged, hurrying to relieve Carrie of her Safeway bags. "Let me take those, Miz Carrie." She was a tall and strong-looking woman with a ramrod posture that General MacNeil himself would have envied, an unlined face the color of *café au lait,* and hair braided from root to tip in thick, gray plaits.

"I can put this away, Rose," Carrie said.

"No, you'd better go in to Miz Althea. She's real fretful, I think."

"Where is she?"

"In the parlor with the other gentlemen."

"Which other gentlemen?"

"I couldn't say exactly who they are. Mr. Tom here will be able to tell you more." Tom stood behind Carrie with the last of the grocery bags. "Just leave them there on the bench, Mr. Tom. I'll get them."

"Thank you, Rose." He settled the plastic sacks on the brocade-padded settee under the stairs.

"Tom, what on earth is going on?" Carrie asked.

He nodded to the housekeeper, who hooked the handles of several additional grocery bags through her strong fingers before heading back into the kitchen. Only when the swinging door had closed behind her did Bent finally face Carrie. "Have you heard from Drum in the last hour or two?" he asked.

"No, I haven't. Why?"

"When did you last see him?"

"Earlier this morning. He was here when I came down to make breakfast for Jonah, which was a bit of a surprise. He left not long after that. Said he had a meeting."

"Where?"

"Over at FBI headquarters. But he was on his way over there when they called to cancel."

"The Bureau called here?"

"No, I imagine they—or his office, I'm not sure—called him on his cell phone to tell him about the cancellation."

"So you have spoken to him since he left home?"

"Yes. I saw him again around nine-fifteen or so at the Asbury Park Rec Center. Jonah's enrolled in day camp there. I had already dropped Jonah off, but then I returned about twenty minutes later because I found his asthma inhaler rolling around my car. I was worried he might need it. That's when I realized Drum had shown up."

"What was he doing at the rec center?"

She hesitated. "He said he wanted to watch Jonah's swim class, except it's not until this afternoon."

"You don't sound like you believe that's the real reason."

"Well, I suppose it's possible. I'm not sure. If it was, though, it's a first. Not surprising he didn't know there was no chance he'd catch Jonah in the pool. Drum usually leaves Jonah's school and extracurricular activities to me to organize and attend. He never even made it to the Christmas pageant last year. Missed Jonah's stage debut as one of the three 'wise guys,' as he called them."

Tom smiled. "That would have been something to see." Then he sobered again. "So, you saw Drum at day camp, and then?"

"He left before me."

"Where did he say he was going after that."

Carrie frowned. "To the office. I'm pretty sure that's where he said he was headed. Why? What's happened?"

"He never showed up."

"What do you mean? Where is he?"

Tom shook his head. "Did you have any sense he was unhappy or worried about anything, Carrie? Did he seem out of sorts at all lately?"

"I'm not—"

Just then, the wood panel doors to the living room slid open. A very large, very bald and very fierce-looking man loomed in the opening. Dressed in a navy open-necked golf shirt and casual gray slacks that seemed decidedly downscale next to Tom's striped Oxford dress shirt, rep tie and Brooks Brothers suit pants, the man nevertheless exuded the kind of authority that comes with great size and a scowling black laser-beam focus.

"Carrie," Tom said, "this is Frank Tucker, also from Langley. He's head of a special security unit the Director set up recently. Frank, this is Drum's wife, Carrie."

Tucker nodded. "Mrs. MacNeil, would you step in here, please?"

Peering around him, Carrie spotted her mother-in-law sitting on one of the chintz-covered wing chairs that flanked the unlit river stone fireplace. A tall, thin, angular woman with pure white hair that she had done every Friday at the same Pentagon City hairdresser, Althea looked peevish and fretful—although there was nothing terribly unusual in that, Carrie reminded herself. Her mother-in-law could find something to bemoan on the sunniest of days. Even when things were going very well, Althea would be sure to predict it wouldn't last, then recount a story about one acquaintance or another who seemed to be on top of the world one day, only to be diagnosed the next with some virulent form of cancer.

"Well, here she is, at last," Althea said. She was dressed in a sleeveless black-and-white-checked blouse, white Bermuda shorts, with white Peds and canvas shoes on her overlarge feet.

"Are you all right?" Carrie asked.

Althea nodded peevishly. "Yes, of course *I'm* all right."

Tucker stood aside to let Carrie pass into the living room. "Come in here, if you would, please, Mrs. MacNeil."

But instead of going forward, she took a step back. "No. First, I want to know if my son is safe."

"Why wouldn't he be?"

Carrie turned to Tom. "Where's Drum, Tom?"

"That's the problem, darlin'. We're not exactly sure."

"Oh, God," Carrie groaned, heart sinking. "That's it, then. I want to go and get Jonah right now."

"You're not surprised to learn that your husband's whereabouts are a mystery, Mrs. MacNeil?" Tucker asked.

"I want my son."

Tucker shook his head. "Not until—"

"No! Right now," Carrie insisted, hooking her purse higher up on her shoulder and gripping her car keys.

"Carrie, I'm sure Jonah's fine," Tom said.

"I'll believe that when I see him. You don't understand, Tom. I went to see a lawyer this morning."

"You what?"

She glanced nervously at her mother-in-law and turned back to the vestibule, lowering her voice. "I'm thinking of leaving Drum. I think he might have gotten wind of it." She glanced behind her into the living room, where Althea was sitting straighter now, watching her through the open doorway with a look of utter fury. Carrie turned back to Tom. "If Drum did find out about it, he might have decided to snatch Jonah to prevent me from getting custody."

Tucker had been leaning in to catch her urgent whispers, but then he glanced over her head. When Carrie looked up for the source of the distraction, she saw the freckled, ponytailed blonde just inside the front door. She hadn't heard her come in.

"Tengwall," Tucker said to her, "I want you to head back over to the little boy's camp. Confirm he's okay, then radio back ASAP, would you? Mrs. MacNeil," he added to Carrie, "Tengwall here works for me."

"I want my son where I can see him."

"Fine. She'll bring the boy back to the house. You phone the camp and tell them to expect her. Tell them there's been a family emergency and you've sent your cousin, Brianne, to pick up your son."

"I'd rather—"

"She's armed and fully capable of bodyguard duty," Tucker said.

Carrie blanched. "Armed? You think that's necessary?"

"Just so you know he'll be okay with me," the young woman said. "I like kids, Mrs. MacNeil. I used to be a camp counselor myself."

Right, Carrie thought. *Just last year, I bet.*

"Jonah will be fine, I promise. I'll have him home in half an hour. Just call and tell them I'm coming, would you? Otherwise they won't let me take him."

"I'd rather pick him up myself."

"I'm afraid that won't be possible," Tucker said. "We have to ask you to stay here."

"And if I refuse?"

Tom put a hand on her arm. "Carrie, it's for the best. Trust me."

"I trust you, Tom, but these people…. Look, can I see some identification, please? I'm not about to let just anybody take charge of my son."

Tucker and Tengwall both produced federal identification cards that matched the one Drum had, identifying them as officers of the Central Intelligence Agency.

"This is insane," Carrie said, shaking her head. "All right, but first, I want to call the camp and satisfy myself that Jonah's actually there."

She reached in her purse, fished out a small address book and looked up the number of the rec center switchboard. Then, withdrawing her cell phone, she put in the call, glanced at her watch as the phone rang on the other end, then asked to be connected to Mindy Steinberg at the day camp program.

"He's in the pool, Mrs. MacNeil," Mindy said when she came on the line a few moments later and Carrie asked after Jonah. "The Sharks just had their swimming lesson and they're on free swim right now. I was just down there watching them. Jonah showed me his trick dive. That's the one where he crossed his fingers, crosses his hands, crosses his legs—"

"And crosses his eyes," Carrie said, smiling as she nodded. "I know. He was showing me at bedtime last night. So he's doing all right, then? You're sure?"

"Sure. In fact," Mindy said, "I'm walking out on the deck now with the portable phone and I can see him…um… hmmm…"

"What?" Carrie felt her heart begin to pound in her chest. "Is he there, Mindy? Can you actually see him?"

"I don't…no, never mind, I do see him. Yup, there he is," Mindy said. "They're playing Marco Polo. Listen. You can probably hear him."

She must have been holding the phone up to the pool, because Carrie could make out childish squeals echoing around the pool's tile walls and voices calling, "Marco! Polo!" in cheerful repetition.

Mindy came back on the line with a deep sigh. "Boy, by the end of the summer, I can tell you, every counselor here positively hates that game."

"I can imagine," Carrie said. She glanced over to where the big man—Tucker—was watching her, black eyes flashing impatience. "Look, Mindy, I'm afraid Jonah has to leave a little early today. We've got a family thing going on here. My…um…friend—" She raised an eyebrow at the young

blond woman, who held up her CIA identification as a reminder "—Brianne Tengwall is going to pick him up in about
fifteen minutes. Can you have him ready to go?"

"Oh, sure. I'll need to see her ID, though."

"No problem. She'll show you a driver's license," Carrie
said pointedly, frowning at the two strangers in turn. That was
all she needed, having someone show up and flash spy cre-
dentials before driving off with her son. Tengwall nodded and
slipped the CIA document back into the pocket of her jeans.

After Tengwall left to pick up Jonah, Carrie let Tom Bent
lead her into the living room, where Drum's mother watched
her approach with the same look of contempt that Samson's
mother must have reserved for Delilah.

"Althea, are you all right? What's going on here?"

"Where have you been, Carrie?" Althea asked angrily.

"Running errands. I told you last night that I'd be out this
morning."

"Errands…ha!" her mother-in-law snorted. Her angry gaze
held Carrie for a moment, and then shifted past her. "My
son's midlife folly. No sense of duty of loyalty, that's what's
wrong with young women today. They all have their own
needs. Got to take care of those. Never mind taking care of
their husbands and children. Well, go ahead, ask her. Ask her
what she's been up to. Ask her what she's done to my son."

Carrie glanced around behind herself to see who Althea
was talking to. There were three strangers in dark suits around
the perimeter of the room, but from the nervous glances they
were sending in the direction of the ferocious one, Tucker,
they seemed to be underlings of his, awaiting orders.

Her mother-in-law's comments, however, had been addressed to a fourth man Carrie hadn't noticed up until now.
He was seated on one of the sagging, down-filled armchairs

set off in one corner. He rose to his feet and nodded as Carrie made eye contact, his ruddy skin seeming to flush even deeper. Like Tucker and Tengwall, he was dressed casually—in his case, in a black T-shirt, webbed, military-style belt and khaki pants. But in spite of his dressed-down state, he, like Tucker, somehow seemed to carry more authority than the flunkies in suits. This man's fair hair was wooly thick, his gray eyes direct and assessing, his face weathered and weary looking.

"Mrs. MacNeil, how do you do?" he said. "My name is Mark Huxley. Your mother-in-law and me were just having a bit of chat. Would you care to join us?"

An English accent. North country. Maybe Yorkshire, Carrie amended. Working class. Inwardly she grimaced. Three years of living in London, and she was doing that British thing—divining background by accent, reading a life into the subtle differences in pronunciation that probably sounded as indistinguishable to the average American ear as they once had to hers.

But never mind that. What was a Brit doing in the Mac-Neil's living room, taking charge like he owned the place?

CHAPTER SIXTEEN

TOP SECRET
CODE WORD ACCESS ONLY
NOT FOR DISTRIBUTION

FEDERAL BUREAU OF INVESTIGATION
INTERVIEW TRANSCRIPTION

(continued)

Just so you know, Carrie, no matter how this investigation may have been handled up before this, it's now officially an FBI file. We're liaising closely with the CIA and MI-6, so Tucker and Huxley here have become my new best friends, whether I like it or not, but this is a national security matter, so the Bureau has the lead and they are no longer running this show.

Well, thanks, Agent Andrews. I'm sure we'll all sleep better, knowing Mr. Hoover's heirs have taken charge. You don't mind if I tell you, though, that your interagency turf wars don't really interest me?

I figured as much. I'm just telling you so you'll know I have the authority to say what I'm about to say.

And what's that?

That you are officially enjoined from discussing this case outside of this room. You will not mention your husband's disappearance or the investigation to anyone.

What am I supposed to say when people ask me where Drum is?

Away on business. Just carry on doing what you would normally do and we'll keep you posted as appropriate as the situation develops.

"As appropriate," right. I won't hold my breath for that.

Needless to say, you shouldn't make any plans to leave town.

It's not quite that simple. At least two people—my best friend, Tracy Overturf, and her partner—know I was getting ready to leave Drum.

You have their legal firm on retainer, I believe.

That's right. In fact, Tracy suggested she come here with me today in case I needed legal advice. You did say I could have a lawyer present any time I wanted, didn't you?

Yes, that's your right, if you think it's necessary.

So, as my legal counsel, I'm allowed to get her advice, right?

As legal counsel, yes, you can consult her.

Good. Because I have already and intend to continue doing so. And while we're on the subject, I presume my mother-in-law isn't included in this non-disclosure injunction of yours, either, since she's been getting grilled, too, about Drum's whereabouts. She's obviously aware of what's going on, given that her house is being overrun and pulled apart by the seams even as we speak.

She was married to a five-star general. She understands about national security.

That doesn't mean she's accepted that her son is guilty of anything.

Do you think there's something she knows that she hasn't told us?

Not that I'm aware of—not that she'd confide in me, anyway. Ever since she found out I'd been speaking to a divorce lawyer, she's pretty much stopped speaking to me, except when it can't be avoided. And even there, most of the time she just passes messages through Jonah or the housekeeper. But it does raise the issue of what I do next. I think I mentioned that I've been offered a house to sit. It belongs to Tracy Overturf's parents. They both teach at Georgetown University, but they're off on sabbatical right now. Even before all this happened, I'd told Tracy I might be interested in taking her up on the offer of her parents' house. Now, given how upset Althea is with me, I'm inclined to take it up sooner rather than later.

We'd rather you stayed where you are.

Well, that may be, but I'd rather not. The atmosphere in that house is so tense you could cut it with a knife. It's not a happy environment for anyone, least of all a six-year-old. He's going to be starting first grade in a couple of weeks. I'm sorry Drum has taken a flyer—sorry and mightily angry about it—but if I'm going to have to move, anyway, the beginning of the school year just makes it that much more urgent to do it sooner rather than later.

Let me put some cards on the table here, Carrie. We think there's a chance your husband may still make contact. If he does, we'd like it to be under controlled circumstances. The surveillance on the Elcott Road house is already in place. We've moved it back into a low-profile mode, at least from the outside. If he shows up there,

there'll be no outward signs that we're still on site. If he comes back, we're well placed to nab him.

He's not stupid. If he really has done something wrong, he's going to stay as far away from that house as he can. Anyway, why would he want to contact me? He obviously doesn't give a damn about how I feel. If he did, he would never have snuck around behind my back, and he would certainly never have disappeared like this without telling me what he was up to.

It's not you we think he'll be back for.

You think he might try to see Jonah?

Not "see."

What do you mean? You mean—oh, bloody hell! You think he's coming back to take Jonah away with him?

Possibly. We think it was part of his agenda until he twigged to the fact that he was being followed the other morning at Tyson's Corner.

Why do you say that?

This was dropped at Nordstrom's that morning.

A passport?

Nobody made the connection at first. It was found by a customer, who gave it to a salesclerk, who stuck it in a drawer, then got busy and forgot about it until the end of the day, when she finally handed it in to store security. They were planning to mail it back to the State Department. When we went out there earlier this morning with a warrant for their security videotapes, I happened to spot the passport on the security director's desk and picked it up. As soon as I saw the picture, I realized what it was.

It's Drum's passport?

Not Drum's. And not a valid document, obviously. A very good forgery, though. The name on it is Jonathan

*Michael Parkes. Date of birth July 28, 1996—the same
as your son. Here, I'll try to open it inside the evidence
bag. Don't touch it. Our fingerprint people still need to go
over it. Hang on...okay, there. You see the picture?*

No! Oh, God, no, no, no!

You knew nothing about this, Carrie? You're sure?

Nothing.

You'd agree that it is a picture of your son, though?

Yes, but I've never seen it before.

You have no idea when it was taken?

No, none. Unless maybe...

What?

It's at least a few months old.

How do you know?

Jonah lost his first front tooth just after Easter. He's still got
them all in this shot.

*A passport photo has very specific size and head angle
requirements. Did Jonah ever mention his dad or anyone
else taking a picture like this?*

I'm not sure. Maybe. Drum took him out one Sunday
afternoon, back when we were still in London. It was one of the
few days he wasn't at the office. He said he wanted to have a
"boys day out" with Jonah. It was a rare enough event, so I
certainly didn't discourage it. When they got back, Jonah
started to say something about getting his picture taken, but
then Drum shushed him up and they got this conspiratorial look
between them. I thought it was some sort of birthday or
Mother's Day surprise they were plotting, so I didn't press for
more information. But now that I think about it, my birthday
and Mother's Day have both gone by and I didn't get any
pictures. I'd forgotten all about it until just now.

Dammit! This was what he needed the picture for? To get a false passport so he could steal my son from me? That means he's been planning this for months. The bastard!

Do you see now why we want you to stay where you are, Carrie?

Because you think Drum's coming back. Coming back for Jonah.

Maybe. But if he does, we'll be waiting.

CHAPTER SEVENTEEN

McLean, Virginia
August 17, 2002—11:14 a.m.

There were eyes everywhere. It had been five days since Drum's disappearance, and Carrie felt them on her at every turn.

She'd once accused him of paranoia. "Even paranoiacs have real enemies," Drum had replied.

Well, if he hadn't had them before, Carrie thought, he certainly did now after pulling that very public vanishing act at Tyson's Corner. What could he have been thinking?

After that stunt, witnessed by dozens of civilians in the mall that morning, his CIA watchers had finally been forced to alert the FBI to his flight and the suspicions surrounding him. The Bureau, furious at having been kept in the dark up to then, was pulling out all the stops in an effort to locate Drum and bring him to task. The house in McLean had been crawling with agents ever since, turning drawers, desks and closets inside out, sifting papers, studying computer disks, examining every crack and crevice for evidence that might reveal his whereabouts, intentions and the extent of his betrayal.

But if Drum was gone, his family was stuck behind like a collection of captive butterflies pinned to a board, wriggling helplessly under the cold scrutiny of federal officials determined to discover what role, if any, Carrie and Althea might have played in what looked to be a serious breach of national security.

If Carrie had been ill at ease on Elcott Road before, trying to find her place in a family that seemed determined to keep her at arm's length, the house now felt more like a prison than anything else. FBI, CIA Security, Fairfax County Police—at this point, there was no keeping track of the officials slipping in and out of the house at will, turning the place into Grand Central Station as they ripped apart everything from Drum's sock drawer to Jonah's toy box looking for clues to the missing deputy's whereabouts.

Althea has spent most of the last few days in her bedroom, pleading a migraine, leaving Carrie on the front lines of this assault on their home life, such as it was. But if these rude intrusions were uncomfortable for Carrie and mortifying to her mother-in-law, who'd always taken such pride in her family's accomplishments, to Jonah they brought only confusion. On Saturday morning, he finally suffered a meltdown.

He'd already been in a funk about missing out on the volcano project at camp. The morning after Drum's disappearance, Carrie had gone in to wake him, determined to keep his routine on as normal a footing as possible, especially after

Tucker and Huxley the MI-6 man, had promised a dedicated security person would stay with Jonah at all times. But when Carrie went up to his room that Tuesday morning, she found Jonah congested and running a low-grade fever—a summer cold, nothing more, but enough to keep him indoors for the rest of that week.

Alternately curious and fretful about the taciturn strangers moving in and out of the house, Jonah had grown increasingly restless as the days wore on. Late Friday afternoon, though, he got a treat when Mindy, his much-loved counselor, came by the house with the papier-mâché volcano he'd made the morning his father disappeared, and which his fellow Sharks had painted for him in his absence.

The camp counselor had seemed unnerved to find so many stern-looking people overrunning the big house she'd thought contained nothing more daunting than a little boy with a summer cold, but Carrie had convinced the watchers to let her come inside to visit Jonah, who at that point was sorely in need of a little distraction. The three of them proceeded to gather ingredients in the kitchen, then mix the "lava" and set off the volcano under the willows out in the backyard. Jonah went to bed happy that night, feeling better than he had all week.

But then, on Saturday morning, he rolled out to find a dreary rain falling. When he went down to the den in his pajamas to play computer games, he found the way barred by burly strangers, the place in a shambles, and the computer packed up and carted away.

"Mom!" he cried, charging back upstairs and into her bedroom, landing on the bed in one tearful leap. "Those people! They took the computer! And all my games!"

"Oh, honey, I know. They had to borrow them for a while."

"But how come? They took the Spidey game! I want to play with it."

"We'll get it back," Carrie assured him. How could she explain to a six-year-old that the FBI thought his father was a traitor who may have hidden stolen intelligence files among his little boy's game CDs?

Jonah was fit to be tied, cabin fever finally taking its toll. With the rain falling outside, adding to the general feeling of gloom, there was no question of sending him out in the yard to run off steam in spite of the fact that his summer cold had dwindled to light sniffles. Instead, after breakfast, Carrie carted down a large bin of Legos and action figures from the playroom upstairs and settled him in the solarium, out of the line of foot traffic, while she set about baking some chocolate chip cookies to cheer him up.

The cookies were just coming out of the oven when Tracy Overturf showed up, as she had every day since Drum's disappearance, officially to provide legal counsel but, more importantly, to offer moral support while the FBI ripped the family's life to shreds.

"Oh, man, does it smell fatal in here," Tracy groaned. Cinnamon and warm chocolate scents permeated the kitchen. "Goodbye diet, hello hippo hips. Hey, there, Jonah!" she called over to the solarium. "How you doing today?"

"Okay," he said, looking up at her over the table.

"His cold sounds better," Tracy said to Carrie. She perched on one of the bar stools at the baker's table. "And look at you, baking cookies like you had not a care in the world. Who'd guess your whole life is being turned upside down?"

"Nothing like denial to get you through the day," Carrie said, as she slid the cookies off the hot sheets onto cooling racks. "I had to do something to cheer things up around here.

Jonah went to pieces this morning when he realized the computer and all his games were MIA. He was already bummed about missing camp this week, so losing his video games was the last straw."

"He might have been better off carrying on with his normal routine," Tracy agreed, grabbing one of the cookies and hot-potatoing it from hand to hand.

"Part of me was kind of glad to keep him home. I was a little freaked about letting him out of my sight. When he came down with a cold, it felt like the fates were sending a message—trust no one."

Tracy glanced back at the game unfolding over in the solarium. "Looks like he found himself a new best buddy."

"Hmph. I was just about ready to tell the whole bunch of them to take a flying leap," Carrie said quietly. "But this one has redeemed himself a little—for the moment, anyway."

Huxley had been at the round oak table in the solarium, reading a newspaper when Carrie had brought down the toys from the playroom. He was sitting in the same chair and the same position as Drum had been in that last morning, and when Carrie had walked in and seen the raised newspaper, only two hands and a pair of legs showing around it, her heart had pounded at the weird déjà vu of it all. For a split second, she'd even allowed herself the fantasy that Drum's vanishing act had been a bad dream. But then, at the sound of footsteps on the terrazzo tile, the paper had dropped, and she'd seen that it was the man from British intelligence.

"Must have kids himself," Tracy said, watching Huxley with Jonah.

"I guess. Whatever. All I can say is that it's a nice change of pace, having one of these guys recognize for a change that there's a little guy here whose life they're completely upending."

Although maybe, she reflected, it was just that the Brit was looking for a little distraction of his own. That first day, he'd been right in the thick of things, asking probing questions about Drum's habits and movements, but ever since the FBI had shown up, Huxley had seemed decidedly under-occupied, his presence in the middle of an American security operation barely tolerated, it seemed. Or was he simply underfoot because he'd been assigned the task of keeping the family under close surveillance?

Whatever the reason, when she'd lugged the box of toys over to the solarium, he'd set aside the newspaper, settled himself on the floor under the windows, and started helping Jonah construct a Lego pirate ship. Before long, the two of them had tipped over one of the oak chairs to serve as a poop deck and rigged up a set of sails from paper napkins, tape and twine that Carrie had found for them in the kitchen junk drawer. They'd been at it for nearly an hour now, their sandy heads, one reddish, one dark blond, bent together as they taped a handmade Jolly Roger to one of the upended chair legs.

Jonah, who'd spent half of his short life living in London under the care of a Cockney housekeeper, seemed completely unfazed by the brawny Brit's thick accent, Carrie noted. He certainly seemed delighted to have found a willing if over-size playmate after being cooped up all week with nothing but grumps for company.

"Be thankful for small mercies," Tracy said.

"Oh, believe me, I am. At this point, I'll take what I can get." Carrie stacked a few of the warm cookies on a plate and headed for the solarium.

Huxley looked up, scrunching one eye as she approached. "Har! Avast, me hearty," he cackled out of the side of his mouth. "Here's a wench bringing treasure. All hands on deck."

"Har!" Jonah cried, brandishing his toy Spider-Man like a sword. "Hand 'em over, wench."

"You don't call your poor old mom a wench," Carrie protested.

"Better hand 'em over or you'll have to walk the plank!" Jonah said, giving her his gap-toothed grin.

"Well, as long as you put it like that..." Carrie set the plate between them on the underside of the oak chair poop deck. Jonah dove for a warm cookie which he proceeded to share with his Spider-Man figurine. "Would you pirates like a little milk to go with those? Or coffee," she added to Huxley, a little self-consciously. It was a pretty absurd scenario, all things considered.

"Aye, I'll thank-ee for that," he growled, staying in character. On the other hand, Carrie thought, maybe he was just a couple of sandwiches shy of a picnic. "Milk for me mate here and a little of the black brew for me, neat. Eh, me hearty, what do you say?"

"Aye, matey!" Jonah sputtered through chocolate-smeared, cookie-crumbed lips.

"You're a messy bunch, you pirates," Carrie said.

She went back and got them their milk and coffee, then returned to the kitchen to put together a breakfast tray for Althea.

"At least you don't have to worry about Drum sneaking back and carrying him off," Tracy murmured, watching the two over in the solarium. Jonah was grinning as Huxley's broad fingers struggled to fold a paper napkin into a makeshift pirate kerchief and tie it around Spider-Man's small plastic head.

"No," Carrie agreed, "not with all these heavy hitters swarming the place. On the other hand, Drum did manage to give them the slip once, so it's not beyond the realm of the possible that he could do it again."

She sliced an English muffin and dropped it in the toaster, then pulled a serving tray out under the island. Lifting a banana and some grapes out of the three-tiered wire fruit basket hanging over the island, she set them on a blue flowered plate and folded a napkin alongside. When the toaster popped a few moments later, she put the English muffins and some marmalade next to the fruit.

"I can't tell you how it froze my blood to see Jonah's picture on that fake passport Drum dropped at the mall," she said quietly. "Who knows? Maybe the only reason he hasn't shown up yet is that he's getting another one done up as we speak. He's got the connections to get as much phony documentation as he needs, and these guys know it, too. Not only that, he used to brag about how the technical support guys at the Agency could teach you how to make yourself unrecognizable. A little hair dye, a pair of glasses, a prosthetic nose, some body padding. He said he'd been on jobs where his own mother wouldn't know him. Creeps me out, thinking he could be out there, just waiting for the chance to make his move. Makes me want to take Jonah down in the basement and hide out for the next decade."

"Has Jonah asked where he is?" Tracy asked.

Carrie picked up a knife. It glinted under the overhead pot lights as she sliced the muffin halves down the center. "Not until last night when I was tucking him into bed, funnily enough." She wiped her hands on the front of her green bib apron and walked over to one of the glass-fronted cabinets, withdrew a small tumbler that she filled with orange juice from the fridge. "The thing is, Drum was gone so much of the time anyway, that Jonah thinks nothing of the fact that he's not around now."

"So, what did you tell him last night?"

"That Daddy was away on a business trip. The only thing to recommend those deadpan FBI guys," Carrie added quietly, cocking a thumb at the kitchen door, beyond which they could hear hammers and crowbars at work as a team of federal agents pried apart the wood paneling in Drum's study, looking for hidey-holes, "is that they're so closemouthed they haven't let slip that his dad's done a bunk. Jonah thinks they're here because Drum lost some important papers and they're trying to help him find them."

"Did you ever find out why Drum really showed up at Jonah's camp that day?"

"Oh, yes, I meant to tell you. Jonah finally told me last night. He asked me if Drum was going to be home today because they were supposed to be going to go out to look at boats."

"Boats?"

"Yeah. Big hero. Promises his son a boat the very day he's planning to fly the coop. They were supposed to be going out shopping for one today, Jonah remembered, but I had to tell him it wasn't on. That's when he decided it was his fault."

"What was his fault?"

"That Drum had canceled out on him. Jonah said his dad had come by camp that morning to say he had some free time, so they could do the boat shopping right away. Jonah was reluctant to leave, though, because they were making these working volcanoes at camp." Carrie smiled. "And also, just between you and me, because he's got a big crush on his camp counselor, although he'd die of embarrassment if you ever suggested it. Anyway, Drum told me he was there to see Jonah swim, but Jonah now says that wasn't it at all."

"Jesus. You know what that means, don't you?"

"Yes," Carrie said grimly. "Drum was planning to take him with him into hiding that morning. If I hadn't happened to show up when I did, he might have pulled it off, too. They could have been anywhere in the world by now. Makes me realize how sharp your partner is. Heather had just finished telling me she was worried about the possibility of Drum kidnapping Jonah. I break into a cold sweat just thinking about what almost happened. That's why I can't help worrying he might be back."

"You should just try to relax, kiddo, take this one step at a time."

"Relax? Ha!" Carrie reached back for one of the mugs hanging under the kitchen cabinets and lifted the coffee thermos, pouring out a cupful. "Do you want a refill? I'm going to run this tray up to Althea and see how she's doing this morning."

"No, you go ahead, I'm fine," Tracy said. "I'll go watch the pirates. Maybe they'll let me swab the deck."

Her mother-in-law's door was closed when Carrie went up the stairs with the breakfast tray, but when she knocked softly and got a mumbled response, she entered to find Althea out of bed, dressed in a sleeveless yellow linen shift, sitting at her skirted dressing table and trying to fasten a string of Mallorca pearls around her neck. The flesh under her pale, stout arms jiggled as she struggled with the catch. The room, done up in dark blue floral motif, smelled as flowery as it looked. Althea's hair had been teased and sprayed into the white helmet she usually presented to the world, and a shaky line of pink lipstick ran across and beyond the line of her thin, disapproving lips.

"You look nice this morning," Carrie said, setting the tray

on a padded settee at the end of the narrow four-poster bed. "Here, can I help you with that?"

Althea tried to hook the catch once more, then gave up with an exasperated sigh. "Oh, all right. I'm all thumbs. I just can't seem to get the blessed thing done up."

Carrie took the two ends of the pearls from her arthritic hands. When she slipped them together and locked the catch on the first try, Althea shot an irritated look at her daughter-in-law's reflection in the mirror.

"I always find those things hard to do up on myself, too," Carrie said.

"They make them too small."

"Yes, they do. How's your migraine this morning?"

"Better. Still there, but not so bad."

"I'm glad. That dress is a good color on you. And you've got your nice pearls on, too. Were you planning to go out this morning? It's raining, you know."

"I know. No, I'm not going anywhere. It doesn't do to look dowdy when there are strangers in the house. These people need to keep in mind who they're dealing with."

Althea glanced up once more, frowning at their reflections. Carrie checked herself out in the mirror—sandy red hair pulled back in a quick ponytail, flour-dusted green apron tied over an orange tank top and white clam diggers, old leather clogs on her feet. Definitely dowdy, especially next to linen and pearls—and, Carrie noted, looking down, tan pumps on her mother-in-law's feet. She'd even put on panty hose this morning.

"What are they doing down there, anyway?" Althea grumbled. "Surely they should have finished by now? Why don't they just leave? When Naughton was alive, they wouldn't have dared barge in here like this, throwing around these wild accusations."

"They seem pretty intent on finding something down there," Carrie said, "and the warrant seems to give them the authority to take as much time as they need to do it."

"It's not right. I feel like a prisoner in my own home."

"I don't think we're required to stay put. I haven't been out for the past few days because of Jonah's cold, but it's not like we're under house arrest or anything. You and I haven't done anything wrong."

"Oh, and Drummond has? Is that what you're saying?"

"No. I don't know that for sure—although it would be nice to have some idea what he's up to. You're sure he didn't mention anything to you that might shed some light on why he's run off like this?"

"I don't believe he's run off. They're just saying that. Drummond wouldn't do anything illegal. He's just...I don't know...gone away for a while, I suppose, to think things over."

"What things?"

Althea turned on her. "Well, I should think *you'd* be the one to say, Carrie. I certainly don't know what was going on between the two of you. I know about the lawyer, though. And that friend of yours—Tracy. She's here again, isn't she? Why is she always here? And that was her partner you had an appointment with the day Drummond went away. I'm not totally senile, you know."

"I never said you were."

"Oh, no, but you think it."

"No, I don't think it at all. Look, I brought you some coffee and a light breakfast. Shall I put it here on the dressing table?"

"Eat? At a time like this? I couldn't possibly."

"Well..." Carrie hesitated. "I'll just leave it, then, in case you change your mind."

Althea watched her in the mirror, her gnarled hands shredding a tissue. "I don't understand," she fretted. "I don't understand any of it. Why is this happening? And why on earth did he marry you?"

Carrie had started for the door, but she stopped and pivoted. "Excuse me?"

"Why did he marry you? Did you tell him you were pregnant and then proceed to have a convenient eleven-month pregnancy?"

"That's a rude question, don't you think? Especially after all this time, and with your grandson right downstairs?"

"I'm just curious. You weren't the right woman for Drummond, anyone could see that. He had such poor judgment. First Theresa, who, Lord knows, was as neurotic as they come—although she, at least, was the daughter of an ambassador, so she might have been expected to know things required of someone in her position. She was a sulker, though. Spoiled. Always in a snit about something until finally— well, she did it to punish him, you know."

"Drum said they ruled her drowning an accident."

Althea gave an irritable wave. "An accident—well, in a manner of speaking, maybe. She'd been drinking, but there was nothing new in that. She'd taken pills with booze once before—tranquilizers—but Drummond found her in time and got her to hospital. Had to have her stomach pumped, but, oh, didn't she love all the attention? Poor, sad, misunderstood Theresa. She probably thought he'd rescue her again that night, but he was working late. Then that storm blew up and she got caught out on the river. Stupid girl. Stupid, selfish girl." Althea sighed heavily. "And then, you. I could tell as soon as he brought you home from Africa that he wished he hadn't gotten himself tied down. But by then, of course, there was the baby, so what could he do? He looked dreadful when he came back home, I thought. I'd told him not to rush into another marriage, but what could I do?"

"Oh, Althea," Carrie sighed wearily. "We got married because we fell in love, improbable as that may seem to you. Not because I seduced him or tricked him or anything else. I loved him. I thought he loved me. And if he was stressed when we came back to the States that time, he had good reason to be. The embassy in Tanzania had been bombed. You know that. You know Drum and I were both in the building the morning it happened. It was a horrible day. And afterward, he felt he had to answer for the security lapses that allowed the bombing to happen in the first place."

"It wasn't his fault."

"No, of course it wasn't. It was a string of bad luck and lack of foresight right across the board, here and overseas. But that didn't change the fact that Drum felt, rightly or wrongly, that he was being put on the hot seat. He was under a lot of strain, but it's hardly fair to blame me for everything, don't you think?"

And yet, Carrie thought, it was almost as if Drum, too, had blamed her—not for the bombing, of course, but for having had the bad taste to see him panic afterward. He'd hardly been able to look her in the eye for months, and the resentment seemed to have festered in him ever since.

"A better helpmate would have supported him through it," Althea said. "His father went through crises, too. Korea, Vietnam. And we had other problems, as well, over the years. Despite appearances to the contrary, things weren't always perfect with Naughton and me, you know. But I always stood behind him, kept the home fires burning. That was my job. That's what a wife is supposed to do, and I'm not a complainer. Never have been."

"I did what I could, too, Althea. I really did. Maybe it wasn't enough. I don't know."

"Ha. You were going to leave him, weren't you?"

Carrie hesitated again and considered denying it, but what would be the point? "I was thinking about it," she said, nodding. "I wanted us to go for marriage counseling, but Drum refused. At this point, I was out of ideas, so yes, I thought it might be better if we separated."

"And so now, if anything has happened to him, you think you're home free, do you?"

Carrie felt the blood drain from her face. "I'm not going to dignify that with a response. I know you're worried about Drum and upset about everything that's going on—all these people barging into your home, tearing things apart—so I won't—"

"You think you'll get the house. Get Drummond's money. Put me out in the street, too, I suppose."

"Nobody's putting you out on the street. For God's sake, Althea, lower your voice and get a grip. Jonah's downstairs in the kitchen. I don't want him hearing nonsense like this from his Nana. Look, you're obviously upset, so I'll leave you alone. If you need anything, just call. If you want to get out of here for a while, visit friends or do some shopping, that's probably a good idea. I'm sure nobody would object and you'd feel better for it. We've all been cooped up too long and we're under a lot of stress. Just try to relax, all right?"

Her mother-in-law only glared at her in the mirror. Carrie hesitated for a moment, then gave up, turned and walked out. She was halfway down the stairs when a flash of yellow linen appeared at the railing overhead.

"You wanted to leave?" the older woman screamed, her voice quavering with rage. "So leave! Nobody's stopping you! Just don't think you're fooling anyone, Carrie, because you don't fool me for one minute!"

Carrie's face was burning when she slipped past the cotton-gloved federal agents who'd come out into the hall, hammers and crowbars in hand, their work interrupted by the commotion. They stared at her curiously, then up the stairs. Carrie gave them an irritable wave and headed down the short passage to the kitchen.

Tracy met her at the door. "Well, that sounds like it went well," she murmured.

"No kidding." Carrie glanced over to the solarium across the room, where Jonah, oblivious, was swinging his pirate Spider-Man across the net of twine that he and Huxley had strung between the chairs and the latches on the windows. The Brit, however, was nowhere to be seen. She turned back to her friend. "Dammit, Trace, she's under a lot of strain and I'm sorry for that, but so am I. I'm not sure I can handle being around her anymore."

"You don't have to. I told you, my parents said you're more than welcome to use their house in Georgetown."

"I'm really tempted to take you up on the offer, too, but the feds are telling me to stay put. I can't do it, though. It's not fair—to me, to Jonah. Not even to Althea. If we can't help each other get through this, then there's no point in my being here. School starts in a couple of weeks. If Jonah's not going to do first grade in McLean, then I need to get him registered somewhere else. I'm out of time. This has to be taken care of now."

"I think you're right," Tracy said. "I was talking to that English guy while you were upstairs with the dragon lady. We've come up with an idea. He's gone across the road to try to sell it to the big fellow from CIA Security and the Bureau guy. Come on in and sit down, Carrie. Let me pour you a fresh cup of coffee and I'll tell you what we were thinking."

CHAPTER EIGHTEEN

McLean, Virginia
August 17, 2002—12:22 p.m.

Huxley paced back and forth across Bernice Klein's sculpted pink Chinese living room carpet. "I think we should let her take the boy and get out of there. Maybe MacNeil's coming back for the kid, maybe he's not. But if he is, we should force him to make his move on turf we control."

"We control the ground right here," Andrews said. The FBI supervisor was sitting on the Kleins' overstuffed sofa, flipping through documents, sorting them into cardboard storage boxes marked "MacNeil—Bank Statements," "MacNeil—Stock portfolios," "MacNeil—Real Estate Holdings." All the financial records from the house across the road were being readied for shipment to the Bureau's forensic accounting specialists, who would study them line by line in an effort to spot the smoking gun—hard, prosecutable evidence that Drummond MacNeil had received payoffs for intelligence he'd leaked to the Zurich broker they already knew had been reselling western security secrets to a well-bankrolled assortment of enemy states and terrorist organizations.

"MacNeil knew he was under surveillance," Huxley argued. "That's why he took off the other day. This is his turf, and somehow, he twigged to it. We could sit here from now till doomsday. If he does decide to come back for the boy, he'll bide his time, then grab him a few months down the road from school or a park or a playmate's house. In the meantime, that old crone across the road is making her daughter-in-law miserable."

"Hey, my heart bleeds," Andrews said. "Look, she made her bed when she married MacNeil. Now she has to lie in it. Tough luck."

"Not the little boy's fault, though," Tucker said quietly.

The old bruiser from the CIA was sifting through a box containing the contents of the Jaguar MacNeil had abandoned at Tyson's Corner, mostly insurance papers and maintenance records, it would seem. But he paused, frowning as he smoothed out one piece of crumpled paper pulled from the bottom of the box, then set it aside.

"I tend to agree with Huxley," Tucker added, looking up. "We've done the background security check on Tracy Overturf and her parents. There's no red flags there. I had an answer back from our station in Rome, by the way. The parents are right where she said they'd be, camped out in a rented villa in Tuscany. Mom's an English prof at Georgetown University, using her sabbatical year to put the finishing touches on a novel. Dad teaches Romance Languages and is apparently a gourmet cook on the side. Our station over there says he's doing the rounds of Tuscan inns, gathering recipes, writing a kitchen guide of the region." Tucker held up a dog-eared issue of *Bon Appetit.* "I found an article here that Professor John Overturf did a couple of years ago. It's on Italian cooking class vacations abroad. Probably sparked the idea for his book."

Huxley smiled to himself. Trust Tucker to have uncovered that little detail. That was something else Huxley had learned about his gruff colleague in the months they'd been working surveillance together. Tucker was something of a gourmet himself, as evidenced by some of the meals he'd whipped up right here in Bernice Klein's well-stocked kitchen. Huxley and Tengwall both thought they'd gained weight on this job.

"I was talking to Ms. Overturf just now," Huxley added. "She said the reason her parents didn't rent out their house while they're away is because it's needing some work. They didn't think a renter would want to put up with the bother of having carpenters underfoot. If Mrs. MacNeil and her son were house-sitting, though, that might provide a handy cover to keep someone inside the place."

"You have anyone in particular in mind?" Andrews asked.

Huxley shrugged. "Me old dad's a joiner. Been around hammer and saw all my life. Depends what needs doing, but I could make a passing fair stab at the job."

Andrews smirked. "So you're volunteering to baby-sit the lovely Mrs. MacNeil?"

"For a bit, maybe, until we decide whether it's worth the candle or not. My brief—which both your front offices have signed off on, by the way—is to stay on top of this until Mac-Neil turns up, dead or alive. It's not like I'm over-employed at the moment. I'd like to earn my keep."

"You know, that's what I like about the cousins," Tucker said, grinning to Andrews, "you can always count on 'em to pitch and help with the dirty work."

"Here, now," Huxley protested. "Who was it held Hitler and the real bloody 'Axis of Evil' at bay for three years while you lot sat back and filed your nails, then?"

Tucker played an imaginary violin.

"We'll see about letting Mrs. MacNeil move out and how that might unfold," Andrews said. "Before she does, though, I'll want the place in Georgetown checked out from top to bottom."

"Meantime," Tucker said, picking up the crumpled paper he'd set aside, "did you see this?"

"What's that?"

"A letter from the brokerage firm handling Carrie's investment account from her parents' estate. You remember she said she had her own money to live on so she wouldn't need alimony if she divorced MacNeil?"

"Yeah? So?" Andews cocked his thumb at the boxes of paper. "We've got her brokerage statements. Looks like there's just over a million-four there, including a decade's worth of accumulated interest. Most of it's in bonds and mutual funds. Fairly conservative stuff."

"It was," Tucker said.

"What do you mean, 'was'?"

"I just came across this letter from her broker. It was under the seat in MacNeil's car, apparently. Seems to be a response to a request to liquidate her account, and it's dated July 28— three weeks ago."

"Why would MacNeil be carrying around a letter from her broker?" Huxley asked.

"Didn't she say that money was hers alone?" Andrews added.

"The letter was addressed to her," Tucker said, handing it to Andrews. Huxley moved over onto the couch next to the FBI man to read over his shoulder. "It confirms that they've started liquidating the account as per her instructions."

Andrews scanned the letter and read, "'As requested, proceeds of your account have been divided into a series of laddered transmissions as scheduled to the accounts listed in the attachment to this letter (Annex A). These transmissions are to begin on this date and continue daily for the next eighteen weeks.'" Andrews flipped over the paper, scowling. "The attachment's missing."

"Yeah, but think about it. A series of daily financial transmissions over eighteen weeks…" Tucker pulled a pen from his pocket and began scribbling on a piece of scrap paper. "That's…umm…one hundred and twenty-six individual cash transfers."

"No big deal, these days," Huxley said. "It's just a computer algorithm. You set it up once and the electronic banking networks handle the rest. I don't get it, though. Why dribble it out like that?"

Tucker was still calculating. "Because assuming the million-four and change was divided up into equal chunks, that would make each international transaction about….yup, just as I thought."

Andrew smacked his thigh. "Son of a bitch! Puts them under the ten thousand dollar mark that triggers the federal reporting requirement. Godammit! And you guys think she's not in on her husband's dirty dealing?"

"Wait a minute," Huxley said. "Even assuming that she is transferring her money offshore, it doesn't necessarily make her a co-conspirator with him." He waved a hand over the boxes strewn about the room. "We're looking for MacNeil's payoffs from the Zurich broker. This money came from her parents' estate. Maybe what was going on here is that each of them, unbeknownst to the other, was planning to take a scarper, only MacNeil beat her to the punch and got out of town first."

"Whatever," Andrews said. "Either way, she hasn't been truthful with us. There's obviously more going on here than meets the eye. I think I'd like to see how she explains herself on this one." He folded the broker's letter and got to his feet. Before the others could follow, a tinny bleat sounded from his hip pocket. The FBI man withdrew a cell phone and flipped it open. "What's up?...Shit. I'm on my way!" He jammed the phone back in his pocket and headed for the door.

Huxley and Tucker were close on his heels. "What happened?"

"Across the road," Andrews shouted, as he threw open Kleins' front door. "MacNeil's been spotted!"

The rain had let up and a brilliant summer sum was breaking through the black clouds that had hung over the city all morning. The air was turning steamy, as the pavement dried and puddles evaporated. The cicadas, which had sounded muted from inside the closed up houses, were piercingly loud out in the oak and sycamore trees that arched over Elcott Road, as if shrieking in delight at the rain's end.

Huxley, Tucker and Andrews sprinted across the street and up the MacNeils' white rock drive, taking the brick stairs at the front door two at a time. Inside, the front hall was empty, and as they wove from living room to dining room to den, looking for someone—anyone—they found the place apparently deserted. They ran down the short access hall to the kitchen. Rounding the corner, Andrews's wet, leather-soled shoes skidded on the glossy terrazzo flooring.

The kitchen was empty, too, but across the way, on the far side of the solarium, the French doors leading out to the terrace stood open to the early afternoon sunshine. On the sloping lawn beyond, leading down to the dock, they saw three agents in blue knit golf shirts with FBI stenciled in yellow across the back moving up and down the riverbank. Carrie MacNeil and her friend and son stood on the dock, peering downstream.

"What happened?" Andrews asked as they reached the edge of the lawn.

"I'm not sure," one of the agents said. "We were working in the den when we heard Mrs. MacNeil yell. When we came into the kitchen, she was already outside, chasing her little boy across the lawn. Her friend said the boy spotted MacNeil down by the dock."

"Shit," Andrews said. "Where's the outside detail? Did they see him?"

"They were in the garage. They'd been doing the rounds of the houses, but when the sun came out, they went to dump their hot rain gear in there. They couldn't have been inside more than a couple of minutes, though."

"Where are they now?"

The agent pointed to the riverbank, where two more agents were moving up and down through the tangled underbrush at the water's edge.

"For God's sake," Andrews said, disgusted. "Get on the radio, right away. Get a description out to the air patrol. I want overhead recon, stat."

Huxley was already down on the wooden dock, his eyes scanning the murky river. The rain had freshened the air, setting dust and washing down the summer-weary leaves, but on the water, bits of brown gunk and green algae could be seen floating just under the surface. In those moments when the breeze died a little, the Potomac breathed a ripe and slightly sour odor of decaying animal and vegetable material. You wouldn't want to take a swim in this soup, he thought.

Carrie, meantime, was down on one knee on the wooden dock, examining her son's leg. Jonah's gray-green eyes sparkled with unshed tears and his lower lip was trembling. Beneath his denim shorts, his shin was bleeding through a grass-stained abrasion.

"Hey, matey, are you all right?" Huxley asked.

Jonah shrugged unhappily. "I slipped. The grass was wet."

"Ouch. Yeah, that happens to me all the time. Is he okay?" Huxley added to the boy's mother, who was dabbing at the bleeding shin with a tissue.

"It's just a scrape," she said, but her voice, too, was quavering and her hand was shaking. With mother and son both struggling to maintain a brave face, it was hard to tell who was working harder not to upset the other.

"Here, let me." Huxley pulled a clean cotton handkerchief from his pocket and folded it lengthwise in half, then in half again. "Looks like that leg needs a pirate bandanna. Hold still. We'll just put this on until we can clean it up at the house, okay?"

He knelt in front of the little boy, who put a hand on his broad shoulder to steady himself while Huxley tied the handkerchief around the bloody shin. The mother had pulled out of his way, but as she hovered nearby, Huxley could almost feel her nerves thrumming and hear her heart pounding in her chest.

"So, Jonah," he said, keeping his eyes down on the loose

knot he was fastening, "what did you see that set you off running like that?"

"I saw my dad. He was in a boat, a real fast one."

"A motorboat, hmm? What color was it?"

"I think it was black. And it had a stripe on the side."

"Like a racing stripe?"

"Yeah. And a roof and everything."

"No kidding. That sounds like quite a rig. And was your dad running it?"

"Uh-huh. I was at the window in the breakfast room, fixing our nets. That's when I looked out and saw him."

"You saw him pull up to the dock?"

"He was already there. The boat was just kind of bobbing on the water at the end. I think he came to give me a ride, Mark. He must've bought the boat today like he said. He told me we were gonna get one. Soon as I saw him, I yelled, but he couldn't hear me 'cause the windows were shut, so I ran to the door, but it was locked. After I got it open, I ran down, but the boat was already leaving and it was noisy, so he didn't hear me calling. And I fell, and he didn't see me." The six-year-old's composure finally abandoned him and he started to cry. "I wanted to go for a ride, Mom! How come he left? I wanted to go for a ride in the boat!"

Carrie crouched down next to him and brushed his sandy red curls back from his sweaty forehead. "Shh! Sweetie, it's okay. I don't think it could have been Daddy. I told you, he's away on a business trip."

"No, it was him! He had hair just like Daddy, and sunglasses just like Daddy. And he was wearing a blue golf shirt, Mom, the one we bought him for Father's Day."

"Maybe it just looked like him and that's why he left? Because the man realized he was at the wrong dock? You think?"

"It was Daddy. I'm pretty sure it was..." A hint of doubt seemed to creep into his voice now, but maybe it was just frustration. In any case, the tears flowed freely and he threw his arms around his mother's neck.

Huxley watched as she rocked him, stroking his hair while her own nervous eyes darted up and down the river. Then she stood, lifting the little boy in her arms.

"Come on, sweetie," she said quietly, "let's go up to the house and put a purple Band-Aid on that leg." He wrapped his legs around her green apron, burying his face in her shoulder as she carried him back up the lawn and in through the solarium doors.

Tracy Overturf had followed the others down to the water's edge. She frowned at the men on the dock, now, then shaded her eyes as she, too, scanned the riverbanks, upstream, then down. Finally, head shaking, she went after her friend into the house.

Huxley and Andrews were sitting on bar stools at the baker's table when Carrie came back downstairs about half an hour later. Her mother-in-law had come down briefly to see what the commotion was about. Then, with a snort of disgust, she'd retreated upstairs to her room once more. Carrie had spotted her on her way down from the third floor, and she thought Althea had seen her, too, but her mother-in-law had marched into her bedroom without a word and slammed the door behind her.

Downstairs, Tucker stood over at the solarium windows, still watching the sun glint off the Potomac, watching fruitlessly for Drum's return. Tracy was emptying the dishwasher, and from the steam and the smell rising off the coffeemaker, Carrie concluded that her friend had put a fresh pot of coffee on to brew. Even with the house shut up once more against the saunalike heat and humidity that had descended like a wet towel after the rain, Carrie could hear the low thump-thump-thump of rotor blades as a helicopter made passes up and down the river.

Huxley looked up when she walked in. "Is the little guy all right?" he asked.

Carrie nodded. "I let him lie on my bed to watch cartoons and he fell asleep. He's still fighting that cold, and crying got him all crouped up again. He has problems with asthma, too, so when he gets upset like that, it doesn't help. He used his inhaler, though, and that seemed to help."

"The sleep will probably do him good," Tracy said.

Carrie turned to Andrews. "Did you find anything out there? Was it Drum?"

"I don't know. That's our search copter now, checking out the traffic on the river. We've got a patrol boat out, too, but so far, they haven't spotted him—if it *was* him," he added. "You think there's any chance the boy imagined it?"

"I don't know," Carrie said. "I was at the kitchen counter and I didn't realize anything had happened until I heard him yell as he struggled to get the patio door unlocked. The next think I know, he was running out the door and down the lawn. If there was a boat, I didn't see it. I've never known Jonah to make up stories before, though."

"There was *something* there," Tracy said firmly. "I saw a wave sloshing around the dock. Some kind of boat had to have gone by, but I couldn't see anything through the willows on the banks. Jonah's a bright little guy," she added. "I mean, look at the level of detail—he remembered that the man he saw had hair like his dad and sunglasses like his dad. Even a similar golf shirt, for crying out loud. I've seen people convicted in criminal cases on less complete witness testimony."

"Lots of men wear golf shirts and sunglasses, Ms. Overturf, especially in boats."

Tracy's shoulders assumed a stubborn square. "Jonah wouldn't say there was someone there if there wasn't."

"But you didn't see this boat yourself?" Andrews asked. "And you didn't, either, Mrs. MacNeil?"

They both shook their heads, but Tracy wasn't backing down. "I think it's time Carrie move somewhere safer and more comfortable. The situation here sucks, to put it bluntly. It's not secure, and it certainly isn't a happy or stable environment for a six-year-old, especially with Cruella De Vil up there on a rampage the way she is. As her lawyer, I've advised Carrie she's under no legal obligation to stay in this house. As her friend, I insist you people back off. Let her do what's best for her little boy. Whatever Drum has or hasn't been up to, you've got no grounds to be casting suspicion on his family and making their lives miserable like this."

Tucker stepped forward, a deep frown bisecting the high dome of his forehead. "I don't know about that," he said. "Mrs. MacNeil, did you not tell Agent Andrews the other day that the reason you weren't going to ask for alimony if you divorced your husband is that you had resources of your own to fall back on?"

"That's right," Carrie said.

"An investment account, I believe you said. Was that being managed by the Stanley-May brokerage house?"

"That's right. My father used them for years. Why?"

"And you said the account was in your name alone, I believe. That your husband had no interest in it."

"No, no interest at all, legally or otherwise. When tech

stocks started to tank a few years back, I asked Drum where he thought I should move my money. Stocks and bonds weren't exactly my forte, either, even though I'd done a business minor as an undergrad. I always ducked the courses on financial markets. It was the art markets I cared about. And Drum was even less inclined to deal with that stuff than I was. I could have been asking him what brand of panty hose to buy, for all the interest he showed. Finance made his eyes glaze over. He told me to call the brokers, tell them I wanted to park the money in some conservative shelter and ride out the storm. That's more or less what I did."

"So you parked the money and you haven't touched it since?"

"That's right."

"No, I don't think so," Andrews said. He withdrew a folded piece of paper from his pocket. "You've been in the process as we speak of quietly cashing out and moving your money offshore."

"What? No way!" Carrie said indignantly. "I told you, I haven't touched that money since I got married."

"That's not what this letter from your broker says."

"What letter?" Carrie took the letter from his hand and read it, then sank onto one of the bar stools.

"Carrie? What is it?" Tracy asked, coming around the island.

Carrie handed her the letter. "It's not true, Tracy. I didn't order this. Where did you find this letter?" she asked Andrews.

"Among your husband's things. The annex is missing, though. How convenient. Won't do you any good, though. We'll find out where the accounts are."

"But these transactions are still underway," Tracy said, re-

reading the letter. She looked up angrily. "It's obvious what's happened. Drum forged her signature and set out to steal her money. But it's not too late to stop it, Carrie. You need to call the brokerage right now and terminate these transfers. With luck, you can even get the ones that have already gone through reversed."

Carrie took a step toward the phone mounted on the kitchen's brick wall, but Andrews held up a hand.

"Don't bother, Mrs. MacNeil. I've already got my people working on a warrant to freeze your accounts and seize your broker's files. The rest of your money's not going to be leaving the country any time soon, and neither are you. If you want to move your son over to Georgetown, we might consider that. But Georgetown is as far as I'm prepared to see you go until we get to the bottom of this."

CHAPTER NINETEEN

The next few days were the most uncomfortable of Carrie's life, with the exception of the period immediately following the death of her parents and sister. With Tracy's cautious agreement, she agreed to submit to a polygraph examination in which she was grilled on everything from her financial dealings to her sex life—both pretty much nonexistent, she was able to say and apparently pass electronic muster. Her personal correspondence was examined and retained for analysis, both content and handwriting. Her closets and drawers and jewelry box were pulled apart for evidence of recent purchases or other evidence of plans to skip the country.

Federal agents delved into every aspect of her life, and no matter how much Carrie argued that there was no evidence to be found, she got the distinct impression she was guilty until proven innocent—of what, she wasn't sure. As for the letter of instruction to her financial broker, Carrie could get nothing out of Agent Andrews, who seemed to have warned Tucker and Huxley, too, against telling her what they'd decided about that business. The broker, when she quietly telephoned, wouldn't take her call. Obviously, he, too, had been warned about colluding with shifty redheads.

Finally, though, Andrews agreed to let her take Jonah and move across the river into Tracy's parents' house in Georgetown. She could only hope that meant they'd decided she wasn't lying about not having instructed the broker to send her money overseas.

Drum, meantime, made no return appearances—if it had indeed been him Jonah had seen at the dock that morning. Jonah was bitterly disappointed, but as he and Carrie made plans to move yet again, he seemed to sense the pressure she was under and the fear she was feeling, and he never mentioned his father's name again.

With Althea not speaking to her in earnest now—not merely grumbling, as she had since Drum's disappearance, but responding with icy silence to all approaches—Carrie was down to Jonah and Tracy as her last remaining allies in her battle to hang on to her good name and her sanity. And, she conceded, maybe Huxley, who was kind to Jonah and reasonably polite to her—although he was probably just playing good cop to Andrews's and Tucker's bad. Since he was the only bright point in poor Jonah's long days, though, Carrie was willing to give the Brit the benefit of the doubt. She might as well. She needed all the foul-weather friends she could get.

The feds seemed to have backed off a little for the moment, but it was small enough comfort, given that she was effectively broke, abandoned, and still under suspicion of God only knew what.

"But it's a bit like being repeatedly poked in the eye with a stick," she told Tracy the day she and Jonah were finally given the go-ahead to relocate across the Potomac to Georgetown. "It feels so good when it finally stops that you almost forget you're bleeding, blind, and a butt ugly pariah to the rest of the world."

Washington, D.C. (Georgetown)
October 27, 2002—9:25 a.m.

Sunday morning, and a cool breeze wafted through the tall windows that Carrie had flung wide open that morning, setting the creamy shears in the Overturfs' front rooms to dancing like drunken wraiths. Somewhere nearby, somebody had a fireplace lit—or was burning leaves, maybe. Were people allowed to do that anymore? Whatever it was, the air carried that smoky autumn undertone that always made Carrie's heart skip a beat.

For the first time in weeks, she found herself humming under her breath as she moved from room to room, tidying the clutter that seemed unavoidable when you lived with a six-year-old. She pulled a rag from the back hip pocket of her jeans and dusted surfaces in each room she passed through, liberating them temporarily from the perpetual film that seemed to accompany the renovation work being carried out in Tracy's parents' absence.

Other people, when asked to name their favorite season, might choose spring with its green promise of rebirth or maybe "those lazy, hazy, crazy days of summer." For her part, Carrie thought, give her a crisp fall day any time to spark hopes for new beginnings and better days to come. This warm fuzzy feeling was probably rooted in her happy childhood, she decided, when her mother would take her and Izzie shopping for matching back-to-school outfits as Labor Day approached. Then it was lunch at Anderson's Pea Soup, with its full-size, turning windmill, and on to their father's drug store, where each twin would be allowed to wheel her own shopping cart through the school supply aisles, picking out shiny lunch boxes and pencil cases and all their other goodies for the coming school year. Best of all were the new crayons, one big box for each girl because their dad owned the store, so no need to settle for smaller packages of twelve or twenty-four. For the Morgan twins, only sixty-four brilliant colors with a built-in sharpener in the bottom of the box would do.

After Jonah's first day at Elmwood Elementary, Carrie took Jonah shopping for supplies on the list his new teacher had sent home. As they walked through the aisles at the Georgetown branch of Staples, Jonah paused and gave her a very strange look when he caught her sniffing Crayolas. "What are you smelling the crayons for?"

"Because they smell hopeful," Carrie told him, closing her eyes and inhaling the innocent, waxy smell of indigo, cerulean and apple-green.

"Hopeful?"

"Uh-huh. Like a promise that anything's possible. That the future belongs to you, if you believe in it and commit yourself to it with all your heart." She held up a notebook and riffled the pages under his nose. "Newsprint, too. The smell of it, and all those nice, clean blue lines. A big, fat promise that it's a new day and ours to make the most of."

"Mom?"

"What?"

"You're really weird, you know that?" He moved ahead of her in the aisle, distancing himself, curly head shaking as he passed Tengwall, who'd accompanied them that morning while Huxley hung back at the house. If the FBI was keeping its distance, it didn't mean that Carrie had been completely abandoned by the watchdogs.

Tengwall laughed at the dramatic roll of his big gray-green eyes. "Oops. What was that about?"

"It's happened," Carrie said ruefully, as she pulled her cart alongside the young woman. "I've made the transition from 'she who can do no wrong' to 'she who suffers from terminal dorkiness.'"

"Bound to happen, I guess. Past a certain point, parents are uncool by definition."

"Tell me about it. We're into the 'my teacher knows everything' phase now. As if I didn't already feel like a complete idiot, after totally screwing up my life to date, now I get a daily reminder from a six-year-old."

"You think it's bad now. Wait till he gets to be a teenager."

"Oh, joy," Carrie had said ruefully.

But that Sunday morning, it was impossible not to feel cheerful. The air felt especially cool and refreshing after a long, oppressively muggy summer that she'd feared would never end.

Objectively speaking, she had little enough reason for optimism. Drum was still AWOL, a third of her savings had vanished into offshore accounts, the rest was in legal limbo, and she and Jonah were only temporarily settled in digs that sometimes felt more like a construction site than a home. Yet, despite the uncertainty of her situation, Carrie had been finding herself more and more often irrationally upbeat—for brief stretches, at least, until reality crashed in on her once again and she remembered that she was effectively broke, adrift, abandoned, and under suspicion of God only knew what. She was working on developing Zenlike patience, though. She might as well, since at this point, the situation was largely out of her control. All she could do was take care of her son and try to come up with a workable plan for managing on her own while she waited to see what developed on the legal front.

She moved into the dining room, gathering up Jonah's crayons and paper. Already reading, thanks to the advanced kindergarten experience he'd had at the International School in London, he'd been honing his skills on the daily comics in the *Washington Post*. The night before, he'd decided that his ambition was to draw the Peanuts trip. His first efforts at Snoopy and Company were still scattered across the long oak trestle table. Carrie smiled as she stacked them on the side buffet, picking out a couple to stick to the kitchen refrigerator, then pulling out her dust rag to wipe down the table. Tracy's mom, who taught nineteenth-century lit in Georgetown's English Department, was an avid collector of antiques, and the two-hundred-year-old trestle table had once seen service in the dining room of the Jesuit fathers who'd founded the university on the hill. The stories this table could tell, Carrie thought, smiling as she ran a dust rag over its deep, golden grain.

As much as she'd hesitated to uproot Jonah once again, she should have known the move to Georgetown would work. This house had always been lucky for her. It felt like a special trust, caring for it while Tracy's parents were away on sabbatical. From the time she'd first arrived at Georgetown University and discovered that her assigned roommate was the daughter of two popular professors, she'd always felt welcome in the big old place on O Street. That fall of her freshman year, despite battling homesickness and missing her left-behind twin, she'd fallen happily into the routine of Sunday night dinner with the shifting crowd of students, professors, neighbors and relatives who always seemed to show up for Tracy's dad's hearty concoctions.

And then, there was the sheer comfort of being back in Georgetown again, with its quaint brick and stone houses, arching trees and funky shops. Although the area's fortunes had risen, fallen, then risen again in the past three centuries, physically it was little changed from its earliest days as a tobacco port town. Take away the cars from the narrow streets and the bright signage of the trendy coffeehouses and fashionable eateries, and Thomas Jefferson would probably still recognize Georgetown—named not for the first President, as many people believed, but for the mad English king who'd lost America for his heirs.

The Overturfs' three-story house was federal-style, tall, narrow and deep, constructed of red-brown bricks that had been formed, like most of those in Georgetown, from the very soil on which the house had been built. Built in 1801 by a tobacco trader, the single family home had been converted to apartments in the late 1800s, and was a rundown tenement when Tracy's parents had bought it nearly thirty years earlier. Now, after years of renters and renovations, they were almost done converting it back to its original residential elegance.

Carrie moved out of the dining room and across the hall into the library. After her parents and sister had died, the Overturfs had practically adopted her. She'd even lived with them that first summer after the fire, when going back to California had seemed terrifying and unthinkable in so many ways. Now, this big old house on O Street had become a safe haven once again as she tried to put her shattered life back together.

She picked up a glass Jonah had left next to the computer on the library desk, pausing to turn off the machine. He'd been playing a Star Wars game when she'd come downstairs a short while earlier to make his breakfast. The computer belonged to Tracy's parents, and the game was one Tracy had bought as a welcome gift when Carrie and Jonah had moved in at the end of August. Their own computer and Jonah's games were still impounded by the FBI as they searched for hard evidence of Drum's treachery—being none too quick about it, Carrie thought, reminding herself to ask Agent Andrews when they planned to return her machine.

Coming out of the library to return Jonah's glass to the kitchen, she nearly collided with Huxley, who'd appeared out of nowhere. "Yikes!" she cried. "I didn't know you were here."

She'd accepted by now that they were under twenty-four-hour-a-day surveillance, even when she couldn't spot the agents tailing them, but Huxley's comings and goings seemed to follow no particular schedule, as if he thought the element of surprise might somehow encourage Drum to appear out of thin air. As it was, barring the unexplained incident at the Elcott Road dock, there'd been no confirmed sightings of her husband since the morning he'd given Huxley the slip at Tyson's Corner. As for missing him, Drum had been around so little even before his disappearing act that neither Carrie nor Jonah really noticed he was gone. If it hadn't been for worrying he might still show up to claim Jonah, Carrie might almost have been able to relax and accept that Drum was out of their lives for good. It was grim but revealing evidence of how hollow the marriage had become, Carrie thought, that its ending cast so little shadow over her heart.

Huxley stepped aside awkwardly in the doorway, weighed down by a heavy canvas sheet, rags, brushes and what appeared to be a can of paint. "Sorry," he said. "Didn't mean to startle you."

"No, you go ahead," she countered, pulling back into the room. "You're more loaded down than I am."

"Yeah, well, thanks," he grunted, coming through the doorway.

He set the supplies down and proceeded to spread the drop cloth over the hardwood in front of the floor-to-ceiling bookshelves that ran along one entire wall. The shelves were empty, stripped and sanded down to the original oak in readiness for staining and varnishing.

"I didn't know you were planning to be here this morning," Carrie said. "It's Sunday. Don't you ever get a day off?"

For a few moments there, she'd almost allowed herself to forget he and Tucker and Tengwall were still underfoot, much less what their presence signified—Drum, betrayal, suspicion, her life in disarray. In England during World War II, she'd read, there had been a period between the declaration of war in the fall of 1939 and the beginning of the Blitz in the summer of 1940 when the idea of battle had seemed a little unreal, as if the newspapers had made up the whole thing in a bid to boost circulation. The Phony War, people called it—until the bombs started to fall and it became gruesomely real.

She was living in her own personal Phony War these days, a deceptive lull between Drum's defection and the legal firestorm that was bound to erupt when he was eventually tracked down, as he surely would be sooner or later. Meantime, the ongoing presence of Huxley and the two CIA watchers, as well as the periodic reappearance of FBI Agent Andrews with more questions to which she had no answers only served to remind Carrie that the battle lines drawn by Drum's defection had yet to be crossed.

Huxley pulled a hammer out of the tan carpenter's apron knotted around his waist. He was dressed in a paint-spotted black T-shirt, stained jeans and his ever-present combat boots.

"I thought I'd get at this first thing." He glanced around. "Where's Jonah?"

"Upstairs, taking a shower—theoretically, at least, if he hasn't been distracted. I heard water running a few minutes ago, but that's no guarantee of anything. He sees his toys or has an idea for a new game, and the next thing I know he's engrossed and completely forgets what he's supposed to be doing. Spider-Man could be deep-sea diving in the bathtub, for all I know."

"The two of you are going out this morning, I hear?"

"Shortly."

"And where was it you're going?"

"The National Cathedral. Tom Bent's father-in-law—you remember Bent, the CIA Liaison Director?"

Huxley nodded.

"Right, well, anyway, his father-in-law is bishop at the National Cathedral. There's a special service this morning to mark the fifty-year anniversary of his ordination."

"Well, so much the better. I'll be able to get at this while the two of you are out of the house." He dropped onto one knee, using the claw end of the hammer to pry the lid off the can. "What time are you leaving?"

Carrie glanced at her watch. "In about half an hour. The service starts at eleven. You could come along if you wanted—not that you guys need an invitation, of course. But if you haven't seen it before, the cathedral's quite a spectacular building, a tourist draw in its own right." She shrugged. "Of course, it's not old or anything. It was only finished in the mid-1990s, and it's modeled on the sort of Gothic extravaganza you're used to, anyway, I suppose, with all the nice cathedrals you have back in England. Seen one, seen 'em all, right?"

"I'm sure it's very nice, but I'd better get at this while the weather holds and the windows are open. I don't know if the fumes will bother Jonah, but they're calling for rain in the next couple of days, so just in case…"

"Right. Should I move the computer out of the way?"

"I'll toss a drop cloth over it. It should be all right."

She nodded. He seemed to be waiting for her to leave, but instead, she settled on one corner of the heavy oak library desk. He hesitated a moment, but when she didn't explain herself, he just frowned and turned away. A man of few words, Carrie thought—unlike Drum.

Drum's voice was deep, mellow, FM-quality, and he's always likes to hear himself talk. His height and good looks telegraphed authority, too, so that people tended to hang off his words. The brightest ones figured out pretty quickly that the whole was less than the sum of the parts where Drummond MacNeil was concerned, but the average person, herself included, took a little longer to tumble to the fact that Drum was nobody's best friend but his own.

Huxley, by contrast, was positively taciturn—around her, at least, although he seemed relaxed and chatty enough with Tucker and Tengwall. With Jonah, too. But whenever the two of them were alone, Carrie noted, Huxley retreated into a shell of disapproval. She watched him work, the sleeves of his spattered black T-shirt stretching taut over his upper arms as he pried the lid off the can and began stirring the contents. A metallic paint smell rose from the dark honey stain. Huxley was shorter than Drum, dense and muscular, with weathered features like someone who'd spent a lot of time outdoors. But doing what? Carrie wondered. She had no idea.

In the eight weeks since she and Jonah had moved over to Georgetown, the Brit had been nothing but kind to her son, nothing but cool toward her—tarring her, she suspected, with the same black motives as her husband. Hardly fair, since she was as much a victim of Drum's duplicity as everyone else who'd foolishly trusted him. More so, in fact—although what did that make her except outstandingly stupid? No wonder Huxley had so little respect.

"So," she ventured, "you're not on surveillance duty today?"

"Not today, no. Tengwall will be along shortly. She'll drive you and Jonah to your event and stay with you there."

Carrie frowned. "So, we do still get baby-sat. And you're going to stay back here to stain bookshelves?"

"That's right."

"Okay," she said slowly, watching the top of his fair, wooly head as he stirred the stain.

The tone of her voice made him glance up. "What?"

"Nothing. It's just…look, forgive me, I don't mean to snoop, but this is a little confusing."

"What's confusing?"

"You. Here. I mean, don't you have anything better to be doing?"

"Worried about the waste of British tax dollars, then, are you?"

"I'm just not quite sure what your real job is, Huxley. Are you just liaising with your CIA brothers over here? Looking to nab Drum for the greater glory of MI-6? Watching me in case I decide to skip out of town, too, with God-only-knows what deep, dark secrets? Or are you really just a frustrated woodworker passing yourself off as an international spy?"

"All of the above, I guess."

"Don't you have anyone back in England who wonders where you are?"

"Sorry?"

"Family…a wife, children. I notice you seem to like kids. You've been really good to Jonah during all of this, by the way. I want you to know I appreciate it."

"Jonah's easy to like. He's a fine young fellow." Huxley looked up at her sideways. "You're doing a good job with him," he said.

It was just about killing him to say it, too, Carrie noticed. But there was no point in confirming his worst suspicions about her by pointing out his all-too-evident reluctance to let a friendly word pass from those stubborn lips to her compliment-starved ear. "Thanks," was all she said. "So, you didn't answer my question. Do you? Have family back in England?" she added when he pretended to forget what she'd asked.

"I have my mum and dad, and a brother."

"In Yorkshire?"

He glanced up, eyebrows raised. "Yeah. Bravo. Not many Yanks would figure that out."

"Ah, well, accents. It's a talent, I guess. Not a terribly useful one, but there you go. Story of my life." She pursed her lips. "So, Mr. Huxley is a Yorkshireman, he has a mum and a dad still living. And a brother. But he's not married?"

"Not. Not anymore, at least."

"Aha, I see. Another marriage bites the dust, falling victim to the demands of the global espionage. It's a dirty job, but you guys have to do it, right?"

Huxley said nothing, only grimaced and went back to stirring the thick, viscous liquid in the can.

"And so this week," Carrie went on, "you've been assigned to spend your Sunday morning staining shelves and—what? Planting bugs? Is that why you're really hanging back here today?"

The lines in his weathered face deepened as he rested an elbow on one thigh and frowned up at her. "No. Nor microphones or cameras or any other surveillance devices. I'm staining these shelves...uh—" He lifted the tin and read the label "—deep golden brown, satin finish, because I said I'd do it as part of the deal with your friend for keeping the real workmen out of her folks' house while we watch over you lot and wait to see if that hubby of yours decides to show up again. And I'm doing this on what, technically, I guess, you could call a day off—or at least, a few hours off—because your son has asthma and the weather's cooperating. It seemed like a good idea not to leave it for a rainy day when the windows have to be shut up tight. Do you have a problem with that?"

Carrie felt her face go warm. "No, I don't. I appreciate it, actually."

"Well, good. Glad to hear it." He put the can back on the tarp and gathered up his brushes.

"It's going to be nice," Carrie said.

"What?"

"The stain. On the shelves."

"Oh, yeah." He glanced around the room. "It's quite the place, this." He glanced back at her. "Must be nice to have friends in high places. Bishops, CIA bigwigs, Georgetown profs with fancy digs. Me, I've never had that talent for cultivating the right people."

Carrie frowned, but ignored the personal dig. "Those friends—they've worked for what they've got. This place, for example. It didn't always look this good. It was a run-down tenement when the Overturfs bought it. I've seen pictures. The place was a dump. It had four ratty little apartments, and they lived in one with their three young kids while they rented out the others to pay off the mortgage. They only started renovating the place five or six years ago, and they've built up a lot of sweat equity in the place, turning the four apartments into two. My friend Tracy and her boyfriend lives in one, her parents in the other. It was only last year, when Tracy and Alan bought a place of their own over in Alexandria, that her folks decided to return the house to its original state."

Huxley only nodded.

She got to her feet again. "Anyway, I'd better go make sure Jonah's getting ready upstairs. Can I get you anything before we leave? Some coffee, or something to eat, maybe?"

"I've had my breakfast, thanks."

"Oh...well, all right. I'll let you know when we're leaving. We should be back by about one or one-thirty, at the latest."

"Oh, joy," he muttered.

He went back to stirring the nut brown liquid stain in the can. Carrie frowned at his back, then left, returned the glass to the kitchen and went upstairs, trying to remember what it felt like to have a life that wasn't under twenty-four-hour-a-day scrutiny by snippy Brits.

CHAPTER TWENTY

Washington National Cathedral
October 27, 2002—10:37 a.m.

Tom Bent phoned to make sure Carrie and Jonah had received their second official invitation to the special service marking his father-in-law's golden jubilee, and that they'd be coming. The first, apparently, had gotten "lost in the mail," although there was little doubt that it had actually arrived at Elcott Road but not been forwarded on by Althea to Carrie's new address in Georgetown. If Tom hadn't been keeping as close tabs on Carrie and his godson, the occasion might have passed without their even knowing about it.

So a few days after the second invitation went in the mail, Tom had followed up with a phone call, during which he'd told Carrie there would be a parking space held for her in the cathedral's staff lot. When Carrie and Jonah arrived at the cathedral that morning, she happily bypassed the long line of cars waiting to enter the main parking area and showed her ID to the traffic cop on duty, who directed her into the small lot on the north side of the cathedral.

As the Passat pulled in, Carrie saw Tom talking to a younger man outside a carved side door that she knew led directly to the cathedral's administrative offices. When he saw her, he smiled a welcome and pointed out an empty space nearby.

"Hey, Tom, thanks for the priority parking," Carrie said, climbing out of the car.

Tom gave a dismissive nod to the fellow at his side, who slipped off his sunglasses, followed the direction of Tom's gaze, then turned away and headed inside. He seemed vaguely familiar, she thought. Was this someone whose name she should know?

When she and Drum had first married, she'd felt gawky and shy on the diplomatic cocktail circuit, but her husband had been adamant on the importance of schmoozing and small talk and remembering the names and foibles of potentially useful people—so much so that it was a reflex now to slip into vigilance mode every time she found herself out in public, lest she commit some social faux pas that might embarrass him. But, Carrie thought, catching herself in mid-neurosis as she racked her brain to remember where she'd seen that man before, surely desertion was a fairly major breach of etiquette? And as for treason—well, also a bit of a social blooper, was it not?

If there was one, small silver lining to this whole grim episode, she decided, it was that Drum had lost all claim to superiority in the realm of social graces. Never again would he have the power to make her feel like the girl from steerage skulking in the shadows of the first-class deck, praying no one would notice.

But that said, why *did* that fellow at the door look so familiar? Was he one of the cathedral's deacons, maybe someone she met at a previous service? No, he didn't have a deacon's air of rumpled geniality. Also, priests and deacons tended not to wear sunglasses, she'd noticed—blurred their insight into other people's souls, maybe. However, they were standard issue for poker players and spooks. And now that she thought about it, his pinstripe suit did look like a bad James Bond knockoff.

That was when Carrie remembered where she'd last seen him.

As Tom pulled up alongside her, she leaned in to accept his kiss, then cocked a thumb at the closing door through which the other man had passed. "Are you expecting trouble here this morning?"

"What do you mean?"

"That fellow you were talking to—I recognize him. He was at the house the morning you guys showed up to tell me Drum had absconded."

Tom sighed and nodded. "CIA security detail."

"You have a bodyguard now?"

"Off and on. It's routine whenever the threat level goes up—all that color-coded nonsense, you know. I can never keep track of it. I think we're at puce or chartreuse or something this week." He waved a dismissive hand, but Carrie wasn't so easily put off by nonchalance, no matter how reassuring it was intended to be.

"There's been a threat warning? About another terrorist attack?"

"Well, nothing specific. But…" He sighed. "It's because of this business with Drum. Some people think the information he took with him when he disappeared must have hit the buyer's market by now."

"So, he *did* steal critical intelligence? That's been determined for sure?"

"Hard to be certain—so much is stored digitally these days that it's hard to trace what might have been copied or downloaded. But the default assumption is that he had a shopping list of some of our most critical secrets. We also have to assume that the shopping list included the names and addresses and other pertinent information on certain senior or undercover officials. I hardly belong among those top operators that anyone's going to target, but—" Tom sighed again. "Because of my proximity to the Director, the security people have opted to err on the side of caution."

"So now you have to have a bodyguard with you everywhere you go?"

"It's all overblown, as I say. Fortunately, I am senior enough that I can tell these eager beavers to back off when they start to get too annoying."

"Oh, Tom, I'm sorry."

"No reason to be. It's nothing you did. Anyway, seems to me that if someone wanted to do me harm, they've had plenty of opportunity before now, given all the traveling I do. If I wanted to spend my life hiding under the bed, I wouldn't have got into this business, would I? Hey, there's Jonah!"

Carrie turned to watch Jonah, who was grinning up at the grotesque stone faces projecting from the cathedral's gutters high overhead on the building's limestone walls, showing them to Tengwall, who'd driven them over.

The cathedral's official name was the Cathedral Church of

Saint Peter and Saint Paul. Completed in 1990, eighty-three years after construction began, it was the sixth largest cathedral in the world and the second largest in the U.S.A., after Saint John's in New York City. Although it was the seat of power of the Episcopal bishops of both the U.S.A. and Washington, the cathedral had been built through private subscription with the intention of welcoming all the nation's faiths, and had been the site of many an interdenominational service of both celebration and mourning. As long as two football fields, the nave was as tall as a thirty-story building from its marble floor to the Indiana limestone vaulting overhead. The top of the cathedral's central tower was the highest point in the District of Columbia.

Carrie knew all this because not long after their return from London, Bishop Merriam himself had given her and Jonah a "backstage tour" of the cathedral's towers, carillon, pipe organ and stained glass windows, as well as the inside scoop on some of the hundred and ten uniquely carved gargoyles which served as downspouts to carry rainwater away from the building's foundation. Some had been carved to resemble the cathedral's financial patrons, while others were self-portraits of the carvers or models of fanciful animals. There were also numerous stone caricatures of cultural icons of the day, including Darth Vader, a placard-toting hippie and a Yuppie carrying a briefcase. Every time they'd been back since, Jonah had delighted in revisiting his favorite "garglers."

"We tried to get here a little early," Carrie told Tom. "He likes to explore—although maybe it's not such a good idea for him to wander this morning. There's quite a mob lining up out there to get into the main parking lot."

"Ah, well," Tom said, "the bishop's very well connected, don't you know. Half the cabinet's expected to show up. You

know how these politicians like to stay on the side of the an-
gels. That way, they can feel confident telling the world God's
on their side." He leaned down and rubbed his hands together
as Jonah and Tengwall approached. "Hey there! How's my
godson?"

"I'm good, Uncle Tom."

"You look real handsome, I must say," Tom told him.

Jonah's eyes dropped and he smoothed his navy jacket
proudly. "I got a new suit."

"So I see. Very impressive."

Carrie smiled. The suit came from the juniors department
at Brooks Brothers. When she'd heard that her mother-in-law
had also been invited to Bishop Merriam's jubilee, she'd
called to offer Althea a peace offering in the form of a ride to
the service.

"No, I'll make my own way over," Althea had replied
coolly, making sure Carrie understood that she wasn't for-
given for the mortal sin of having stood up for herself. Carrie had thought she was going to have the phone hung up on
her, but then Althea came back. "Am I going to see my grandson at the service?"

"Yes, I think so."

"Well, that's something, anyway. I know you'd prefer to cut
me out of his life—"

"No, Althea, not at all. You're welcome to visit him anytime you like. I did invite you for his birthday party last
month."

"I'm sure I wouldn't dream of invading your privacy, Carrie. Just so long as I can see him on Sunday and know he's
all right, I'll have to be satisfied with that, I suppose. He will
be properly dressed, I hope?" she added testily. "Just because
he's young doesn't mean he shouldn't show respect and dress

accordingly on an important occasion like Bishop Merriam's jubilee."

Like she was in the habit of sending him out in rags, Carrie thought irritably. Still, she'd tapped into her limited funds to buy him a suit, and she'd been sure to get his hair cut, as well, so that her mother-in-law would have no reason to find fault.

For her own part, she'd dressed conservatively in a light wool suit. The Kelly-green jacket had Chanel-style black frog closures up the front and a matching straight black skirt that almost reached her knees. Her shoes and bag were likewise black and conservative, while her hair was twisted into a modest knot at the back of her head. She looked like her own mother, Carrie thought, but she was taking no chances.

Jonah, surprisingly enough, had seemed genuinely delighted with his new suit that morning, proudly hooking his clip-on bow tie to his collar all by himself. Poor Jonah. Ever since Drum had gone MIA, he seemed to feel it was his job to play man of the house. A little boy should be a little boy, Carrie thought, anger rising in her once again. But then, at the sight of Jonah standing next to his godfather, who rarely wore anything but Brooks Brothers, she had to smile. They looked like a preppy Mutt and Jeff.

"Tom, do you know Brianne Tengwall? She's one of yours," Carrie added quietly. Behind her dark glasses, Tengwall appeared to be casing the joint, as if she expected terrorist assassins—or the erstwhile Operations Deputy—to leap out from behind the flying buttresses.

"I do believe we met on Elcott Road last month," Tom said, a hint of a frown crossing his smooth, ruddy face. It vanished almost immediately, though, his natural charm winning out over whatever had sparked his disapproval—

Tengwall herself or the knotty problem of which she was another reminder. "Welcome," he added.

Tengwall nodded, blushing nervously through her freckles as she stuck out her hand. "How are you, sir?" She'd dressed for the occasion in a conservative black business suit and wrestled her frizzled blond hair into a black plastic clip. But despite that and her sober vigilance, she still looked all of seventeen, Carrie thought. Far too young to be playing spy games.

"I do just fine," Tom said. "I hope you know, young lady, that this young fellow here is my godson. I take a very particular interest in knowing he's being handled gently."

"Yes, sir. No worries there. Jonah and I are good friends, aren't we?"

"Yup," Jonah said firmly. "You wanna go check out the garglers, Bree? Mom, can I show Bree the garglers?"

Carrie glanced at her watch. There was still twenty minutes or so until the service. "I guess that would be all right, if you're very quiet about it and don't get in the way of people trying to get in. Just for a few minutes, though.'

Tengwall looked hesitant, as if she wasn't sure she should let Carrie out of her sight, but Tom nodded to her. "You can meet us inside. I want to have a word with Mrs. MacNeil, anyway." He turned to his godson. "Jonah, Aunt Lorraine's inside the building with her mother. The three of us are going to be sitting in the first row of chairs, right in front of the pulpit, and there are places for you and your mom and Ms. Tengwall right behind us. Your names are on the seats. Do you think you can find them?"

"Yup, I'll find 'em," Jonah said. "I can read now."

"You don't say," Tom exclaimed. "Well, you are just getting to be so grown-up, I can hardly keep track. You keep a close watch on your friend there, you hear?" He said it to Jonah, but from the raised eyebrow he directed at Tengwall, there was no doubt that he meant the reverse.

She nodded soberly. Young as she was, Carrie thought, this was a girl who knew on which side her bread was buttered. Tom's position near the top of the CIA organization chart made him a figure she shouldn't cross if she valued her career. Although Tom and Drum had risen together through the Agency's ranks, in the case of the coal miner's son from West Virginia, it was hard grinding work and not just fortuitous birth and connections that had gotten Tom into Yale and onto that escalator to the top of the D.C. power structure. Drum had told Carrie once that the current Director, an outside political appointee, never made a move without Tom Bent's advice, relying on Tom to serve as his personal tugboat through the Capital's dangerous shoals. It was entirely conceivable, Carrie thought, that Tom himself could end up being named to some top post one of these days. Tengwall would do well not to alienate him.

They watched Jonah take her by the hand as he pointed out some of his favorite garglers. "There's a robot, see? And a computer? And that one's a hamster." He laughed. "Did you ever see a hamster and a computer on a church before?"

Tengwall shook her head as they walked off, hand in hand.

"He's really grown," Tom murmured. "How's he been since the move? Settled in?"

"Surprisingly well, actually," Carrie said. "It's one advantage of having been a foreign service baby, I guess. He's so used to moving around and to housekeepers, nannies and *au paires* that he seems to have taken it for granted that we move from time to time and that our household should include a few strangers. The fact that these people occasionally pick him up from school or attend his soccer games if I'm tied up in FBI interviews only seems to confirm his general impression that they're hired help."

"He's liking his school?"

Carrie nodded. "He was going to be in a new school, anyway, so he handled the last-minute switch to Georgetown better than I could have hoped. Of course, it helped that when Tracy took us over to the house for the first time, we discovered a little boy just his age living right next door. They've ended up in the same class, and he's Jonah's new best bud. The two of them are going out together for Halloween later this week. Jonah's going as Spider-Man, of course."

"What about the business with Drum? You said on the phone that you'd told Jonah about it? How did he handle that?"

"I soft-pedaled what really happened. I just said Drum had gone away and forgot to tell anybody where he was going and for how long, so people were a little upset with him—including me, by the by, which Jonah had already figured out, since he'd overheard me arguing with Althea." She slapped her forehead lightly. "Idiot that I am. I could have handled that better."

"This has been hard on all of you."

"Have you heard anything, Tom? Nobody's telling me a thing, but surely they must have picked up Drum's trail by now?"

Tom glanced around, then took her by the elbow and led her over to a wrought iron bench in the shade of a locust tree. "So far," he said as they settled on the bench, "they've discovered there were at least two other non-sanctioned sets of identification he'd had done up for himself, but there's no trace of travel under those names. Who knows how many others he had, though? He'd also been setting assets aside for at least a year. Your money was the least of it, Carrie. You know they caught most of that before it could be transferred out of the country?"

She nodded. "Agent Andrews told me. Not that it does me any good. They've gotten a court order to freeze it."

"You'll get it back, Carrie, I'm sure, just as soon as they've cleared you, which they're bound to very soon now."

"I sure hope so. That money was my insurance policy."

"I know I've said this before, but I want you to know the offer still stands. If you need a loan—"

"No, Tom, thanks," she said. He was a kind, generous soul, but Tom, she knew, had only his CIA salary and very little else by way of financial resources. Nor did his wife come from major money, however well-connected the Merriams might be through the bishop's high-profile position in Washington. "Drum did leave a little money in our household account that the feds are letting me tap into for living expenses. And the Overturfs are letting Jonah and me stay in their house rent-free, so that helps."

"They're good people."

"They sure are. This isn't the first time they've been there for me. Anyway, now that Jonah's at school, I've been thinking about getting a part-time job. I've met with the manager of the Oxfam Gallery in Georgetown in connection with my poor, neglected thesis, and they might have something for me there. So really, Tom, I thank you for your offer, but we're all right for the moment. I wasn't planning to take any round-the-world cruises in the near future, anyway."

"Well, just so you know we're here."

"I just wish this had never happened. Would you ever have believed Drum would take off like this?"

"No. And to pull a stunt like that on his mother, at her age—"

"Disappearing, you mean?"

"Well, that, too, but the business about the house," Tom said. When she shook her head, confused, he added, "You didn't know?"

"Know what?"

"The house on Elcott Road. It turns out that in addition to forging your signature on that letter of instruction to your broker, Drum had also mortgaged the family home last spring, then transferred the money out to offshore accounts in the Caymans and the Isle of Man."

"Oh, my God, Tom! Does Althea know?"

"Turns out that she'd known about it since shortly before he disappeared. She'd intercepted a statement from the bank. It was addressed to her and Drum both because her name's also on the title deed. She said she thought he must be in some sort of financial trouble to have done that behind her back. Then, when he vanished, she didn't say anything about it because it looked so suspicious and she didn't want him in any more trouble than he already was. She's been quietly making the payments, though, because the bank was threatening to seize the place."

"Poor Althea. She never breathed a word to me. That explains a couple of things, though."

"Like what?"

"Oh, cracks she's made about me spending Drum's money, that sort of thing. She probably thought I was driving him to the poor house and that's the reason he did what he did. She's convinced herself this is all my fault. I tried calling and offering to drive her here this morning, but she wasn't giving an inch."

"You have to forgive her, I suppose. She's old, and Drum is her son, after all. She doesn't want to believe ill of him, so who's she going to lash out at?"

Carrie shivered. "Maybe I shouldn't have come today. What if she makes a scene? I'd hate to ruin the bishop's special day."

Tom shook his head. "Not going to happen. Althea phoned first thing this morning to send her regrets. She said she'd come down with a cold, but my guess is she decided discretion was the better part of valor."

Carrie nodded. "Well, I could say I'm sorry to hear it, but honestly, I was terrified at the thought of seeing her." A leaf fell on her skirt and she brushed it away. "Have you heard anything else about the investigation?"

"Not a whole lot, no. You didn't see this coming, either, Carrie?"

She sighed and glanced around as a couple of choir members stepped out the cathedral's side door for a quick cigarette. "No, but maybe I should have. He hasn't really been right since Dar es Salaam."

"How do you mean?"

"Since the bombing." Carrie frowned and watched a squirrel run across the lawn. "Something happened that morning, Tom. I never said anything about it before this happened, but that day the bomb went off, it destroyed more than real estate. It killed several people and, frankly, it killed my marriage, I think."

"How so?"

"Because Drum panicked that day. I was in the building when the bomb went off, as you know. Afterward, I found Drum out in the parking lot, hysterical. It passed, but I think he was humiliated that I'd seen him that way. He never really got over it. It was all that 'son of General MacNeil' nonsense he always had to deal with, you know."

"You never knew the General, did you, Carrie?"

"No, he died long before Drum and I ever met. From what Drum tells me, though, I gather he was quite a tough customer."

"Actually, I don't think he was."

"Really?"

Tom shrugged. "Oh, he was all Army, that's for sure, but he wasn't just some hard-ass character strutting around and showing off his chest candy. He was a leader, and a really good man. I think you would have liked him. Drum idolized him, I think. You know, just between you and me, Carrie," Tom added, "Drum's problem was he really wasn't the man his father was, and deep down, he knew it and worried that everyone else knew it, too. But for a while, there, it was possible to get away with being a fake hero—for all of us, I guess. Unlike the General, we didn't have a real battleground we had to prove ourselves on. We were the post-Vietnam, post–Cold War generation. We could play our spy games and not worry about the fact that we were untested. Then the bombs started going off and September 11 happened, and suddenly the ground had shifted under us. Before that, there was a brief time we could strut around playing king of the world and hope nobody noticed we were buck naked. Didn't last, though." He looked around sadly, rubbing his hands together as if trying to ward off a chilly wind. "It's a new world we're living in now, Carrie, and a dangerous one. There's no more getting by on charm and a name. It's time to put up or shut up."

Carrie nodded. "Drum couldn't assume anymore that people would give him a pass just because he was General Mac-Neil's son."

"That's a fact. You know, when he came back to testify before the intelligence committee after September 11, I think it shocked him to realize there were senators there who'd barely even heard of his father. Nobody was going to cut him any slack on that score."

"It was more than that, though," Carrie said. "It wasn't just that he was afraid of taking the blame for what was going on, Tom. I think he was genuinely afraid of being killed."

"Rightly so. Look, the Israelis have the best intelligence in the world and the tightest security net, but they're losing people all the time. That's what happens when you make implacable enemies. They may be unsophisticated, their methods may be low-tech, but that just makes 'em more dangerous. They find a way to get under the radar. Not every time, maybe, but even if they only succeed one time out of ten, people are still going to die. America's at war now, and there are going to be losses. But Drum and I—well, we cut our baby teeth on the Cold War and we thought we were pretty tough, but that was just pretend. Now, we're in it for real."

Carrie nodded. "He's not a brave man, Tom. I guess I realized that after the bombing in Dar. No wonder he decided to pack it in. The game got too dangerous. Maybe the only surprise is that he waited until now to do it."

"You may be right. I think that last attack in London finally did it. The one where that young girl was shot outside the embassy? Must have struck too close to home."

"Do you think I really was the target?"

"That seems to be the conclusion. Maybe it was a way to strike at the CIA Station Chief. Either that, or…" Tom hesitated.

"Or what, Tom?"

"Oh, Carrie, what does it matter now?"

"It matters to me. What's the other theory about the attack in London?"

"Well, given the fact that it looks like Drum had been thinking about taking Jonah—"

"You think he arranged the shooting. He wanted me dead, is that it?"

"I don't know that for sure. But somebody hired that hit man, Carrie. Maybe it wasn't him. Maybe Drum was afraid he was being targeted. Or maybe he thought the blame was going to come back to him. One way or another, I think he decided after that the game was over and it was time to get out."

"God, Tom! I knew he was cheating on me with other women, but how dumb have I really been?"

"You weren't dumb, Carrie. Drum wasn't cut out for constancy. I guess I've always known that about him. He's been one of my closest friends for a long time, but let's face it, he's a party animal, looking for the good time and the easy way. He's a charmer, and that was always enough to get him by. Except once you get to a certain level, charm's not enough. You've got to step up to the plate and accept responsibility. Drum liked the glory, but he didn't like the heavy load that came with it. I guess I've sensed for a while that he was looking for a way out, but I never expected this. When the Brits came to the Director and said they suspected him of selling out, I was the first one to shout 'em down. Said they were just trying to cover their own butts, that the leaks could just as easily have come from someone on MI-6."

Tom's shoulders slumped and he looked as unhappy as Carrie had ever seen him. "I don't know, Carrie. Maybe if I'd confronted Drum right back then, things wouldn't have gone this far."

Carrie shook her head. "You can't blame yourself, Tom. I lived with him and I didn't see this coming."

Just then, the cathedral's carillon began to peal in the central tower high overhead, ringing out a celebratory chorus that must have echoed all the way over to poor Althea sitting alone in her beautiful, mortgaged home on Elcott Road, Carrie thought sadly.

"I guess we should go in," she said.

"I guess so," Tom said wearily. "Just one more thing, darlin'. So far, we've been lucky the press hasn't gotten wind of this. The whole affair's being played very close to the chest. The Director's terrified of publicity. The last thing the country needs is a security scandal right now, with the President and Cabinet running around telling other governments how to clean up their acts." Tom rose and held out a hand to her. "There's going to be a fairly large crowd in there, though, including one or two from the upper levels of the intelligence community who've heard Drum's run into a spot of trouble. Don't be surprised if you get a few odd looks. Just keep your chin up and don't give 'em the satisfaction of looking whipped."

"I don't know, Tom, maybe it would be better if I didn't go in."

"Nonsense," he said firmly. "We want you there, darlin', Lorraine and her mother as much as me. And the bishop, I happen to know, plans to offer a special, if subtle, prayer for you and Jonah and Althea, and for Drum's safe return. He won't mention Drum by name, for obvious reasons, but you'll know it when you hear it. So come on in and be with folks who love you."

Carrie, teary-eyed now, let herself be lead into the great limestone cathedral.

CHAPTER TWENTY-ONE

Washington, D.C. (Georgetown)
October 27, 2002—3:11 p.m.

Huxley was half-drunk on fumes. Since Tengwall had left to drive Carrie and Jonah to the cathedral, he'd worked his way around the two library walls that held floor-to-ceiling book-shelves, applying golden brown stain. Over the past couple of weeks, between surveillance stints on mother and son, he'd stripped the shelves down to the original bare oak and sanded them to a soft, smooth sheen. Now, moving from top to bottom of each section, climbing up and down an aluminum stepladder, he brushed stain with the color and texture of liquid honey on each of the thirty-six individual shelves, topside and underside, as well as on all the upright pillars and decorative moldings adorning the units. It was repetitive work, physically exhausting, but satisfying, too, in its own tortuously painful way. His knees creaked as he rose at last from the final corner. He stepped back to admire his work, the shelves golden and gleaming, the oak's coarse grain tiger-striping through the stain. Stretching out knotted arms and legs, he looked the place over with frank admiration.

The tall, French-paned windows were at the front of the house, but vehicle traffic tended to be light. While other Georgetown avenues had long since been resurfaced to make them car-friendlier, the cagey residents of O Street had cleverly resisted all efforts to upgrade their thoroughfare, knowing that improvements would only increase the number of cars running by at all hours of the day and night. Georgetown drivers, Carrie had told him, knew to avoid O Street, with its lumpy cobblestones and wheel-wrecking old streetcar tracks.

Because the traffic was light, though, the street attracted walkers, including vast numbers of students strolling off the campus of nearby Georgetown University. Across the road now, Huxley spotted a young, jean-clad couple loitering under the spreading branches of a red-hued maple. They carried backpacks and looked like students, but even as the boy pulled the girl toward him in a hormone-fueled embrace, Huxley couldn't help wondering if they might be an FBI's surveillance detail, still keeping the house and its occupants under close, albeit subtle, scrutiny. If so, they were good, he thought wryly, watching the girl slip her hands under the young man's thick sweater. Nothing like making sacrifices for national security.

He turned back to the room and started gathering up his drop cloth. The refinished oak floors were scattered with richly patterned wool prayer rugs, and he slid one back into its original position in front of the bookshelves. The sprawling wood desk angled across the opposite corner from the shelves looked like it might have seen duty in an old rural post office, its pigeon-holed secretary unit and built-in inkwell providing an archaic contrast to the sleek gray computer monitor and keyboard on top. The desk chair was high-backed and tapestry covered, while a couple of deep, comfortable looking green leather armchairs surrounded a brick-lined fireplace mounted with Tiffany-style wall sconces angled just right for long evenings of fireside reading. A low wooden table between the two armchairs held a backgammon board and, oddly, an antique brass mortar and pestle.

Like the rest of the renovated house, the room was cozy and inviting—and even more appealing, Huxley thought, now that he knew that the owners themselves had spent the past thirty years renovating and refurbishing the place mostly with their own hands. Sweat equity, Carrie had called it. The Overturfs must take great satisfaction in seeing the fruits of their labors.

A home of one's own—what would that be like? It wasn't anything Huxley had experienced, not since leaving his childhood home in North Yorkshire nearly twenty years earlier. The older he got, though, the more appealing the notion became, after living in temporary digs in far-flung locales, some of them primitive in the extreme. Sure, he'd had adventures. That's what he'd hungered for as a young man. But now, here he was, half his life gone, and what did he have to show for it?

Generations of his family, by contrast, had lived, worked, raised families, died and been buried in and around Scarborough, on England's east coast. Huxley's father had spent his entire life there, working as a finish carpenter from the age of sixteen until his forced retirement that past summer at the age of sixty-eight, when his gnarled hands and battered knees, spine and ankles flatly refused to carry him through any more jobs. Still, idleness wasn't in his nature. When Huxley had telephoned on his mother's birthday a few days earlier, she'd reported that the old man was still getting up at five-thirty every morning and heading out to his tool-lined, thatched-roof workshop behind their rural home overlooking the North Sea.

"What's he doing out there?" Huxley asked.

"Making toys," his mother said.

"Toys?"

"Wooden trains and ships and what not. For the grand-children. Some of it, anyway. The extras he takes over to the children's ward at the hospital, or gives 'em to charity. Who-ever can make use of 'em. And he made a lovely rocking horse for Simon's birthday."

Simon was one of Huxley's nephews, the youngest of his sister's three kids. She and her husband lived in the heart of Scarborough, just a couple of miles from their folks, as did his brother and his brood of five. Simon would have just turned three, Huxley calculated, feeling a tug of melancholy. He hadn't seen any of them since Christmas at a gathering of the entire close-knit clan, which included an extended net-work of aunts and uncles and cousins. He himself was one of the few who'd ever left Yorkshire, joining the military right out of school, his work in the Special Air Services, then MI-6 taking him far afield. If he'd once thought of return-ing to live among the relations, he no longer allowed him-self that fantasy. Being around them, pleasant as it was, brought too many reminders of what he himself had almost had, then brutally lost.

Shaking off the thought, Huxley gathered up his brushes and cans and drop cloth and headed for the back of the house.

He left the tins and cloth next to the pantry and went out the back door. In the small garden, he rinsed the brushes in mineral spirits and spun them dry as his lungs took in the fresh air.

The temperature had dropped precipitously in the past couple of hours and the wind had picked up, whipping fallen leaves into a red-orange frenzy. A bank of ominous-looking clouds was moving in from the west, probably bringing rain, as predicted. He'd finished not a moment too soon. He'd have to keep an eye on the sky, he thought, maybe walk around the house and close up the windows if the rain moved in before Carrie and Jonah got back.

Back in the kitchen, he gathered up the tins and drop cloth once more and headed down to the cellar via a door next to the pantry. The staircase was narrow and steep, without a handrail, forcing him to balance the supplies precariously as his boots negotiated each squeaky, unforgiving step. Hewing close to the wall lest he lose his balance and tumble off the side, his bare arm scraped against the rough stone foundation, but he made it safely to the bottom.

It was as much crawl space as cellar, really. The packed dirt floor had an uneven cant, and the low ceiling joists and steel ductwork of the central heating system seemed sadistically designed to thwack any unsuspecting skull that made the mistake of turning too quickly in the cramped space. Most of the foundation had been retrofitted with a thick layer of plastic-wrapped insulation to keep out the damp and cold, but the dank space held the must and dust of two hundred years.

The ductwork system must have been fairly revolutionary when the house was built two hundred years earlier, Huxley thought. He had to crouch a little to avoid the fat, snaking metal tubes that carried warm air from a compact gas furnace nestled against the street-side wall. The gas unit was a new addition, obviously installed well after the original, massive coal furnace, which stood uselessly alongside. The big old monstrosity gave off a faint creosote smell and loomed over the dreary space like a giant, cast iron spider. Next to it, a wooden bin held a few dusty leftover coal nuggets—probably delivered decades earlier by way of the coal chute that was padlocked but still accessible to the cobblestoned street.

The refurbished upper floors had given a glamorous facelift to this grand dame of a residence, Huxley thought, but this creaky, dusty cellar was a potent reminder of how much work had gone into tarting the old girl up.

He stored what was left of the wood stain on metal canning shelves under the staircase, then packed away the brushes and other tools he'd been using. He was just rolling the drop cloth into a tight wad when he heard a floor joist squeak overhead. He paused, listening. The floor squeaked again. Tucking the cloth quietly away, he crept to the bottom of the narrow staircase, dodging a hanging strip of ancient, cloth-wrapped conduit—another orphaned fixture, this one left over from the building's first electrification at least a century earlier, long since replaced by modern copper wiring.

Peering up the stairs, Huxley saw only the blue patterned wallpaper of the kitchen wall opposite the pantry. "Carrie?" he called. "Tengwall?"

No answer.

"Jonah?"

Silence.

He started up, taking care to step at the inside of each tread, close to the wall, where there was less likelihood of audible protest. He paused briefly at each step, listening to the rustle of someone moving through the upstairs hall. The front door was self-locking, Huxley recalled. And the back door to the garden? He'd closed and relocked it after cleaning the brushes out back—hadn't he?

He was just lifting his foot to the top step when a dark shadow tumbled across the cellar opening. Even though he'd been expecting someone, Huxley was startled by the suddenness of the looming black shape. He regained his footing only at the last second, then let out a gasp of exasperation.

"Bloody hell, Tucker! Did you not hear me call?"

"Sorry," Tucker said, stepping back to let him up into the narrow passageway outside the door. "I wasn't sure anyone was here. I let myself in," he added, holding up a key.

It was one of the conditions that Carrie and her friend, Tracy, had agreed to when Carrie had moved over to Georgetown—that the watchers would have a key to the house. Tracy had given them one, which they'd promptly copied.

"What are you doing down there?" Tucker asked.

"Cleaning up. I was finishing the library shelves this morning while Carrie and the boy were out."

"Where did they go?"

"National Cathedral. Tengwall drove them over. They should be back soon."

Even as he said it, Huxley realized he'd been keeping an eager eye on his watch all afternoon, anticipating their return. He told himself it was because he wanted to have the stain as dry as possible before the little boy got back so as not to stir up his allergies. He reminded himself that he'd promised Jonah they might kick the soccer ball out back for a while if there was time before the sun set. He admitted to himself, as well, that he genuinely liked the little guy and was quite happy to give the kid a bit of much-needed male companionship as long as he was on the job here anyway.

What Huxley would barely concede, even to himself, was that Carrie, too, was beginning to get under his skin. He'd been watching her for months now, and much as he'd wanted to write her off as that traitor MacNeil's equally feckless trophy wife, the more he saw of her, the less fault he could find. True, her taste in husbands was abysmal, and that went for her choice of mothers-in-law, too—although admittedly, it was a package deal so she couldn't really be blamed for that one. But back before her husband had gone on the lam, Huxley had also hated the way Carrie tiptoed around MacNeil, carefully groomed, polished and deferential, as if terrified of putting a foot wrong around the bastard.

Ever since MacNeil had disappeared and Carrie had moved away from that museum of a house on the Potomac, though, a subtle transformation had been taking place. The shyness that Huxley had once put down to snobbery seemed to have melted away. That morning, when he'd come in and found her dusting the library, was a case in point. Dressed in jeans and a sweatshirt, her hair tumbling around her shoulders, wearing no makeup, humming under her breath as she worked, she'd looked so relaxed and cheerful it had taken his breath away. When she'd settled on the edge of the desk, dangling her foot casually, watching him with those stunning gray-green eyes, he'd hardly dared look at her, so tongue-tied and flustered did he suddenly find himself. He'd covered his discomfort with grumbling until she'd finally gotten the hint and left him in blessed peace.

Later, when she'd poked her head in to tell him they were leaving, she'd been dressed to the nines again, the way she so often was for MacNeil—polished, primped and utterly unapproachable. Thank God, Huxley had thought. Looking like that, she made it so much easier for him to remember what he was there for.

"What are you doing here?" he asked Tucker now, shaking off thoughts he had no business thinking. "I thought you had another engagement today."

"Not till this evening. I spent the day catching up on paperwork."

"So, got a hot date tonight, do we?" Tucker had mentioned once that he was a widower—something else the two of them had in common.

"In my dreams," the older man said. "No, it's a family thing at my daughter's. I could get out of it, though, if you need me here."

"No, I'm footloose and fancy-free. I can do the night watch. I think Tengwall said she had a date later."

"She can cover here if you want the night off."

"No, let the kid have some fun. She's been hanging around old codgers for months, now. I'm sure she needs a break. Can I get you—" From down the hall came a faint buzzing sound.

"What's that?" Tucker asked.

"My mobile," Huxley said. "I left it in the library. 'Scuse me."

He sprinted up the hall and got to the library on the third ring, though it took one more before he remembered where he'd left the cell phone—propped inside the brass mortar on the coffee table near the fireplace. He grabbed it up and flipped it open before the call could bounce to the voicemail system. "Huxley."

"Mr. Huxley, this is Mr. Greenwood's office," a male voice announced. The accent was British, not surprising. Greenwood was the cover name of the MI-6 liaison officer at the British Embassy over on Massachusetts Avenue.

"Yes, what is it?"

"Mr. Greenwood was hoping you could drop by for a short visit. In thirty minutes, to be precise. Three p.m."

"Did he say why?"

"No, sir, but he was most anxious to see you."

Huxley sighed. "All right. I'm on my way."

"Very good, sir. I'll tell him to expect you at three."

Huxley ended the call and looked up to see Tucker's black eyes watching him closely. "Problem?"

Huxley frowned. "No, not really. I'm not sure. I have to run over to the embassy."

"What's it about?"

"Don't know. Liaison man's probably just catching up on his own paperwork, looking for a debriefing for his overnight cable to the mother house. I don't imagine I'll be long."

"No problem. I can hold the fort here till Tengwall gets back. If you get hung up, don't worry. Between the two of us, we can cover off the night watch. She'll just have to take a rain check on that date of hers."

They'd been taking turns camping out on the living room couch. Tonight was Huxley's turn on the rotation.

"Tell her I'll try to be back in time." Huxley headed for the door.

He was on his way out when Tucker called after him. "Hey, Huxley?"

"What?"

"You think maybe they're going to call you back to London? Surely they've got better things for you to be doing than carpentry work."

"I don't know. I suppose it's possible. Bound to happen sooner or later."

"We'll be sorry to lose you. Been a good team."

"Yeah, it has. Wish we'd accomplished a little more, but there it is. Win some, lose some. Maybe next time."

"Right, next time. Well, catch you later?"

"Cheers."

* * *

National Cathedral
2:55 p.m.

Carrie sat at the end of a long luncheon table. The table had already been cleared, only a few scattered china cups and dessert plates remaining on the food-spotted white linen cloth. A few guests were still milling around in the cathedral meeting hall, although most of the attendees at the luncheon following Bishop Merriam's jubilee service had left. The bishop and his family, including Tom and Lorraine, were at the door, saying goodbye to the stragglers.

Carrie glanced at her watch, hoping to make her own escape, but Jonah was off with Tengwall, showing her a few more of his favorite "garglers." If they didn't show up in the next two minutes, Carrie decided, she was going to track them down so they could say their own farewells. She felt a sharp pressure building at her temples from the tension headache that had been creeping up on her since the moment they'd pulled into the parking lot. She wanted to go home, get Jonah organized for the evening and for his next week of school, then maybe take a long, hot bubble bath. Through the window, she could also see black clouds moving in. Huxley had been right. It was going to rain.

Sitting at the table, she was safeguarding Tom's camera while he helped Lorraine's family see the guests off. It was a digital camera, and Tom had shown her how to scan the file of pictures he'd shot that afternoon. There was Bishop Merriam in his robes and miter, looking apostolic. Lorraine and her mother flanking him, looking proud, Mrs. Merrian snowy-haired, Lorraine, who so resembled her, well on her way to pure white, as well. The bishop with Jonah and Carrie, looking avuncular. Jonah under the Space Window on the Cathedral's south aisle, pointing up at the piece of lunar rock embedded in the celestial stained glass. The moon rock had been presented to the cathedral during its construction phase by the astronauts of Apollo XI.

"Phew! Glad that's over."

Carrie looked up, startled. "Oh, Tom! Yikes, I nearly fumbled your expensive camera here."

"Sorry, didn't mean to scare you. But you can't really hurt the camera. It's pretty resilient."

"All done with the farewells?"

He nodded. "Pretty much."

She frowned at the doorway. "We really need to get going, too. I don't know where Jonah and Brianne have gotten to."

"We were just going to head over to the rectory for a glass of sherry—or something stiffer. Why don't the three of you join us?"

"Oh, thanks, Tom, but it's a school night. I should really get Jonah home. It's been a lovely afternoon, though. Lorraine and her mom have been positively beaming."

They looked over to where Tom's wife and mother still flanked the bishop. Lorraine was very active in cathedral committees, as much a support to her father as her mother was. It had severely limited Tom's foreign posting opportunities, in fact, because Lorraine didn't like to live away from Washington. The Bents had never had children of their own. Maybe that was why Lorraine, at fifty, seemed so childlike in her attachment to her parents, Carrie thought. But even as the notion passed through her mind, she felt petty and ungrateful. She liked Lorraine well enough, even though her personality was a little on the bland side. She was a kind person, and not stupid, by any means. So what if she was devoted to her mother and father? With no extended family of her own,

Carrie could only envy the good fortune of still having loving parents at hand.

The Merriams, too, had always been good to her and Jonah, as well as Drum—as little as Drum had ever appreciated it. Today, the bishop had taken special notice of them during his personal celebration and, as Tom had said he would, offered a subtle prayer on behalf of Carrie's errant husband and Jonah's negligent father. What was there to criticize?

You are an obnoxious bitch, she thought. She sighed. She was tired. She was frustrated. She was scared.

Just then, Jonah and Tengwall came through the door, and she got to her feet gratefully. "There they are now. We'll say our goodbyes to Lorraine and her folks." Tom rose and she turned to hug him. "Tom, thank you so much, as always, for everything."

He held her tight and patted her back. "There is nothing I wouldn't do for you, darlin'—and for my godson, of course." He pulled back and held her at arm's length, looking at her closely. "You call me anytime. I mean it. I'm here for you, Carrie."

She handed him back his camera. "I know. I appreciate it."

British Embassy, Washington, D.C.
3:12 p.m.

Huxley arrived at the Massachusetts Avenue entrance to the embassy by 3:00 p.m. as scheduled, Sunday traffic being light in downtown D.C., but it took another ten minutes before he was finally admitted to the wood-lined office of Greenwood, the MI-6 resident. When Huxley was finally shown in by a thin, acne-scarred young aide with the same Midlands-accented voice that had delivered the cell-phone summons a short while earlier, he found Greenwood on the scrambler, talking to London.

"Yes, sir, he's here now," the resident said, waving Huxley over to the desk. "Shall I put you on the speakerphone?" He frowned. "Well, no, of course not, sir…. Yes, certainly. I have an extension for this line—" His frown deepened. "Very good, sir. I'll just put him on, then. Yes, sir, I will. Thank you."

Greenwood stood and motioned Huxley to a chair in front of the desk. As Huxley approached, Greenwood pressed the mute button on the base of the heavy white phone. "This is Sir Roger on the line, Huxley."

"Sir Roger?" Huxley paused, confused, until it dawned. "Sir Roger Cambridge, you mean?"

"Yes, C himself." The chief of MI-6. "He'd like a word with you."

"Good Lord. What for?"

"I'm not privy to that, I'm afraid. I was summoned to the embassy this afternoon and told to have you here at 8:00 p.m. GMT for an incoming call. You're late, by the way."

"I've been waiting in the bloody outer office for ten minutes."

"I see. Well, you'd better get on the line. Sir Roger's waiting. I'll be outside. When you're done, just let me know." Greenwood thrust the phone into his hand, poked the mute release button, and walked out the door huffily, taking care, however, to close it quietly behind him.

Frowning, Huxley put the white receiver to his ear. "Huxley, here."

"C here, Huxley. Sorry to call you in suddenly like this."

"It's all right, sir. I'm on duty."

"Still keeping MacNeil's family under surveillance?"

"Yes, sir, but no sign of the man himself. I'm not sure this is very fruitful, as operations go."

"Yes, well, I'm inclined to agree, but for reasons you won't be aware of. We've uncovered some troubling information. We're going to have to play things very close to the chest from here on in, I'm afraid."

"Close to the chest? In so far as the cousins are concerned, do you mean?"

"Exactly so. Tell me, have they still got you liaising with that Frank Tucker fellow over there?"

"Yes."

"What do you know about him?"

"He's an old Soviet section head, ex-Navy. I understand he's the Director's handpicked choice to head up this security detail. The Yanks are also playing this very close to the chest. They're terrified of press play."

"And this Tucker is the only one assigned to you?"

"There's one other full-time operative, sir, a young woman by the name of Tengwall. Very young, actually. Turns out her mum and dad were both CIA ops people, though, so I guess she gets the nod for that."

"Yes, well…" The tone of the MI-6 chief on the other end of the secure Transatlantic line suggested he or someone in the room with him was doing some checking. Huxley thought he could hear a keyboard tapping in the background, but he couldn't be certain if it was a keyboard or just static on the line. Eventually C came back, however. "We know about this Tucker fellow. He got in a spot of trouble a while back, it seems."

"Trouble, sir?"

"Personal stuff, but nearly washed out over it, it seems. Been on the back burner ever since. First time he'd really been brought out to play, oddly enough. How do you find him? Think he's dodgy at all?"

"Not that I've picked up, sir, but it's difficult to say."

"Well, there's been very little action from that end these past few months, which is not a good sign. Not good at all. It might mean someone wants us to do nothing but spin our wheels. As for the woman...your Miss Tengwall—"

"Not my Miss Tengwall, sir."

"No, of course. Any case, we don't seem to have anything on her. We're looking into it, though."

"What's this about, then?"

"We've finally got a lead on the shooter at the American Embassy last April. Russian fellow—Georgian, actually. Name of Markov. Sergei Markov. I'm having a dossier secure-faxed over for you to take a look at as we speak. Greenwood should have it for you at that end by the time we're done our call. This Markov is a contract assassin known to be associated with the Zurich broker who's been burning our joes. He was engaged here in London to take out Carrie MacNeil, just as we suspected. Killed the cabbie, stole the cab, did the job—but botched it, took down the student instead of Mrs. MacNeil—then ditched the cab and went to ground."

"Have we got him in custody?"

"Unfortunately, not. In fact, it looks like he's over on your side of the pond at the moment. Our people spotted him coming into JFK but didn't realize until too late that he was a 'person of interest,' as the American cousins like to say. As of today, however, we've traced his movements to the Washington area. He may be over there to finish the job he botched last April, or he may have another mission planned. Frankly, we're just not sure."

Huxley sank into the chair. The job Markov had botched— murdering Carrie. "Have we alerted the U.S. authorities?"

"Well, that's the 'close to the chest' part, I'm afraid. We don't think it's a good idea to let the cousins know we're on

to this Markov. There's a distinct possibility this entire operation has been compromised."

"I'm not following you, sir."

"Let me back up and explain. But the main thing you need
to remember, Huxley, is that at this point, none of your CIA
contacts should be considered secure."

"None of them?"

"For the moment, until we figure out how far this infection
has spread inside the Agency—no, not one of them."

Huxley sat on the edge of the chair, feeling the blood drain
from his face as the MI-6 chief outlined the dilemma in which
they suddenly found themselves.

Georgetown
7:42 p.m.

Carrie was in the kitchen, cleaning up from supper, when
she heard the front door open. Tengwall was helping her load
dishes into the dishwasher, but at the sound in the front hall,
her face passed through a comical progression that Carrie, in
spite of weariness and the tension compressing her skull like
a vice, found hilarious. Tengwall's split-second facial con-
tortion encompassed joy, relief, and guilt before settling back
into the blank mask of alert officialdom.

"Gee, Brianne," Carrie said, chuckling. "Why do I get the
sense there are places you'd rather be than baby-sitting us?"

Blush washed out freckles as the younger woman grimaced. "It's that obvious?"

"Oh, yeah, most definitely," Carrie said, nodding. "So, is
he cute, I hope?"

"I think so."

"You *go,* girl. No, really, I mean it," Carrie added, as the young woman kept loading dishes into the machine. She gave her a soapy backhand, scattering detergent bubbles across the kitchen tile. "You go, girl. Get outta here."

Tengwall hesitated. "Well...I'll see if it's okay. Thanks, Carrie. I mean, not thanks, but...."

"Yeah, I know. You don't answer to me. Look, just have a good time, all right?"

"I will. See you tomorrow."

"You betcha."

Tengwall walked out the swinging door into the front hall. Carrie heard her talking, and then Huxley's unmistakable Yorkshire lilt in response. They spoke quietly for a few minutes before the front door opened and closed once more. Carrie waited, expecting Huxley to come through to the kitchen, but there was only silence. Finally, curiosity got the better of her and she went into the front hall.

Nothing.

She frowned. She could hear water splashing upstairs where Jonah was taking a bath. She was just about to sprint up the stairs when she heard a thump from the direction of the library. When she walked in, she saw Huxley slumped in one of the armchairs by the fireplace, staring glumly into the cold hearth.

"Hi,' she said.

He glanced up, startled. "Hi."

"You're back."

"Uh-huh." His weathered face looked more lined and wearier than ever, Carrie thought, like someone who had lost his best friend or a really great poker hand. Physical exhaustion. She glanced around the library, taking in the gleaming golden bookcases.

"The shelves look fabulous," she told him. "You did a great job on them. The Overturfs are going to be really pleased."

He looked up, confused, as if he'd forgotten what book-shelves she was talking about. Then he glanced at them and nodded. "Right. Good, then."

"Are you hungry?" Carrie asked.

"I'm all right."

"I only ask because I reheated the lasagna I made yester-day, but Jonah and I were still too full from lunch to eat much and Brianne was holding out for a better offer. There's still plenty left and if you don't eat it, it'll probably just end up going to waste."

"Oh. Well, all right then, I guess I could eat a little. Don't go to too much trouble, though."

Carrie arched an eyebrow. "I wasn't planning to go to any trouble at all. It's in the fridge, along with some leftover salad. The lasagna's probably still warm, but if not, you can throw it in the microwave for a minute. There's some bread in the bread box, too. Help yourself. I'm going upstairs to check on Jonah."

"Right. Sorry, I didn't mean…"

She'd already turned back toward the door.

"Carrie?"

"What?"

"Are you angry? Did I do something wrong?"

She watched him for a moment, as if wrestling with her-self. "Yes, I'm angry, but with myself, not with you. Why would I be angry with you? You haven't done anything wrong. You're just doing a job here. If a little boy spends a couple of hours with his nose pressed to the window because someone promised to play soccer with him when he got home, that's certainly not your fault."

Huxley winced. "Oh, bloody hell, that's right. I'm sorry. I got tied up."

"Yes, at your embassy, I heard. Well, no problem. That's who you answer to, of course. Jonah's not your concern, he's mine, and I've handled it badly. I've let him get attached to you, which is a stupid, stupid thing for me to have done. He doesn't need one more person in his life to disappoint him. He's had quite enough of that already. My mistake was standing by and letting it happen. So, no, Huxley, your conscience is clear. You've done nothing wrong. So just go away and do your job and I'll try to do mine a little better than I've been doing, all right?"

"Can I tell him I'm sorry? I'd planned to be here, but I got called away and it took longer than I expected."

"It doesn't matter. Kicking a soccer ball with a six-year-old doesn't fall within your job description, I'm sure." She then exhaled heavily. "Look, just go ahead and get your food and forget it, all right? I need to go upstairs and make sure he's finished his bath. He'll be down shortly for a bedtime snack. But, Huxley?" she warned. "Don't make him any more promises, will you?"

"No, no more promises. But, I like him a lot, Carrie. I mean that. He's a good little fellow. He really is."

"Good God. Don't you think I know that? Why do you think it pisses me off so much to see his feelings trampled on?"

He had the grace to look contrite, she thought as she turned on her heel and walked out the door and up the stairs. Fat lot of good contrition did.

But when push came to shove, it was right, what she'd told him. This was her fault, not Huxley's. What kind of mother let a stranger—a spy, for God's sake, the most lying, conniving, unreliable of human beings—move in on her life and earn her son's trust? Was she a total idiot?

And yet, and yet…. After a while, as she'd gotten to know him a little better, Huxley had seemed so different. Straightforward. Uncomplicated. Trustworthy. Trust—worthy.

Ha. You really are an idiot, girl.

Jonah was still in the bathtub, making water geysers between his cupped hands. Carrie rapped on the door frame, then walked in, flipped down the toilet seat and settled beside him. His hair was wet, soapy ringlets clinging to the nape of his neck.

"Hey, buddy. You washed your hair?"

"Uh-huh."

"I think you missed a little soap when you rinsed. Can I pour some water over your head to get it out? Otherwise it's going to be all sticky in the morning." When he nodded and lifted his knees, resting his elbows on them while he covered his eyes, she took a plastic bucket from the side of the tub and poured a couple of loads over the spots he'd missed. "Okay, I think that's it." Taking the soapy cloth he'd left on the side of the tub, she rubbed his back gently.

"I heard Mark downstairs," Jonah said finally.

"Yeah, he came. He got called into his office, it seems, and couldn't get away."

Jonah nodded.

"I think he wants to talk to you."

"It doesn't matter. He doesn't have to play with me."

"I think he wanted to, though. He's sorry."

"Like Daddy," Jonah said quietly.

Carrie was still rubbing his back gently, but she paused. "Are you missing Daddy, honey?"

He shrugged. "I don't know. Sort of, I guess. Not really."

"Are you mad at him?" When he didn't answer, Carrie rinsed off his back, then said, "Because it's okay if you are a little mad at him. You know what? I'm kind of mad at him my-self."

His enormous gray-green eyes rose to meet hers. "I thought you wanted him to go away. That's what Nana said."

"Oh, sweetie." She sighed. "You know, I love you more than anything or anyone in the whole, wide world. And Daddy loves you, too. None of this is your fault. I really don't know why Daddy went away the way he did. But as much as he and I love you, we probably don't love each other as much as we'd like. Maybe that's part of the reason he's done what he has. I'm sorry he did it without telling us, though. I hope he comes back soon so the three of us can talk this over and stop being mad. It makes my stomach hurt. How about you?"

Jonah nodded. "Am I gonna stay with you, Mom?"

"Yes, absolutely. Is that okay with you?"

"Yeah, that's what I want to do."

She dropped onto her knees beside the tub and put her arms around him. "Then that's exactly what's going to hap-pen. You and I are stuck like glue, kiddo."

"Good." He leaned into her briefly, then flicked some water at her, a smile finally breaking through the overcast and light-ing up his face.

"Hey!" Carrie jumped back. "Now, would you get out of that tub before you shrivel up like a big old prune? This water is free-eezing!"

He grinned. "Remember when I was little and I thought I was going to go down the drain when you pulled the plug?"

She cackled and waved her hand over the stopper chain, chanting, "Oh, my goodness, oh, my soul! There goes Jonah down the hole…"

He shrieked with laughter and beat her to pulling the chain.

* * *

Carrie took Jonah downstairs after his bath, scrubbed, combed and wearing flannel pj's to ward off the chill on a fall night that had suddenly turned wintry. They found Huxley in the kitchen, just finishing his dinner. He looked up when they came in and put down his fork, swiveling on the chair to face Jonah.

"Hey, there, Jonah. You look very smart."

"I had a bath."

"Mmm. Look, mate, I'm really sorry I was so late getting back. I know we were supposed to kick the ball out back, but—"

"It's okay. It was kind of too cold, anyway, and I wanted to play on the computer."

"Right. I guess soccer season's pretty much over, anyway."

"Yeah." Jonah climbed up onto a chair while Carrie poured him a glass of milk and set out a couple of oatmeal cookies for his bedtime snack. "Hey, Mark?" Jonah said.

"What?"

"You want to hear me read a book before I go to bed? I can read, you know."

"No kidding. That would be great—if it's all right with your mum," he added, looking up at Carrie.

She shrugged. "I suppose, just this once."

"And then you can read me one," Jonah added to Huxley.

"That sounds fair."

"And then my mom can read one," Jonah said.

"Three books? Don't push your luck, buddy," she said. "Tomorrow's a school day."

"You know," Huxley said, "while I was cleaning out back this morning, I noticed a woodpile back there and I brought some in. Your friend Tracy said the fireplaces are working and cleaned. How about if we make a fire in the front room? Would that be all right?"

"Yeah, a fire!" Jonah said. "That would be cool, hey, Mom? We can read by the fire."

"I suppose," she said reluctantly. "But you have half an hour till bedtime, and not a minute more."

Jonah was asleep on the couch by halfway through the second book.

"So much for the readers' marathon," Carrie murmured.

"I do believe he finds my reading boring," Huxley said, rising off his chair. "Do you want me to carry him upstairs?"

"No," Carrie said, jumping up. "I'll do it. Thanks, though," she added as an afterthought.

"He's not too heavy?"

"I've done it lots of times. I'm used to taking care of him on my own, and I can do it just fine now, thank you very much."

He sat back down as Carrie lifted Jonah in her arms and took him up to his bed, settling him in as sleety rain sounded a soft tattoo in the window. He rolled over onto his side, pulling his knees up into his chest. Carrie tucked the covers around him and leaned down to kiss his cheek, a lump forming in her throat as she inhaled his clean, baby soap scent.

When she came back downstairs, Huxley was crouched on the rug in front of the hearth, rearranging the logs with a poker. She stood in the doorway for a moment, watching his back, debating saying good-night herself and then going upstairs to take that long bubble bath she'd been promising herself all evening. But when he suddenly seemed to sense her presence and turned around to look at her, Huxley's expression was worried, his gray eyes sad in the light of the flickering flames.

She sighed and moved into the room, settling into an arm-chair near the hearth and tucking her blue-jeaned legs up under her. "I'm sorry," she said quietly.

"For what?"

"For snapping at you. And for sounding so insufferably self-pitying."

"You don't sound self-pitying. You sound angry. You have a right to be."

"But not with you. This isn't your fault. So, for what it's worth, I'm sorry."

"No problem." He cocked his thumb at the ceiling. "All tucked in?"

"Gonzo. He was tired. We had a long day."

"I'm glad I got a chance to see him before…" He hesitated. "Before he went to bed."

She watched him. "You're surprisingly good with kids."

"Surprisingly?"

"For someone in your business. Drum wasn't. He loved Jonah, but he really didn't understand kids all that well or relate. Anyway…" She stared at the flames for a few minutes.

"Big family," Huxley said.

She frowned. "Pardon."

"I come from a big family. Huge, as English families generally go. I've got eight nieces and nephews. Cousins by the dozens, too."

Carrie nodded. "Lucky. I had one sister and my parents. And that was about it. There were a couple of uncles, some cousins in the wings somewhere, but we didn't see them all that often even before my family died, and afterward…" She shrugged.

Huxley settled more comfortably on the floor and they sat saying nothing for a while, just watching the flames and the occasional shower of sparks as air pockets exploded in the wood.

And then, out of the blue, Huxley said, "I was married. My wife was killed two years ago."

Carrie watched his lined face in the glow of the embers.

"She was a nurse. She was working in the Middle East for Doctors Without Borders. We met in Lebanon. She was Irish, from Dublin. She had blue eyes and flaming red hair and freckles. Not as many as Tengwall, mind you, but a fair lot, just the same."

"How long were you married?"

"Nineteen months and twelve days. She died in a helicopter crash over northern Israel. They were flying medical supplies to Gaza." He poked the fire once more. "Somebody put a bomb on board. The Palestinians blamed the Israelis and the Israelis blamed the Palestinians. Tel Aviv didn't like the fact that medical supplies were going in to the camps, but there were some radical Islamic groups who thought the medical charities were a cover for western spies. They never quite worked out who got access to the cargo. There were various theories, but in that kind of situation, everybody's got an agenda. It's a liar's market."

"A pox on all their houses," Carrie said quietly, angrily. "I'm really sorry."

"Yeah, me, too. She was a great girl. We'd just found out she was pregnant," he added quietly.

"Oh, God. Mark..."

He exhaled heavily. "Life's a bitch, and then you die."

"It doesn't make sense."

The fire crackled and outside, thunder rolled ominously.

"Mark," she ventured. "What happened?"

"What do you mean?"

"Something happened this afternoon, didn't it? Tucker said you were called to your embassy. And now, you seem... I don't know...worried. What happened?"

"Nothing."

"Nothing? Or nothing you can talk about?"

"Both. Neither."

"Is it Drum? Has he been spotted?"

"Not that I know of."

Carrie sighed. "Fine, don't tell me. Christ, I am so tired of riddles and bloody spy games."

He looked up at her. "I'm not playing games, Carrie. I just don't know where your husband is."

"Well, nothing new in that. I didn't know where he was most of the time we were married, either." She drummed her fingers on the arm of the chair. "There's nothing else you can tell me about what's going on?"

"Nothing."

"Please? This situation is driving me crazy. You must know by now that I didn't play any part in whatever Drum was into. This suspicion in the air, though—I'm living in suspended animation here. It's like one of those bad dreams when you feel like you're running through syrup and you just can't get anywhere. You can't give me any idea how to get out from under?"

He studied her for a moment, then shook his head slowly. "Carrie, I'd like to help. I really mean that, but I can't tell you a thing." He put a finger to his lips and glanced around the room.

She stared at him for a moment, and then it dawned on her. She slipped off the chair and onto the floor, took the poker out of his hand and started prodding at the logs. She could feel him watching her, wanting her to understand...what?

"They're calling you back to London, aren't they?" she said quietly.

He nodded.

"When?"

"Right away."

She felt the bottom drop out of her stomach.

He took a deep breath, then reached out and laid his hand on hers. "But I don't want to go," he said quietly.

His fingers were warm. His body, close to hers, was warm. They both sat very still, watching the flames dance. Then, almost imperceptibly, she leaned in toward him and their shoulders touched. With his free hand, he took the poker out of her other hand and set it aside. He studied her soberly for a moment.

"Mark—"

He put a finger to her lips again and got to his feet, walking over to the stereo sitting on a table on the other side of the room. A moment later, Ella Fitzgerald's smoky voice drifted over the room to a warm jazz beat.

Huxley came back and settled beside her on the rug once more and took her chin in one hand. She thought he was going to kiss her and found, surprisingly, that she really wanted that to happen. And he did, but lightly, on the cheek and not on the lips, and then she heard him murmur in her ear.

"Things are going well on this case. I can't give you details, Carrie, but my office wants to cut our operational losses. They're pulling me out now to go back to help do damage assessment."

She nodded, closing her eyes.

"But I don't want to leave you," he added quietly.

"I don't want you to go," she whispered back.

He'd been holding his breath, she realized, but when she said that, he sighed and wrapped his arms around her.

It was stupid and pointless, she knew, but suddenly, she really didn't want him to leave, even though there was nothing in the world she could do to stop it—anymore than she'd been able to change anything else. She felt like a bit of flotsam on a vast, roiling sea. She wanted to scream and kick and fight against the unfairness of it all. And she would, dammit. She would fight, for herself and her son. On her own, by her own effort. She'd take care of Jonah, and she'd get a job, and they would get through this somehow. She didn't need to be taken care of by anyone.

But right now, a pair of surprisingly gentle arms was around her. Tomorrow he'd be gone, and she'd continue picking up the pieces of her life, moving on without him, without anyone but her son.

But that was tomorrow. For tonight, there was this man beside her who wanted her, and whom she wanted, too. It had been so long….

So, just for tonight…

"I give up," she said.

He pulled back and peered at her. "What?"

"I'm tired of trying to figure it all out. I'm tired, period. Just for a little while, do you think you could hold me, and let me hold you? Could we just forget about the rest of the messy world for one blessed night?"

He nodded. "I'd like that." He took her face in his hands and kissed her on one cheek, then the other, then, softly, on the lips.

"We have to be quiet," she murmured, running her fingers over his chest.

He nodded and lay her back gently on the rug. "I know."

CHAPTER TWENTY-TWO

Washington, D.C. (Georgetown)
October 31, 2002—7:15 p.m.

Hollywood had a lot to answer for—encouraging America's love affair with guns and violence. Lowering the level of civility in public discourse. Turning staid old Georgetown into a lunatic asylum every Halloween.

Of course, students didn't need much excuse to cut loose, Carrie conceded, and parties probably got wild in every college town at Halloween. But ever since Georgetown University and the surrounding neighborhood had been tapped as the location for the filming of *The Exorcist,* students there had felt a special obligation to turn October 31 into a particularly insane spree.

She had vivid memories from her own college days of the

traditional screening of the movie at Healy Hall, during which the costumed audience hooted and cheered at every recognizable landmark. Then, once the devil-possess priest had been fatally dispatched down the spooky "Exorcist staircase" (which actually stood beside a renovated Georgetown streetcar barn and nowhere near the house used in the film shoot), the entire campus population would spread out onto the surrounding streets, thousands of pixilated ghouls creating total gridlock until the wee hours of the morning.

So, when Jonah and his buddy Sam started making excited plans for trick-or-treating in the neighborhood, Carrie was skeptical. Sam's mom, who'd been living next door since before her son was born, assured her the boys would be fine.

"As long as they go out early, there's no problem," she said. "The college kids don't really hit the streets in force until nine or ten at night. I don't know about Jonah, but Sam's fast asleep in bed by then—even if I have to scrape the little sugar-devil off the ceiling to get him there."

"Come on, Mom," Jonah pleaded. "I've never been trick-or-treating in my whole, entire life."

"You went to Halloween parties when we lived in London," she said.

He'd been not quite three the summer Drum was posted to the British capital, too young to have trick-or-treated before that. The embassy community traditionally hosted indoor Halloween celebrations for the diplobrats.

"It's not the same," he said. "We didn't go around to houses. The kids at school think it's really weird I've never gone out before."

"Yeah, well, I bet they didn't get to go to the Tower of London on Halloween like your class did last year," Carrie said. "Hey, Sam? Doesn't that sound cool?"

Sam furrowed his brow. "What's the Tower of London?"

Jonah threw up his hands. "See, Mom? Nobody goes to the dorky old Tower of London. You gotta go trick-or-treating."

She sighed. "I suppose we could go out for a while. But here's the deal—we have to be home by eight and you still have to be in bed by eight-thirty. It's a school night."

His tousled head bounced up and down. "I promise," he said, "cross my heart."

She smiled. "All right then."

The two six-year-olds went shrieking up the stairs. "Yay!"

Sam's mother was a lawyer with the Justice Department. His father, Carrie guessed from the few clues she'd picked up, was an anonymous sperm donor. His mom employed a full-time live-in nanny who, at sixty, was sweet, kind and loving, but she wasn't up to Carrie's standards when it came to body-guard duty to protect Jonah from drunken students on George-town streets—much less from the machinations of his duplicitous father. She volunteered herself to accompany the two of them out on their Halloween rounds. And where Car-rie went, Tengwall was right behind.

Although, the young security officer told her as the two of them followed the boys that night, there was little chance Drum would show up after all this time. "My bosses think he's long gone," Tengwall said. "MI-6 thinks so, too. That's why they pulled Huxley back to London."

Carrie nodded and said nothing, although she could feel Tengwall studying her out of the corner of her eye, waiting for her to add something on the subject of Huxley. Maybe she knew—probably she did. Well, so what if she did? Carrie thought. By now, her life was an open book, no chapter too personal that some stranger didn't feel justified in peering at it. She was getting used to standing naked in front of the world, all her faults and stupid acts laid bare. So maybe Tengwall did know she'd slept with Huxley, but even if she did, what was the point of discussing it?

She and Huxley had one night, coming together out of mutual need and frustration—and attraction, admittedly. It had been a long time since anyone had made her feel so wanted, Carrie thought, or held her so close. But they both knew there was no future in it. By the time Tucker and Tengwall had shown up the next morning, she and Huxley had been awake for hours, saying their regretful farewells. He'd spent extra time with Jonah before he left that morning, gently explaining that he had to go back to London for his work, but promising to write via snail-mail and e-mail, hoping he would get back to D.C. soon for a visit. Jonah had been disappointed, but had taken it bravely. It wasn't right, Carrie told herself angrily, that at such a young age, her little boy already knew so much about abandonment.

And it wasn't just his father and Huxley, she realized suddenly, as her wandering mind focused back on what Tengwall was saying to her.

"...ordered to report back to work at Langley on Monday morning myself."

She looked over at the young woman. "They're pulling you off surveillance here?"

Tengwall nodded. "I think they're shutting down this part of the investigation altogether. It's just not producing anything useful, and resources are tight."

"What about the FBI? Have they pulled back, too?"

Tengwall shrugged, as two pairs of superhero feet came flying toward them.

"Hey, Mom! We got Mars bars!" Jonah cried, showing her

his pillowcase haul. He was dressed in a red-and-blue spandex Spider-Man costume. Sam was the Hulk, tricked out in green latex foam that bulked up his skinny six-year-old arms and legs. Both of them had chocolate-smeared lips from sampling the wares of their increasingly heavy load.

"Whoa!" Carrie said, peering into his bag. "What a haul. We'd better give some of this stuff a taste test, make sure it's not poison. You think, Bree?"

Tengwall nodded and looked over her shoulder. "Yeah, I think so. Better let me test one of those Snickers bars. They look pretty dicey to me."

"Yeah, I don't like the look of these Almond Joys, either," Carrie said, mock soberly, as she pulled a couple of bars out of the bag.

Jonah rolled his eyes. "You guys can have some. I've got *tons*. Hey, Sam? Race you!" he shrieked in delight.

The two boys took off at a gallop up to the next house on their route.

"Slow down," Carrie called after them. "And don't forget to say thank you."

"We won't," came the chorused reply.

She tore the wrapper off the end of the chocolate bar and stuffed the paper into the pocket of her down jacket. She was wearing a heavy wool green turtleneck and jeans under it, a multi-hued knit scarf knotted around her neck and long johns under her jeans and boots. A killing frost had settled over the city, and her wispy breath was making ice crystals in her loose hair.

"Man, one more block, and then I think I'm going to rein these guys in," she said. "I'm freezing."

"You've got that thin California blood," Tengwall said. "I grew up in North Dakota. This is nothing."

"Yeah, I'm a total wuss, no doubt about it."

They walked along a little farther, watching the parade of small witches and wizards, princesses and superheroes on the street—as well as some of the oversize characters who were starting to emerge from the nearby campus. There were students dressed as knights and nuns, pimps and Playboy Bunnies, as well as a variety of handmade costumes that had obviously been put together from odds and ends in assorted dorm rooms. One fellow was a bulletin board, decked out entirely in paper flyers. Another in an advanced party spirit was walking down the middle of the street wearing jeans and a T-shirt to which were pinned dozens of fuzzy yellow stuffed Easter chicks. The T-shirt had two words emblazoned across the front: CHICK MAGNET.

Across the street, a group of elaborately costumed adults was streaming up the sidewalks of a large, brightly lit home with loud music spilling out its open windows. A young D.C. Metropolitan cop stood on the doorstep, handing out what Carrie guessed would be the first of multiple warnings about noise levels. It was going to be a long night for law enforcement.

Under the lamplight at the corner, a tall man was dressed as the Phantom of the Opera, in a long, red-lined black cape, wide fedora and a gleaming white mask bisecting his face. He seemed to be watching them, but when he spotted Carrie looking back, he spun on his heel, cape swirling, and started up the drive toward the party.

Carrie's heart began to pound. "Brianne? See that guy across the road? He looks like Drum."

"Which one? Where?"

"The one in the Phantom costume, heading up the walk. His gait is identical to Drum's."

The Phantom mounted the steps, and paused at the door, joining the conversation for a moment before the cop waved him through. A moment later, the music turned down, the cop came back down the sidewalk and drove off in his cruiser.

Carrie exhaled heavily. "I guess it was just my imagination."

"I'm telling you, Carrie, he's gone. You can relax."

"Maybe you're right." She frowned at the younger woman. "So, anyway, you're leaving us? Jonah will be sorry to see you go."

"I won't be far away. Maybe I can drop by to see him. I really like the little guy."

"He really likes you."

Tengwall hesitated, then said, "I'm sorry you've had to go through all this."

Carrie nodded. "Me, too, believe me." She waved to Jonah and Sam. "Hey, guys, it's getting late and I think you've got enough candy there to last you until next Halloween."

They grumbled, but turned back, peering in their bags and pulling out sustenance for the walk home.

After they got back to Sam's house, Jonah and Sam spread their loot out on the floor to let Carrie and Sam's mother sift through it, removing anything with an open wrapper or that looked in any way dicey. Then, Carrie and Jonah said goodnight and headed back next door with Tengwall. It was a happy little boy she tucked into bed—after he'd brushed his teeth under very close scrutiny.

"That was so much fun, Mom!" he breathed happily. "I wish every day was Halloween."

She snuggled beside him on his narrow bed, breathing in his soapy, chocolatey scent. "If every day was Halloween, it would get boring. It's having it just once a year makes it special."

"I'd like to get candy every day. That wouldn't be boring."

"Sure it would—boring as those peas you never want to eat. I'd have to say, 'Jonah, eat your Snickers bars, or no spinach for dessert,' and you'd say, 'Mo-om! Do I have to'?"

He rolled on his side sleepily and pulled the covers up under his chin. "We should try it and see. Could I have jelly beans for breakfast?"

"In your dreams," she said, kissing him. "Go to sleep, doofus."

He grinned and closed his eyes. "Night, Mom."

"Night, sweetie. I love you."

She lay with him for a few minutes, humming softly, savoring the quiet. Thinking how different this was from those long colicky nights when he was a baby and she'd walked him up and down the floor for hours, wondering what she'd done wrong to produce such an unhappy infant. Now, she couldn't imagine what she'd done right to have been blessed with such a lovable son.

At the faint sound of murmuring downstairs, she rolled gently away from his sleeping form and headed for the door, switching off the lamp as she went. Tucker must have shown up for the night watch. She was losing track of which one of them was on duty when—although from what Tengwall had told her, maybe she and Jonah would soon be left on their own, at long last. It couldn't come a moment too soon. She could no longer remember what it was like to have a life that didn't include the perpetual presence of suspicious eyes.

And yet, by the end, these people had become familiar and almost comfortable—especially Huxley, she admitted, feeling a small ache that she had no business indulging. Their lives were on different paths. Those paths might have briefly intersected, but she wanted no more of the world to which Huxley and the rest of them belonged.

Been there, done that. No, thanks.

Down in the library, though, was proof that if Carrie was done with treachery, it wasn't done with her.

She saw Tengwall standing with her back to the open door, talking to someone on the far side of the room, out of her line of sight.

"I was going to make her some tea," she said. "I thought we agreed that was the best way to handle it."

"Handle what?" Carrie said, stepping into the library.

Tengwall spun around, her blond ponytail flying, her gaze leaping from Carrie to the desk, then back again. When Carrie saw who it was sitting at the desk, she froze, her heart leaping into her throat. "Drum," she breathed.

He rose to his feet. His silver hair was slicked back and there was a white half-face mask lying on the desk next to a broad-brimmed fedora, and a red-lined cape tossed over the back of the chair.

He followed her gaze to the costume, then smiled. "Yup, that was me in the street. You almost had me there, Carrie. Fortunately, there were so many people at that party that no one thought anything strange in one more costumed stranger walking into the place. It's what I always used to tell you— if you carry yourself like you belong, nobody questions your right to go anywhere you want. Takes a little confidence—" He punched a fist lightly in the air "—but it can be done."

"What are you doing here?" she asked coldly.

"I came for my son."

She backed up into the doorway. "No way. No bloody way. He's staying with me."

"I don't think so."

"This wasn't how it was going to go, Drum," Tengwall protested. "I could have brought Jonah to you once she was out. You shouldn't even be in the streets. She recognized you. Somebody else might, too."

"That's sweet of you to be concerned, honey." He came around the desk and put a hand to her cheek, smiling. "But I changed my mind. I didn't want to leave this all on your shoulders. It didn't seem fair. The traffic is wicked out there tonight. It makes more sense for us to do this together."

"You're in on this, Brianne?" Carrie asked. "How could you? Isn't it obvious the man's a total snake?"

"No, he's not. You don't understand, Carrie. He didn't do what they said. And," she added, "I love him."

"Good God. *He* was your hot date the other night? How long have you been seeing him?"

"A couple of months. I admit, I was ready to turn him in when he first showed up. But after he explained what happened, I knew I had to help him."

"What *happened*?" Carrie repeated. "What happened is that he betrayed his country. You know that."

"No, I didn't," Drum said. "I would never do that. You should know better, Carrie. I'm a MacNeil. MacNeils aren't traitors. My family has served this country for generations."

"Unbelievable," Carrie said, shaking her head as she backed out the door. She had to get to a phone. She had to keep him away from Jonah.

"Carrie, don't make me play the heavy," he warned. "Come in here and sit down and let me explain."

"You need to leave right now, Drum."

"I can't do that. Now, get back in here and sit *down,* dammit." This time, he pulled a gun out of his pocket and aimed it at her for emphasis.

Carrie froze for a moment, racking her brain, trying to think what to do. He had a silencer on the gun, but the streets were so loud with revelers it wouldn't matter how much noise they made, no one would hear anything. Except Jonah, maybe. And the last thing she wanted was for him to walk in on this.

She moved back into the library and settled on the table near the fireplace. "So now what happens?" she asked. "You shoot me? That's a great way to make it up to your son for being a lousy father. God, this is so typical of you, Drum. And you, Brianne. You're every bit as dumb as I was. Don't you see what's going on? He uses women. Do you think he's going to walk off into the sunset with you and live happily ever after? Get real. He needs you now, but how long do you think it'll be before he moves on to greener pastures. He'll dump you, or start cheating on you, the ways he's cheated on me—and on his first wife. How did that go, by the way, Drum? How did Theresa really die?"

"She drowned. You know that."

"After ingesting alcohol and tranquilizers. Is that what was going to happen to me, too? That's what Brianne meant about making tea for me?"

"Nobody's going to hurt you, Carrie," Tengwall said. "He just wants his son. You can understand that."

Carrie gave her a scathing look. "No, Brianne, I take it back. You're much dumber than I was if you can't see what he's got planned here."

Drum stepped between them. "Brianne, you need to go upstairs and get that bag over there packed with a few things for

Jonah. I'll be right up, and I'll help you carry him down. Would you do that for me?"

"Drum, are you sure—"

"It's going to be fine. I'll just talk to Carrie, and then we'll be off. Go on now. Scoot!"

Tengwall moved away, reluctantly. He watched her gather up a duffle bag by the door and head out. Then, Drum turned back to Carrie. "It's not what you think. I am not a traitor. I've been set up, but with this much suspicion hanging over me, there's no way I'll ever clear myself now. And frankly, I can't be bothered, anyway. I've had enough of the business. I'm ready to retire."

"You mortgaged the house out from under your mother. And you forged a letter to my broker and tried to steal my money."

"The house is mine, Carrie. I can do what I want with it."

"And my money?"

"Well, that, I admit, was a little over the top. But I had to do it, once I realized how bad things were, and that they were going to try to pin this bogus espionage rap on me. You'll be all right. You're young and bright and beautiful. You'll find someone else. I hear there's an MI-6 character sniffing around. That's great. You liked England, didn't you? You'll be fine, Carrie, but I need—"

Three loud bumps sounded from the front hall, like a punching bag being bounced down the stairs. The first thought that occurred to Carrie was that Tengwall had tried to carry Jonah down by herself and dropped him. Drum must have thought the same thing, because he bounded for the door.

Carrie was right behind him, but she paused just long enough to grab the heavy brass pestle out of the mortar sitting in the low table, sticking it up the sleeve of her oversize sweater. Tracy's mother had bought the mortar and pestle in an antique market in Marrakech. It was a kitchen utensil, really, but the mortar had a crack in it, so Mrs. Overturf had polished it up to use as an attractive paperweight in the library instead. As weapons went, a blackjack in her sleeve was better than nothing, she decided.

In the front hall, they found not Jonah but Tengwall collapsed on the staircase. Carrie came around Drum to get a better look, and saw the young woman's head draped over the landing, a trickle of blood beginning to pool next to it.

Carrie clamped a hand over her mouth as a freezing draft washed over her. She caught movement out of the corner of her eye and turned to find a large man just inside the open front door, his right arm raised. It held an automatic weapon fitted out with a silencer. He was big, like Tucker, but this man wasn't bald. Rather, he had thick black hair, a heavy moustache and a couple of days worth of stubble on his swarthy cheeks. He was wearing a black leather jacket over a blue shirt and brown corduroy pants.

He pivoted in one smooth movement and pointed the gun at Drum. "You will drop your weapon, please," he said in heavily accented English.

Another voice, this one familiar, piped up behind him. "I would do what he says if I were you." Coming through the vestibule door, his cheeks ruddy, his brown eyes bright, was Tom Bent.

"Bent," Drum said grimly. "I should have guessed."

"Your weapon, Mr. MacNeil," the brawny one repeated.

Drum tossed it over onto the hall rug, and Tom crouched down and retrieved it. He stuck it into the left pocket of his overcoat, then reached over to the right side and fished around that pocket until he found what he was looking for. Another weapon, also silenced.

"Tom, what's going on here?" Carrie asked. "Who is this?" She wanted to feel relieved that help was at hand, but it was small comfort, with Tengwall bleeding profusely, quite possibly dying on the staircase.

"This fellow's name is Markov," Tom said. "Sergei Markov, and he works for me, don't you, Sergei?"

The big bruiser nodded, while Carrie tried to remember where she'd heard that name before.

"But," Tom added, "there's really no need for you to remember his name."

A sharp hiss of air sounded, and Markov's free hand flew to his chest like someone with a sudden, severe case of heartburn. He looked down, apparently stunned to see a field of red suddenly blooming on the front of his shirt. And then, his knees buckled and he dropped forward like a stone. As the man fell, Tom managed to retrieve the gun that slipped from his failing hand. When Markov hit the carpet, Carrie saw a small hole in the back of his leather jacket, its edges still smoking. The smell of gunpowder in the air bit at her nostrils.

"Tom!" she cried. "What did you do that for?"

"I'm cleaning up loose ends, darlin'. This man's a nasty piece of work—a hired assassin. Look what he did to poor Miss Tengwall there. This is also the fellow who tried to shoot you in London."

Carrie nodded slowly. "That's right. Huxley said a man named Markov had been identified as the shooter from last April."

"I hear Drum here hired him to kill you," Tom said, "only Markov botched the job."

"That's a damn lie, Tom," Drum said indignantly. "Carrie, I didn't, I swear. That's what I mean. You see? They're trying to pin this all on me."

"It's on you, Drummond," Tom said. "The jig, as they say, is well and truly up. You tried to have Carrie killed. And poor Alex Lee in Hong Kong? They're saying you threw her off her balcony—and on her birthday, no less."

"But I didn't! You know I didn't. I told you I was going to stop off in Rome on the way to that Delhi conference to see Francesca."

"Who's Francesca?" Carrie asked, and then answered her own question. "Oh, my God, Francesca Gambini, the Italian ambassador's wife? Who was always sending over wine from her father's vineyard? Godammit, Drum, you were screwing her, too?"

But Drum was shaking his head in disbelief, staring at Tom. "You were the one who did this to me. Christ, Tom, how long have we been friends? I even shared Alex with you, and—"

Tom's face contorted. "You *shared* her with me," he sneered. "So magnanimous. Crumbs from the table of the great Drummond MacNeil."

"Oh, hell, now I see," Drum said. "You killed her, and then set me up to take the fall. And I thought you were trying to help when you warned me CIA Security was taking a hard look at me. He was the one who called me in a panic that last morning when I took off at the mall, Carrie. He was my friend, he said, he had a backup car waiting to take me to cover while everything got straightened out."

"If you'd had nothing to hide, Drummond, you'd have had no reason to be rattled."

"Everybody has something to hide, Tom. A little fudging on expense accounts, a couple of under-the-table deals—"

"Keeping mistresses on the Company's tab, making payments to non-existent informants, trading in black-market currency," Tom added, head shaking. "You just kept digging yourself in deeper and deeper." He turned to Carrie. "I hate to say this darlin', but this man you married is smooth but not real bright. The more rattled he got, the more stupid mistakes he made, until he just ended up looking so sleazy that the security folks were ready to believe anything about him—including that he compromised operations."

"But I don't understand," Carrie said. "I was told that operations really were damaged. They said people were betrayed and killed because secret intelligence had been sold. Information that could only have come through the London Station Chief. That was Drum."

"Oh, operations were blown, all right, all over the world," Drum said. "And somebody went to a lot of trouble to make sure that the common element in every single case was that *I* knew about them. There wasn't much that doesn't pass through the London station. But it all goes across the Director's desk, too. And guess who had access to everything the Director saw? Our friend Tom, here. So what did you do, Tom? Copy every damn document that had my name on it?"

"Pretty much. A digital camera's a wonderful thing. You photograph, you download it at an internet cafe and send it off to Zurich, and then you erase the disk by recording over it—say, a picture of a little boy with a piece of moon rock? What could be more innocent? Ain't technology grand?"

"You set me up."

"Oh, bull! You were looking for an excuse to run, Drummond. You weren't cut out for this business and you know it. You're a fraud and a coward. Even Carrie knows that, don't you, darlin'?"

She shook her head. "Tom, I can't believe it. You did this to us?"

"I did it to *him*, the smug bastard. Always got everything, did Drum—a beautiful wife—two beautiful wives, actually. A nice little boy, the best jobs. Did he appreciate 'em, though? No. Whereas I, who worked my tail off, at Yale, at Langley— well, I have to say, it just sticks in your craw after a while, you know? And there was all this valuable information passing across my desk every day. Worth a fortune, you know, if you understand the market and know where to find the right buyer. I knew that once the intelligence got out there and ops started being blown, somebody was going to trace it back. All I had to do was make it look like Drummond here was the source. And then, when I quietly warned him that MI-6 was making allegations about his nefarious activities and that the Director was appointing a special security committee to look into it, it was only a matter of time until he bolted like a jackrabbit with a stick o' dynamite up his behind."

Drum leapt across the hall at him, fury and arrogance combining to make him forget how outmatched he was, since Tom still held a gun. A single shot dropped him right next to Markov.

"Let this be a lesson," Tom said, looking down into his fading blue eyes. "You act guilty, Drummond, people are going to believe you really are guilty."

Carrie backed herself against the library doorframe, shaking with terror at the realization that there was only one way this could end. Tom couldn't let her get out alive, not knowing what she did. If she could get away from the house and get him to come after her, though, then at least Jonah would be safe.

"Tom, you don't want to do this," she said.

"No, I know I don't, Carrie, but unfortunately, I've got no choice."

"This can't possibly end well for you."

Tom was patting his pockets, a frown of concentration on his face. "Actually, it can. I've put a lot of thought into it, and I think it can work out very well, indeed. Aha! This is the one," he added, pulling Drum's gun out of his pocket. "This is how it's going to play out—Drum came back with Markov to finish you off. Markov took out your young bodyguard there, while ballistics will show that Drum shot you." He waved the gun in his hand. "With this weapon here. Now, stay with me, because it gets a little more complicated. I happen to show up, bearing a Halloween gift for my godson. But sadly, I get here too late to save you. But when Drum pulls a gun on me, I defend myself and manage to take down him and Markov. It's all very complicated, I know, but it will wash, believe me. I've thought it through very carefully."

"You've always been a very meticulous person, Tom. And then what? You just carry on as if nothing happened?"

"Oh, no. This is a tragedy, after all. I had to shoot my oldest and dearest friend. Drummond and I have known each other since college days. And walking in on all this mayhem he caused here? Well, I wouldn't be surprised if I came down with a bad case of post-traumatic stress syndrome and had to retire—on a full disability pension, of course. And then, after a short time, I'll probably tell Lorraine she deserves better than to spend the rest of her days with an old mope like me, and I'll take myself off somewhere to lick my wounds. The Bahamas, maybe, or Fiji."

"And live well off the money you made selling out those intelligence operations."

He nodded. "There you go."

"And all that stands between you and this plan is me." Carrie had let the brass pestle slip unobtrusively down her sleeve until it rested in the palm of her hand.

He nodded again. "Fraid so, darlin'. You and my godson, unfortunately."

"You bastard!" She pitched the brass hammer with all her strength, and it struck Tom in the forehead. As he stumbled, hand to his head, she turned and ran.

The front way was blocked, but if she could just get to the back door—

The first bullet passed so close that she felt hot air whiz by her temple. She ducked as wood splintered off the back door. A second shot took out the window. He had a clear sight line from where he stood in the front hall directly to the back door. She could hear his boots as he tore down the hall after her.

Carrie had no choice but to veer right, throwing open the cellar door and heading down the perilously narrow stairs. She could only hope that he would follow her and stumble in the dark. Anything to get him as far away as possible from Jonah.

She was able to make it to the bottom of the stairs by the light spilling from the kitchen, but down below, the cellar was pitch-black. She felt her way along the wall, stumbling on the uneven dirt floor, and managed to duck behind the big old cast iron coal furnace just as Tom found the switch at the top of the stairs and flicked on the overhead light. The stairs creaked as he moved slowly down one step at a time.

"Carrie," he called softly, "there's no way out. You might as well come up. I promise it'll be quick and painless. You won't feel a thing."

Her body was shaking uncontrollably, despite her heavy sweater and the heat coming off the rumbling gas furnace near by. Carrie crouched deeper in the shadow of the big old coal unit, bracing her arms on the ground as her shaking knees threatened to topple her. A stone bit into the palm of her hand.

No, not a stone, she realized. A lump of coal. Her fingers closed around it.

"I know," Tom said quietly, "it's not fair. I tried to think of a way to avoid this, but it just can't be done."

Another step creaked, and then she heard his boots hit the dirt floor. He was circling around, looking.

"Oh, Carrie," he crooned, "come out, come out, wherever you are!"

He'd moved away from the bottom of the stairs, she realized. If she could distract him long enough to get back up the staircase, she might be able to get the door shut and lock him down here.

Tom was circling slowly, apparently peering into every nook and cranny. "Maybe I could take Jonah with me, Carrie. That might be something good that comes out of this, hmm? I'm his godfather, after all, and with the bishop's influence, I'm sure I could arrange for custody."

Bastard! Carrie thought furiously. *You're not fit to be near my son!*

She peered around the furnace and saw him on the far side of the cellar, looking under an old workbench. Her hand closed around the rock of coal and she waited for just the right moment...then lobbed it at one of the cellar windows. The glass shattered. As Tom leapt out of the way, ducking flying shards, he stumbled on the floor's uneven cant and fell backward onto his butt.

Carrie took her chance. Scrambling out from behind the furnace, she charged for the stairs and started up. She was halfway to the top when she felt his hand shoot out from between two steps and grab her ankle, yanking hard. Her foot skidded on the tread, and she tipped, falling backward, her spine and skull striking the wooden steps painfully, knocking the wind out of her.

She lay there helplessly sprawled on the staircase, one foot caught between two treads. Tom came around from the underside. "Godammit, Carrie, you are not making this easy."

She finally worked her foot free and her body bumped back down the steps. As she lay in a heap at the bottom, he looked down at her, head shaking. He had a cut on his forehead from where the brass pestle had struck him and he was sweating profusely.

"Girl, I would gladly shoot you where you lie, I am that annoyed, but I need you to be upstairs with Jonah, where it'll look like Drum did the nasty, and I am not about to carry you and have you bleed all over me."

"You bastard. You never had any intention of leaving Jonah alive."

"I wanted to, but it just isn't practical. Now, for heaven's sake, get up, would you?"

She rolled over painfully and sat up, rubbing her ankle where it had gotten caught in the stairs. "If you think I'm going to walk up to help you stage your little scene, Tom, you're nuts."

He sighed. "I was afraid you'd say that."

He glanced around, then yanked at a piece of cloth-wrapped electrical conduit hanging from one of the ceiling joists overhead. A couple of feet of wire broke off in his hand. He planted a boot on her back and pushed her down on her stomach, then dropped himself on her back, pinning her in place. Carrie struggled mightily, but he was heavier and stronger. Grabbing her wrists, he wrapped the wire tightly around them, then rolled off of her and pulled her back up to a sitting position, and then onto her feet.

As she struggled to get blood back into her legs after being painfully folded under him, he pulled a drop cloth off the metal canning shelves, shook it out and threw it over her head. Carrie felt his arms go around her, and the next thing she knew, he had picked her up and thrown her over his shoulder.

"Now don't wriggle, girl, or we're both going to crack our skulls on these damn rickety stairs," he said, starting up.

One, two... She counted as he made his way up the steps, thinking, calculating. *Four, five...* She'd been up and down those steps dozens of times, but how many were there? *Six, seven...* She had to time it just right. If she could kick just as he reached the top step, with luck, her feet might find the landing while he went backward. *Eight, nine...*

There couldn't be more than ten, she decided. She stiffened her knees, then brought them up hard into his groin. He bellowed and his grip loosened. Carrie felt him start to go back, and at the last minute, her feet found the kitchen floor. She heard the thump as he went down, but then, she knew there was no way she wasn't going right after him. The tarp was still over her head. She couldn't see, and with her hands tied, she couldn't regain her balance. Her feet scrambled for purchase, tangling in the cloth, tripping over the top step. Helpless, she was going down.

And then something shot out in front of her and blocked her fall. She felt herself yanked back from the precipice. As the drop cloth was ripped off her head, she lost what felt like a handful of hair. When a hand brushed it out of her watering eyes, she found herself looking into the worried, weathered face of Mark Huxley.

He pulled her farther away from the cellar door, then shouted past her, "Clear!"

Carrie turned to see Tucker straddled across the cellar opening, his arms outstretched and holding a gun in a two-handed grip aimed down the stairs. They all stood absolutely still. And then, after a moment, Tucker stood down, his fierce scowl relaxing.

Huxley steadied her and they moved next to Tucker, following the direction of his downward gaze. Tom Bent lay at the bottom of the stairs, his head flattened awkwardly against the foundation, smashed against bloodied two-hundred-year-old Georgetown bricks.

From the front hall came more footsteps, and Carrie looked up to see FBI Agent Andrews coming through to the kitchen, followed by several other men in black FBI windbreakers.

"My son?" she asked anxiously.

"Sound asleep in his bed upstairs," Andrews said. "He must have had a great Halloween."

CHAPTER TWENTY-THREE

McLean, Virginia
November 8, 2002

It was a freezing, windswept November morning, the kind of dark and gloomy day that seemed fitting for nothing else but a funeral. The sky was a roil of blue-black clouds rimmed in shades of purple—an angry, unforgiving sky.

In spite of her heavy black woolen coat and the cashmere scarf bundled around her neck, Carrie felt the damp cold slice through to her bones the moment she stepped out of the black limousine in front of St. John's Episcopal Church in McLean, home parish to six generations of MacNeils. High overhead, a single bell in the church tower pealed somberly.

Pushing a wind-tossed strand of hair out of her eyes, Carrie reached a leather-gloved hand back behind her. Her mother-in-law gripped her hand tightly for support as she climbed awkwardly out of the back seat. Then, she dropped Carrie's hand and took the arm of her daughter, Eleanor, who emerged from the limo behind her. Eleanor sighed and nodded to Carrie, then turned and led her mother forward toward the entrance.

Althea was still angry, Carrie knew, convinced her daughter-in-law was somehow to blame for Drum's downfall. But nothing would prevent her from putting on a show of family solidarity for her son's funeral.

It was going to be a small service, unlike his father's. Eighteen hundred people had filed through the National Cathedral's triple set of pierced bronze gates to pay their respects when General Naughton MacNeil had passed away in 1990, including the President of the United States, several cabinet ministers, and all the Joint Chiefs. Drum's service, by contrast, would be primarily a family affair. The CIA Director had sent flowers on behalf of the Agency, as well as condolences, but was unable to attend due to heightened security concerns, his office reported.

The official Agency line on the deaths of Drummond Mac-Neil and Tom Bent was that they had fallen in the line of duty, felled by the same terrorist assassin who had attacked the U.S. Embassy in London the previous April. Some of the press reports mentioned in passing that a junior CIA official had also been seriously wounded in the Georgetown attack. Tengwall would be in hospital for several weeks, it seemed. The FBI wanted to bring criminal charges against her for her part in helping Drum, but Carrie suspected that the young woman would end up being fired and told that a whopping load of legal grief would come down on her like a ton of bricks if she ever breathed a word about what had happened that Halloween night in Georgetown.

The national security community didn't wash its dirty linen in public. There was nothing to be gained by revealing the seamier side of the story, the powers that be had decided. The Agency had a job to do, America had a war on terror to fight. The British cousins were satisfied that the leak in the western intelligence net had been closed. End of story.

Carrie turned back to the car as Jonah's tousled head emerged. He leapt from the jump seat to the curb, then seemed to remember the solemnity of the occasion. He stood patiently while Carrie tugged down his parka.

"You can take your jacket off inside," she told him.

He nodded. His Brooks Brothers suit was getting its second workout in a couple of weeks. It had almost done triple service, but in the end, Carrie had decided not to take him to his godfather's funeral, although she had gone herself, in memory of the friend he'd once been to her. She'd stood quietly at the back of the almost empty National Cathedral and slipped away as soon as the service was over, but the sad smile Bishop Merriam had sent in her direction on the recessional expressed the family's gratitude that she'd even come. Althea, not surprisingly, had refused to attend.

Hand in hand, Carrie and Jonah followed his grandmother and aunt up the steps and into the church. Carrie felt eyes on her as she went through the charade of playing the grieving widow. *Only for Jonah,* she told herself. And for his sake, she did genuinely grieve, too. Whatever his faults—and they had been calamitous—Drum had loved his son, and he'd died trying to hold on to him.

CIA and FBI security had quickly set up a protective cordon around the Overturfs' Georgetown home that Halloween night, holding back both inquiring press and the curious crowds, who'd soon figured out that there was something beyond the usual Halloween madness happening on O Street that night. Sequestered inside the house, keeping watch over her sleeping son while the carnage downstairs was photographed, then cleared out, Carrie could only imagine the tense all-night meetings that had gone on while senior government officials on both sides of the Potomac tried to work out what, if anything, to say about what had happened.

Tucker, it turned out, had begun to become suspicious of Tengwall weeks ago, and had followed her the night that Huxley had stayed with Carrie. When he realized that she was working with MacNeil, he'd convinced Huxley to stay on long enough to let MacNeil's scenario play out so they could determine who else was in on the conspiracy. They'd bugged Tengwall's Virginia apartment and overheard the two of them planning to meet there on Halloween night, after Tengwall had drugged Carrie and kidnapped Jonah.

Only at the last minute had Tucker and Huxley realized that the escape was going down from the Georgetown house instead of Tengwall's apartment. They'd called in Andrews's FBI team for backup as they'd fought their way through the crowded streets of Georgetown, only narrowly arriving in time to avert total disaster—although by then, Carrie had managed on her own to bring Tom Bent's treachery to an end.

It was fair to say that absolutely no one on the American side had guessed Tom's role in the betrayal—not the CIA, not the FBI, not even the Russian assassin Tom had engaged the previous April when he'd supposedly gone to Harrod's in London to buy Oxford marmalade for his wife. Only the British "cousins," studying security tapes from Harrod's tearoom months later, had spotted the Russian assassin meeting with an American from the CIA Director's staff. At that point, Sir Roger Cambridge had decided to pull Huxley off the case, no longer knowing who their allies were.

Only the paranoid survive, Drum used to say. So how had he fallen so far, so fast? Carrie wondered. Had he left his paranoia at home like a forgotten umbrella? A little less paranoia, a little more loyalty would have taken him much further, she thought grimly.

As for her, she was numb, carrying on only because Jonah needed her to. As she moved up the aisle in the church, Drum's flag-draped coffin standing in front of the altar, she spotted Huxley and Tucker among the mourners. Jonah's fingers lifted in a subtle wave, and Huxley nodded, smiling gently back at him. Then, his eyes met Carrie's.

There was a world of meaning in that look, but she'd already told him to give her time. She needed to stand on her own feet for a while. She needed to help Jonah deal with his father's disappearance and death. She wasn't sure she ever again wanted anything to do with people in his line of work.

"I don't have to do this for the rest of my days," he told her. "I've been thinking myself that it might be time for a change. And if it's England you don't fancy, it's not a problem. I can live anywhere."

"You need to decide what you want for yourself, Mark," she said. "Do what you need to do, and I'll try to get Jonah and me back on some kind of even keel. Then if our paths should happen to cross again—"

"Oh, they will. Count on it."

She'd nodded slowly. "Good. I hope they do. And we'll see what happens then."